Letting Go and Holding On

D.M. ROBERTS

DEDICATION

To everyone who asked me, "Sooo, how's that book coming along?"

ACKNOWLEDGMENTS

My first thank you goes to my supportive friends and family, especially my dad for hounding me about a theme. A second big thank you goes out to my boyfriend, for not only joining in on my 2 a.m. conversations about my book, but for also not being there when I needed to get some work done. Next I need to thank my readers, who read a first time author's book and offered their critiques without being paid to do so. Along with that I thank Barbara Rose for offering her knowledge of child psychology. I also have to thank my friend and cover artist, Grant Sarber, for getting so excited about drawing an ink blot. Even more thanks go to all of my English teachers for not making me feel it was a waste of time earning an English degree. And lastly, I want to thank my craft group, for reminding me that writing *can* be fun, but only when combined with watching Internet videos.

"The madman is the man who has lost everything except his reason." G.K. Chesterton

CHAPTER ONE

"Uh, Mom, Dad, I gotta talk to you."

Evan Little sat at the kitchen table with his parents, as he had done every day for the last 19 years. Tally, his mother, stood at the stove, hastily making eggs so everyone could get to work on time. His father, Frank, read the newspaper, grunting at the prospect of yet another union strike. The worn-out clock on the wall loudly ticked down the minutes to the start of another work day. Every day, the same useless conversation. Every day, the same dull routine.

And every day, Evan tried to talk to his parents about his plans to break free.

"Looks like the upper management shitheads at the factory are trying to cut our hours again," Frank snorted. "Doesn't matter where you work these days. They're always trying to squeeze more outta ya with less pay."

"Did you hear me? I have to talk to you guys about something."

"Oh Frank, I forgot to tell you. Chad called the other day while you were at work."

"Chad? How's he doing? Broken any records at that school yet?"

"You know I never ask him about that stuff. I just want to make sure he's still passing."

"Babe, the only thing he needs to be passing is the football down the field. That's why they wanted him. As long as he's healthy, his arm is the only thing that's gonna get him anywhere."

Evan watched as Tally brought the plate of eggs to the table, spooning a couple onto each plate. His face grew warmer as he stared at the runny yolk spreading over the plastic dish. His parents' voices melted into the yellow

3

center growing wider and wider. It was happening again, another discussion about his brother's triumph overshadowing Evan's frustration. He closed his eyes and waited; waited for a break in the stream of praise that often followed in his brother's name; waited for his parents to acknowledge that he was even there; waited for his chance to be heard. He felt he spent his whole life, waiting.

Shut up. Shut up. Shut up!

"Mom, I gotta talk to you!" he exclaimed, interrupting them.

"All right, Evan, there's no need to shout."

"Jesus, kid, we're talking about your brother. You know, the one who *made* it into college."

Evan could feel that familiar ache start pulsing in his head.

"Frankie…"

"Well, if this one stopped playing video games all the time, he would be doing more with his life than working at the mall."

"Oh, like what, Dad? Working at the steel mill, washing dishes at Mom's restaurant?" Evan asked sarcastically.

"Hey!" Frank snapped. "That's what people do, kid. They make a living. You're getting a free ride here. Don't you forget that. At least your brother is making his way on his own."

"Yeah, he's lucky people value a guy who can throw a touchdown pass," Evan muttered.

Frank turned and grabbed Evan roughly by the arm.

"Frank!"

"You listen here smartass, you don't have to stay here. You're 19 now, which means you're old enough to be a man. And a real man can provide for himself. Chad knew what his strength was and he's out there, making us proud. What are you doing?"

Evan opened his mouth to retort when Tally reached over and put her hand on her husband's. Frank yanked it away, downed the last of his coffee, and abruptly left the table. Evan whipped his head around and shouted after him.

"Sorry I'm not Peyton Manning! I guess I'll have to get by being average like most people I know!"

Shaking her head, Tally picked up her hand from Evan's arm and began to clear the table. Evan grunted in disgust toward the stairs and turned back to his mother. This wasn't how he wanted to begin the conversation, but his father never allowed him to follow through on anything that mattered. The irony of that situation was never lost on Evan, though it was always lost on his father.

But now that Frank was out of the room, Evan finally had the chance for a real conversation. And all Tally had to do was listen.

"Honey, why do you test him like that?"

Evan looked up at her in shock. *Damn it, Mom! Not you too!*

"Me? Are you kidding? He started it!"

"You see? That's why he doesn't respect you. You have to start acting like an adult. You're not in high school anymore, Evan."

"Damn straight. High school sucked."

"Well, if you weren't getting into fights all the time... and that poor boy."

"Jesus, Mom. I didn't start any of those either! And trust me, he was no 'poor boy.' Dad was the one who told me to stop being a pussy and stick up for myself."

"Evan, language!"

"Oh, so Dad can swear all he wants but I have to be above that crap?"

Tally turned around and looked Evan squarely in the eye.

"You can always be better," she said sternly. "Do you hear me? You can always change things."

Evan snorted, looking around the cramped kitchen in their tiny two-bedroom home.

"Just like you guys did?"

"Hey! There were very special circumstances that brought us here. You know that," Tally exclaimed. "But you, you're young enough to do anything you want with your life. Isn't that what the psychiatrist keeps telling you? That's why we put you on the meds, so you could control your anger."

"That's just it, Mom. I've been trying to tell you guys. I feel really messed up. I mean, I don't think the new dose is working."

"What do you mean, not working?"

"Well, at first I just felt numb. But now, I don't know. It's like I'm angry all the time and I just want it to be over."

Tally turned around, alarmed.

"You want what to be over?"

That was what Evan had been trying to figure out for months now. He always knew he came in second to his brother, ever since Chad showed off his athleticism by third grade, but it never bothered him. He wasn't interested in any of it, and all of Chad's games kept his father off his back. But as they grew up, it became clear that Chad was their golden ticket while Evan became just another mouth to feed. He would never amount to the same paycheck that Chad would most likely bring in some day.

But that realization was only the beginning. Evan soon had to endure his father's constant barrage of put downs, in private and public. Others would laugh it off, trying not to show their embarrassment for Evan, but it hung over his head wherever he went. He would never be known as anything more than "Chad's brother", and even that was too good a title by Frank's standards.

That's when Evan was put on the medication, and almost immediately he began to feel a bit more numb to all of his father's provocations. It was a great first step in what he hoped would calm the chaos in his head. Maybe once he graduated from high school and his brother finally moved out, maybe then he would find some peace. It was almost enough to get him through the day without wanting to hurt himself or any of the kids who taunted him on a daily basis.

But he soon discovered there were too many pent-up thoughts and emotions to control with one pill. Other ideas simply grew louder, causing a change in dosage and therapy appointments. What were once simple fantasies now seeped into his dreams, creating nightmares from which he was unable to awake. His restraint was failing, along with whatever allowed him the hope of escape. It was nothing more than a faint memory now, slowly drowned out by his father's constant mantra that he had no money, no skills, and most of all, no help.

What do I want to be over? Uh, how about my shitty lot in life? Of course, I can't tell her that. She'll just say I'm not "applying" myself. Same spiel, different day.

"I don't know, Mom. There's all this noise in my head and it never stops," he muttered. "I just don't like the way I feel all the time."

Tally sighed in relief.

"Oh honey, I know what you're going through. I felt something like that when I first started taking the meds. I was confused and scared, because I didn't know what was happening to me. But you'll get through that. You just need to talk to the doctor about it. I'm sure he'll know what to do."

"But I'm trying to talk to you guys, Mom. And you're not listening to me…"

Frank came bounding down the stairs, throwing his jacket over his shoulders.

"Tally! Is my lunch ready? We gotta get going here."

"Honey, can you give us a minute?"

"Jesus Christ, Tal. I can't be late to work again because our son can't get his ass in gear."

"Frankie," Tally pleaded.

There it was, pounding, pounding, pounding. Evan thought his head was going to explode. The walls began to pulse as the kitchen fell in on him. He was trapped, cornered, and the only way out was through his father. He slammed his hand on the table and stood up, knocking the chair onto the floor.

"You know what, Dad? Fuck you!" he yelled. "Don't you get it? I'm trying to tell you guys…"

But Frank didn't wait to hear any more. He stormed over and grabbed Evan by the collar, shaking him.

"Don't you ever, EVER, take that tone with me!" he roared. "I'm sick of your crap! I oughta throw you out on the street. Then maybe you'd learn what it's like to live in the real world."

Evan shoved his dad off of him and jumped to the other side of the table, out of his reach.

"I can't even talk to you anymore!" Evan yelled. "All you do is call me a screw-up and compare me to Chad, who's going to school to throw a stupid ball! Who cares? I'm trying to tell you my meds are all messed up and you can't get over the fact I'm still at home and working a stupid mall job! When are you gonna take your head outta your ass and see that I'm drowning here?"

"Drowning? Don't be so melodramatic!" Frank shouted. "God, everything's the end of the world with you! I'll tell you what it's like to be drowning. Try paying a mortgage, utilities, credit cards, raising two kids. Then you can tell me about 'drowning.' But right now you need to get your butt in the car so we can all avoid getting canned for laziness."

Evan glared at his dad, his chest heaving. Frank mirrored his stance. The table was the only thing standing in the way of the two bulls, squaring off at opposite ends of the room. Tally stood in the middle, shaking silently, her eyes closed and her hands in the air.

"All right. All right," she said quietly, grabbing onto the back of a chair. "We need to calm down here. Evan, please go upstairs and get your stuff. We'll finish our talk later. Right now, we just need to make it through the day. That's all. Let's just make it through another day."

Silence.

"I don't think I can do that, Mom," Evan replied, his eyes locked on his father. Without another word, he turned and walked up the stairs.

"Evan? Are you going to get your stuff?"

All she got in return was a door slam. Frank punched the table and turned around, swearing to himself. After a few seconds he looked at Tally, shaking his head.

"Fine. If he doesn't want to go to work, he'll have to learn the consequences."

"But Frank, if I can just talk to him…"

"Forget it," he answered gruffly. "Talking doesn't matter anymore. Let's go."

Evan watched his parents pull out of the driveway in his father's weathered pick-up truck. When they were finally out of view he collapsed onto the bed. He tried to slow his breathing, but the stale air only stifled his lungs even more. He looked around his room, stopping on every item he had hanging on his walls or sitting on a bookshelf. It wasn't much, with his brother's trophies arranged like a shrine along one wall. A few tattered comic books and auto magazines, posters of scantily clad models, some science fiction DVDs, and his TV hooked up to his video game system with a small heap of rented games sitting underneath. It was all mindless distraction from the shallow existence he lived, or more accurately, limped through, on a daily basis.

7

Is this all there is to my life? he thought incredulously. *When are things supposed to get better? Does that ever happen? It never did for my parents. And now they're living vicariously through my friggin brother. He's their only way outta this hellhole and they know it. No way I'm gonna end up like that.*

His thoughts raced along with his heartbeat. All of the anger and frustration that had been building up for years had finally reached its boiling point. It was all too much to bear.

They've always ignored me. Well they won't be able to ignore this. Evan stood up and began to walk with purpose for the first time in months, maybe years; or perhaps, for the first time in his life. He opened the bedroom door.

Today's the day, he thought. He knew.

Today's the day.

CHAPTER TWO

BANG! BANG! BANG!

"Dude, those are the most agile zombies I've ever seen," said Zoey Young.

"I know. I thought they were supposed to be sluggish," added her best friend, Laura Simmons. "And aren't you supposed to knock their heads off or something? What good does shooting them do?"

"Hey babe, where'd you put the leftover pizza from last night?" Aaron Mason, Laura's newest boyfriend, shouted from the kitchen.

"Where would anyone put old pizza? In the fridge."

It was another weekend at Aaron's fraternity house, on what the girls had deemed a "real" college campus. Coming from a town of 3,500 people, with several smaller towns and only one city as neighbors, their idea of a "real" college was modest. Any school that threw large parties fit the criteria, which automatically excluded the community college they attended. And while both schools were in the city, the fraternity served as their best escape from boredom.

Of course, Zoey didn't care about any of that. She only wanted to spend time with her best friend. But Laura needed the social scene to thrive, and had once again convinced Zoey to get out of her parents' house to visit with other people. She didn't often consider frat boys "people", but Aaron seemed normal so she agreed. She found being a commuter difficult enough.

Aaron came out of the kitchen, a cold piece of pizza in one hand and the box in the other. He set it down on the warped coffee table as another frat brother, Hank Foley, reached in for a slice.

"Ugh, cold pizza for breakfast?" Zoey asked. "That's gross."

"Z, you gotta remember, they're guys," Laura said. "They can eat anything for breakfast. They're pigs."

On cue, Hank and Aaron snorted in unison.

"Nice touch," Laura giggled.

"And to answer your question, my dear, you have to shoot the zombies because they spew more ooze that way, which is totally cool. Oh, and it's a good way to slow them down. These guys apparently are mutated zombies, a different kind of breed which is why they're faster."

"I kinda thought zombies already were a mutated bunch," Zoey said.

"Nah, not like a natural mutation," answered Hank.

"Well, duh. I wouldn't consider anything about zombies to be 'natural.'"

"True dat."

"Honey, you're not black," said Laura. "The street slang doesn't really work for you."

"Oh come on. Eminem got away with it."

"Yeah, you're not cool like he was either."

"Oh, snap!" Zoey laughed.

"Ok, now wait a second!" Aaron exclaimed. "She can say 'oh snap' but I can't say 'true dat?' There's gotta be a line somewhere!"

"That's just how I roll."

"Oh that's it. No one disses me in my own place and gets away with it," Aaron said, picking up a pillow from the couch. Zoey reached over and grabbed the other one in defense.

"Go ahead. Make my day," she said in a deep voice. Aaron chuckled, putting the pillow down.

"Nah, you're not worth my time, punk," he grinned. Laura put her hand on his arm, and he leaned down to kiss her. Zoey realized it had only taken three months for them to become more serious, which was quite different from Laura's other boyfriends. She reminded herself to talk to her friend about it later, and turned her attention back to the TV.

"Hey guys!" yelled Dean Robinson, another frat brother, from the other room. "Did you hear about this dude who went all psycho at some mall?"

Dean came into the room and set his laptop down on the table. Everyone hovered around the couch to look at the security picture posted and the article entitled, "Local teen opens fire at mall, killing 10 people before taking his own life." Dean began to read the article aloud.

"Evan Little, 19, was a recent graduate of Smith High School and a cashier at Rich's Clothing Store, where two hours ago he walked in with a sawed-off shotgun and began shooting into the crowd at random. At press time police said he had injured over 20 people and killed 9, customers and employees alike, before taking his own life.

Little had been an employee at Rich's since his graduation last June. One of the employees, Bob Hutchins, had trained Little, and was shocked to witness such a brutal event at the hands of his former trainee.

"Evan was a simple boy, there was nothing that really stood out about him," Hutchins said. "I mean, he was a teenage boy who didn't want to work at the mall, but he was never violent or anything. Like I said, he was quiet, did his job."

Hutchins was working the day of the shooting and managed to lead a group of customers and employees into a back office that had a lock on the door.

"It was unreal," he said. "A mall is not a place you expect to hear gunshots, unless it's coming from the movie theater."

Mall security was on the scene immediately, in time to see mobs of people running out of the store as continuous shots rang out in the background. Suddenly, amidst the chaos outside of the store, there was silence inside, and then a single gunshot. It would be the final shot heard, the bullet that took Little's life.

Marla Richards was shopping toward the back end of the store when she heard the gun shots.

"At first people seemed confused," she said. "All of a sudden the shots got louder and they didn't stop, and people started running to where I was, looking for a back exit. I asked what was going on and this woman said there was a kid shooting people in the store. I joined the rest of the group toward the exit signs and never looked back."

Richards said the local police herded the group of customers and employees she was with to one side of the parking lot for questioning, looking for a description of the shooter. Shortly after, a mall security guard came out and said the shooting was over, and that the shooter had taken his own life before anyone could get to him.

"Thankfully we didn't have to stay much longer after that," said Richards. "The whole thing was frightening."

Details on what prompted Little's shooting spree and why he chose his place of employment are scarce. A group of teenagers hanging out at the mall that day said they knew Little, and that he constantly got into fights at school, mostly during his senior year. They knew he had a brother, Chad, who went to state college on a football scholarship, and that his father worked at the local steel mill, and his mother, as a waitress.

"He didn't really have one main group of friends, not that we could see," said Greg Tyler, a student of Smith High School. "I mean, he'd sit with one or two people at lunch, mostly SPED kids, but he never hung out with anyone. I figured he was skating through school until he could get outta there, like most of us."

Most recently, there was an altercation between Little and Dylan Perry, a three-star athlete at Smith. Also a senior at the time, Perry was well-known in the community for his excellence in football, baseball, and basketball. A month before graduation, Little was arrested for assaulting Perry, but claimed

Perry had taken the first swing. Perry's family decided not to press charges, and the school placed Little in counseling.

"Sure he got into some fights, but if you're not a popular kid that's just everyday stuff," said Tyler. "We don't have gang wars or anything like that, but that doesn't mean there's not a turf. It's all turf here. That's what the parents think anyway."

In a small town where school sports are the main recreational activity for families, it seems Little was seen as an outcast, a loner, with an exceptional athlete for a brother and parents struggling to make ends meet.

This report will be updated as more details emerge."

Aaron clicked on the thumbnail security image of Little on the side of the article. To the group, Evan looked like an average teenager, spiky blonde hair, a dark t-shirt, baggy jeans, sneakers. The only thing that looked out of place was the gun he carried by his side. There was another picture below that, his senior yearbook picture. Wearing a white shirt and black tie, the expression on his face was one of boredom.

"Damn, he barely looks big enough to hold that gun, never mind shoot up the place."

"It's always the quiet ones. Isn't that what they say in the news?" Dean asked. "They'll be interviewing the neighbor of some guy who had 10 dead bodies rotting in his basement, and they're all like, 'This is such a shock. He was always so quiet.' Just once I'd like to hear someone say, 'Oh, that dude? Yeah, he was one scary motherfucker! I knew he was crazy! No surprise here!'"

"Somehow I think if that was the case it would be easier to find these people before they committed a heinous crime," Laura said.

"That's just it. Some people keep things bottled up inside until it becomes too much for them, and then they blow," Dean said. "You can be crazy but not show it until the very end. Then they kill themselves and no one has any idea why, except they were a 'loner.'"

"That's such a cliché, don't you think? It's always the loner. I'm sure there's more to this story than that."

"Yeah, but unless he left a suicide note, how would anyone know?" Zoey asked. "They go out and shoot a bunch of innocent people, and then off themselves, for what? To avoid the consequences? Jesus, someone should tell them there's better ways to vent their anger."

"Obviously this guy was already pretty messed up," Hank replied. "Getting into fights all the time? If he wasn't already a ticking time bomb, then he probably just snapped, like Dean said."

"There's another stupid cliché, 'just snapped.' I imagine he had a plan to have that kind of gun on him," Laura said, looking at the screen. "And choosing the store where he worked? That's a pretty obvious one."

Zoey sat quietly, staring at Evan's picture.

"It's hard to imagine he was our age. You shouldn't have that much anger at 19."

"Are you kidding? Life sucks," Dean interjected, chewing on a slice of pizza. "You spend your first 18 years trying to make it through school, only to have to choose your career a year later in college. Then after busting your ass to get a degree, your reward is a thankless job, maybe one that's not even in your field. You work for 40 years so you can retire on a meager 401k that's been up and down in the stock market so many times you can barely live off it, all so you can die alone in a nursing home."

Everyone turned and stared at Dean. He shrugged. "What? I'm just sayin.'"

"Jesus man, I hope you're not hiding an Uzi under your bed!" Aaron exclaimed.

"Oh please, Dean. You're not poor or homeless, and you have enough money to get a degree to get a job that will keep you from becoming either one of those things," Laura scoffed. "That's way better than a lot of people can say. I mean, just living in the US is a big plus in comparison to other countries!"

"This Evan guy didn't seem to think so."

"Maybe someone in the family beat him or something. They say domestic violence isn't always obvious to other people," suggested Aaron.

"Well, whatever his deal was there was obviously some kind of imbalance," Laura said. "It's like that guy last year, although I think he was a couple years older. He had lived in a juvenile detention hall until he was 18 and look at how much good his 'rehabilitation' did him. He killed what, 8 people or something? Kids are just messed up these days. It goes along with the rest of the world and its messed up priorities."

"Seriously. It's not like adults haven't been doing this stuff forever. Just because their actions dominate the news doesn't mean they're the only ones doing violent things. Why should it be such a surprise when people our age do it?"

"Because people our age aren't expected to have that much to be angry about," Zoey replied. "We're supposed to be out having fun and being young and all that crap. Plus we supposedly have help and guidance from our parents to keep us on the right path. But I guess some people don't stay that innocent for very long."

"True dat."

"Honey, what did I tell you about using that phrase? You sound like an idiot!"

The conversation eventually turned away from Evan and back to socially acceptable slang terms. But Zoey couldn't stop looking at the picture of the teenage boy in a white shirt and tie.

CHAPTER THREE

"How awful."

The next night Zoey sat down to dinner with her parents, and as usual couldn't wait until they were finished. She knew the shooting would most likely be the topic of conversation with her mother, but one more trite statement about how much tragedy there is in the world and she thought she would scream.

"It's such a tragedy," said her mother, Connie. "He was so young. He had his whole life ahead of him. It's such a shame."

Zoey stuffed another piece of meatloaf in her mouth to muffle the high-pitched sound rising in her throat.

"Yes, hmm," muttered her father, Walter. That was his only response to Connie whenever he was deep in thought about his next book project. Currently he was working on a new piece of fiction with his favorite detective, Monty Teller. He was a teller of secrets, once he discovered them, but Zoey always thought the name sounded more like a game show host.

Her mother sighed. Zoey forked another piece of meatloaf, waiting for the inevitable generic gem concerning the news story they were watching on TV. It was a daily habit she had grown accustomed to over the years. While her father seemingly ignored it, Zoey turned it into an amusing game.

"Oh the poor families of those victims. I can't imagine something so horrible happening in our town," she said. "You can't turn on the news or open up a newspaper these days without seeing a story like this, especially about someone so young. Did you know that kids in this country are 11 times more likely to commit suicide with a gun than kids from 25 other countries combined?"

"Did you know that 72 percent of all statistics are made up on the spot?" Zoey grinned.

"What is this world coming to where kids have guns, and know how to use them?" Connie continued, not hearing Zoey's sarcastic contribution. "Of course, this kid was old enough to buy the gun himself, and since he had no real record it only took a three-day waiting period to get a hold of one. They say guns don't kill people, and it's true that people pull the trigger. But what if there wasn't a trigger to pull? I think Congress should focus their efforts on gun control. Then maybe this kind of violence would lessen."

Zoey was amazed at how much of a conversation her mother could hold by herself.

"Don't you think so, dear?" she asked, turning to Walter.

"Yes, that's right," he responded, seemingly answering a question in his own head rather than his wife's. Rolling her eyes, Zoey asked to be excused. *That's enough of that game.*

"You've been awfully quiet tonight, honey," Connie observed. "How's school going?"

"Fine."

"Oh come on now, your father would be disappointed in you using such a generic term like 'fine'. Isn't that right, Walt?"

"Mmmm," he mumbled, chewing on his meatloaf.

Gee, I wonder where I could have acquired such a generic vocabulary. No wonder Mom has all these solitary conversations, Zoey thought. *Is that how my parents stayed married all these years? I don't see any big romance between them anymore.*

"Now, let's try again. How's school going?"

"Uh, swell?" Connie sighed.

"Would you care to elaborate on your swell classes?"

"I don't know, Mom. The professor talks to us. We talk back. Sometimes they ask questions. Sometimes we answer them. That's pretty much how college works."

"Well, how about boys? Have you met any cute boys?"

What am I, in junior high? Zoey thought. *No, thank god. The last boy I dealt with in junior high tried to feel me up and I had to kick him in the balls. Unfortunately the name "Z Nut Crusher" never went away.*

"No, Mom, there's no one I'm interested in." *And even if there was I wouldn't tell you!*

"What about Laura? She's seeing someone, right? Maybe her boyfriend could set you up with someone."

"Ugh. I'd rather gouge my eyes out with a fork and be blind for the rest of my life than date a frat boy."

"I could've done without the vivid image, dear," Connie replied. "I don't know why you have to be so judgmental about boys who join a fraternity. At least they show an interest in something other than sports. Don't they have to do community service things?"

"Mom, the only service they provide to the community is free drinks to minors."

Connie sighed again.

"You're in college, honey. You should be going to parties and socializing like the other kids."

"You want me to engage in underage drinking and drug use?" Zoey asked, smiling. Connie looked down at her daughter over her glasses.

"All right, smart alec. You know what I mean. You're supposed to be having fun at college, and sometimes I wonder if you even remember what that word means anymore."

"I have plenty of fun with Laura. We go out all the time and hang out and stuff."

Another sigh. Zoey wondered if her mom would ever run out of air the way she expelled it all the time.

"I know, dear, but it worries me that you only have fun with Laura," Connie continued. "You kids have been friends since first grade, and it's wonderful that you're still so close after all these years. But by now you should be meeting new people, expanding your horizons, opening up your social circle."

Geez, three clichés in a row. She must be going for a record.

"Mom, there aren't that many new people that come to town," Zoey replied, exasperated. "I know everyone already and they're not exactly people I wanna hang with on a regular basis!"

Connie began clearing the dishes from the TV trays. She took her husband's plate out from underneath him, including the empty fork that was dangling in his hand. He didn't even seem to notice.

"Honey, your father and I are just a little worried about you, that's all."

Could've fooled me, Zoey thought, looking at her father. Every dinner for the last five years ended the same way, Connie cleaning up after everyone as Zoey tried to imitate her father and escape to her own world. The constant struggle was frustrating for both her and her mother, but for different reasons.

"We just want you to get out into the world, experience some new things, and we thought going to college would do that for you," Connie said. "We want you to be happy. You saw the newspaper article about that boy. There's enough tragedy in the world, and we want you to experience all the good it has to offer. Isn't that right, Walt? Walt?"

Hearing his name a second time jolted Walter from his book-induced coma.

"Hmm? What? Oh yes, sweetie, we care about you very much," he said, getting up from the couch and patting Zoey on the shoulder. He wandered into his study, his thoughts turned to solving crime again. Zoey watched him close the door.

"See? We just want you to be happy."

I would be happy if you got off my back. Zoey pushed her TV tray and stood up, turning towards the stairs. Her room was the one place in the house that offered her safe haven from her mother's endless questioning and trivial concerns. It was all too stifling after a while.

"Ok, ok, you want me to be happy, I get it," she said, walking up the stairs. "I'll be sure to work on that."

Connie watched her daughter disappear into her room. She frowned, looking up at the TV. Evan's schoolbook picture stared back at her.

"Such a shame."

CHAPTER FOUR

On the other side of town, Deirdre Hart was also home to watch the 6 o'clock news, but for her it was a rarity. As a reporter who covered nightly town meetings, she often worked late and was home for the 11 o'clock news instead. But the board of selectmen had canceled their session that night, allowing Deirdre to eat dinner at home. While the TV blared in the living room she stood over the stove, cooking the one thing she always had in the house- spaghetti. Over the years she had learned that she rarely had time to cook anything that involved more preparation than tossing food into a pot and turning on the stove.

As she stirred the pasta she kept one ear turned toward the TV, currently set on one of the 24-hour news channels. Normally she despised those channels, as the "news" they discussed often involved the public's thoughts on scandalous stories of famous people rather than crucial events. It wasn't the kind of hard-hitting information she felt her stories contained. But tonight's discussion was with a psychiatrist offering her opinions on a teenage suicide shooting that had occurred only days earlier, a topic that always peaked Deirdre's interest.

"Yes, Tom, I believe in this case his brother's celebrity status in town did help to isolate Little from his family, and possibly the community," the psychiatrist was saying.

Deirdre grabbed a pot holder from above the sink and brought her spaghetti over to the TV tray in front of the couch. Sitting down she grabbed the remote and lowered the volume.

"There was a history of limited violence, especially with another well-known athlete of the town, which suggests an impulse to lash out against those who had similar interests and talents of his brother," Dr. Patricia Morgan was telling the anchor.

"Dr. Morgan, why do you think Little then targeted the mall, or more specifically, the store where he worked?" asked the anchor.

"Well, the targets are not always so cut and dry unless the shooter leaves a suicide note, which in this case he didn't," she replied. "But my guess is the store represented the community as a whole, a community in which he did not fit in as well as others did. Also, many targets are chosen simply because they're accessible, have poor security, or are often crowded. In this case, Little would have known how many people would be there on a regular basis since he worked there."

"Along with these reports, there are also emerging reports stating that Little was on anti-depressants," said the anchor. "Can you explain to us what anti-depressants do exactly, and if this alleged drug use may have affected Little's actions?"

"Well, Tom, in layman's terms, anti-depressants are FDA-approved drugs which are used to combat depression," Dr. Morgan explained. "The drug affects the travel of serotonin, which is a hormone found in several areas of the body, that works as a chemical messenger in the brain and transmits signals. That's why the drug is called a selective serotonin reuptake inhibitor, or SSRI."

"So what does this SSRI do?" the anchor asked.

"The SSRIs affect the chemicals used in the brain to send signals, otherwise known as neurotransmitters," Morgan continued. "The neurotransmitters not taken up by other nerves are re-taken by the same nerve that sent them, which is called a reuptake. The SSRI prohibits the reuptake of serotonin, allowing more serotonin to be taken up by other nerves. This, in turn, can manipulate the emotions of the patient."

Hmm, violent kids on medication. This could be interesting. Deirdre took out a notebook from her work bag and began to take notes.

"So these drugs can control the way neurotransmitters send signals through the brain, affecting how a person feels?" the anchor clarified.

"That's right," said Dr. Morgan. "But as with any drug, there are side effects that the FDA prints on the label. These side effects, besides simple physical symptoms, can include worsening anxiety or sadness, sleeplessness, increased aggression, or suicidal thoughts or attempts. It's very important, especially with children, to monitor the first couple of months of usage, along with continued psychiatric evaluations and possible dose modifications."

"So, in your professional opinion, doctor, do you think it's possible some of these effects came into play in this horrific event?"

"It is possible," she replied. "Depending on the symptoms Little had when he was put on the drug in the first place, it's possible the drug could have exacerbated any existing feelings of aggression or suicide. But you have to keep in mind, Tom, the FDA statistics reported for such an occurrence were relatively low, about 4 percent, back in 2004 when these kinds of suicide warning labels were required to be put on the drug. And the percentage hasn't increased that much in medical trials since then."

"Do you think we are a society too quick to place our children on such drugs?" asked the anchor. "With all sorts of psychiatric problems being identified, attention-deficit disorder being one of the big ones, do you feel there is any validity to them and the drugs being prescribed for treatment?"

"Well, as a psychiatrist I feel that, yes, there are certain legitimate disorders out there with common symptoms that we can identify and treat in a certain way to help children to grow into functional adults."

Nice non-committal answer, Deirdre thought, smiling. As someone who asked probing questions for her job, she came across such answers every day as an occupational hazard.

"But these kinds of drugs are most often used in conjunction with regular psychiatric visits, which I feel is the more helpful part of that equation," she continued. "Sometimes the child is extremely imbalanced, thereby rendering the therapy almost useless. But with medical science we've been able to develop supplemental methods to improve on such therapy."

"So you believe in prescribing such medication only in extreme cases?" the anchor pushed.

"Again, that depends on your definition of 'extreme', Tom," the doctor answered, smiling.

Deirdre rolled her eyes, when her cell phone rang. She looked over at the caller ID to see it was Rebecca Hart. She hesitated, then muted the TV and opened the phone against her better judgment.

"Hello?"

"Hi, honey," Rebecca said. "I tried you at the office first, of course. I'm surprised you're home."

"My selectmen's meeting was canceled tonight," Deirdre replied. "Plus I'm in-between independent projects right now. My editor really enjoyed my last article about Alzheimer's disease and some of the new techniques they're using to treat it, so I might do another health issue."

"That's wonderful. But you know I don't like to talk about your work. Too stressful, and I don't want to add any more of that to your life."

Her mother always said that, since Deirdre often talked about work. Writing was the one stable thing in her life, her one true skill. *Why shouldn't I talk about it?*

"Mom, I don't know why you think my job is so stressful," she mentioned, slightly annoyed.

"Because honey, you write about things like disease and war and dirty politics."

"Oh, you mean topics that are important to many people and have some bearing on the world."

"Oh, Dee Dee."

God, I hate when she calls me that. I haven't been Dee Dee for a long time, Mother.

"Does everything you focus on have to be so depressing?" Rebecca continued.

"Just because I take on difficult topics for my job does not mean my life is empty. I am a grown-up, Mother. I can separate my work from real life."

Rebecca paused. Deirdre felt uneasy every time she did that. It was always some subtle gesture, a pause, or a sigh, but it was much worse than anything her mother could ever say. It was a judgment without the sound of the gavel. She was able to plant ideas in her daughter's head without saying a word, and it brought Deirdre back to being that little girl every time.

"Well, it certainly doesn't help in fostering a happy environment."

"Mother, is there a reason you called?" Deirdre asked, exasperated. "I'm right in the middle of dinner."

"Macaroni and cheese or spaghetti?"

Damn she's good. Apparently Deirdre had the same ability to transmit thoughts back to her mother.

"Seriously, Mom," she muttered, ignoring the question.

"All right, fine," Rebecca acquiesced. "I just wanted to let you know that your sister is having a birthday party for your nephew. Remember him? Brown hair, stands about two feet tall, has a two year birthday coming up? Anyway, it's going to be in two weeks, Saturday, around 1 pm. Is that too early for you, darling?"

"I don't know. Is that too early to start drinking?"

"Please tell me you're kidding, dear."

"Well, I'm just saying if you're trying to get me not to go, it's working like a charm."

"I doubt I have to do much for that."

"Oh, Mom, you know I love those two demon spawn."

"Otherwise known as Brad and Karen," Rebecca sighed. "I hope you don't call them that in front of your sister."

"What? Brad and Karen?"

"Demon spawn!"

"Geez, Mom, take the fun right out of it."

"You know, you'd think asking your daughter to attend her nephew's birthday party would be a simple thing."

"Think again," Deirdre smirked.

"So shall I tell my oldest child that the unruly aunt will be attending her son's birthday party?"

"Why didn't Ellen ask me herself?" *She's the perfect one, after all.*

"Gee, I can't imagine."

"All right, I'll be there. So, Mom, is there anything else you'd like to torture me about? Maybe a family reunion with thousands of relatives that's happening in a building with no air conditioning in the middle of hell tomorrow?"

"Wouldn't that make for a depressing new topic for an article?" Rebecca quipped. Deirdre could hear the smile in her voice. She couldn't help but smile too. "No, dear, I think I've had my fun for the day. Have a good night, demon aunt."

"Bye, Mom."

Deirdre hung up the phone. *Survived another call,* she thought. Making a mental note of Brad's birthday party, she grabbed her pen. Turning up the volume on the TV, she returned to listening to Dr. Morgan.

"That's true, Tom. Most mass shootings involving teenagers do happen at school. We've certainly seen a growing number of them over the years, as more and more students are bringing guns to school. And it is where they spend a lot of their time, which can be good or bad. To add to that, bullying is still an issue in many schools, especially with kids being able to bully their peers through Facebook and texting.

"But there have been other incidents in the past, although limited, that happened outside of school. In fact, this shooting mirrors an incident that happened three years ago at the Westdale Mall…"

Hearing the name of the mall caught Deirdre off-guard, and she fumbled for the remote to turn off the TV. The screen went black, but the images of the mall remained steadfast in her memory. She tried breathing deeply to slow down her racing heartbeat as she placed the remote back on the table. Looking down at her pasta, she realized she had suddenly lost her appetite.

I should figure out what I'll be working on tomorrow, she thought. Standing up, she brought her pasta into the kitchen to throw it away, and made her way toward her computer desk.

CHAPTER FIVE

The snow fell lightly around Zoey and Laura on their ritual walk to their first class that morning. Having chosen similar majors, Laura with Communications and Zoey with English, they often had classes in the same building. It was a routine that began in first grade and never faltered in a town with a small school system. And even now in college, Zoey tailored her schedule to coincide with her best friend's to ensure the existence of their daily routine down that sidewalk.

"Oh god, did I tell you I have to go to friggin Utah for my cousin's wedding this summer?" Laura asked suddenly.

"Utah?"

"Yeah. We're obviously not that close to them, but my mom wants to go because we haven't seen them in a while. I don't even know how they ended up in Utah."

"Weird. So, is your cousin the first, second, or third wife?"

"They're not Mormons!" Laura exclaimed. "Although they're probably the one family in the area that isn't. I'm surprised they haven't been suspiciously run out of town yet."

"No, no, the Mormons aren't like the Catholics. I'm just surprised your cousin hasn't been converted yet."

"I wonder if the ceremony will be in English or in tongues."

"Dude, that's the Baptists," Zoey said, trying to stifle a laugh.

"Well, let's see. Is there any way we could bring the Jews or Muslims into this unholy conversation?"

"Only if we wage a religious war."

"We are so going to hell," Laura replied. "Thank goodness it's snowing or else that bolt of lightning wouldn't seem odd to anyone."

"Are you kidding? It's New England. The weather doesn't mean anything. We could easily have a thunderstorm come outta nowhere. Then we'd be screwed."

"Even in January?"

"Totally."

"You're right. The people on the West Coast have it so much easier than we do."

"Yeah, except for that whole earthquake thing. Oh, and the random forest fires, those are probably a drag. I guess they're just smitten by different kinds of wrath."

"It's always something," Laura sighed. The girls laughed again.

"Oh, I came across this quote the other day that perfectly fits all religions," Zoey said.

"Wow, don't tell them that. If the different religions found out they had something in common it would be Armageddon. What is it?"

"God is the only being who, in order to reign, need not even exist," Zoey quoted. "It's by Charles Baudelaire, French poet."

"Hey, that's a good one. Got it up on your quote board?"

"Not yet."

Zoey's love of quotes began in high school. Often times when she had trouble articulating a thought, she would turn to someone she felt had more knowledge on the subject, and was able to put into words the most difficult of ideas. Any quote she came across that she felt was applicable to her life, or life in general, went on the homemade quote board that hung in her room. It was one of her few creative outlets, besides her blog.

"I always liked that one by Kurt Vonnegut, the one about if God was alive today he'd be an atheist," Laura said.

"Yeah, that's pretty good too. You bring up that quote a lot in conversation with your parents?"

"Yeah. It's right up there with all the conversations we have about me having premarital sex." Zoey gasped mockingly.

"You sinner! I hope you're going to confession for that."

"Nah, I'm just gonna wait until I'm on my death bed and repent for it then."

"Good call."

In most cases, Zoey considered herself to be agnostic. Her parents were Unitarian and attended services a couple times a month, but Zoey never went with them. That was the one thing she could appreciate about her parents. Unlike Laura, who attended weekly Catholic services with her parents, Zoey's parents allowed her to believe whatever she wanted.

At least Mom doesn't hound me about that crap.

"Speaking of death bed, that pair of shoes I ordered online two months ago is still backordered," Laura sighed. "I'm gonna be on my death bed by the time they get here. And then what good will they be? No one will see my cute feet when I'm in the ground."

"That's a nice morbid thought to start your day," Zoey giggled. "Maybe the casket can hide your wrinkly upper half and only showcase your cuter lower half."

"Oh Z, you always know what to say to make me feel better."

"That's what I'm here for."

"Eww, did I hear you guys talking about coffins?" asked Beth Schumacher, their classmate, who followed them into the building.

"Yeah. Why? You don't talk about coffins with your best friend?" Laura asked.

"You guys are so deranged," Beth replied. "Anyone else listening to you would think you're Marilyn Manson wannabes."

"Hey, I am not that pale," Zoey protested mockingly.

"Yeah. And her boobs are real," Laura added.

"Hell yeah!" Zoey exclaimed. Beth shook her head as the girls continued their giddy banter.

"Seriously deranged," she said, entering the classroom.

Zoey and Laura took their usual seats at the table, as more students began filing into the room. Zoey looked around at the relatively non-racial mix of people in the class, and more noticeably, the entire school. She had always had high expectations for college, hoping it would take her out of the comfort zone that was her life and bring her on an adventure. She didn't know where or what that would be, she only knew that Laura would be her traveling partner. Together they could make any place entertaining.

Except this one apparently, she thought, sighing. *God, this place is so boring. I mean, yeah, it's community college, but there must be other people from other communities with interesting lives. Right? It can't all be mundane crap.* At the same time, she knew she wasn't doing anything to change her mundane existence either.

"You don't think we're that deranged do you?" Zoey asked.

"No, dude, we're just well-rounded."

In comparison to the other students in the class, Zoey accepted that response.

As the professor walked into the classroom, Zoey stifled a yawn. Laura looked at her friend out of the corner of her eye as she searched in her backpack for her notebook. She realized Zoey's lowered eyelids were slowly becoming a new part of their daily ritual.

"Dude, do you ever get any sleep the night before this class?"

"I hardly get any sleep period, you know that," Zoey answered, pulling out her notebook. "Ever since high school it's taken me at least a couple hours every night to fall asleep."

"I'm sure doing your homework last minute at midnight didn't help."

"There's nothing wrong with procrastination. It's a great motivator. I always get my stuff in on time."

"Yeah, but at what cost?" Laura asked, concerned. "I mean, pulling all-nighters is a college ritual, but you gotta catch up on sleep at some point."

"Ah, I'll sleep when I'm dead."

"Okay, Bon Jovi," Laura giggled. "If you keep up your non-sleeping habits that death thing may come sooner than you think."

"Oh, come on. I'm young. I don't think that kind of damage starts until you're at least 30. That's when I hear everything goes downhill."

Laura frowned.

"Have you at least tried those vitamins I suggested? They say they're perfectly harmless, they just help to boost the melatonin in your system to help you fall asleep."

"I've tried everything, L. It's been years since I've had a good night's sleep, unless I can sleep past noon. And I can only do that on the weekends. I'm just an insomniac."

"Then why in the world did you choose a 9:30 class?"

Zoey didn't want to admit to her friend that she needed a similar schedule to hers. Even after all of these years it was the one thing that remained constant in their friendship, mostly through Zoey's persistence. It was her motivation to do well to keep up with Laura's honors classes, and it helped to maintain their bond through changing interests in high school. It also allowed them the same amount of free time, something Zoey was unable to fill on her own.

"It was the only time I could fit it in," she lied.

Laura opened her mouth to say something about the afternoon class when Zoey cut her off.

"By the way, you still owe me a birthday present," she said, changing the subject as quickly as she could. "Don't think I haven't forgotten about that."

"What? I totally gave you a present. You know, it was that awesome thing," Laura smirked.

"Uh huh. Don't try to get out of it. I got you those concert tickets for your birthday."

"Oh please, that concert was as much for you as it was for me. You can't bullshit a bullshitter."

"I could say the same thing to you!" Zoey exclaimed. The girls laughed as the professor started her lecture, pulling them out of their own world and back to reality.

CHAPTER SIX

Deirdre sat at her desk in the press room, muttering to herself as she scanned the latest newspaper story about Evan's shooting. While other reporters were busily making phone calls, taking notes and writing up stories, she was buried in a sea of old articles about suicide shootings. A week had passed since the mall shooting, but the topic was still fresh for the media. It clearly was for Deirdre, who had spread the various articles around her desk, cut up and spilling onto the floor. Many of them happened within the last decade, but the oldest one was dated seven years before the Columbine shootings in 1999.

"Wow," she murmured to herself. "There may be more to this than I thought."

Pulling out her notebook Deirdre began to write down the dates of each incident, along with the name and age of the shooter. As she worked her way backwards she began to expand the information to include how many people were killed, where the incident took place, and the kinds of guns that were used.

The most disturbing detail that stood out immediately was the age of each shooter. There were kids as young as 14 involved in school suicide shootings, where the gunman killed himself after either targeting people at the school or shooting seemingly at random. Dating back to 1992, there was at least one school shooting a year, sometimes more, acted out by a teenager, and more than a dozen of them ended in the shooter committing suicide.

I wonder how far back I can find these kinds of stories. It seems to be happening at a more alarming rate. Or maybe it only seems that way because of how the media plays out each one. Of course, if it's not an uncommon thing would that make it any less of a scary concept? Hmmm. Would I be bringing something new to this issue or adding more to the unnecessary hysteria surrounding it?

Well, I guess I won't find that out until I do more research.

27

Besides, there's so much more to this issue than just the stories themselves. There's the gun control issue, that's always been a hot button topic with these things. Every day there's a new bill in Congress about the kind of guns that can be sold. And violence in the media often goes along with that: movies, TV shows, video games, etc. Oh, and the family dynamic. More and more kids coming from "broken" homes.

Let's see, what else? Bullying in schools? That's an obvious one. High school cliques have been written about and immortalized in movies for decades. I wonder if peer pressure has changed over the years. Do people even use that phrase anymore? Maybe when talking about drugs…

But who's to say there has to be a standard reason for this anyway? Each individual case is different. Maybe it's not solely environmental; it could also be psychological. The world is pretty different from how it used to be 100 years ago. Hell, it's different from how it used to be 10 years ago. With Child Psychology, medication, therapy, kids could simply be growing up different from how they used to. They're subjected to a lot more stimuli from a lot more sources. That could affect the way they view the world as a whole.

God, these kids are just, well, kids. Where does all this rage come from?

And do I really want to find out?

Deirdre was so involved in her notes she didn't notice her editor, Neil Stanfield, standing over her desk.

"Deirdre, what in the world is this mess?" he asked. "I know you become obsessed with your stories but this is ridiculous!"

Deirdre grinned, looking down at her island of chaos.

"I know, I know. It does get a little, um, out of hand," she said sheepishly, putting down her notebook. "And I know I told you I wanted to work on another health issue, Neil, but I think I've got something even better."

"Well, it looks like a doozy. What is it?"

Deirdre paused, trying to figure out a tactful way to put it.

"Teenage suicide shooters."

Neil looked down at her over his glasses.

So much for tact, she thought.

"Jesus, old people losing their memories wasn't depressing enough?"

God, he sounds like my mother.

Deirdre ignored his comment and started picking up some of the articles littering her desk. The first one she handed him concerned a 20-year-old who, last year, caught national fame after killing his parents and then eight other people in the grocery store where he worked. He lived in a juvenile detention facility for four years before he was released after turning 18, which raised questions about the effectiveness of juvenile facilities successfully integrating the teenage dependents back into society.

"Neil, just take a look at this. I'm sure you remember this kid a year ago. His suicide note said he was 'unprepared' for how lonely life would be once he left the institution. What he thought would be freedom turned out to be more isolation."

"Yes, I remember. That story raised quite a hell storm about the nature of the juvenile justice system and whether or not it actually worked in rehabilitating kids. Weren't there some who argued that there wasn't enough education in the system or something?"

"I think so. And I think it was recent enough that most people will remember it, which gives this incident at the mall even more punch. You can see all the articles I have here go back at least 10 years, and all of them are under 21. It almost seems like the problem of youth violence, and more specifically young suicide shooters, is escalating."

"You say problem as if this is an epidemic that comes from somewhere and has a solution."

"It could, we don't know," Deirdre said awkwardly. "There are a lot of factors to look at, a lot of changes that have taken place over the years. It's such a complicated issue that right now I have a lot more questions than answers. Let me do some research and I'll tell you if that's the case."

Neil looked around the office, searching for something. He found a chair in the middle of the cube farm and pulled it towards Deirdre's desk. Sitting down, he leaned forward and clasped his hands together.

Uh oh, she thought. *He usually just says ok and moves on to the next person. He never sits down unless he's concerned about something.*

"Neil, if you're worried about the subject matter I certainly know how to…"

Neil held up his hand to stop her mid-sentence.

"Deirdre, I know you know how to handle sensitive issues. You've been working here for 5 years. I'm just afraid that this particular topic might, well, how can I put this gently? It has the potential to consume *you.*"

Deirdre shifted in her seat.

"What do you mean?"

"Come on, you know what I'm talking about. Don't tell me your current interest in this has nothing to do with your past."

Deirdre looked down at her notes. She hadn't really thought about her motivation until now, and Neil's memory suddenly made her question herself.

"Look Neil, I know what happened after that, um, incident, but this has nothing to do with it. I'm just seeing a pattern here and I'd like the opportunity to explore it more…"

"Deirdre, whatever happened is over, and I know you've moved on," Neil interrupted. "I just don't want to see you get your hopes up over something that might turn out to be nothing. No matter what you think or where you're at now, I know what the temptation is. And I don't want to see you get hurt again, especially if there are no answers out there for you to find."

"You don't know that," Deirdre said, fighting to control the tone in her voice. "There's a lot of information here, Neil, and I'm already seeing many similarities. And the fact that these are all younger people, under the age of 21, well, doesn't that make you wonder why?"

Neil paused, thinking over her question. It was intriguing. But it wasn't the first intriguing question Deirdre had asked with the potential to take over her life completely. She was one of those reporters who was relentless when it came to hunting down a good story, and she knew how to tell it too. But often times what began as a simple spark ended in an explosion, which he understood all too well.

"I don't know, Deirdre. I think you're reaching on this one. It's like asking that age old question of why humans kill at all."

"But this is a specific kind of killing, Neil. It's not only gang violence or some random cult following. And they're not terrorists or kids who happened to fall in with the wrong crowd," Deirdre countered. "It's individual kids, some with close family and friends, murdering innocent people."

Neil frowned. He knew she had a point.

"I know how it sounds, Deirdre. But right now there are plenty of stories out there about these individual incidents, all of which you apparently have on your desk," he said. "Why not distance ourselves from the rest of the pack and keep going with what's getting good responses?"

"Neil, you know anything I wrote would be a hell of a lot more comprehensive than just the who, what, when and how that everyone else writes about," she said, exasperated. "I think people are afraid to dig deeper into this issue, including you apparently."

"Hey, you know I never shy away from the tough sell! But in this case, I think you'd be in over your head. You have an obligation to keep up with a certain number of stories and I expect you to maintain that. Besides, we got such a great response from the Alzheimer's piece and I think you have a real knack for health stories."

"Why do I get the feeling I'm not going to like your final answer."

"Look, why don't you keep this idea on the back burner for now and look for something else," Neil offered. "There are plenty of diet and exercise fads out there, or if you're looking for something more exciting you can research new medical technologies."

This was not the reaction Deirdre was expecting. After working with Neil for all these years, she was hoping for a little more support.

Is this really that much of a dangerous topic for me? Am I really not as healed as I thought I was? Deirdre didn't know what to think now.

"Are you telling me I can't work on this?"

"As your editor, I'm telling you, no," Neil replied. "As your friend, I'm asking you, please don't go down this road. You may not find an end to it."

Before she could protest, Neil stood up and walked into his office, shutting the door behind him. He never did that either.

CHAPTER SEVEN

"Dude, this is so cool! You gotta check it out!"

Zoey and Laura were hanging out in Zoey's room, pretending to study for an upcoming exam. Their study sessions always began with good intentions-open books, open notebooks, talking about the subject at hand. But often times their discussions would diverge into their social lives or private jokes, and eventually they would both end up online looking at videos. There was an overabundance of entertainment at their fingertips which interfered with their concentration on other subjects.

That included Zoey's blog, which she used as a way to connect with other people whose lives were as mundane as hers. Many of her posts had comments from the same group of people, whose blogs were also bookmarked on her page. It wasn't anything deep or meaningful by society's standards, but for her it was all she had besides her friendship with Laura. It was nice to know she was not the only small town girl looking for something more.

Besides, I know I could never be a professional writer. They say "write what you know", and all I know is boredom, not exactly compelling drama. And I can't tell Dad about it either. That would be way too much pressure to actually produce quality work. The blog was the only way for Zoey to express what little she knew in a forum accepted by many.

Setting down her laptop, Zoey jumped off her bed and walked over to her desk, where Laura had set up her computer. The video showed a group of boys jumping off ledges and running up the sides of buildings.

"What the heck is that?"

"The video is called 'Parkour', whatever that means. Look it up."

Zoey sat on the edge of her bed and grabbed her laptop, opening a new window to look up the term.

"Apparently, it's this way of using your body to get around as quickly as possible," Zoey explained, scanning a website. "I think it originated in France or something. There's a whole movement behind it."

"No pun intended," Laura said, causing both of them to start giggling.

The sound of the two girls giggling echoed down the stairs as Connie walked up with the latest load of laundry. It was an all too familiar scene, one she had hoped would change over the years to include a larger population, at least of girls. She supposed she should be happy that Zoey agreed to attend college in the first place, since it would take her out of her usual element somewhat. But Laura would always be the anchor keeping her grounded here.

I suppose it's better than being in her room alone.

Connie stopped at the door, shaking her head. It took a couple loud knocks to get the girls attention.

"Ugh, I bet that's my mom," Zoey sighed, turning toward the door. "Come in!"

Connie opened the door, pushing aside the usual mound of clutter. As she walked further into the room she noticed Zoey quickly close the browser on her laptop. That happened every time Connie caught her daughter off-guard. She finally understood why her own mother was constantly nosing around her room during her teenage years.

"Honey, when are you going to clean this mess?"

Zoey pretended not to hear her.

"Zoey, I asked when you were going to clean your room," Connie repeated, exasperated.

"Come on Mom, I'm in college," Zoey said. "It's not like I need to do it to get an allowance anymore."

"That's true," Connie replied. "However, you do still live under this roof."

"Oh god Mom, the 'under this roof' excuse? Really?"

"Hey, if the shoe fits..."

"Then buy two pair," Zoey joked, making Laura giggle. Connie didn't find it as amusing.

"You know, I do an awful lot of work around here, and it would be nice if, while you were living here, you pitched in once in a while."

"Why? Dad doesn't."

"Your father makes a good living to provide for his family, of which you are a member," Connie said. "When you start to do that, instead of letting us pay for your education, then you can make up some of your own rules. Until then..."

"Geez Mom, fine, I'll clean my room," Zoey muttered, cutting her off.

Connie sighed. She could never get her daughter to actually follow up on those words.

"What are you two watching?" she asked, trying to change the subject.

"It's these kids doing parkour," Zoey explained. "It's a French movement."

"Like the can-can," Laura joked. Both girls snickered again.

Connie rolled her eyes. *If I could get Zoey to study as much as she laughed with Laura, I'd be raising a rocket scientist.*

"Well, that's very interesting and all, but don't you girls have some studying to do?"

"We already did, Mom," Zoey lied. "We're just taking a break between subjects."

"Fine," Connie said. "I just want to remind you that your scholarship…"

"God, Mom, I know! You don't have to remind me every day!"

Startled by her daughter's outburst, Connie opened her mouth to scold her for talking back to her mother. But seeing Zoey glance over at her friend with the look of, *Can you believe her,* she decided against it. That look came up more often than Connie wanted to admit.

Setting down the laundry on the bed, Connie turned and walked quietly out of the room. Once Zoey heard her mother's footsteps disappear, she groaned.

"Sorry about that," she said to Laura. "I don't know why she has to freak out on me all the time. You'd think having a daughter who does nothing but hang out with her best friend at home and study would be comforting. There are way worse things I could be doing, and she's on my case all the time!"

"Are you kidding? She's a dream compared to my parents," Laura said. "They're freaking out over me dating Aaron because he's not Catholic. Can you believe that? I'm surprised they let me out of the house wearing skirts that show my ankles, never mind my knees."

"I wish I had someone to drive my parents crazy," Zoey replied. "Then maybe they'd stop focusing on me and all the stupid stuff I'm not doing."

Laura looked at her friend sympathetically.

"Considering you're not 'doing anything,' you talk about it a lot. Are you sure you're just not upset about your life being boring?"

"Laura, whose side are you on?"

"There aren't any sides here. I'm just making an observation, that's all. You rip on your parents for ripping on you for having nothing to rip on."

"Yeah, that makes sense," Zoey replied sarcastically.

"Geez, I'm not judging you or anything," Laura said, holding up her hands. "My life is boring as hell. The one thing that's worth talking about is Aaron, and I don't even know how I feel about him right now. I mean, he's a frat guy and he's nice, but there's not a lot more that I see in him. On the other hand, being with him alone makes me wanna jump his bones. It's very confusing."

Zoey turned her head toward Laura, catching her sideways smirk.

"You're not even being serious about this!" Zoey exclaimed, throwing a pillow at her. Laura ducked.

"Oh come on, someone had to break the tension," she said, laughing. "It's a fact of life. Parents nag their kids. Even when we graduate and finally get outta here, they'll still be on our case about something. Where we live, what kind of job we get, why they don't have grandkids yet. It's never ending, Z."

"I guess."

Laura turned her attention back to the computer screen, blatantly taking a sip of her soda to avoid further conversation. Zoey glanced over at her.

"Sooo, how's jumping Aaron's bones going?"

Laura tried not to choke.

"I was wondering when you were gonna ask me about that!"

"Well, I wasn't really sure how much of that you guys were even doing. But after what you just said…"

"Hey, I only said that to change the subject!"

"Oh come on, you could have said anything to do that! You chose to bring up Aaron."

Zoey crossed her arms mockingly, waiting for Laura to break out the latest story of her date with Aaron. Laura grinned.

"Oh fine. So we went to the movies last night…"

*   *   *   *   *   *   *

"I'm telling you Walter, it's incredibly frustrating trying to talk to her sometimes," Connie said, standing behind her husband in his office. "I just don't know how to get through to her. Maybe you could try next time."

Walter had been typing furiously on his laptop when Connie entered, as she always did, without knocking. He found it extremely frustrating, especially when he was in the middle of an important chapter. Although he was constantly thinking about his new project, it was only through fleeting moments of inspiration that he wrote down character descriptions and dialogue. He had tried to ignore her to show that he was working and didn't want to be disturbed. But she was already in her own world of exasperation, so she could ignore the fact that he wanted to be alone in his.

"Walter, what do you think? Will you talk to her?"

"About what, exactly?" he asked, taking a break from typing.

"You know, about the way she's been acting lately."

"What, you mean like a typical teenager? Honey, she's hanging out with her friend, watching videos online. The fact that she doesn't want to tell you she'll clean her room in front of Laura is a simple power play. Your nagging her about it will only make things worse."

"I'm not nagging her about it, Walt. I'm merely reminding her about it because she never does it."

"That's just semantics, dear."

"Geez honey, whose side are you on?" she asked. Walter grunted. He never wanted to take sides when it involved his wife and daughter, yet somehow that ended up being the case every time.

"You always stick up for her, don't even try to deny it."

"Connie, for god's sake, I'm not on anyone's side. There shouldn't even be sides in the first place."

"Oh, that's such a cop-out. There's always sides. You just hate making a commitment to one."

"Are you serious?" he asked incredulously. "I make commitments all the time. I'm committed to being a faithful husband to you. I'm a committed father to Zoey. And right now I'm trying to be committed to finishing my next book so I can get another paycheck to afford all these commitments."

Connie walked to the other side of the room, keeping her back to Walter.

"Well, I'm so sorry all these horrible commitments are keeping you from living your life."

"Did I say that? Did I say any of that?" he asked angrily. "I was just trying to defend all the commitments I make on a daily basis to prove that your point is moot."

"I love how you make it seem like you're the sole person who makes a living around here. I too have a job you know, and I've also made sacrifices for this family."

"No one said you didn't," Walter countered. "I mean, honestly Connie, what the hell are we fighting about here?"

Connie turned around to face him. In reality, she wasn't sure herself. All she knew was that dealing with Zoey on her own was extremely time consuming and exhausting. Every day she could feel her only daughter slipping away, with no idea how to stop it.

And hearing Walter's reaction, he didn't seem to feel the same way she did. She didn't know which was more disheartening.

"Walter, aren't you worried about her?" she asked. "She's going to be 20 soon, and she has no sense of direction. The only friend she has is Laura, and who knows what will happen to their friendship after college. It's like she has no social skills without that girl. That's no way to send her out into the world."

Walter dropped his guard. He knew Connie was constantly battling with their daughter, especially within the last couple of years. It wasn't easy for him to have a simple conversation with her either, but he knew one day she would start to distance herself from them. He stood up and walked over to Connie, leading her to the couch against the wall of his office. As she sat down he joined her, putting his arm around her shoulder.

"Honey, I understand your concern," he said, gently. "I think about that stuff too."

"You do?"

"Yes, of course I do," he answered. "I'm sorry if that doesn't come across on a regular basis. But honey, I'm not sure how much we can do on this subject. She's old enough now where she's making her own choices, and we're not as much a part of them as we used to be. I think this is a natural fear that every parent has. But we need to have at least some faith in the way we raised her, right?"

Connie looked up at Walter, shaking her head.

"You're right. You're right. She's not a child any more. Although the way she gets with Laura sometimes that statement is questionable."

Walter chuckled, causing his wife to smile back.

"If you're that worried about her, I can have a talk with her," he said.

Before Connie could answer they heard a door slam, followed by the girls' footsteps down the stairs.

"Mom, Dad, we're going out for pizza," Zoey called to them.

"Well, I guess now's as good a time as any," Walter said. Connie nodded, as they both stood up.

"Hey, Zoey, can you wait a second?"

"Dad, we're on our way for food. I'm starving."

Walter opened the door to his study and motioned for her to enter.

"It'll only take a second."

Connie walked out of the office, passing Zoey who looked at her in confusion. Connie patted her shoulder.

"Don't worry, you're not in trouble."

"Are you guys?"

"No honey, of course not," Connie replied on her way to the kitchen. Zoey watched her disappear and turned to Laura.

"Wait for me outside?" Nodding, Laura went out onto the front stairs and sat down. After the front door closed, Zoey walked into her father's office.

It had been years since Zoey spent any time in that room. Her father treated it like his own sanctuary, a place he could go to get away from everything and simply write. Her mother never treated it that way, but Zoey knew better. She understood. She couldn't wait for the day she too, had her own sanctuary.

"Sit down, honey."

Zoey sat down on the couch Indian-style. As her father sat down behind his desk, she couldn't help but wonder if her mom had been fired, or if he had been fired. Walter seemed to be lost in thought, as if he was unsure how to begin the conversation.

"Dad, did something happen? You can tell me."

"No, no, honey, it's nothing like that. Everything's fine. We're just a bit concerned about you, that's all."

"Oh, Jesus," Zoey muttered under her breath. Walter ignored that.

"Now I don't want you to get all defensive or anything. We know you're a good kid and you're keeping up with your school work, and that's what every parent hopes for when they have a child in college," he began. "The one thing we are concerned about is your withdrawal from us, that's all. Your mother and I just want to make sure you have a sense of direction, and we can't know that if you don't talk to us once in a while."

"Come on Dad, are you really worried about all this? Isn't this Mom's whole thing? Why isn't she asking me about this?"

"Zoey, this is a concern for both of us," he answered. "And I don't like your assumption otherwise. This is our biggest concern, that you don't seem to be taking anything about your future seriously right now. I know you're only a sophomore, but we were hoping by now that you would be involved with more than just whatever Laura is doing."

"Are you kidding me, Dad? I knew that was gonna come up!" Zoey exclaimed. "What do you guys have against Laura?"

"Hey, you know we have nothing against Laura. We like her very much, as if she was our own daughter," Walter said. "You know that's not what this is about. This is about you having your own life, honey. Obviously Laura is a very important part of your life and having friends like her is wonderful. But we feel that you're limiting yourself by not trying new things on your own."

"Dad, I'm not a recluse or something. We do things with other people."

"Do you hang out with these other people when Laura isn't around?"

"What does that have to do with anything?"

"Well, honey, that would say to me that you're capable of entering into new social situations on your own, without needing Laura there to guide you."

"You know, you keep telling me to go out and 'explore my horizons' or whatever, and then you complain about the way I do it. Make up my mind here, Dad."

Walter frowned, frustrated by Zoey's response. She often became defensive any time they discussed her relationship with Laura. Over the years Walter had become increasingly concerned that their friendship was interfering with Zoey's social development. Now that she was old enough to go out on her own, he realized it had finally happened.

But for Zoey, her relationship with Laura was the life raft that saved her from drowning in apathy. She could never understand her parents' objection to that.

At this point, Walter realized that no matter how he tried to phrase his response to his daughter, there was nothing he could say that didn't involve Laura. He knew that wouldn't accomplish anything. *How am I supposed to talk to her when she's already on the defensive?*

After a minute of silence, Zoey stood up from the couch.

"Dad, Laura is waiting for me. Is there something else you want to control about my life or can I go now?"

"Hey, you don't need to be rude young lady," Walter said, sternly. "I'm still your father who brought you up to treat your parents with respect."

Even when they're being ridiculous? She could see her father waiting for an apology. *Ugh, my only way out.*

"Fine, sorry," she mumbled. "Are we done?"

Walter knew there was nothing more he could say to change her mind. He sighed.

"Yes, you can go."

Thank God, Zoey thought. She turned and walked out of the room, closing the door behind her. Opening the front door she joined Laura outside.

"Everything ok?"

"Yeah, just my parents going mental," Zoey muttered, "reminding me how much fun it is to be a teenager."

CHAPTER EIGHT

Philip Smith sat in his room, staring at a blank blog entry. It matched his current feeling about life. Empty.

You would think at age 17, there would be more to my life than church, he typed. He stared at that sentence for a moment, then continued.

And it's not even a church with a religion I believe in. It's my parents' church, my parents' beliefs, my parents' morals. Well, so-called morals. The morals their religion tells them to believe so they can root out the "immoral" ones who don't believe the same things. Well that would be their son. I am immoral in the eyes of their god.

I can't believe how naïve my parents are, to believe that this kind of a god even exists. The world has gone to shit and its people with it, yet they remain constant in their faith that we are simply not wise enough to understand God's ways. Well, isn't that convenient? We're human, and no human could ever comprehend such an intricate plan. Bullshit. I don't feel my life or my choices should be based on such a lousy explanation.

But, because I haven't reached 18 yet, my parents get to inflict their own moral code upon me without needing my permission to do so. They can teach me whatever they want and make me believe in whatever they want. There's no legal paper they have to sign to allow them to be parents. Just being human gives you the right to have a child, whether or not you're a good human. And being the automatic elder, they get to do whatever they want to you until you're able to get out of their house. If you're ever able to get out of their house.

And even then they have the right to keep track of you, or at least they feel like they do. It's like they can't relinquish their control after having it for so long. This religion they force you to join follows you wherever you go, they make sure of it. So this thing that's supposed to bring you comfort ends up only bringing you pain and confusion.

Why do we have to have religion anyway? We're born, we live, we die. What's so friggin complicated about that? Why does there have to be a place to go afterwards? There was a time when we weren't here, and that time will come again after our death. Big deal. Right now, I'd rather be in that empty space than living in this hell.

But that's not allowed, of course. We're not allowed to choose our own destiny if it involves permanently escaping from this hell hole. We're not even allowed to choose our own destiny if it goes against God's teachings. We can't love who we want if that person doesn't fit into some standardized mold that someone else tells you they need to fit into. We can't even be who we want because of that same mold. There's only one true and righteous path we can take, and if we don't want it then we're screwed.

And this god is supposed to be a loving, caring god? Shit. Complete shit.

A knock on the door interrupted Philip's writing.

"Not now," he yelled, annoyed.

"Honey, I need to talk to you," his mother, Martha, called out on the other side of the door. Angrily, Philip minimized the screen.

"Fine. Come in."

"Hello, Philip," she said as she entered the room.

Great, she never calls me by my full name. What sin have I committed now?

"I came in here to talk about the church's next retreat," she said, sitting on his bed. "I just heard from the pastor that you got kicked out of youth group. What on earth happened?"

"Mom, it's not that big a deal. I hated youth group anyway."

"Not a big deal? It's a huge deal. Youth group was the one place you could go hang out with other kids your age. You know, be yourself."

"Myself? Are you kidding?"

"Now, Philip, I understand…"

"You don't understand anything, Mom. You guys never have!" he exclaimed. *Why don't you ever listen to me? And I mean actually listen!*

"Oh, Philip. Just tell me what happened."

Philip paused. He thought about lying, but he was sick of lying just to protect his family from something that they didn't want to see. He couldn't hide who he was any more.

"Fine. So this one kid told me he knew I listened to this band, Lamb of God, and how it's the devil's music," Philip began. "So I asked him how he knew what kind of music the devil listened to. That's when he called me a heathen, so I pushed him. He fell back into a table and cut his arm. That's all. It was no big deal."

"Lamb of God? That sounds pretty Christian to me."

Philip tried not to smirk about the heavy metal band. Martha frowned.

"I assume by that look they don't play Christian music?"

"Uh, no."

"Well, obviously this child was concerned for your well-being and he didn't know how to express it. You shouldn't have put him down for that. Nor should you ever resort to violence."

"Are you serious?" Philip asked, incredulously. "He's the one who put me down first for liking a band that he doesn't like. And all I did was push him away. Don't you think you're being hypocritical?"

"That is extremely disrespectful!" Martha exclaimed, sternly. "Apologize right now."

"Mom, I'm trying to tell you I never fit in there. I have nothing in common with those kids."

"I don't understand why not. You're all the same age, you're in the same church, you're from the same town. How can you not have anything in common with them?"

"You know why," he mumbled.

"What was that?"

"You know damn well why," he said louder. *You're going to hear me now.*

"Don't you swear at me," Martha scolded, surprised. "Explain yourself, right now."

"It's the same reason you sent me to that place. You know, that straight camp or whatever ridiculous name they give it," he said angrily. "That place that's supposed to save me from myself. From being who I really am."

"Philip, that's not who you are," Martha said quietly. "We discussed this. You're just young and confused. And that boy led you astray."

"That boy is the only person I've ever cared about! He was the only true thing in my life!"

"That is not true. You have your family. And you have your faith."

"No, I have *your* faith," he shot back.

"Oh Philip, please, do we need to have this talk again?" Martha asked, exasperated. "We barely made it through Easter last week with your talk of how religion isn't even a part of the holiday anymore and how no one cares about the resurrection of our Lord."

"Mom, we never have the talk I want to have. You tell me about God and his plan for me and how I need to pray more and all this crap. It has nothing to do with me!"

"It has everything to do with you. I don't understand why you're so resistant to your faith. If you look deeper you'll find the meaning you're searching for. You just have to trust in God's will."

"How can I trust in God's will when I don't believe in him!"

"Philip! I don't want to ever hear you say that! Not in this house, not anywhere!" she exclaimed. "Tomorrow morning we are going to meet with the pastor and you are going to talk to him about your feelings. You're obviously hurt by what happened with the youth group. You merely need some guidance to get back your bearings."

That was all his parents ever had to offer, sending him to the priest for another lecture on how he'd "lost his way". Philip had endured those conversations all of his life, ever since he went to Sunday school and was teased by the other children for dressing differently and scoffing at sports. Back then his mother still had some influence over his clothes so she was able to suppress some of the "unusual" outfits. But she didn't have the same luck with his behavior.

As he grew older, Philip always found ways to rebel against their wishes, whether it be the music he listened to or the books he read. Martha hoped over time he would be influenced by his brothers, who both dated girls from their youth group and were currently at the same Bible college. Philip was well aware of their hopes, and he knew there was no room for his "colorful" individuality. But now he was beginning to lose patience with the status quo.

"This is ridiculous," he said. "I'm not going to talk to the pastor who kicked me out for liking a certain kind of music."

"You know it was for more than that," she answered. "I can't believe how difficult you're being right now. Your brothers and sisters never talk to me this way. I thought home-schooling would keep you kids away from all the evil in the world, but obviously you found a way to be influenced by it. I knew it was a bad idea letting you have your own computer."

"Why? Because it allows me to see how the world really is, uncensored? Because it shows me how people live? Because it makes me want to get the hell out of here as soon as possible?"

"That's it!" Martha said sharply. "You are grounded. No TV and no computer. In fact, I think we need to take the computer away permanently."

Philip jumped out of his chair and grabbed his laptop. It was the only source of comfort he had in a home full of oppression, his single link to the outside world.

"No!" he yelled back. "You can't do that. It's mine!"

Martha stood up, reaching out her hand.

"Philip, the computer. Now."

"Get out! Just get out!" he shouted. "I said, GET OUT!"

Martha backed up a couple feet. She had never heard him shout like that before, not to anyone. She walked backwards slowly to the door.

"Your father is not going to be very happy when he hears about this."

Philip sat back down on his chair, setting the laptop gently on the desk.

"This is nothing," he replied. Martha looked at him, alarmed.

"Philip, please tell me there isn't something else we need to know about."

"Not yet."

"What? What do you mean?"

"Get out!" he yelled again. She gasped and hurriedly closed the door.

Philip waited until he heard her footsteps disappear, and turned back to his computer to maximize the blog entry. His fingers shook as he held them above the keyboard. All those years of telling him what to think, what to avoid, who to love, had been building ever since he discovered a world without those boundaries. His first love had introduced him to that world, a place where they could be together without fear of judgment and retribution.

Is that so much to ask? He wondered. *How could something that feels so amazing be so horrible?*

It's them, he thought, staring at the words in his blog. *They're trying to mold me into some mindless robot they can control and use to spread their hateful doctrine. They want me to shed my real personality so they can clothe me in whatever confining identity suits them best. I'm not a son to them- I'm just a disciple.*

Well not any more.

Philip listened as his mother's footsteps retreated down the hallway and stopped in front of the table with the phone. He could hear her feverishly pushing buttons, and he stood up to listen at the door. But from his desk he could hear the concern in her voice as she repeated, "But Father, this was different. He sounds so much more hateful!" He stopped in the middle of the room, concerned for a moment that something might actually come from their conversation. But he knew that his real father wouldn't be back from his business trip until tomorrow, and the pastor would be able to do nothing except offer empty "guidance" in the way of prayer.

And prayer won't help them now, he thought.

CHAPTER NINE

"Now do you think there's something going on?"

Deirdre stood in the doorway of Neil's office. He was reading the front page of their newspaper. An Associated Press article underneath the picture of a church massacre described a shooting rampage done by 17-year-old Philip Smith. The headline read, "Second teenage suicide shooting in four months".

Neil looked at her over the top of the paper.

"What did you have in mind?"

CHAPTER TEN

"Dude, will you stop on something already?"

"If there was anything decent on the 400 channels we get I would."

Laura and Zoey sat on the couch in Laura's living room, flipping through channels on the television. Zoey was relieved to be out of her house for a while. Ever since that conversation with her father about her future, Zoey wasn't able to talk to him like she used to. That was the ironic part. He was worried that she wasn't communicating with him, and now she was avoiding him more than ever.

As Laura flipped by each channel, passing baseball game after baseball game, a bad movie, another game, another bad movie, Zoey tipped her head back and stared at the ceiling. Over the years Laura's home had become her second home whenever she needed a break from her parents. It was never an issue in the beginning if Zoey wanted to sleep over there. She had a feeling her parents were simply thrilled she had found such a good friend. But as the two of them got older that feeling seemed to change from contentment to concern, even though their relationship remained the same.

Sigh. Why do they worry so much? I'm fine! Geez, do these conversations ever come to an end?

"Whoa. What the heck is this?"

Zoey tipped her head back down as Laura stopped on a breaking news story interrupting a baseball game. The picture in the corner of the screen showed a teenager at a church Christmas event, but the story the news anchor was telling sounded very different.

"The only information we have right now is that Smith entered his parish during a wedding ceremony with some sort of hunting rifle and began firing into the crowd," the anchor said.

"Holy shit," Zoey muttered. Laura turned up the volume.

"The total we're hearing right now is 12 injured, 5 killed, including the gunman," the anchor continued. "We go now, live, to Sharon Birch who is just outside the police perimeter at the scene. Sharon, what can you tell us about this incident?"

"Well, Hugh, it definitely is a gruesome scene here," Sharon observed. "Police are still going through the crime scene, logging in evidence and talking with the guests to recreate the horrible event that played out this morning. As you can see behind me, there are clear bullet holes in some of the stained glass windows which indicate the shooter walked straight into the church spraying bullets back and forth as he walked toward the front of the building."

"Does that suggest the shooter did not have any intended victims at this ceremony?"

"It's possible, Hugh."

"Sharon, do we know yet the names or ages of the victims?"

"The police have not officially released the names yet, as some of their families are still being notified of their loved ones being in the hospital," she answered. "But it is confirmed that the bride and groom were two of the people who were killed."

"Is there any indication that the shooter specifically targeted the couple or had any relationship to them?"

"At this point, everything is considered speculation, Hugh. It may have been that the couple was simply in the middle of the aisle and were easy targets for the gunman."

"There seems to be some kind of commotion going on behind you, Sharon. Can you tell us what's happening?"

"Many of the parishioners have gathered around the perimeter in a massive prayer group with the pastor urging them to pray for the families of the victims," she said. "The pastor sustained a minor wound, as the bride and groom shielded him from the gunman who entered from the back of the church."

"Do we have any additional information on the 17-year-old shooter?"

"Well, we know he was a member of this parish, along with his parents, two brothers, and two sisters," she said. "His father is a lawyer and his mother is a Catechism teacher here at the church. It seems until recently, Smith was a member of the church's youth group, but he was kicked out due to a violent incident involving one of the other members. We're hoping to get more on that story as further details emerge on this young man."

At that moment Laura's cell phone rang. Both girls jumped.

"Wow, Mom, you scared the heck out of us!" Laura exclaimed as she answered it. She stood up and walked into the other room.

"Honey, I've got some bad news," her mother said. "Your cousin's wedding has been postponed for a few weeks. It seems there was a terrible incident that just happened at the church where they were going to have the ceremony."

"Oh my god, were they gonna get married at the church where that guy shot up a wedding?" Laura asked incredulously.

"How did you hear about that?"

"Mom, we're watching it on the news right now! It's crazy."

"Oh my goodness, I was watching it too when your aunt called me to tell me about the wedding being postponed. It's so frightening. I mean, can you imagine if that was your cousin's wedding? And we were there?"

"They're saying they don't know yet whether this couple was targeted specifically, like a vendetta, or if they were just really in the wrong place at the wrong time."

"Well, whatever the case, it's a horrible story," her mother replied. "I'm gonna let you go so I can call some of the other relatives in the area, see if we can get more information. Talk to you later, honey."

Laura hung up the phone and walked back into the living room, taking her place next to Zoey.

"Dude, that's where my cousin's wedding was supposed to be!"

"Seriously? That's messed up!"

"No kidding!"

"This whole thing is totally crazy," Zoey said. "They said they may have come across a blog he wrote that slams his religion, and religion as a whole. I guess it had all this stuff about religion not allowing you to be who you really are, and how his parents forced him into believing their faith. It's pretty obvious he was an atheist."

"I'm sure that went over well with the parental units," Laura said, turning her attention back to the TV.

"Well, it just shows he was so heavily against his parents' religion that he wasn't afraid to tell the whole world. Too bad no one even paid attention. I bet his family didn't even know he had a blog."

"Are you kidding? I bet there are still parents today who have no idea what a blog even is, never mind paying attention to whether or not their kid has one."

"The blog also indicates the shooter may have been gay, although it's never stated directly," Birch was saying in the background. "There is mention of a specific boy that the shooter was involved with until his family ended their relationship."

"I assume their religion does not support gay rights, Sharon?"

"That's correct," she answered. "But again, we're still waiting for more information as the police conduct their investigation. Right now the authorities are still questioning the wedding guests, along with the pastor, other parishioners, and members of the gunman's family. We'll be updating this story throughout the day as it develops. Back to you, Hugh."

Laura shut off the TV.

"Can you imagine? Right in the middle of a wedding. How sadistic is that? This seems even worse than that mall shooting."

"Seriously. It's like you can't go anywhere in public these days, even church!"

"Maybe I can use this as an example as to why my parents shouldn't make me go to church anymore," Laura grinned. "Or get married in one for that matter."

"That's awful!" Zoey said, stifling a laugh. "Besides, if you use that logic then they won't let you go to the mall again either."

"Damn, you're right. I'd totally be shooting myself in the foot then."

"Or someone else would be."

"Dude! That's horrible! And you call me awful! I think your mother would be very disappointed in you!"

"Oh god, add it to the list," Zoey muttered, rolling her eyes. "What do I do that doesn't disappoint my mother? Or my father these days, apparently."

"Still not on good terms with him, huh?"

"Nope."

"Well, I wouldn't worry about it too much. You've always had a good relationship with him. I'm sure this will all blow over soon."

"Maybe."

The two girls sat silent for a moment, mulling over the news story.

"I can't believe that even in the year 2009 gay people are still being persecuted," Zoey said, breaking the silence.

"I know. Not that that excuses what he did, of course."

"Of course not! That whole story is mind-numbing. It's just, well, you know how your family can hound you on stuff. It's enough to make anyone lose their mind sometimes."

"Especially when it comes to someone you love," Laura said quietly. "Whoever that boy was, he was probably his first love. And he can't even have a simple crush on him, never mind an actual relationship. It's crazy to even try to comprehend that."

"I know. We really do have it good, L. We really do."

CHAPTER ELEVEN

Zoey didn't want to leave her best friend's house that night, but Laura's parents had scheduled a dinner with other relatives so she didn't have a choice. She knew she would have to start interacting with her parents again at some point, but they kept returning to the same argument and she didn't have the energy to go around in circles again. When she got to her front door, she turned the handle quietly and tiptoed into the hallway. Shutting the door softly behind her, she tried to sneak upstairs without her parents noticing.

"Zoey? Is that you?"

Damn it. Maybe if I run I can avoid interrogation.

"Yeah, Mom. I'm going upstairs to do homework. I have a lot due next week."

"Honey, can we just talk to you for a sec…"

As Connie made her way into the hallway she noticed her daughter had already disappeared into her room. She frowned and began to climb the stairs, but stopped midway. She knew they wouldn't be able to have a meaningful conversation until Zoey had time to cool down from the previous discussion with her father. And Walter's immediate reaction wasn't any better. He threw himself back into his book as he always did, whether there was an ongoing issue or not. It seemed her role as mediator was growing with every argument.

Connie sighed, turned around, and walked into the kitchen.

Zoey stood at her door, listening for footsteps. She heard the creak of the stairs for a minute, then nothing, then creaking back down in the other direction. She let out a sigh of relief and sat down in bed with her laptop. Opening up a new window for her blog, she sat for a minute, her fingers poised over the keyboard. She thought of the boy she had heard about on the news and began typing.

I can't imagine what it's like to be in love.

She stared at that sentence, sitting back against her pillows. She wondered if anyone truly knew what love was like at her age. To her, true love seemed to be just a phrase, something she heard about but didn't know if it actually existed, like in The Princess Bride. It was always something seen in movies, but rarely in real life.

Real life seems too messy to allow love to exist, she typed. *Relationships may start off wonderful but that's because there are no long-term concerns or challenges to deal with at the beginning. You get to know a new person, learn all these new things, and still keep an element of mystery in the whole process. Everything is exciting.*

But it seems no one can maintain that level of excitement for very long, and if there's nothing else to the relationship then it simply fails. There has to be some sort of intense connection to keep the people coming back for more, even if there isn't a lot more there. And if there isn't a lot more there, should you even stay together? Although I suppose if that were the case, then no one would ever get married.

Of course, what do I know? Going on a couple random dates, my best friend by my side doubling, doesn't really qualify me to talk about any of this. And seriously, if I met someone right now, would I be ready to date them the way you're supposed to? Or do you have to stumble through the first couple relationships to learn what to do? And is there even one thing you're supposed to do, or is every relationship different? Ugh. Life can be so annoying without any of these questions. Sometimes I wonder if love is even worth the effort?

I guess according to that kid in Utah, it is. And the fact he couldn't have it, well, we all know what happened.

Zoey stopped typing and reread her entry. She wasn't sure what her point was, but it felt good to get all of those thoughts out of her head and onto the screen. When she wasn't sure what to think, it helped to put those questions out into the void, even if no one responded to them. It was as if she was adding her own opinion to a social conversation that always welcomed new members, no matter who you were in real life. You could be whoever you wanted online, and you could always find a group to accept you.

She sighed, unsure of what to write next. She thought about Laura's relationship with Aaron, how the two of them seemed to be progressing toward being an actual couple. Laura was so popular and was always dating other people and simply having fun. But now it seemed different, as if she had found someone who encompassed everything she had been looking for in her previous boyfriends. It made Zoey smile, but at the same time she worried how that would affect their friendship. Laura wasn't acting any differently, and there was never any mention of Aaron being tired of Zoey's company. But as things grew more serious, would that remain the case?

Of course it will, she thought, shaking her head. *She's my best friend.* Cracking her fingers, Zoey began to type again.

Sometimes I wonder how anyone does anything in this world? It seems there's always someone there to knock you down just when you think you're heading in the right direction.

Sometimes it's so frustrating I want to walk outside and scream, scream until the sky falls down and the houses collapse and there's nothing left but emptiness, and quiet, and me.

The only light at the end of the tunnel is that, although they try, others can only dictate your actions for so long. Eventually you become old enough to make your own decisions, and that's when your life truly begins. Of course, that's when you also discover that life is very different from what you see on TV or read in books. Having no real knowledge on the subject, all you can do is throw yourself out there and see what happens, and cling to the fleeting moments of happiness and peace, if you find them. And you've got to be able to find some- otherwise, what the hell is the point?

Zoey paused, then hit the Enter key to post her entry on the blog. Reading it one last time, she frowned. She knew it wasn't one of her better posts, but the entries about love rarely were. They merely acted as one more reminder that the concept still eluded her, even after entering college.

It always seems I'm waiting for my own life to begin, she thought. *Hopefully I'll recognize if that ever happens.*

CHAPTER TWELVE

It was approaching 11 p.m. and Deirdre sat at her desk in the living room, surfing the Internet for ideas for her article. It had only been a couple days since the church shooting, but she was completely engrossed in numerous sites with information on teenage violence. Nowadays it was easy to find the statistics she was looking for. The Internet offered access to sites from the Federal Bureau of Investigation, the U.S. Department of Justice, and the Center for Disease Control, which offered information on the prescription drug issue. Her printer was working overtime as she made hard copies of various articles detailing past suicide shootings from news web sites, while she bookmarked other articles dealing with youth violence as a whole.

There were several headlines that caught her attention. "More teenagers than ever before claim depression or anxiety", "Teen suicide rates on the rise", "Is gun control making a dent in this country's violence?" Each new statistic, each new piece of information she encountered, made Deirdre even more interested in her topic. Despite her initial pitch to her editor, she knew she also had a morbid fascination with the subject matter. Judging by the endless number of web sites she discovered, she realized she was far from alone.

The easiest information to find, of course, was all of the articles written about various school shootings in the past. After Columbine there seemed to be an influx of studies and articles dealing with the students' personalities and home life, and how schools could better prepare to handle such a situation. But this most recent shooting was quite unlike the others, in that it had taken place in a church. While a large number of teenage shootings occurred in schools, the last one was at a mall, and then this. It seemed as though school was not the only major factor dictating the actions of these shooters anymore, and Deirdre wondered how this story would fit into her assessment of an escalating phenomenon.

Looking at her list of bookmarked sites, Deirdre smiled.

Jesus. I hope the government isn't watching what sites I'm checking out, she thought, looking over the varied assortment of violence-related topics. *I'd look like a friggin psychopath.*

As she bookmarked another site, her cell phone rang.

Who would be calling at this hour? she thought, glancing at the clock on her laptop. She looked at the caller ID.

Oh God.

She stared at the phone as though afraid of it. She didn't want to pick it up, but she also didn't want to hear what kind of message would be left if she didn't. Gingerly, she reached out and opened the phone.

"Hello?"

"Hey, Deirdre. Sorry to call so late, but I figured you'd be up."

"Yes. You know me too well, Ben," she answered softly, struggling to keep her voice from wavering. It had been several months since their last phone call, when he told her about Veronica. Deirdre assumed it wasn't serious at the time. He had dated a couple women since they separated, and no one had lasted more than two or three months.

But the time of day and tone of his voice suggested he had some news to tell her. News she wasn't ready to hear.

"I was catching up on some email," she lied. "Um, how have you been?"

"Well, that's what I wanted to talk to you about." Deirdre cringed.

What is wrong with me? I knew this day would come, she thought. *I just didn't think it would happen so soon.*

"You know I've been seeing Veronica for a year now," he began.

A year? Has it been a year already? Wow. I guess it wasn't that soon. We have been separated for three years.

"And things are going, well, great," he continued cautiously. "She's always understood our, um, situation, and it's never been a problem. However, I would like to be able to move things forward with her, and with us too, I guess."

Deirdre bit her lip.

"Deirdre, I think it's time we finalize the divorce."

There it was. Divorce.

Of course he wants to get a divorce, she thought. *Unlike me, he's moved on completely. He found someone else. He's finally happy again. Bastard.*

Ben sat quietly on the other end of the line. When Deirdre didn't say anything, he continued.

"I know we've been holding out on this issue for a long time, Deeds," he said. She'd almost forgotten that nickname. She always liked it, since he was the only one who used it. "But we both know we can't hold out any longer.

53

We tried to make it work and it didn't. There's nothing else we can do. This is just the final step in that process."

Deirdre hated that word, process. As if their entire relationship could be broken down into parts like that. When they first met their junior year of college, living apart for a year before settling down in her hometown, working hard to afford a home, and then making enough to raise a family. It was perfect until the incident. That's when the real "process" began.

"I never wanted to go through all that in the first place," Deirdre muttered.

"What?"

"Nothing."

"Come on, you know we both agreed to separate."

"You say that as if it was my choice," she replied.

Ben sighed.

"Jesus, Deirdre, this whole victim thing is starting to get old."

Deirdre went silent. She couldn't believe he was belittling what happened to her, what happened to them. *Has he forgotten already?*

"Excuse me? I don't have to play the victim here. I *was* the victim. And our relationship was next. Or don't you remember any more?"

"Deeds, come on. There's no need to get melodramatic. Let's not make this harder than it already is."

"That's easy for you to say."

"No, it really isn't," he replied, his voicing rising slightly. "And you know it. Don't make me out to be the bad guy here. You know I hung on as long as possible. Things weren't healthy for either one of us anymore. And no amount of outside help was going to change that."

"What about us, huh? Never mind the 'outside help.' What happened to us working things out?"

"I don't know, Deirdre. You tell me."

Deirdre was speechless. It sounded as if he was placing all the blame on her.

"What's that supposed to mean?"

Ben sighed again. This wasn't the conversation he was hoping to have. Bringing up old memories, especially these specific memories, was something he wanted to avoid. It had happened three years ago, but for Deirdre, she spoke about it like it was yesterday. For Ben, it was something he needed to move on from or else he would go insane over the loss. But what she couldn't, or maybe wouldn't, see, was that he had always been there to listen, he had tried to be there for her, and it wasn't enough.

He knew it wasn't going to be easy. And it wasn't the first time a seemingly simple conversation turned into the same full blown argument. But he wanted it to be the last.

"Tell me what you meant by that!" she demanded.

"Deirdre, do we have to go through all this again?" he asked. "We went through that ordeal together, remember? We both said things we can never take back, and we'll have to live with that. So don't pretend you're the only one with a burden to carry here. I tried for a year to keep things together. I took responsibility for my mistakes. I paid my dues. And now I'm ready to try again, with someone else. And I don't feel I need to apologize for that."

He was right. Deirdre knew he was right. *God, I hate when that happens.* She paused, trying to keep her voice steady.

"You're going to ask her to marry you, aren't you?"

This time Ben paused.

"Yes."

Deirdre knew from the beginning it would end like this. Years of separation were enough for him, but they would never be enough for her. No matter how hard she worked, or how often she went out with friends, or visited with her family, her life was not her own any more. It would never be again. She lost control when she lost the baby.

And Ben would never understand that. He couldn't. He wasn't there. No matter how great a loss it was to him, and she knew it was devastating, he would never comprehend the pain and remorse she would feel for the rest of her life.

But there were no words left to say. They were out of ideas. And she was out of options.

Ben waited for her to say something, anything. Deirdre took a deep breath.

"Do you really love her?"

The question took Ben by surprise. He'd said "I love you" plenty of times to Veronica, and it felt good being able to say it again. But Deirdre would always be his first love and that made her special. He hoped she would realize that one day.

Even though he didn't need to think about it, he needed to let her know he meant it.

"I do," he answered. *And I want to explain so much.* But Deirdre would never understand, nor should she have to. He knew it was painful for her. And he knew she would never see the leap of faith it took for him to love again- he would never be able to do it justice.

There was just too much for either one to try to explain to the other. And now it was too late.

Deirdre could hear the sincerity in his voice. It was heart-breaking, but it was also what she needed to hear.

"Ok," she said. "When do you want to meet?"

CHAPTER THIRTEEN

"Aaron, don't be ridiculous. I already have my job here."

Laura was getting tired of having the same discussion with her boyfriend about their summer plans. *We haven't even been dating for a year, yet he's being so adamant about the whole thing.*

"Oh come on, Laura. You know the restaurant isn't gonna fall apart without you," he insisted, walking over to her on his bed.

"It's not the restaurant I'm concerned about. It's Zoey."

"Zoey? What? You think *she's* gonna fall apart? She's a big girl, L."

It was almost the end of the semester, and Laura and Aaron hadn't spent a day apart in months. Zoey tagged along on the lesser date nights, like when they went to see the latest action movie, or the frat guys threw a party at the house. And Aaron didn't care. He thought Zoey was cool, once you got to know her. But it suddenly became apparent that her presence was going to ruin his plans for the summer.

"Laura, this is an awesome opportunity," he pleaded. "I mean, the whole summer working for Dean's family at their resort in Florida? Think about it. We'd be hanging out at the beach for three months and getting paid for it! How sweet is that?"

"You just like the thought of me hanging out in a bikini all summer."

"Absolutely! Come on. You know you'd rather do this then waitress at some boring restaurant all summer."

Laura couldn't deny the temptation. She'd never had a boyfriend before that had such connections. She'd never known *anyone* who had these connections. Usually she and Zoey were forced into working the same monotonous jobs at the same tired restaurant, she taking orders and Zoey clearing tables. And it wasn't the best paying job either.

But for their town, it was the best offer they had, and one that was left open for them each summer. She knew Zoey wouldn't be able to afford to go to Florida for three months. Aaron and his friends were able to split an apartment, but she and Zoey wouldn't have that option. However, if she went alone, she could easily be another roommate in the house, staying in Aaron's room.

It was a wonderful opportunity, but only for her.

"Aaron, you just don't get it," Laura said, standing up. "Maybe if Zoey could come, too, I'd do it. But she can't afford it. And I can't afford to leave her for the summer. We've never been apart for that long."

"Jesus, you make her sound like a pet," Aaron mumbled.

"Hey! That was a shitty thing to say! I told you, you don't get it, Aaron. I don't know why you're not accepting no for an answer."

"Because you're not giving me a valid reason," he said, angrily. "You keep talking about Zoey, like she'll friggin self-destruct if you're not here. And that's ridiculous. If she's as good a friend as you say she is, she'll understand that you have this really cool chance to get away for the summer, do something fun. She wouldn't want to deprive you of that, would she?"

"That's not the point, Aaron."

"Oh yeah? Then what is? Explain it to me. Tell me what I'm not getting. Because right now you sound pretty egotistical, thinking that Zoey wouldn't be able to live without you. I mean, are you guys planning on living near each other forever? Because stuff happens. You can't put your whole life on hold because of Zoey."

Laura knew no one could fully comprehend her relationship with Zoey, no matter how hard she tried to explain it. Her parents understood it on some level, watching the two of them grow up together. They knew the relationship was extremely tight, and that they had been best friends for a long time. Zoey's parents understood the same thing, although they saw it as a detriment to Zoey's growth as a person. And maybe it was in some sense.

But Laura learned something, when they were much younger, that brought about a deeper understanding of who Zoey was, and how difficult it was for her to interact with others on a regular basis.

Zoey told her one night during a sleepover at Laura's house. They had just met in first grade. After watching a movie they were supposed to go to bed, but instead played house with some of Laura's stuffed animals.

"This is boring," Laura said, putting down the stuffed bear. "Let's play Truth or Dare. I saw it on TV."

"Ok," Zoey said. "You first."

"Truth or Dare?"

"Truth."

Laura thought for a moment.

"Tell me something no one else knows."

Zoey looked down at the floor. She traced a circle pattern into the carpet in Laura's room. Laura could see she was trying to choose her words very carefully. She knew this was going to be a big truth.

"My dad didn't want to have me."

"What?"

"A couple months ago I heard my parents yelling," Zoey began. "I couldn't really hear what they were saying, but I know they were fighting. It was the first time I ever heard my parents fight so loud."

Laura nodded, encouraging her to continue.

"Anyway, my mom was sad about something, and my dad started yelling. It was scary. Even when he's mad at me, he doesn't yell. But he was yelling."

Zoey paused, as if she was back in the moment.

"That's when he said something about not wanting to have a kid in the first place."

Being in first grade, Laura didn't know how to respond to that statement.

"I'm sure he didn't mean it," she told Zoey. "People say stuff like that all the time when they're mad."

Zoey wanted to believe her, wanted to believe that the man she adored had always wanted a daughter just like her. She was sure other kids heard their parents say terrible things when arguing with each other, and it wasn't a big deal. There are worse things a parent can say or do to cause physical or emotional harm to their own child.

But ever since that day, Zoey felt like her existence was a mistake.

It was the kind of story only a best friend would know, and Laura never broke Zoey's confidence. And over the years it became obvious their friendship was the one thing Zoey knew wasn't a mistake.

Even Laura would never fully understand Zoey's pain until they got older. As she developed faster than her favorite counterpart, physically and socially, she could see Zoey struggle to keep up with her while still maintaining some sense of individual identity. Everyone noticed Laura, but no one spoke to Zoey until Laura introduced them. Only through Laura's upbeat personality was Zoey allowed to join the rest of the group.

And it was something Laura always regretted, for Zoey was the most loyal person she knew. No matter what new group she joined or what sport she chose to play, Zoey was always there to support her. And over time, Zoey would be able to open up and be her funny, playful self around other people. But until Laura created that opportunity, her best friend was lost in her own world of doubt and insecurity.

So once she discovered she had the power to help, Laura gladly took on the responsibility of maintaining Zoey's happiness. She knew Zoey would do the same for her if the circumstances were reversed.

"There are things you don't know about, Aaron, things I can't tell you without breaking Zoey's trust in me," Laura stated, turning to look at him.

"Just please believe me when I tell you, I'm not being egotistical or melodramatic or ridiculous. She relies on me for certain things, as I do her, and this is one of them. It's non-negotiable."

Aaron looked Laura in the eyes, and saw that she had made up her mind. Whatever this great secret was, she wasn't going to tell him, even if it was seemingly the only excuse she had not to join him in Florida. He watched his hopes of getting even closer to her over the summer slip away.

"Well, I guess I have no choice," he said, trying to hide his disappointment.

"I'm glad you understand, honey," she said. She knew he didn't, but she hoped in time he would get the chance to.

CHAPTER FOURTEEN

"Wow, that's quite the invite!"

"I know, it's crazy."

"What did you say?"

"I said no, of course. We already have our jobs here for the summer."

"Wow."

Zoey wasn't sure what else to say to Laura as they drove down Main Street. She knew it was a huge opportunity for Laura, to work on the beach all summer in Florida. *Beats the hell out of staying in this lousy town.* But at the same time, she was relieved her friend had turned him down.

"Dude, that's like, a serious relationship offer," Zoey noted. "I didn't realize you guys hit that level yet."

"Ugh, I never know if we're on the same level or not," Laura sighed. "I was totally taken off-guard when he asked me. To be honest, I was kinda freaked out by it."

"Too much too soon?"

"Oh yeah."

They drove along in silence for a couple minutes.

"Remember when we went to the movie last weekend?" Laura asked suddenly. "And there was that one couple that kept flirting with each other to figure out what the other one was thinking without asking? Well, that's definitely us. When it comes to our relationship, I have no idea what's going on."

Zoey grinned.

"I think most relationships start off that way. Isn't that what they mean when people talk about keeping the mystery alive? That's the game playing part, when everything is still up for grabs. I thought that was supposed to be the fun part."

"Well, I think it starts off as the fun part because nothing is that serious at the beginning," Laura replied. "But before you know it, your boyfriend is asking you to live with him in a different state so you can work together for the entire summer. No idea where the transition period was for that development!"

"No kidding."

They drove in silence again for a couple miles, each one caught up in their own thoughts. Laura wondered if she was actually caught off-guard by Aaron's invitation, or if she simply wanted a better excuse than Zoey not to go. Zoey glanced over at her, wondering the same thing.

After a while it was too quiet for her. There was more of an opportunity for Laura to change her mind if they continued that discussion.

"Dude, I can't wait till the end of the year," Zoey said, breaking the silence. "I think junior year is gonna be way better than this year."

"What? Oh, yeah. Three more weeks to go. But who's counting?"

"I have this 10 page paper due in a week that I haven't even started yet. It's on Hamlet, which I've read, like, three times now. I'm so sick of people making a huge deal about that play. I mean, yeah it's a great play, but there's only so much you can say about it. Is Hamlet crazy? Yes or no. That's it."

"I'm sure Shakespeare had bigger intentions for his audience than that."

"Well then, he shouldn't have made Hamlet so crazy," Zoey laughed. Laura snorted, causing the girls to laugh even harder.

"Don't do that! I'm laughing so hard I'm crying! I can hardly drive here."

"Well, you should stop driving anyway because we're coming up on a red light," Laura said in-between giggles. "I'm pretty sure that means stop."

"Ugh, I hate this light," Zoey said, catching her breath as she brought the car to a stop. "It's the worst life-sucking light out there."

"Life-sucking? Like the machine in the Princess Bride?"

"Yeah, kind of, without the straps and water wheel. It's like it's taunting you by not letting anyone go anywhere. You can see the light is red for everyone and there's nothing you can do about it. I feel myself growing older by the minute waiting for this thing to turn green."

"Dude, you are growing older by the minute."

"You know what I mean."

Another minute passed as the light remained unchanged.

"Jesus, I could've made it to Utah and back by now!" Laura exclaimed. "Not that I'm upset the wedding didn't happen this weekend. But I see what you mean."

"Just think, you could be sitting in a hot church right now listening to some priest ramble on about the sanctity of marriage. Thank you repressive religion."

Another few seconds, the light finally changed. Zoey stepped on the gas pedal.

"We need some tunes," said Laura, leaning forward to turn on the radio.

That's when Zoey saw the pick-up truck, right before it slammed head first into the passenger's side of the car.

The sudden impact sent the car flying sideways. The airbags deployed, throwing the two girls back against their seats. Zoey could hear the truck slam on its brakes, as they careened into the other lane of traffic. She struggled to gain control of the vehicle, as cars coming from the other direction swerved recklessly to avoid them. It didn't matter, she couldn't see or do anything as she was thrown around with the rest of the car. Her screams blended with the deafening squeal of tires, until she felt another jolt from the front of the car. It was the last thing she felt before passing out.

"Zoey! Hey, Z!"

"Laura? Where are you?"

Zoey felt herself teetering on the edge of something, but there was nothing to see. She could hear Laura's laughter, but couldn't tell where it was coming from. It seemed to be coming from everywhere. The one image Zoey could make out was a faint light in the distance. She strained to see beyond it.

"Come on, Z! Look up!"

"What? I can't see you!"

"Sure you can, silly. I'm right here."

Zoey put her arms out, frantically reaching for something, anything, that she could hold onto. Nothing.

"I can't open my eyes, L. Where are we?"

"You have to open your eyes, Zoey."

"Laura? Please, talk to me. What's happening?"

"Open your eyes." Her voice was getting fainter.

"Wait for me! Laura! Wait!"

"Miss? Miss?" Someone was suddenly shouting above her. "Can you hear me?"

When Zoey came to, everything was blurry. She strained to see where they were, what was happening. The smell of smoke hung thick in the air. She could hear sirens coming from somewhere, and a distant voice calling out above her. Her head was already turned to the side, and she could barely make out a person standing on the other side of the door. He was yelling something, but she couldn't understand him. The sirens grew louder.

Zoey's head was pounding. She tried to move her arms but they felt like lead. She couldn't even feel her legs. She looked down to see one of them pinned underneath the flattened hood of the car. She felt nauseous.

"Miss? If you can hear me, we're going to get you out. Just don't move."

Don't move. Okay, I can do that. That's all I can do.

Suddenly, Zoey remembered that Laura was in the car with her. She tried to turn her head, but the pain shot down her entire back. The man outside the door kept yelling at her to remain still. She tried again.

Slowly, her head fell forward, and she was able to use the momentum to turn her head to the right. Laura lay crumpled in her seat, the metal frame completely crushed around her. She was strangely close to Zoey, even though she was on the other side of the car. There was a lot of blood. A lot of blood.

Zoey tried to touch her, but the pain was immobilizing. She tried to call out to her, but nothing came out. Stale air.

She struggled to swallow, the pounding escalating in her head. She tried again.

"Laura," she croaked. "Laura."

"Hold on miss. We finally have the equipment we need. We'll have you outta there soon."

"No, Laura. She needs…" Zoey's voice trailed off, as she slipped in and out of consciousness.

"Miss… Real soon… It's okay…"

"Laura…"

Suddenly Zoey heard a terrible ripping noise, as if someone was drilling a hole in her head. She could feel the car's weight shift. She opened her eyes in time to see Laura's limp body slump forward against her seat belt. It was the only movement she saw.

"Laura," she whispered, a little louder than before. No response. "Laura!"

* * * * * * *

Zoey's parents were sitting at the kitchen table, catching up on the day's newspaper, when the phone rang. Connie got up to answer it.

"Hello?"

The voice on the other end of the line was hysterical. Connie couldn't make out a word the girl was saying. But it sounded vaguely like Zoey.

"Zoey? Zoey, honey, is that you? What happened?"

Walter looked up from the paper, alarmed.

"Zoey, slow down. I can't understand you, honey. Where are you? Are you all right?"

The next words came out crystal clear.

"Laura is dead!"

CHAPTER FIFTEEN

That Saturday was a beautiful day. The sun rose to a cloudless sky, inviting spring to begin its bloom. The trees rustled in the light breeze. Birds, coming home from a long flight, called out their greetings. The grass looked greener, the flowers, brighter, and the dismal grey of winter, nowhere to be seen.

Nowhere, except in Zoey Young's eyes.

It had been five days since the accident. Zoey sat on her bed, her ankle in a walking cast. She spent three of those days in the hospital to ensure she didn't have a concussion. The driver of the truck was arrested for his 5th drunken driving charge, which meant his license was permanently revoked and he was in jail. The police said they could take comfort in knowing he was off the streets. The doctor told Zoey's parents she was extremely lucky there were no other major injuries, minus a few bumps and bruises.

And my best friend.

She looked down at her faded black dress, confused. She hadn't worn a dress in years.

Why am I wearing this dress? I hate this dress. Laura would totally razz me about it if she saw me.

But she won't.

I want to ask her what she thinks I should wear. Is that what I'm supposed to think about before her funeral? All these strange thoughts swirled around in Zoey's brain, none of them relating to Laura's death. It didn't matter, but of course, it did.

Down the hall, Connie finished putting on a necklace to complement her outfit. She could see Walter in the mirror standing behind her as he straightened his tie. She couldn't tell what he was thinking, but she rarely could. Everything was so unreal she didn't even know what she was thinking. *Maybe I should see how Zoey is doing.*

As she stood up and turned toward the door, Walter walked over and put his hand on her arm. She looked up at him, trying to hold back her tears. He was doing the same.

"It could've been her..." she whispered.

"But it wasn't."

He gently wiped the corner of her eye as she bowed her head.

"It's okay," he murmured, lifting up her chin. "There's no right answer here."

Connie nodded and made her way past him into the hallway. As she walked toward Zoey's room she could see the door was open slightly. It was so quiet she could hear the floor squeak under her feet. The silence was unnerving.

I can't believe I used to be annoyed by their laughter, she thought. *What mother is bothered by that?*

When she got to the door she grabbed the handle to push it open further. That's when she caught a glimpse of Zoey in her mirror. She sat motionless on her bed, looking down at the blanket. Connie had never seen such a lifeless expression on her daughter's face before. The sharp wit, sarcastic grin, mischievous eyes, they were all gone. It was as if a shell of Zoey's body was all that remained.

Connie opened her mouth to say something, but nothing seemed appropriate. *Would anything ever be appropriate for this?* She shook her head, let go of the handle, and walked past the room.

Zoey didn't even notice.

* * * * * * *

Hours later, hundreds of people huddled around Laura's grave site as the priest offered the final prayer. Zoey recognized all of them and knew many, but spoke to no one. It was as if she was a part of one of Laura's dreams, where everyone who knew and loved her got together to celebrate life as Laura lived it. Nothing seemed real, and their presence without Laura only strengthened that sense of disbelief.

It began with the church ceremony. Dozens of pictures of Laura covered a poster board that sat near the casket, surrounded by brightly colored bouquets of flowers. Zoey didn't look at any of them. What was the point? She had plenty of her own photo albums, trinkets, concert programs and real memories they had created together. That was why she hadn't gone to the wake the night before either. It wasn't her friend any more in the casket. She didn't know who that person was.

Across from her Zoey could see Laura's parents. Her mother sobbed uncontrollably, her shoulders shaking. Her father held his wife tightly, clinging to the only immediate family he had left. The pain flowed through their eyes, the grief being too much for their bodies to contain. They were burying their daughter. Their only child was gone.

My only friend is gone.

After what seemed like hours, the crowd began to clear. Zoey could see people looking at her as they walked by, shaking their heads. *Poor girl. She was always hanging around with Laura. What was her name?* They continued to their cars.

"Hey, Zoey," she heard someone say behind her. She turned around to see Aaron.

"Oh. Hi," she said awkwardly. It was the first time they had ever spoken to each other outside a familiar setting.

"I just can't believe it. I can't believe she's gone," he said, his voice breaking. "It feels like I'm at someone else's funeral, and she'll be calling me later today."

Zoey nodded, not knowing what to say. She had never seen Aaron upset, or even anything but happy and laidback. They were no longer in the comfort of the frat house or the local hang-out, or even in Laura's presence. He suddenly felt like a stranger.

"Are you going to her parents' house now?" he asked.

Before Zoey could answer, Connie and Walter approached them.

"Honey? Do you want to go to the Simmons' house for the reception?" Connie asked, putting her hand on Zoey's shoulder. Zoey shook her head.

"I just, I can't. I want to go home now. Bye, Aaron."

She turned and began walking toward the car. Connie followed her.

"I'm sorry about that," Walter said, turning to Aaron. "She's obviously upset right now. I'm her father, Walter. Do you go to school with Zoey?"

"No. I'm Aaron, Laura's boyfriend. I mean, I was," Aaron said, straining to hold back more tears. Walter frowned.

"I'm so sorry, Aaron. Laura touched the lives of many people. We will really miss her."

"I know. That's the part I'm not ready for."

"No one ever is," Walter said. "Well, I should catch up with Zoey. It was nice meeting you, Aaron."

Walter turned to see Mrs. Simmons stop Zoey and Connie on their way to the car. He walked over to join them.

"Oh, Connie, Walter, thank you for coming," she said tearfully. "It means so much to us and I know it would mean so much to Laura."

"Of course, don't think anything of it," Connie replied, taking her hand. "I can't even imagine the pain you're going through right now. There are no words."

Mrs. Simmons nodded and leaned over Zoey to hug her. It was the first time since Zoey had met her that they hugged.

"Oh, honey, I'm glad you're all right," she sputtered, pulling back to look at Zoey. "I'm glad you were with her when…"

Her voice trailed off as she began to sob again. Mr. Simmons walked over and put his arm around her shoulder.

"I'm sorry. We're, well, you understand."

"Yes, of course," Connie replied. "We just wanted to let you know how truly sorry we are for your loss. Laura was like a daughter to us, and we will miss her so much. Unfortunately I think this has taken quite a toll on Zoey, so we won't be able to make it to the reception."

"Of course," said Mr. Simmons. "Thank you again for coming. And Zoey, please, don't be a stranger. In fact, we would like you to come over some time and take a look through her closet and her room. You can take whatever you like. We'd rather give her things away to people close to her than strangers."

Why would I want to take anything out of her room? That's where it belongs, Zoey thought. She nodded anyway.

"Good," he said. "Well, we should get back to the house. Again, thank you for coming."

As they walked away, Connie and Walter looked back at the grave one more time, taking each other's hand for comfort. Zoey never looked back.

The three of them rode home in silence, neither Walter nor Connie knowing what to say to their daughter. The sun shone brightly on her face through the window, but she didn't notice the warmth, nor did she see any of the new signs of spring. In the rearview mirror Connie could see the look of confusion and helplessness on Zoey's face. Trying not to cry again, she turned away.

When they reached the house, a package sat on the front steps. Walter got out of the car and walked over to pick it up.

"It's addressed to you, Zoey. There's no return address though."

Zoey took the box and looked at the top left corner. "Surprise" was all it said. The handwriting was familiar.

"I'm going to my room." .

"Sure, honey," Connie said. "Let us know if you need anything."

How about my only friend back? she thought. She carried the package to her room.

Sitting down on the bed, Zoey placed the box on the floor and took off her shoes. She picked the box up again and set it down next to her. Sliding her fingers along the sides of it, she ripped the brown paper that covered the box and opened the top flaps.

A note sat on top.

"Surprise! You thought I had forgotten, but I didn't! I knew you wanted these boots and I ordered them weeks before your birthday. But of course they were back ordered, so I had to use the excuse that they were for me so you wouldn't find out! Happy birthday buddy! I can't wait to see you in them! Love, Laura."

The box fell to the floor as Zoey collapsed beside it, sobbing.

CHAPTER SIXTEEN

"Thank you for meeting with me, Dr. Stephens."

Deirdre walked into the office of the psychologist she was interviewing for her article. Dr. Carla Stephens was one of two psychologists in town, and was managing all calls while Dr. Loring was on vacation. Deirdre was surprised the doctor had time for an interview, with all of the town's "crazies" left in her hands alone for an entire week. Of course, Deirdre would try to refrain from bringing that up, especially the word "crazies."

"Please, come in, Miss Hart," Stephens offered. "I read your column all the time. Very enjoyable."

"Thank you."

Deirdre looked around the office with interest. There was nothing unusual- a dark wood desk with some pictures on it, a tall bookshelf filled with textbooks, degrees hanging on the wall, and two wide leather chairs next to each other. It brought Deirdre back to the days when she was in therapy after she lost the baby. They weren't pleasant memories, but that was mostly due to her failing relationship with Ben at the time. He thought she needed the therapy, but he didn't. She thought if they went through it together it would help bring them closer.

Maybe he was already checking out of the relationship by then, she thought, taking out her pen and notebook. But now was not the time to re-analyze that situation.

"So, you mentioned on the phone you're working on a new piece about teenagers and violent behavior," Stephens said, gesturing for Deirdre to sit down in one of the chairs. She took the other chair next to her. "What can I do for you?"

"Well, I've been doing a lot of online research about various tragic incidents involving teenagers over the last 20 years or so," Deirdre began.

"The Internet is a wonderful source of news from all over the country. But I also wanted to interview someone who is trained to deal with these kinds of situations."

"When you say 'these kinds of situations,' you mean the teenagers committing the violence?"

"Yes. I suppose I should come out and say that. I'm most interested in those kids who end up as suicide shooters."

Stephens shifted in her seat.

"That's a pretty specific topic, Miss Hart. I'm not sure what kind of information I can offer. I mean, to my knowledge I've never counseled anyone who has committed such an act after our sessions."

"Oh, of course not," Deirdre stammered. "I mean, talk about bad advertising."

Stephens shifted in her seat again. Deirdre cleared her throat in embarrassment and continued.

"I think my intention came out wrong. I'd like to talk to you about these kids in general. Various reasons, mental, emotional, scientific, whatever, that would cause a teenager to commit such a crime."

"Ah. Well, that I can probably help you with."

"Great," said Deirdre, relieved. "First, I thought we could start with some statistics. I've read in a couple different reports that while adult violence is in decline, adolescent violence is on the rise."

"I wouldn't be surprised if that were true, although the definition of 'violence' is probably different in each study. There are a number of very specific events, such as school shootings, that seem to bring this question to light every time they happen. The 1990s especially seemed to be fraught with school shootings, Columbine being only one example of course."

"So you believe this kind of violence has been consistently on the rise?"

"Well, there are some pretty early cases that are somewhat well-known, and sporadic cases throughout the 1980s, but not many. Is that where your research picks up?"

"Yes," Deirdre answered. "From what I can tell, there's at least one case per year through the 90s of a shooting happening, mostly involving teenagers at a school, although some of the shooters were older."

"Ok."

"So, that growing number of teen shooters makes me question whether or not the media is to blame for creating the kind of hysteria that often follows these incidents. I mean, it's not like they're making up these stories or statistics. The facts are there, happening year after year."

"True again. However, the most recent information from the CDC shows that less than 1% of all homicides and suicides among school-age related kids happens at or around school grounds," Stephens said. "Teenagers exhibit all sorts of violence, yes, but our schools are really no more at risk than they have been in the past."

"Ok, well, what if we ignore the school setting altogether. The last couple of suicide shootings that were in the news happened outside of school."

"Well, again, let's look at the statistics," Stephens said, getting up from her chair. She crossed the room and scanned her bookshelf, grabbing a large report from the Centers for Disease Control and Prevention from the top shelf. Thumbing through, she stopped on one page and began to read aloud.

"The closest year we have for this kind of information is 2007, which says juveniles made up 16 percent of all violent crime arrests," she dictated. "You can further break it down to 1,350 being arrested for murder. They don't break it down into suicide shootings, of course, but in general that's what you're looking at for the amount of violent behavior that kids exhibit in this country in comparison to adults."

"Do you know if that's an increase from previous years?"

"I've read some reports that say adolescent violence has risen more than 100% in the last decade or so. But again, those kinds of percentages tend to differ depending on who you talk to and how they define violent behavior."

"What about suicide rates?" Deirdre asked. She was hoping there were more concrete statistics on that topic.

"Well, let's see," said Stephens, returning to the report. "It says here that suicide accounts for about 12% of adolescent deaths, and that the number of suicides has recently increased after a 15-year decline. Well, I would believe that."

"Why do you say that?"

"Teens today have a number of issues they're dealing with. Gang violence is more prevalent in the cities, but there's also alcohol and drugs and sexual experimentation," Stephens answered, returning to her chair and placing the report beside her. "Kids are doing these things at a much earlier age than before, believing they have the adequate knowledge to handle the consequences. But just because they know of these things at an earlier age, that doesn't mean they have the emotional maturity to deal with them responsibly."

"Do you think their introduction to these issues contributes to the rising gun violence done by today's youth?"

"It's possible," Stephens agreed. "Kids see guns everywhere. TV, movies, video games, the news their parents are watching. Today the news is either war stories showing military personnel firing their weapons in a heated battle, or gun-related incidents happening in and around their own community. Their perception of guns is probably quite different from our parents' generation when they were growing up. In fact, I would say the general public's perception of guns is different from what it used to be."

As Deirdre furiously scribbled down her notes, Stephens stood up and placed the report back on the bookshelf. When she sat back down she turned toward Deirdre.

"You realize, Miss Hart, that even with all of these environmental factors, teenagers across the decades still share similar traits, right?"

"What do you mean?"

"Well, no matter when they grow up, they all have raging hormones and identity crises to deal with once they hit puberty," Stephens pointed out. "They're trying to break away from their parents and find their own sense of identity, while needing guidance from their parents at the same time. It's probably the most confusing time in a person's life, no matter what generation you're from."

"Do you think that has more to do with the rise in violence than anything else we talked about? It seems to me that outside forces would have more of an impact on this kind of behavior, especially if the rate at which it's occurring is changing."

"I'm just saying if you're going to write about this subject, you need to look at all of the factors," Stephens suggested. "Your focus is on how these kids are growing up, which does play a major role, but you also have to look at the kids themselves. Teenage brains begin developing differently. Certain parts of the brain grow sharper while other sections are still struggling to catch up. That's why teenagers can be easily influenced by minor details in their lives. And the way they deal with them indicates their personality type."

"Personality type?"

"Most often people are broken down into introverts and extroverts, I assume you've heard of that?" Stephens asked. Deirdre nodded. "Well, people who are introverted would probably deal with their depression by suicide, or some kind of act they would do alone. Extroverts, on the other hand, get their cues from the world around them. They would probably be the ones to go out and shoot others before committing suicide, showing the world how much it hurt them."

"I kind of got the idea that many of these kids were isolated, which caused them to lash out for one final act to do exactly what you said," Deirdre interrupted.

"Isolation can be one catalyst to drive a person to commit such an act. Neglect can be much more damaging than abuse," Stephens agreed. "But it's the person's reaction to the isolation that shows their true personality. Many people believe an individual's personality is formed before birth, and that environmental factors merely add to the personality type already in place."

"Seriously?"

"Oh yes," Stephens smiled. "Things such as intellect are shaped throughout a person's lifetime, but who they are is thought to be well ingrained at the beginning."

Deirdre stopped writing to ponder that idea. She was often told that people can change if they put enough effort into it. Now she had something to tell them whenever someone made reference to her stubborn behavior.

It still seemed odd to her, though.

"So if that's the case with personality, that would suggest that it isn't environmental factors that affect the teenagers who commit that kind of violence."

"Well, as I said before, people often cite environmental factors as being the reason for committing the crimes they do," Stephens replied. "But that's not the only contributing factor. You have a number of individuals to investigate, and I'm sure they're all different in ways other than where and how they grew up."

Stephens paused.

"In fact, if you really want to get involved in this issue, it probably wouldn't hurt to do some research on psychopaths as well."

"Psychopaths?" Deirdre asked, puzzled. "You don't think that's too, well, extreme?"

"Not at all," Stephens answered. "Eric Harris was deemed a psychopath after people read his journals. He didn't target specific people or groups of people by popularity or how they treated him. He thought most people were beneath him, period. I mean, not all people who kill are psychopaths and vice versa, but they certainly are in a class by themselves. It's all about personality with them."

"I guess I never thought about it that way."

"It's not uncommon. Many people don't think about young people when they hear the term. They think of the adults who have been written about the most in the media."

"You're right. The media is very influential in that case."

"Indeed," said Stephens. "But studies have been done on the minds of psychopaths. And they say there is visible evidence that shows the increased development of certain parts of the brain, such as those that influence intelligence, and decreased development in other parts of the brain that affect emotions."

"Huh. That kind of uneven development sounds similar to that of a teenager's brain," Deirdre noted, sounding surprised.

"It's true. Not that there's an automatic correlation of course! I'm simply saying brain development is another area you might want to explore."

"I will definitely add that to the list." Deirdre capped her pen and placed her notebook in her purse. "And with that, I think I have enough information for one interview. You've given me a lot to think about, some of which I never would've considered."

"I hope that's a good thing," Stephens said, standing up. Deirdre stood up and shook her hand. "If you have any other questions, please feel free to call or email. I'll give you my card."

"I'm sure as I go through all my notes I'll have one or two follow-up questions," Deirdre said, taking the card. "It's been quite a whirlwind!"

"Well, you asked for it," Stephens smiled.

"You have no idea."

CHAPTER SEVENTEEN

Zoey sat in her bed, staring out the window at the clouds rolling by over the house. Her backpack leaned against her desk under the weight of the textbooks that hadn't been taken out since she last went to school almost a month ago. It had been that long since she opened a notebook, her laptop, or the front door. She didn't know what day it was, and she didn't care. All she knew was that there was no reason to do any of those things anymore, and it was time to tell her parents.

They aren't gonna be happy with me.

Who cares? It's my life.

They're gonna care. They are paying for it, after all.

Well, now they won't have to pay for it any more.

So what the hell do I do instead?

There's always the restaurant.

True. I just don't know if it'll be good enough for them.

Will it be good enough for me?

Zoey had been going around with the same questions in her mind for the last hour. She knew what she wanted the final answer to be, she just didn't know how to make it possible. And since her parents wouldn't understand she needed a solid game plan. But coming up with something tangible was harder than she thought it would be. She felt a headache start to build.

I just have to go down and tell them I want to drop out of school, she thought. *The rest can be worked out later. I mean, my life was completely ripped apart. They can't expect things to stay the same.*

Zoey's retreat into her own world of solitude had caused her parents to plead her case for an extension on her final homework assignments and exams. She couldn't care less. It was hard enough getting out of bed in the morning, since all she wanted to do was sleep. *Who cares if I never write that paper*

74

about Hamlet? Just thinking about it reminded her of her last conversation with Laura. She would never be able to talk to her best friend again. That was all that mattered.

And talking about it wasn't going to change anything. Her parents tried to break her out of her self-induced coma, tried to get her to open up about her feelings. But the truth was they had never understood how she felt about Laura when she was alive. So why would they think they would understand now that she was gone? Zoey knew it was all nonsense.

This is who I am now, and they're going to have to accept that.

Taking a deep breath, Zoey walked downstairs.

Her parents were sitting on the couch watching the news. When Zoey was younger they would let her stay up with them as long as she watched "appropriate shows." To this day she still didn't know what defined a show as "appropriate," but she had loved getting to stay up with them. Now she couldn't wait for dinner to end so she could run upstairs to her room. She couldn't remember the last full night she spent with her parents. It was even worse now that Laura was gone.

"Hi, honey," Connie said, looking up as she entered the room. "What have you been up to?"

Zoey had thought about how she should approach the subject, but nothing seemed to fit. She had never before attempted such a serious discussion with her parents, never mind one that involved changing the entire course of her life. She knew it wasn't going to be easy. She knew her parents were going to object. But she also knew it was the right choice.

Ugh, just say it.

"I'm dropping out of college," she stated. She was almost surprised at how easy the words came out of her mouth.

The sentence shook Walter out of his news trance. He looked over at Connie, who stared at Zoey in disbelief.

"What? Zoey, what are you talking about?"

Zoey shifted her feet, trying to stand her ground.

"I know you guys won't understand this, but I've decided to drop out."

"Honey, sit down," Connie said, concerned. "We need to talk about this."

"Mom, I've made up my mind."

"Sit down, Zoey," Walter ordered sharply.

His tone of voice caught Zoey by surprise, even though she was expecting a confrontation. She sat down slowly in the recliner across from the couch. Walter turned off the television.

Here we go. Stay strong.

"We understand where this is coming from, honey," Walter began. "The last couple of weeks have been very difficult, and it was great that all your professors agreed to give you an extension. I think once you finish out this year you'll have all summer to think about this. But for now, I think you should focus on finishing out your sophomore year."

"Absolutely, sweetie," Connie agreed. "You're still grieving so you're not thinking straight. And that's going to last for a while, which is why you shouldn't make any rash decisions right now."

"This isn't a rash decision, Mom. I've been thinking about this for the last couple of weeks, and I'm positive. I can't go back to school right now. I just can't."

"Honey, listen to what you're saying," Walter said gently. "You're using the word can't as if it's a physical impossibility. And I know right now it feels like that. But you need to slow down and think rationally about how this decision will affect the rest of your life."

"Why should I? I didn't make the decision to lose my best friend," Zoey snapped. "She was just taken from me. There was nothing I could do about it. But I do have some control over this and I'm taking it. I've made up my mind."

"Zoey, you realize you can also take control by deciding to stay in school, right?"

Zoey shook her head. *I knew they wouldn't understand.*

"Do you guys even know what I'm going through?" she asked angrily, struggling to hold back tears. "Because you can't say anything to me unless you understand. And obviously you don't or else you wouldn't even ask me these questions."

"Hey, you're not the first person to deal with a loved one's death, young lady. Your mother and I have both dealt with the loss of our parents, and they weren't that old when they passed. You know that. Of course we understand what you're going through. That's why we can say these things to you. We've been down this road too."

Could've fooled me, Zoey thought. She kept that to herself.

"Listen baby, all we're saying is that you have time to make this decision, and you should take it," Connie said. "Just get through your finals and then you can take all the time you need to figure out when you want to go back."

"Who said I even want to go back?" Zoey asked. "I mean, seriously. I'm not good at anything. I never have been. That's the only reason I picked English, 'cuz I didn't know what else to do. But what good would getting an English degree do?"

"Come on, Zoey, you know having a degree is very important for getting a job," Walter lectured. "Especially in this day and age. It's all about having a good balance of a degree with job experience."

"Some jobs. I don't have to have a degree to work at the restaurant."

"Is that your plan? Working at the restaurant for the rest of your life?"

"I don't know. To start with, yeah. It's a job for now."

"Well, that's fine for the short-term," Connie replied. "But you don't want to do that forever."

"Why not? You guys always had these high expectations for me, and I always knew I'd never live up to them. Why can't you accept that? I have."

"Don't be ridiculous," Walter snorted. "The only thing we've ever wanted for you was to be happy. We have never pushed anything on you. If anything, I think we've been too easy on you, kiddo."

"Are you kidding me?" Zoey gasped. "Me going to college was practically your idea. The only reason I agreed to go was because Laura decided to go there too."

"You see? We've hardly had anything to do with your decisions. Laura has always been the catalyst in your life," Walter said. "Even now, in her death, she's affecting your decision to quit school. It's always been about her."

"And that's the only reason you have a problem with this, isn't it?" Zoey asked defensively. "You've always had something against our relationship."

"Honey, that's not true," Connie began to say, until Walter interrupted her.

"All right, this is pointless. We've had this conversation before and it gets us nowhere. You are not changing the subject, Zoey. As your parents we have a legitimate concern about you wanting to drop out and completely throw your future away, especially when you have such a great scholarship."

"Well, now they can give the scholarship to someone who actually wants to use it. I don't care about it that much anymore. Besides, plenty of people don't go to college, Dad, and they make it just fine."

"Oh really? How many of these people do you know?"

"The world runs on those people."

"Oh, how profound," Walter retorted, rolling his eyes. "You have plenty of opportunity to make the most of your life, and we're not going to sit back and watch you throw that away."

"That's just it, Dad. It's my life. Haven't you guys been telling me that I'm old enough to go out and make my own decisions now? Well, welcome to my first one."

Walter and Zoey stared at each other across the coffee table, waiting for the other to back down. It was one of many personality traits they shared that often got in the way of their relationship. Connie found herself constantly dealing with it from both sides, making a compromise almost impossible. But after a minute of silence, she couldn't take it anymore.

"All right, let's take a second to bring everything down a notch," she urged, placing her hand on Walter's knee. "It's no use arguing about this. We're going around in circles. Walter, I think we should tell her what we've been discussing."

"I don't know, Connie. It might make things worse."

"I think it's worth a shot, honey."

"I think we should wait until she's thinking clearly."

Zoey looked back and forth between her parents in confusion.

"Jesus, what is it?"

"Ok, this is something your father and I have been discussing, so I want you to hear us out," Connie said. "You've been so resistant to talking about what happened that we're very concerned about how you're dealing, or maybe not dealing with everything. We were afraid something like this would happen eventually, we just didn't think it would happen this soon."

"What your mother is trying to say is that we think it might help if you went to see a therapist."

The word therapist caught Zoey by surprise. She stared at her parents in disbelief.

"So now you think I'm crazy?" she asked, her voice wavering.

"Of course not!" Connie exclaimed. "I don't like that word to begin with. People go to therapists whenever they're having trouble dealing with things. They specialize in traumatic experiences, and we thought it would help for you to talk to someone like that."

"We think it would be helpful to talk to a professional, since you haven't really spoken to us since the funeral," Walter replied. "And we haven't pushed you on that because everyone grieves in their own way. But this school discussion changes things, and I think it's time you dealt with Laura's death openly."

Maybe I would if you guys stopped judging me all the time, Zoey thought. Since the car accident she felt like she had been put under a microscope. All they did was ask how she was doing, what she was doing, to make sure she was doing something other than distancing herself from the rest of the world. Of course, all it did was make her distance herself from her parents even more.

"I don't know why you think talking to a stranger is going to help me deal with this. Why can't you guys let this go? I want to quit school. It's not the end of the world."

"Zoey, I don't think you're ready to make such an important decision. I don't think you can right now," Walter said. "And that's not an insult. Anyone in your position would feel the same way. But there are healthy ways to deal with this. If you don't think it's helping, then you don't have to go. But please, try a few sessions. We'll pay for them, of course."

"It won't hurt to meet with the therapist," Connie suggested.

"How about this? If you don't get anything out of the sessions, then you can quit school," Walter offered. "Just give us this one thing first, as a trial run."

All Zoey could think was that she and Laura often made fun of people who started their sentences with, "My therapist says..." Now her parents wanted to make her one of them, as if they had tried their best but couldn't "handle" her any more. She felt like they had hardly tried at all, but she knew they would never see it her way.

If it'll help me win my case to quit school, then I can manage for a few weeks.

"All right. I'll go for the summer. But you won't back down if I want to stop going, to therapy or school, right?"

"Absolutely," Walter agreed. "We will accept your decision then."

Zoey looked over at Connie.

"Yes, honey. We're all agreed."

Zoey wasn't sure how she felt about the agreement, but it was a step in the right direction. She knew her parents would never back down until she put some effort into something, anything, that would at least get her out of the house.

But that's all they're going to get from me.

"Ok then," she said, standing up from the chair. "I'm glad you at least listened to me."

Before either one of her parents could reply, Zoey turned and left the room. Connie and Walter listened to her footsteps on the stairs. When they heard the door close, Connie turned to her husband, a look of exhaustion on her face.

"That's the most extensive conversation we've had with her in a long time," she sighed, shaking her head. "And of course, it wasn't about how she's doing or what she's feeling. It had to be about her dropping out of school."

"At least we were somewhat prepared for it. Even if she's not communicating with us, at least you and I are on the same page. This wasn't that much of a surprise."

Connie sighed again.

"Even after all these years, I don't think we'll ever be fully prepared for this stuff."

CHAPTER EIGHTEEN

"So, Zoey, tell me why you're here."

Zoey sat in the same chair as Deirdre had at Dr. Stephens' office, but for a very different purpose. She couldn't believe she was actually there, in a therapist's office, having to talk about things that would make anyone upset. *But if it means freedom from my parents nagging me all the time, then I'll have to grin and bear it. For now.*

She didn't know if that was appropriate to bring up at her first session though. She was unsure of how honest she wanted to be, or if she should play the part for a while. *Only time will tell, I guess.*

"Well, um, my parents think I need to be here," she answered tentatively. "That's why they made the appointment."

"Ok. Why do you think your parents want you to talk to me?"

"I know why. They're freaking out because they think I'm not handling Laura's death well."

"And Laura is?"

"She's my best friend. Well, she was my best friend," Zoey said. Then after a moment, "No, she is my best friend."

"I see. And she passed away?"

"Yeah, last month."

"So you think your parents are concerned about your reaction to her death?"

"That's what they told me."

Stephens settled back in her chair, grabbing a notebook and pencil.

"Do you think you need to be here?"

"Honestly? No, not really. They're just pissed because I want to drop out of school. But it's not a big deal. I have a job for the summer which I can keep until I can figure something else out."

"Why do you want to drop out of school?"

"Because, my best friend just died! Why does nobody get that? Isn't it obvious?"

"Well, Zoey, everyone deals with death or any kind of tragedy differently. There's no obvious answer when it comes to these things. There's always the possibility that there are underlying circumstances also affecting your decision. I imagine that's what your parents are concerned about."

Zoey bit her lip. It was her very first session and already she felt like the therapist was acting judgmental, just like her parents.

"But since this is our first session, I'd rather talk about you," Stephens said, changing the tone of the conversation. "I'd like to get to know your background and family history, various relationships, health issues, that sort of thing. Is that all right?"

"Yeah, ok."

Stephens paused before setting her notebook down on the desk next to her.

"There is one necessary component in therapy that I would like you to understand before we proceed," she said. "If we're going to make any progress in our sessions, then we both have to be willing to work at it. If the person doesn't want to be here then there's not much I can do. I can't make you want to talk about things, and if you don't want to then there's no reason for you to be here."

"Are you kicking me out or something?" Zoey asked, confused.

"No, Zoey, I would never do that," Stephens replied, smiling. "All I'm saying is that you have to want to be here, and be willing to talk to me about whatever is on your mind. You suggested that your parents are the ones who feel you should be here, while you disagree, so that's not really going to work."

"You don't understand," Zoey pleaded. "Me dropping out of school will only happen if I come to therapy for a while. They said I couldn't do anything until I gave this a try."

"And you agreed to that?"

"Well, yeah, if it's the only way I can do it."

"All right," Stephens said. "If you did agree to those conditions, then part of that means you have to be involved in our sessions. You have to willingly come here to work on whatever you want."

Zoey thought about those last three words, "whatever you want."

"Yeah, well, I don't know about the last part. My parents really want me to talk about Laura and our relationship and her death."

"Well, your parents aren't here," Stephens replied. "These are your sessions. I let you take the lead on wherever you want to go. If you don't want to talk about something, you don't have to. My role isn't to force you into anything. This is your time, and you get to decide what you want to do with it."

That last part caught Zoey by surprise.

"But, don't you have to tell my parents how things are going, and what we're talking about and stuff?"

"Of course not. You have complete client/doctor privilege here. You're not a minor so anything we talk about is confidential."

"Huh. I wasn't expecting that."

"Well, hopefully I've been able to answer some of your questions." Zoey nodded.

"So, do we have an agreement? You'll play your part and I'll play mine?" Zoey nodded again. "Good."

Stephens picked up her notebook and sat with her pencil poised, ready to write.

"Ok, why don't you tell me about your family? Any brothers and sisters?"

"No, it's just me. I don't think my dad could've handled any more kids."

"What do you mean?"

Zoey caught herself off guard. She couldn't believe she had said that so candidly to a stranger.

"Well, um, I just mean that, I think my parents were fine with one kid."

"I see," said Stephens, writing something down. "Is that something they told you?"

"Uh, no. I don't think they tried again after me."

"Ok. So how would you characterize your relationship with your parents?"

"I don't know. Fine, I guess."

"That doesn't really describe anything."

Zoey tried not to snicker, thinking back to all the conversations she had with her mother that involved the word "fine." Connie often had the same reaction to the word. *Must be a mom thing,* she thought. Then she realized she didn't know if Dr. Stephens was a mother. She looked at her ring finger and saw a wedding band. *I'm sure she has kids. God, what's that like, having a psychiatrist for a mom?*

Suddenly Zoey realized Dr. Stephens was looking at her expectedly.

"Sorry, I kinda zoned out," she said sheepishly. "My parents. I don't know. We normally get along, it's just that I don't like hanging out with them anymore. I guess you could say we used to be close."

"Used to be? Did something happen to change that?"

"No, nothing really changed. I mean, isn't that what you're supposed to do? Grow out of being with your parents all the time and do stuff with friends?"

"It is a healthy part of growing up," Stephens agreed. "But that doesn't mean you have to grow apart from your parents. It's possible to do both."

Zoey had never thought about that option.

"Well, I guess it's more than that," she began slowly. "It's not like it happened suddenly or anything. Laura and I have always been close and my parents think that's bad for some reason. We've argued about that for years, and it got kinda old after a while."

"Why do you think your parents were concerned about your relationship with Laura?"

"They think we spent too much time together and that she stopped me from living my life. But it was the exact opposite," Zoey said, exasperated. "She was the one who brought me places I never would've gone and helped me meet people I never would've talked to."

"Can you tell me about a specific argument you had with your parents about Laura?"

"Sure, because they all came down to the same thing. They thought she was holding me back from having more friends and new experiences on my own. But I don't get why they thought that when we were out doing new things all the time."

"So you hung out with other people besides Laura?"

"Of course."

"Without Laura there?"

Zoey paused.

"Well, no. We all hung out in a group."

"Did you hang out with the group without her there?"

"No. They were mostly her friends. I knew them through her."

"So your parents' concern was that you met people only through Laura?"

"Yeah, I guess so. But I still don't get why that's such a big deal."

"Well, I can see why your parents would be worried right now. Your best friend is gone and you want to drop out of school, which is where your main social circle is," Stephens said. "Maybe they're afraid you'll shut down and not go out into the world anymore."

It was the second time Stephens reminded Zoey of her mother. It was beginning to get annoying. At the same time, Stephens could see the look of unease on Zoey's face. She decided to change the subject.

"We can put this aside for now if you want. Why don't we get back to your family background?"

"Ok," said Zoey, almost relieved to go back to that subject.

"How about your extended family? Are you close with them?"

"Well, all of my grandparents are dead," Zoey said. "My mom's parents both died pretty young of lung cancer, which is why she was always on my case about me not smoking. I was never interested in it anyway, so that made it incredibly annoying. And my dad's mom died of breast cancer, which became another thing for my mom to freak out about. 'All this cancer makes me nervous' she'd say, as if she was talking about the weather rather than a disease."

"And your dad's father?"

Zoey thought for a moment, as if she wasn't sure of the answer.

"All I know is he died a month later," she answered slowly. "Dad doesn't really talk about it. I just figured he had a heart attack or something. Grandpa wasn't that healthy, another reason for my mom to go ballistic about my eating habits. She's a ridiculous ball of health and nutrition pamphlets."

"Well, I can understand with that kind of history in the family," Stephens noted. "Both of their parents dying at such a young age, it's enough for anyone to be paranoid about the genes being passed down to themselves and their children."

"Yeah, but she treats it like an extreme sport."

"What about aunts, uncles, cousins?"

"My mom's an only child, and my dad has a sister. But she lives in California, so we haven't seen her in years," Zoey said. "I guess my mom was never really close with Grandma's side of the family. We still see Grandpa's side, like his two brothers and their kids, maybe once in a while for someone's wedding."

"Do you ever talk to your parents about whether or not they were close with their parents?"

"Sometimes," Zoey replied. "My mom mostly talks about how it was growing up with two people you knew weren't going to last that long. She doesn't like to talk about it because 'it's so very depressing.' And my dad, well, he's always off in his own little world."

"Would you say he works a lot?"

"Kind of. But it's more like he'd rather be somewhere else."

"What do you mean?"

"I don't know. He spends most of his time in his study, and my mom is constantly busting in on him with whatever's worrying her that week. I can't tell if she's just being melodramatic or if he's just so laidback it makes her look worse."

"Is that how you would characterize their relationship?"

"Sometimes. But then there are those times when they're both harping on me for something I don't think is a big deal but they both do," Zoey said, rolling her eyes. "So at least they're consistent in their nagging."

"They're a united front when it comes to you."

"Yeah. Lucky me. I think I'd rather be one of those kids who can pit one parent against the other when they want something."

"I think most parents strive to have the balance your parents have," Stephens smiled. "It generally helps to keep everyone on the same page."

"Maybe. But I think my dad spends a lot of time on his own page, pun intended."

"Does it bother you?"

Zoey had never given much thought to her father's so-called absence. She automatically assumed his thoughts were anywhere else but in the conversation she and her mother were having, but she could understand why. It was a strange paradox to be just like her father while resenting him at the same time.

"Sort of," Zoey said. "But it's not like I don't get it. I like spending time in my room, just chilling by myself. So I can see why he would do the same thing in his study."

"Do you think it bothers your mother?"

"Oh, totally! But she acts like it's not a big deal and walks in on him anyway. That's the same thing she does with me."

"Like she feels out of the loop?"

"I don't know. She doesn't really talk about it. Or if she is then she's using some combination of clichés that I don't understand."

"Moms are good like that," Stephens said, smiling again. Glancing over at the clock, she noticed their session was almost finished.

"All right, Zoey, I think this was a good start. What did you think?"

"It was fairly painless," she replied, shrugging her shoulders.

"Well, I'll take that," Stephens said, standing up and extending her hand to Zoey. "So, shall I see you the same time next week then?"

Zoey stood up and shook Stephens' hand. It was strange, but she almost looked forward to coming back for a second session. She was genuinely curious to see where this was heading.

"Yeah. See ya next week."

CHAPTER NINETEEN

Ben will be here in half an hour and the place is a mess.

As usual, it was the first night Deirdre had been home in weeks. Just as her editor predicted, her new topic had completely taken over her life, not that she would ever admit that to him. There was so much ground to cover, and not enough hours in the day for research and a good night's sleep. Hence the messy apartment.

I don't know why I'm so worried, she thought. *It's not like he's never lived with me before. He knows I'm a messy person.*

But for some reason, tonight was different.

She grabbed all the newspapers and magazines strewn about the living room and threw them into the bedroom, closing the door behind her. She knew there was no danger of him going in there. Then she moved onto the dishes, hastily washing the accumulated stack of plates and bowls overflowing onto the counter. As she dried the last dish, she heard the doorbell ring.

Damn. I guess the vacuuming will have to wait. Not that he'll even notice. Oh god, what if he notices? Jesus, just get the door.

She paused before grabbing the door handle, taking a deep breath. She opened it to Ben holding a bag from their favorite Chinese place.

"I probably should've called to see if you'd eaten yet," he said. "But Chinese food is always good the next day so I took a shot. Sweet and sour chicken and pork fried rice, right?"

Deirdre exhaled gratefully. With all the cleaning she had completely forgotten about dinner.

"Thank god, I haven't eaten since breakfast."

"I figured. I know how you get when you're working. But I didn't want to come out and say that."

"Please, come in."

Ben walked past her, setting the bag down on a TV tray. He took out the individual boxes as Deirdre brought out paper plates.

"All your dishes dirty?" he asked, looking over at the sink. "Wow, it's empty! Now that I wasn't expecting."

"Actually, I just finished drying the last dish when you rang the bell," Deirdre admitted sheepishly. Ben laughed.

"I guess some things never change. It's kind of reassuring."

"Like you bringing me my favorite Chinese food," Deirdre said, trying to keep her voice even. Ben looked down at the table.

"Yeah, I guess so." After an awkward silence he asked if she had any silverware.

Deirdre turned to grab a couple of forks, biting her lip. It had been so long since they had spent any time together, never mind alone, that she wasn't sure what the boundaries were. She handed Ben a fork, letting their fingers touch. If he felt the same electricity she did, he didn't show it.

"Thanks."

What am I doing? She thought. *We're not in grade school any more. We were married for five years! Why can't I relax and be myself?*

Because "being myself" is why we're getting a divorce.

Suddenly she realized Ben was staring at her, with a quizzical look on his face.

"I'm sorry, did you ask me something?"

He smiled, scooping some rice onto his plate.

"No. I just recognize that look," he said, sitting down on the couch. "There were many times I wondered what was going on in your head."

"It's part of my charm," she joked. "That's how I keep the mystery alive."

"Kept me on my toes."

"Then my plan worked."

Deirdre grabbed her plate and sat down next to Ben, dragging another TV tray over for her food. She settled into the cushions as she felt herself start to relax. *We're just eating dinner,* she thought. *Nothing stressful about that.* But as she brought the fork to her mouth for her first bite, he reached into the bag and pulled out the divorce papers.

Might as well get this over with, he thought.

We're going to do this now? Deirdre hoped they would at least make it through a pleasant dinner first.

"So, here they are," he said. "My lawyer looked them over. Since we already split the house profits and had kept our finances separate, it's a fairly simple process from here. Just sign and date."

"Simple process, huh? Well, I'm glad at least one of us sees it that way."

"Deeds, come on. You know what I mean. There are plenty of people getting divorced these days who have way more to talk about. We kinda lucked out here. We don't have any joint accounts, we sold the house, we each had our own car, and we don't have any…"

Ben let the sentence trail off.

"Go ahead. Say it," Deirdre said accusingly. "We don't have any kids. Because if we did we wouldn't even be talking about divorce right now. We'd be sitting here eating Chinese food and watching TV with our daughter."

"Hey, I'm not the one who gave up on that," he pointed out defensively. "Why do you think things fell apart? You didn't want a family anymore."

"Of course I want a family," she shot back. "But you can't expect after everything that happened for that to remain a realistic dream. How can anyone want to bring a child into this world? How can you?"

"Deirdre, plenty of people raise children in 'this world,'" he said, exasperated. "You can't expect one incident to change my desire to have kids."

"Incident?" Deirdre couldn't believe what he was saying. "I was shot, Ben. We lost the baby because some teenager decided to target a bunch of innocent people eating lunch in a courtyard. That was my one job, to protect our child, and I failed."

"I can't believe you're still blaming yourself for this," he exclaimed. "There was nothing you could do."

"I just sat there when he started shooting," she cried out, getting up from the couch. "I was so terrified I froze. I didn't even get down like the other people around me. So you're right, Ben. I couldn't do anything."

"We've been over this so many times, Deirdre, with people at the hospital, friends, therapists. And you still can't move past it. Eventually you have to accept what happened and move on. You were a victim, but you survived."

"You call this surviving?"

"Yes!" he insisted. "You're still here, living your life. You talk about your pain in all of this, but what about me? Do you know how terrified I was when I got the call from the hospital? At one point they weren't sure they could save either one of you. And in that one instant, that one second, my whole life could've been turned upside down forever. I would've lost everything, and there was nothing I could do about it. Do you ever think about that?"

Ben pushed the table away from the couch and abruptly stood up, turning his back to Deirdre. He started pacing back and forth, running his fingers through his hair. She didn't know how to respond to his question. She didn't think he still fought with these demons any more. She took a deep breath.

"That's why I don't understand how you can try again. A new relationship, still wanting kids. Nothing is a given, Ben. Terrible things happen that we have no control over."

"So we should just stop living our lives, is that what you're saying? We should lie down and give up? Why not put yourself out of your misery, huh? Wouldn't that solve everything?"

Deirdre looked up, startled.

"Ben, of course that's not what I'm saying…"

"You might as well be," he said accusingly. "The only thing you did when you got out of the hospital was work. I tried to talk to you about what happened, but you just shut down. I needed you, Deirdre. You were the one person who knew what I was going through, and you left me."

"I never left you! I was right here!"

"Physically, maybe. But mentally, emotionally, you never came back from that courtyard."

Ben sat back down on the couch and stared at the floor. Deirdre stared at him, speechless. After all of their conversations, all of the therapy sessions, she couldn't believe she was hearing this for the first time.

"Look, there's nothing more we can say to each other," he said softly. "What's done is done. You had your way of dealing with the situation and I had mine. There was no way for us to come together on this, and I've accepted that. And whether you like it or not, you have to as well."

It was that last statement that brought Deirdre back to the conversation. She narrowed her eyes.

"No, I don't."

Ben raised his head in surprise. "What?"

"I don't have to accept any of this," she stated matter-of-factly. "I couldn't talk to you when I got home from the hospital, and everyone said that was fine. You told me you understood if I needed time. But what you didn't tell me was that there was a set limit on how much time I could take."

"Deirdre, that's absurd."

"Is it? After a while I did try to talk to you. I told you about my work, about how that was the only thing that could get me through another day without my child. Writing about someone else's life helped me to forget about my own."

"Yes. You ran away from everything, including me."

"Ran away? I still can't run away, Ben. I have a constant reminder of how empty my life is," she answered, tears rolling down her cheeks. "I can still see the gun pointing at me. I can still feel the bullet rip through my stomach. And I can still feel our baby stop kicking. That, I would give anything to have left behind in that courtyard."

It was Ben's turn to be speechless. These were all details he knew, all things she had said afterwards in the hospital, to her parents, in therapy. The story was old, yet it was still fresh in Deirdre's mind. He had no idea how much she still wrestled with the pain that he was finally able to put behind him. All he could do was close his eyes and bow his head.

"So you see, Ben, there is no amount of time that will allow me to move past what happened. And if you understood that, then I wouldn't have to accept any of this."

Deirdre sat back down, fighting to slow her breathing back to normal. It had been a long time since these feelings had been brought out into the open, for both of them. There were instances that caused Deirdre distress, such as hearing about the incident on the news, and she tried to avoid them at all costs. But this went beyond the shooting. This was the last piece of Deirdre's life being taken away from her. Ben shook his head.

"Tell me what you want me to do, Deirdre. Because I don't have a time machine to travel back and do everything the way you wanted me to. I can't take back the way I dealt with my grief, or the way I dealt with yours. So tell me, what do you want?"

"Not this." It was all she could say.

"Well, this is all we've got. That, you do have to accept," he said, sighing. "I'm with someone else now, someone who wants the same things I do. I know it's not a perfect world, but I also know there are endless possibilities in it. I just want the chance to raise a child who understands that. And maybe, just maybe, they can bring some good to it. I know they would bring some good to me."

Deirdre looked over at him. She knew it was no use. He wasn't going to change his mind about the divorce, no matter what she said or wanted. Still, she wasn't sure she was ready to let him go.

"I don't know any more, Ben. This downward spiral keeps getting longer and longer, but I don't want it to end this way. I feel like, I still need you. Like I'll always need you."

"I know, Deeds," he replied softly. "Even now, I can't imagine you not in my life. But we began as friends, and I was hoping we could go back to that."

"Come on, Ben. You think Veronica will be comfortable with that?"

"She has faith in our relationship. She has faith in me. She already told me she understood."

"Well, isn't she perfect," Deirdre muttered.

"What?"

"Nothing," she said quickly, trying to keep the conversation from turning any uglier. "It would be great to be able to talk to each other like normal people again."

Ben grinned.

"So, where does that leave us then?"

Deirdre thought for a moment, and reached over to pick up the papers.

"Do you mind if I have a lawyer look these over?"

"Not at all," Ben answered, relieved. "Take your time."

Oh I will, Deirdre thought to herself. *Don't you worry about that.*

CHAPTER TWENTY

Connie was sitting in the kitchen cutting out coupons when she heard the front door close. It was her way of looking busy until Zoey came home from her therapy session. She stood up and hurried into the hallway, hoping to catch her daughter before she ran up to her room once again.

This time she caught her at the bottom of the stairs.

"Hi, honey," she said, trying to block the stairway. "How was your session?"

Damn, I need to work on coming into the house more quietly, Zoey thought.

"Good," Zoey mumbled, walking around her mom.

"Zoey…"

"I'll see you later."

Connie watched her daughter jog up the stairs and into her room. She knew once the door was closed that that would be the last she would see of her for the rest of the night.

This isn't working.

"Walter!"

No reply.

Sigh. He must be in his office. That's the one thing those two have in common- they both love their own spaces. It's a shame I have to break into them. But how else can I get them to talk to me? It's like I'm not allowed in their private club sometimes.

"Walter!"

Connie got to the door of Walter's study and knocked once before entering the room. Walter was furiously typing away as he always was when the door was closed. He was so involved with his book he couldn't even hear his wife when she was loudly yelling his name. At least, that's what Connie thought.

"Honey, I'm sorry to interrupt you but we need to talk."

"Mmm. Just give me a second."

I've heard that before, Connie thought, as she sat down on the couch. *A second turns into a minute which turns into several minutes which eventually becomes an hour, and by then I'm not concerned any more, I'm angry. And not angry with Zoey, but angry with Walter.*

But Connie waited patiently as Walter finished the paragraph he was typing. He picked up his tape recorder and pushed a button.

"Don't forget, he has to find the key first before he can accuse her."

Walter hit the button again and set the recorder down on his desk. He took a deep breath and looked up at his wife.

"Yes, dear?"

"The book is going well, I take it?"

"Absolutely. I think I have a great premise here."

"That's great, honey. Unfortunately, I don't think you've noticed that Zoey has been going to her sessions for a month now and we have no idea what's going on with them."

"What do you mean?"

"What do you think I mean?" Connie asked, exasperated. "She's seen Dr. Stephens four times now and we know nothing about her progress, or if she's even making any. Wasn't that the reason we wanted her to see someone, so she could talk out her problems with a professional? That's part of our deal and we don't even know if she's holding up her end of the bargain."

"Connie, the only thing she had to do was give therapy a try," Walter pointed out. "All of that other stuff is what we were hoping she'd get out of therapy, but it was never a specific condition. She's going to the sessions week after week, so she is holding up her end of the deal. There's nothing more we can do except hope the therapist is helping her in some way."

Connie stood up, shaking her head.

"Walter, that's not going to work," she argued. "You know as well as I do we had other expectations for these therapy sessions. I don't want her to think we sent her off to talk to some stranger without also wanting to get involved. You heard what she said. She asked if we thought she was crazy. I wasn't expecting that kind of response, were you?"

"Well, I wasn't that surprised by it," he replied. "You know how Zoey reacts to things she doesn't understand right away. She becomes defensive. Hell, most people react that way, never mind a teenager who just lost her only friend. We need to give it time, Connie. We need to give her some space."

"Are you kidding? She has plenty of space. We're not asking anything of her! She goes to work, she goes to therapy, then she comes home and has dinner in her room, where she remains for the rest of the night. How is that not giving her space?"

"Honey, I know you're concerned. I am too. But what do you want to do? Drag her down here and tie her up until she tells us about her session? I thought the whole idea was for her to talk to someone without feeling pressured to talk about things she doesn't want to?"

"Well then what's the point of sending her to therapy? We do that here every day."

"Connie, I think the therapist will be able to get her to open up. It just takes time," Walter said. "They have to establish a rapport first. When I did that book about the therapist who was murdered by one of her patients, I interviewed Dr. Stephens about the procedures of working with a new client. She explained that the first 2 or 3 sessions often consist of getting to know the person's background, their family, their interests, their routine, etc."

"You are a bizarre wealth of knowledge," Connie said, shaking her head again. Walter smiled.

"Look, honey, I know it's frustrating spending all this time and money on something that we don't even know will do Zoey any good. But you're right. She's not talking to us, and when she is, it only leads to an argument. At least this way she's dealing with someone she has no previous relationship with, no prior grudges or feelings of any kind."

Connie sighed.

"I know that's why we wanted her to go. I just thought, well, I don't know."

"You thought if she opened up more with someone else, she might also open up more with us."

"Yes."

"That would be nice. Unfortunately it's not a given."

Connie sat back down on the couch, her shoulders slumping forward as she leaned against the cushions.

"I remember when she'd come home from grade school; she couldn't wait to tell us all about her day. Of course, her day consisted of spelling quizzes and history projects and art class. Now, well…"

"Things are different now."

"Yes," Connie said, closing her eyes. "They certainly are."

Walter stood up and walked over to Connie, sitting next to her. He squeezed her shoulder softly.

"I know you still think we're losing our daughter. But I won't let that happen. And I know you won't either. All we can do is keep trying. Let her know that we're still here for her, even if she doesn't think we can help. That's all we have left at this point."

Connie rested her head on his shoulder.

"I've never felt so helpless as a parent before."

"I know," he replied, looking out the window behind his desk. "I know."

CHAPTER TWENTY-ONE

P... S... Y... C... H... O... P... A...T... H

That was the first thing Deirdre saw as she walked into the classroom of Professor George Tate. After her discussion with Dr. Stephens, she decided to take the doctor's advice and research psychopaths as part of her teen violence study. Several phone calls later, she found a summer psychology class at one of the local colleges that featured a lecture specifically on psychopaths. Seeing that word on the chalkboard, she knew she was in the right room.

"Professor Tate?"

"Yes," he answered, turning toward her. He recognized Deirdre from her picture in the newspaper and extended his hand. "Ah, you must be Miss Hart. Welcome to the world of crazies."

Deirdre laughed, shaking his hand.

"Thank you. I really appreciate you allowing me to sit in on your discussion today."

"Of course. This lecture is my absolute favorite."

"Oh? Why is that?"

"Well, it's the only one where I encourage the students not to do any preparation," he answered. "The idea is to discuss the label of psychopath as it's understood by society, rather than just explaining its clinical meaning. In the 20 years I've been doing this lecture, the definition of the word hasn't changed, but the kids' responses have. Their answers will eventually lead the conversation, and that is every teacher's dream."

"It sounds intriguing."

"As does the article you're writing. I can't wait to read it."

"Me too!" Deirdre laughed again, offering her standard reaction to anyone who showed interest in her work. "So, where should I sit?"

"If you'd like you can take a seat in the back, that way you can hear everyone's comments. Also, I told the class you'd be coming in today, so feel free to talk to some of the students afterward if you'd like."

"Oh, great!"

As the hands on the clock moved closer to 3 pm, Tate's students began to file in and take their seats in the lecture hall. Deirdre thanked Tate again and walked up the aisle to take the first seat in the last row. Pulling out her own notebook, she noticed Tate organizing a handful of note cards, which seemed to be more of an afterthought than anything else. She watched as more students entered the classroom.

"Hi Professor Tate."

"Aaron, welcome back," he responded to one of the students. "I was so sorry to hear what happened. How are you holding up?"

"All right," he answered tentatively. "I was just glad I could finish the course over the summer. Throwing myself back into school helps a little."

"I'm sure."

"What up, Professor Tate?" asked two other boys behind him.

"Hi Hank, Dean."

By the time the clock read five after three, most of the students were in their seats and ready with notebook and pen in hand. Tate took his place behind the podium and tapped his cards on the top of it.

"Afternoon, everyone," he said. "I'm sure you were all wondering why I didn't assign any reading for today's lecture, and we'll get to that in a minute. As you can see on the board, today's topic is psychopaths, and the characteristics that describe this four percent of the population. But before I begin the lecture, I'd like you to first write down five words or ideas that come to mind when you read that word, and then we'll share them to see how similar or different they are. I don't want you to take a lot of time on this, so you'll have about five minutes. Go."

Deirdre watched as some of the students looked around the room, seemingly confused by the change in the usual routine. Others grinned mischievously, ready to use this as an opportunity to come up with something outrageous to offer some entertainment to the class. The rest thought about it for 30 seconds or so and began writing. Deirdre thought about it as well and wrote down her own list.

1) violent 2) mentally unstable 3) calculating 4) emotionally stunted 5) Hannibal Lecter

Deirdre smirked at the last one.

Tate made some last minute changes to his notes as he waited for the students to finish. When the five minute mark passed, he asked them to put down their pens.

"All right," he said, rubbing his hands together. "Who would like to share first?"

The student who Tate addressed as Aaron raised his hand. Tate called on him.

"Should I read the whole list?"

"Read them one at a time, so other students can tell me if they have it. I'll keep track of them on the chalkboard."

"Ok. The first thing I wrote down was killer."

"K...i...l...l...e...r. Ok, good. Raise your hand if you wrote down killer or something similar, like murderer."

"What if you wrote down violent?" someone called out from the back.

"I'll put that as a separate issue," Tate answered. "First, who wrote down killer?"

Tate counted 45 raised hands out of 50 students. Writing the number on the board, he then asked how many put down violent in some form. All of the students raised their hands.

"Wow, we have a unanimous one already. Ok, Aaron, continue with your list."

"I also wrote down cunning."

"Good word. Anyone else have that word, or something else like smart or manipulative? Calculating maybe?"

Thirty-six students raised their hands.

"What's next?"

"I didn't know what word to use, so I put 'thinks they are superior.'"

"A superiority complex. How many wrote down something like that?"

Tate wrote the number forty next to the phrase, and asked Aaron for his final entry.

"Cold-hearted."

"All right. How many people have that?"

"I wrote down detached. Does that count?" another student asked.

"I think that fits under this heading." Again he received a unanimous vote.

"Very good. Thank you, Aaron. Let's go to someone else who has something different written down. Yes, Helen. What've you got for us?"

"Honestly, the first thing I thought of was crazy," suggested a female student in the front.

"Wow, another popular word," Tate said, counting forty-seven people. "Do you have anything else new?"

"I also put down mostly male. That's my only other one."

Tate smiled.

"Gender specific, good. Anyone else put that down?"

Tate wrote twenty next to the entry.

"Ok, let's keep going. What else is out there?"

"Christian Bale!" called out another student. Everyone laughed, including Tate.

"Ah, yes, Dean, good ol' American Psycho," he chuckled, writing down Bale's name on the chalkboard. "Any other takers for that one, or the movie title?"

Four other students timidly raised their hands. Tate asked if there were any other movie-related entries, and another student called out Silence of the Lambs. Two additional students raised their hands. Deirdre tried not to snort out loud, having it on her own list.

"How about Dexter?" another student asked.

"Dexter's a serial killer, not a psychopath," Dean snorted.

"What's the difference?"

Tate smiled again. *Now the real discussion begins.*

"Excellent question, Hank. First of all, how many people had Dexter written down?"

Twenty-six students raised their hands. Tate asked if they all watched the show to which they all responded yes. When asked if any other students watched the show, another eight raised their hands.

"Good. This will fit nicely with the psychopaths in the media portion of the lecture." A couple students giggled. "All right, let's start with the various definitions of the word psychopath."

Tate turned back to the board and began to write.

"The origin of the word psychopath, psychopate, was introduced in 1885 in Germany to describe those who did not fit into any of the known classified mental disorders," he explained. "They were often identified by two characteristics- their cruel indifference towards others and their ability to hide that indifference. In most cases it's believed that psychopaths never really develop emotions, they simply learn how to mimic others. The only emotions they may truthfully exhibit have to do with their own welfare, such as anger, frustration, and rage.

"In 1941, Dr. Hervey Cleckley wrote 'The Mask of Sanity,' in which he uses words such as charming, intelligent, and impressive to describe psychopaths. He also describes how dangerous these personality traits are in a psychopath because it helps him to blend into the world almost seamlessly."

"Him?" Helen asked. "Does that mean I was right about them being mostly male?"

"That's right. You win the gender guess," Tate said. "It's estimated that over 80 percent of psychopaths are male."

"Nice," she replied.

"Now, the English dictionary gives the definition for psychopath as, 'A person with an antisocial personality disorder, manifested in aggressive, perverted, criminal, or amoral behavior without empathy or remorse,'" Tate continued. "That's fairly comprehensive, although most psychologists would add their own spin to it. There is no one clinical definition for the word, but rather a checklist created by Robert Hare in the 1970s to determine if someone can be considered a psychopath."

Turning back to the podium, Tate grabbed a stack of Xeroxed papers and began to pass them out to the students. On the sheet were written the twenty characteristics included in Hare's psychopathy checklist.

"Ok. The way this works is, all the items on the list are given a rating from 0-2. The number 30 is the required score for a psychopath. Your average criminal scores a 20," he said. "Now, how many of the words listed on the board are included in this checklist?"

"Technically, only three of them are on this list," Aaron answered.

"Technically?"

"Yeah. The superior thing matches with 'grandiose estimation of self,' cunning is on there, and cold-hearted goes along with 'callousness and lack of empathy.'"

"So what's the technicality?"

"Well, some of these things could involve violence or being a killer, like 'lack of remorse or guilt' or 'failure to accept responsibility for their actions.' There's also 'impulsive' and 'irresponsible,' or 'juvenile delinquency' and 'criminal versatility.' Any of those things could include violence."

"But according to the list, it's not a requirement," Tate pointed out.

"Um, no."

"There are also very specific traits on there, such as 'lack of realistic long-term goals,' 'sexual promiscuity,' 'pathological lying,' and, my favorite, 'many short-term marriages'. I'm not sure the quantity of 'many' in this case, but I know two friends who might squirm at that one."

"But Professor Tate, couldn't some of these traits be combined?" Helen asked. "Like, 'poor behavioral controls' and 'early behavior problems.' Or 'superficial emotional response' and 'glib, superficial charm.' Isn't it enough to say they're fake?"

"Well, Helen, there has to be some differentiation in the list because there are different kinds of psychopaths," Tate answered. "For the most part, they are connected by an emotional detachment and, as stated on the list, a 'parasitic lifestyle.' They have a blatant disregard for others and will do whatever it takes to obtain what they want. But for some, that could just mean getting ahead in the business world, while for others it could mean killing for the thrill of the kill. Big difference.

"Psychologist Theodore Millon identified 10 basic subtypes of the psychopath," he continued, handing out the second sheet of information. "You can see that these include unprincipled, disingenuous, risk-taking, covetous, spineless, malignant, explosive, abrasive, malevolent, and tyrannical. And if you read the descriptions, you'll see that only the last two involve violence."

Looking down the list, the students noticed the phrase "most murderers and serial killers fall under the malevolent psychopath."

"So, Professor Tate, is there a difference between a psychopath and a serial killer? It says here both fall under the malevolent psychopath," Hank asked.

"Luckily, there are a couple of criminal justice definitions for a serial killer," Tate said. "The National Institute of Justice defines a serial killer as someone acting alone who commits a series of two or more murders, often as separate events, in which the crimes can occur over a period of time ranging from hours to years. Quite often the motive is psychological, and the offender's behavior and the physical evidence observed at crime scenes will reflect sadistic, sexual overtones."

"So a serial killer can be considered a psychopath, but a psychopath isn't always a serial killer?" Aaron asked.

"That's it," Tate replied.

"So would Dexter be seen as both?" Dean called out.

"Ah, good question," Tate said. "What do you guys think?"

"Well, he's obviously a serial killer because he has a pattern of killing like the definition said," Helen answered. "As for a psychopath, I think he fits some of Hare's criteria, but not really any one of Millon's subtypes."

"I don't know. He kinda fits tyrannical," Aaron suggested. "I mean, he kills people, so he'd have to fall into either the malevolent psychopath or the tyrannical one. But his motive for killing people has nothing to do with not trusting people, and he's not intensely suspicious, so that rules out the first one. But he does enjoy overpowering his victims and he really thrives on the victims' suffering, which sounds pretty tyrannical."

"But he chooses his victims specifically because they're bad guys who escaped the system," Helen countered. "Of course he wants them to suffer because they were almost allowed to go unpunished for their crimes."

"Well, the tyrannical psychopath is very selective about his victims so he can overpower them, and Dexter is very selective of his victims because of his code," Aaron pointed out. "That's similar."

"But that's just it. We're talking about a character who's a killer but also has a 'moral code,'" Helen shot back. "All of these definitions for psychopaths and killers assume these people have no conscience; they feel nothing about what they do. And yes, Dexter is constantly faking emotion to fit in with the rest of the world, but he also has a system by which he kills. So that almost automatically throws all these subtypes out the window."

"That's an interesting point," Tate said, leaning against the podium. "There has been a lot of discussion in the psychology community about whether or not it's possible to rehabilitate or even train a psychopath to curb his violent nature. They think it's probably impossible for an adult, but if they caught someone early, like what happened in Dexter, some feel it's possible to change one's behavior."

"But just because Dexter has a moral code, that doesn't mean he stops killing," Hank said. "He still has that 'dark passenger' as he calls it. His father gave him a system to take care of his psychopathic tendencies. That's the whole idea of the show. He's a monster but he's only killing those who society would say 'deserve' it."

"There are those who have done scans on the brains of known psychopaths and they believe you can see a physical difference between their brains and a non-psychopath's," Tate said. "That would seem to suggest there are physical ways, maybe drugs or behavioral therapy, to manipulate these psychopathic tendencies as you called them. And if we could catch something like that early in children, whose brains are still developing, who knows?"

"But look at all the controversy over medication for us as it is," pointed out Dean. "That one dude who went out and shot a bunch of people at a mall, they said he was on antidepressants. And if kids' brains are still developing, who's to say that kind of medication wouldn't elevate their condition, make it worse?"

"It's true," Tate agreed. "Science still has a long way to go in dealing with brain function. But you brought up the mall shooting. How many of you think that shooter was a psychopath?"

Everyone looked down at the psychopath subtype sheet again. Several types had bits and pieces that could fit into the story told by the media.

"Maybe the covetous psychopath?" Helen guessed. "He could have felt that life hadn't given him 'his due' so this was his retribution."

"He could also be an explosive psychopath," Aaron offered. "It kinda sounds like he had 'adult tantrums' and he wasn't smooth or emotionally detached. He just lashed out."

"Well, neither one of those include that kind of violence in their description," Tate reminded them.

"Oh yeah," Aaron mumbled. "Well, I guess then I wouldn't characterize him as a psychopath."

"I think many people are quick to use the term psychopath on anyone who commits this kind of heinous violence. I'm sure the boy from Utah was also not a psychopath," Tate said. "As we saw today, even you, my brilliant psychology students, had certain ideas of what it means to be a psychopath. And now we know they are not always killers, and they are not clinically defined as crazy. In fact, the insanity plea does not extend to psychopaths because they are always aware of what they did."

"What about the Columbine shooters?" Hank asked. "Were they considered psychopaths?"

Ah, Columbine. Deirdre wondered if that would be a part of the lecture. She sat up in her seat.

"Well, it just so happens that one of them, Eric Harris, was considered to be a psychopath. After reviewing tapes they made and the notebooks he kept about the whole process, it was obvious he felt superior to pretty much all of society," Tate answered. "In fact, he fit both definitions for malevolent and tyrannical. He was ruthless and cold-blooded with an intense desire for retribution, and he felt no guilt or remorse. He was also stimulated by what he perceived to be weak students and teachers in the school, and he enjoyed making them suffer."

"What about the other one?"

"Dylan Klebold? He was basically seen as suicidal," Tate said. "He kept a journal as well, but it was mostly about his depression and his desire for suicide, even though it conflicted with his religious views. Harris was obviously the leader of the plan. He shot his weapons twice as much as Klebold, who fired about 55 times. It's a classic case of a dyad, or a pair of killers, who feed off of each other. In this case, Klebold fed into Harris's thrill of killing."

"And no one had any idea they were planning it?" Dean asked.

"Well, to that grand a scale, no," Tate replied. "There were students who were aware they had bought guns and sometimes built small pipe bombs, and they were both in a juvenile delinquent program at one point because of a few acts of vandalism. But they didn't reveal their master plan to anyone. It wasn't until after the shooting that the police found Harris' notebooks detailing every moment of the plan.

"But that brings up a good point," he continued. "Hare also created a separate list of traits for juveniles to describe psychopathic tendencies, including defiance of authority figures, unresponsive to punishment, petty theft, constant aggression, cruelty to animals, early experimentation with sex, and vandalism."

"Holy crap, I used to defy my parents and break curfew and steal packs of gum. I'm a psychopath!" Dean called out. Tate rolled his eyes as some of the students laughed.

"Ok, ok, I know some of them sound like typical teenage behavior," he said. "But just as the adult version has a rating system, so does this one. You put a number of offenses together and it can add up to a more violent picture than just regular teenage angst."

"So what are we supposed to do then?" Aaron asked. "How do you know if your friend is a psychopath?"

"Geez, Aaron, I'm not that messed up. Seriously," Dean said. Hank laughed.

"You sure about that?"

"That's an interesting question, Aaron," Tate said, trying to bring the conversation back to the topic. "Studies done on school shooters have discovered that often times the person told someone about how frustrated they were or angry or hurt, and how they wanted to take it out on the world. I know sometimes teens say things like that to express their resentment at not knowing how to make things better. But it doesn't hurt to talk to the person more about it, try to gauge their real feelings and how serious they are. I think if people simply paid attention more to what teens are saying, rather than dismissing it as teen angst, there might be less feelings of isolation and hopelessness."

"All we need is peace, love and understanding," Dean sang. A couple of students giggled.

"That's right," Tate said, shaking his head. "Although I would add patience to that as well, to put up with you guys."

The rest of the class laughed.

"All right, guys, we're getting to the end of the class," he said, looking up at the clock. "Miss Hart, do you have any additional questions or a desire to speak with any of these fine students?"

Deirdre smiled as some of the students turned to look at her. She glanced down at her notes and thought back to her conversation with Dr. Stephens.

"I do have one question for you, Professor Tate," she said. "Is there evidence that suggests psychopaths are born that way, or is it something that could be triggered by a traumatic event?"

"That's a great question," Tate answered. "Many psychologists believe that psychopaths are born that way, that there are telltale signs right from early childhood that are usually ignored or mistaken for something else. The child might be distant or cold, meaning they're not as affectionate with their parents or others, or they can be aggressive, or they don't get along with other children. But of course, no parent wants to think their child could be a psychopath, so unless the child becomes extremely violent, this behavior often times is allowed to continue into adulthood."

"So, if a person is born a psychopath, would environmental factors come into play to determine which kind of psychopath they become as they get older?" Deirdre asked.

"There's certainly evidence out there to support that theory," Tate replied, leaning against his desk. "Many psychologists feel the person's childhood environment helps to mold their psychopathic tendencies. If they grew up with money and privilege, they may become a white-collar criminal, whereas if they grew up in poverty they would be more likely to end up a violent criminal. But the internal traits are usually the same throughout any psychopath. It's simply the way they choose to use these traits that differs."

"I see," Deirdre said, adding more to her notes. "Ok then, that was my one question."

"Excellent," Tate replied. "Anyone else have any intriguing questions for me?"

No one raised their hand.

"Well then, you guys luck out. The lecture is done a bit early," Tate said. "Although I do have some homework for you over the weekend."

Several of the students groaned as Tate held up his hands.

"Hey, come on. I took it easy on you not assigning reading for today, didn't I? This is such an extensive topic that we need at least two class periods to cover everything. So, for next week I want you to read Chapter 15, and I want you to start thinking of a topic for the six-page paper you'll be writing that's due next Friday on one particular psychopath of your choice."

"Someone we made up or a real one?" Hank asked.

"I know you all think you could write an episode of Dexter, but trust me, it ain't that easy," Tate answered wryly. "So for now let's stick with real, clinically declared psychopaths. All right, that's it for today. Have a good weekend and I'll see you next Tuesday."

Tate started to pack up his notes and Xerox sheets as the students collected their things. Filing out of the room various students said "good-bye" and "have a nice weekend" and "thanks for the depressing reading." As the last student walked out of the room, Tate turned around and began to erase the board.

Deirdre put away her notebook and made her way down to the front of the classroom. Tate turned back to her once the board was cleared.

"So, Miss Hart, how'd I do?"

"This class was exactly what I was looking for," she answered. "You were right, the students were quite engaged in the conversation which made it a fun experience. Honestly, I wasn't sure what to expect from a college lecture."

"Well, I hope it was both fun and informative. And if you'd like to take a copy of the sheets I handed out, please, feel free."

"Oh great!" she said, leaning down to take the top sheet. "Thank you again for your time."

"Well, if you have any additional questions you have my office number. It was a pleasure to meet you, Miss Hart. Good luck with your article."

"Thanks again," Deirdre said. As she turned to walk out she looked back at the lecture hall one last time.

Ah, to be in college again.

CHAPTER TWENTY-TWO

Zoey stared out the window of Dr. Stephens' office. She couldn't imagine working in such a stoic building, especially one that only had a view of the convenience store across the street. It wasn't a very lively environment that encouraged lively conversation. *Of course, there's really no place in town that offers that,* she thought.

Dr. Stephens was talking about something, but Zoey couldn't remember what it was. Today at the restaurant one of their regular customers asked her where Laura was. He only came to the restaurant a couple times every summer when he was in the area on business, and he made sure to flirt with Laura whenever he made an appearance.

Zoey told him she wasn't working there that summer, and walked away. *He's not an important person in her life,* she thought. *He doesn't need to know.*

But those moments were becoming more and more frequent, especially from those who never saw the two of them apart. Zoey was almost angry with Laura for forcing her to become the spokesperson for what had happened. She was never good at that, and Laura knew it.

Other times, people just wanted to tell her they read about what had happened in the newspaper, and how sorry they were. Zoey didn't know which was worse.

"Zoey?" she heard Dr. Stephens say. She turned from the window to look at her. "You seem especially distracted today. Did something happen?"

Zoey shook her head, although all day she had struggled with the decision to discuss it in her session. It was something she would have talked about with Laura, and because of that she felt torn. She knew she could never replace Laura, or the kind of fulfillment Laura brought to her life. Laura was the only person who encouraged Zoey to display her true self around others, allowing her to drop her guard and enjoy life. She felt a freedom with Laura that she had never felt with anyone else.

But now that she needed Laura more than ever, she wasn't there. And Zoey didn't know what else to do.

After a minute of silence, Zoey still had nothing to add. Dr. Stephens decided to change the subject.

"You know, one thing we haven't touched upon yet is how you're sleeping. Any changes in your usual sleeping pattern?"

Zoey was hoping Dr. Stephens would never ask that question. She had often struggled with insomnia, as if she was unable to shut down her brain when she got into bed. There always seemed to be too much going on for her to let go and become part of the silence.

But since Laura's death, she was practically asleep by the time her head hit the pillow. And it bothered her tremendously.

Dr. Stephens could sense Zoey's trepidation.

"There's no right or wrong answer here, Zoey," she offered gently. "You know that by now, right?"

Zoey nodded again.

"Okay, then, have you experienced any changes in your sleeping?"

Zoey looked down at her feet.

"Yeah. Actually, um, I've been sleeping really well."

"Is that unusual for you?"

"It is really unusual for me! I don't know what's wrong with me!"

"You're upset because you're sleeping well?"

"Of course I am! I mean, I could never fall asleep before. I had to be so ridiculously exhausted to fall asleep after lying in bed for two hours. And now, I'm practically out before my head hits the pillow. How messed up is that?"

Dr. Stephens wrote something down on her notebook.

"What about dreams? Do you remember any of your dreams?"

Zoey looked at her, confused.

"Aren't you surprised that I'm sleeping this great?"

"Well, since it's a drastic change from your usual sleeping pattern, no," she replied. "It's not unusual for your daily routine to change after the death of a loved one. Your body is feeling the trauma in a certain way, just like your mind is processing it in a certain way. I'm not concerned about what your habit changed to; it's enough to know that it's different."

Zoey didn't know whether to still be upset by the change, or to now be relieved that it was happening.

"So, now that you're getting a good night's sleep, do you remember any of your dreams?"

It was difficult to pinpoint any one particular dream, Zoey thought. They were often a jumble of images that she couldn't quite make out individually.

"I don't really remember having specific dreams. When I wake up, I remember seeing pictures, or people, or places, but not all of them together."

"That's not unusual. The subconscious doesn't always work in a clear manner."

"The subconscious?"

"Yes, the part of your mind that's displaying these images for you. Many people feel that's how you bring your true feelings to light, through the subconscious mind."

"Are you talking about those people who analyze dreams, and tell you that a bird in your dream represents a fear of heights or something?"

"Well, I wouldn't go that far," Stephens smiled. "But I do believe some people project certain thoughts and feelings into their dreams that can shed some light on how they're dealing with things when they're awake. Does that make sense?"

"I guess so."

"Ok. Then let's talk about some of these images. Do you ever see Laura?"

"No," Zoey answered, surprised at the sudden realization. "I do see places where we used to hang out. Sometimes I think I'm in her room, although it doesn't look exactly like her room. It just feels like that's where I am."

Dr. Stephens nodded, encouraging her to continue.

"Other times, I'm playing a game that we used to play when we were younger," Zoey explained. "Like, one time for Halloween I dressed up like a dinosaur, so after that it became our favorite dress-up game. I always hated the frilly dress-up games other girls played."

"Would you say you're seeing mostly things that remind you of Laura, without actually seeing her?"

"It seems like it, yeah."

"Well, I'm not too surprised then that you're sleeping so well," Stephens said. "You immediately send yourself back to a time when Laura was here, and you get to do all the same things you used to do together without anyone interfering or reminding you that she's gone. Your dreams are safe."

"So why don't I see her then?"

"I don't know," Stephens replied. "Maybe even on the subconscious level you know she's gone, and you don't want to have to go through the pain every day of waking up to the realization that she's not here anymore. It's hard to let go of your routine, especially the routine you had with someone who's been a major part of your life, for most of your life, so it plays a big role in your dreams. But reality tends to be much harsher."

"No kidding."

"How do you feel when you wake up in the morning?"

"I don't know. I never really thought about it."

"Well, tomorrow when you wake up I'd like you to think about it," Stephens said. "Take a minute to think about what you're feeling, how you're feeling. It would be great if you could keep a journal every day, recording your thoughts and moods, as well as anything you can remember from your dreams. You can bring it in for the next session."

"Is this like homework?" Zoey asked, wrinkling her nose.

"Only if you think about it that way. I would think of it as research, a helpful tool for our next session."

"If you say so."

Dr. Stephens looked at her over her notebook.

"Ok, ok, it's research," Zoey said.

"Well, it looks like our time is up. I feel we made some progress today. Do you?"

"Yeah. I really didn't know what to think about the sleeping thing."

"Hopefully we can talk about it some more next week then. So I'll see you Tuesday?"

"Yup. See ya next week."

Zoey stood up and walked out of the office, seeing her mother's car through the window in the hallway. It was a new thing, her mom driving her to her sessions and picking her up. Connie told her it was easier, that it coincided with the errands she needed to run for that day. But Zoey knew Connie wanted to get her alone in the car so she couldn't run away.

When she opened the door, the bright sunlight blinded her. As she shielded her eyes, she noticed a young man standing against the wall of the convenience store, facing her. He was tall, his Led Zeppelin T-shirt just reaching the top of his jeans and studded belt. Zoey admired his dark tousled hair, which looked like he hadn't touched it in days, making it perfect at the same time. Zoey couldn't see his eyes behind his dark shades, but he seemed to be looking at her with interest. He smiled. She blushed, realizing she was staring at him, and climbed into the car.

"Hi, honey," Connie said. "How was your session?"

As they drove away, Zoey looked at him again out of the corner of her eye.

Mmmm. Not bad, she thought.

CHAPTER TWENTY-THREE

KNOCK! KNOCK!

"Come in!" Deirdre called out. "I'll be out in a second."

Deirdre's two friends, Haley Johnson and Nina Ashby, wiped their feet on the mat before walking into the living room. Out of all of the people Deirdre had known since high school, they were the only two she remained close with. And in a small town like her hometown, you ran into people you went to high school with on a regular basis.

Deirdre came out of the bedroom tying her hair back into a ponytail.

"Girl, you need to do something else with your hair once in a while," Nina scoffed. "It's so long you'd think you'd be able to do something new with it."

"Nina, you realize the only reason it's so long is because she doesn't take the time to get it cut," Haley interjected. "It's a laziness thing."

"What? I'm not lazy. I'm on the go all the time! You're the one who gets summers off, Teach."

"Summers off? Are you kidding? Not on my salary. It's summer school for me, baby."

"Ugh, that's gotta suck," Nina said. "Not only do you not want to be there but you know the students don't want to either."

"Oh yeah, it makes for an interesting day."

"Well, that's why we go out drinking," Deirdre replied.

"Amen to that," Nina laughed. "There are days I'd love to sneak a Valium or two from behind the counter. Some of the customers are completely tweaked out when they come to pick up their refills."

"Can you blame them? It's not like we live in the big city or anything. Hell, we don't even live in a small city!" Haley added. "There is nothing to do here except raise a family or go out drinking. And sometimes, the two go together!"

"You would know."

"Absolutely."

Deirdre grabbed her jacket as they headed out to Nina's car.

"So, which one tonight? The Pub? Jackson's? McGillicuddy's?"

"You know, for such a small town there sure are a lot of bars."

"I told you, that's all there is to do around here. It's a vicious cycle that keeps feeding itself."

"You know, I'm sure plenty of people find other things to do. They go out to the movies, they stay in and watch movies, they go out to dinner…"

"They stay in and have dinner," Nina said. Haley laughed.

"Ok, ok, I'm just saying there are other things to do. We choose to go out to the bars."

"Well, where else am I gonna meet someone?" Nina asked. "You guys are my wing nuts."

"That's wing men!"

"No, I think I had it right the first time."

"You bitch," said Haley, punching Nina's arm. "See if I wing anything for you anymore."

They cruised down the town's one main road, the three of them waving at different people they knew on the sidewalk. Since it was almost nine, all of the business owners were closing up shop for the night. The only places to go at night were bars, restaurants with bars, the small movie theater, and the one 24-hour fast food joint in town. Despite the lack of variety, Deirdre made sure to get together with the girls at least once a week to maintain her sanity.

Another mile down the road, Nina pulled into the parking lot at McGillicuddy's, which was surprisingly full for a Wednesday.

"Must be some big baseball game going on tonight," Deirdre commented getting out of the car.

"Yeah, because the townies need an excuse to come out and drink on a Wednesday," Haley said.

"Are you serious? We are townies."

"Hey, Nina," a male voice called out.

"Hey, Cal. What are you doing out on a weeknight?"

"Watching the All Star game. It's the only thing going on during the baseball break."

"Told ya."

"Great, a bunch of drunk guys yelling at the TV. I might as well have stayed home."

"Is Paul's brother still staying with you guys?"

"Oh yeah," Haley replied, rolling her eyes. "And it's like they're back in college, the way they drink and talk, especially about Josh's ex-wife. I thought she was perfectly nice, but apparently she asked 'too much' of Josh."

"Is that the only reason he gave you?"

"Yup."

As they walked into the bar, a cheer erupted from the center of the room.

"Too bad that wasn't aimed at us," Deirdre grinned.

"Yeah, we lost that power years ago."

"Hey, speak for yourself," Nina exclaimed. "I'm still single ya know."

"Do you ever wonder why that is?" Haley asked, smirking. Nina playfully punched her arm.

"Don't make me start a bar brawl before I've even had one drink."

They found a small empty table in the corner and sat down. Nina offered to buy the first round, since she was only allowed one beer as the designated driver.

"I don't know why we even drove here," Deirdre said. "We could've walked from my place."

"Honey, we're not gonna sleep over your place afterwards," Nina said. "No matter how lonely you are."

"Shut up." Both women chuckled, as Nina walked over to the bar.

"So, I assume by your mature response you're still sleeping alone?" Haley asked.

"Ben and I aren't officially divorced yet, you know that."

"So? That didn't stop Ben. You guys did separate."

"Yes, I know Haley. I'm reminded every day."

"Well, I'm just saying, you can't use the divorce thing as an excuse anymore."

Deirdre paused, wondering if she should tell her friends about the divorce papers, especially when she hadn't touched them yet. Even though she loved them like sisters, they could still be judgmental if they felt it was for her own good. Deirdre wasn't sure she was ready to listen to reason just yet, but she knew they would find out eventually.

"Actually, it may not be an excuse for much longer. It might really happen."

"No shit! When?"

"I'll tell you when Nina gets back."

"Uh oh. It's that serious?"

"Yup."

After about five minutes Nina finally came back with three beers.

"Jesus, it's a madhouse up there."

"Hurry up and sit down, Deirdre has some news about Ben."

"Oh shit, what's going on now?" Nina asked, handing Deirdre her beer. She paused.

"He's going to ask Veronica to marry him."

Haley and Nina looked at each other from across the table. Haley's eyes slanted as she opened her mouth, but Nina shook her head. Haley took a sip of her beer instead.

"Oh, honey, I'm so sorry," Nina said. "I assume that means he's ready for the divorce."

"Yeah, he brought the papers over to my place last month."

"Last month? So, is your lawyer looking at them right now or something?"

"That's what I told Ben."

Nina glanced over at Haley, who mockingly threw her hands up in the air. Deirdre looked between the both of them.

"Look, I know what you're thinking. This is tough enough without being judged by you guys too."

"Oh Deirdre, we're not judging you," Haley replied. "But it's been three years now, and obviously Ben is ready to start over with someone new. You should be too."

"So now you're an expert on divorced couples?"

"Deirdre, all we're saying is that we want to see you happy," Nina interjected. "And knowing that Ben has moved on, well, obviously that's not easy for you. But it doesn't make things easier when all you have is your work."

"Hey, I have my family. And I have you guys too. At least, I thought I did."

"Come on, Deirdre," Haley said. "Yeah we're fun and all, but we're not moving into your place any time soon. Although depending on how long Josh stays it might come down to that."

Deirdre found herself smiling against her will. Haley smirked.

"See? All I'm saying is you need to get out and mingle. You're gonna be 30 soon and then what? It's all downhill from there."

"Excuse me? We're all going to be 30 soon!" Nina exclaimed.

"Yeah, but you don't have any baggage," Deirdre observed. "I'm only 29 and I will have already been divorced once. I'm like a walking cliché, divorced, no kids, and ridiculously involved in my work."

"It's not a cliché when you're living it," Haley said. Deirdre shook her head.

"Guys, it's not that simple. Ben and I went through this traumatic experience together, and he'll always be the only person who understands that. But at the same time, he's dealing with it differently than I am, and I just can't get past that. I don't know what to do."

Nina reached across the table and took Deirdre's hand in hers.

"Honey, I can't begin to imagine how you must've felt when all that happened," she said. "But at some point you have to figure out what you're going to do next. You've been coasting for the last three years, and we haven't said a word because it's your life. But we're really worried about you, and now that Ben is officially asking for a divorce, well, we're even more worried."

Deirdre frowned, pulling away from Nina to sit back in her chair.

"Look, I appreciate your concern for me, really I do. But this is something I'm gonna have to figure out on my own."

Haley looked at Nina and shrugged helplessly. It was Nina's turn to frown as she took a sip of her beer. After a moment of awkward silence, she changed the subject.

"So, are you working on any hot topics right now? I know they're your favorite."

Deirdre paused, unsure that this was the time to mention her new article. The transition wasn't the best. *Well, I suppose they're going to find that out soon too.*

"Um, well, now that you mention it, I am working on something new," she said, trying to figure out the smoothest way to approach the subject.

"Well?"

"Well, it's basically about youth violence," she began slowly. "I've been doing some research and I've found a number of interesting statistics."

"Deirdre, does this have anything to do with those shootings that happened earlier this year?" Haley asked, looking at her out of the corner of her eye. Deirdre paused again.

"That's a part of it, yes."

"Jesus, Deirdre, no wonder you can't get past any of this shit! You're holding yourself in the past deliberately, and camouflaging it as work. Does that sound familiar?"

"Now, wait a second…"

"No, no, Haley's right," Nina interjected. "This is taking things too far. You are obsessed, girl."

"See? I knew you guys would react like this. You think I'm writing this story for one reason, but it's not the one you think it is."

"Oh no? You're not looking for answers as to why that happened to you?" Haley asked. "You're not looking for something to blame? Something you can point to and say, look what we can fix to make things different. You're delusional."

"Hey, the whole reason I write these stories is to open people's eyes to things they don't want to look at," Deirdre said. "People have different theories about why these things happen, but they're often based in myth or fear. This is an important issue, and the more research I do the more patterns I see to explain why this might be happening."

"Deirdre, you're not going to solve this 'issue' by writing an article," Haley sputtered. "The only thing you're going to do is drag yourself further down this rabbit hole until you hit rock bottom. Remember the nightmares you had any time it was mentioned in the news? And now you're deliberately looking up information on the subject. Why are you doing this to yourself?"

"I'm not doing anything to myself!" Deirdre exclaimed. "As a matter of fact, I've been totally fine throughout this whole process. Doesn't that show that I've moved on from that?"

"Deirdre, the only thing that shows is that it hasn't hit you yet. But mark my words, that whole vicious cycle will start up again. And then what?"

Deirdre had expected this kind of a response from Haley. She had always been upfront and brash with people when she felt they were in the wrong. It was a trait Deirdre both admired and despised about her friend, depending on what side of the issue she was found. But Nina was a bit more sensitive, more understanding when it came to these kinds of delicate matters, and was still able to communicate her opinion openly. Deirdre looked over at her to see her staring at her beer bottle.

"Do you agree with her?"

Nina put her elbows on the table and leaned forward to look Deirdre in the eye.

"Honey, I think you need to take a long, careful look at why you are so vested in this topic. That's my only advice."

"I can't believe you two."

"Well, can you blame us?" Haley asked. "Don't forget, we've been down many a road like this before with you, Deirdre. We've seen you get extremely close to your subjects, and this is about as close and personal as it gets. I can't believe Neil is even allowing you to work on this."

"Trust me, he had his reservations," Deirdre admitted. "But we can't ignore the fact that this kind of stuff happens all the time, and that kids are doing it at younger ages. It's an important issue, guys, plain and simple, and I'm going into it as a journalist. Scout's honor."

Haley sighed, trying to decide whether or not to trust her long-time friend. She glanced over at Nina, who was studying the expression on Deirdre's face. She too wanted to believe her. But both of them had witnessed how much Deirdre struggled to put the pieces of her life back together, not only after the shooting but also after the dissolution of her marriage. They were there for the long lunches and late night phone calls and weekend crying sessions. And even though this was a broader topic, it was rooted in a situation that had ruined Deirdre's life for years. It was not something either one of them wanted to see their friend bring upon herself again. Nina held out her hand.

"Promise me, Deirdre. Promise me right now, that you will not allow this article to affect your life in any way," she said sternly, looking her in the eye. "Now is not the time to return to that day, or the days that followed. You need to move forward, are you listening to me? Forward."

Knowing the only thing she had to go home to were divorce papers, that would not be an easy promise for Deirdre to make. But she also knew her friends were not going to leave her alone until she agreed. *That will have to do for now,* she thought.

"Fine, I promise," she agreed, shaking Nina's hand. "I will be very careful in my travels."

"You better mean that, girl."

"Yes, for Christ sake, I mean it!"

"All right then," Haley said. "After all that, I think we need another round!"

"Amen!" called out the other two in unison. Deirdre pushed her chair back and stood up, relieved to have an excuse to end the conversation.

"Ok guys, next round's on me."

As Deirdre walked away, Haley sat back in her chair and ran her fingers through her hair. She looked over at Nina, who was watching Deirdre as she ordered their next beers. Haley knew by the frown on her face that she didn't believe Deirdre either.

"We're going to have to keep an eye on her, you know." Nina nodded.

"Way ahead of ya, sister."

CHAPTER TWENTY-FOUR

Finally, some peace and quiet.

Zoey leaned against a tree in the park down the street from her house. She told her mom she had to go to work early, but the truth was she couldn't stay in the house any longer. Not that she could be honest. Her mother was constantly on edge, questioning everything that Zoey thought or felt. *It's bad enough I have to keep track of my dreams and how I'm feeling at the start of every day for Dr. Stephens. Now Mom needs to know too.*

It's exhausting being on display all the time.

Zoey wondered how therapy was supposed to help if it was taking over her life. She only went once a week, yet she felt it was the only thing defining her existence. If her parents weren't asking her about a session, they were bringing up topics in everyday conversation that Dr. Stephens had discussed with her. She knew they were trying to become more involved with her life, but she felt they were taking the wrong approach.

They're not asking me the right questions, she thought. *Everything with them is a technical question concerning my life, rather than asking about my actual one. They talk about concepts and lessons I should be learning and coping mechanisms. They don't talk about anything that's real. Even talking about my future would be better than this crap.*

Hell, I might as well go back to school if all I'm gonna get is lectures.

Every day Zoey counted the tips she earned from work, putting most of the money into her savings account. She used to save it for spending money during the school year, since her parents could only afford to pay for tuition and books. But now her goal was to save up for her own apartment. It was a dream she thought she would have to put on hold, with her first choice for a roommate gone. They had talked about it for after graduation, and for a while after Laura's death Zoey believed it was no longer an option. But now it was very clear. *I have to get out of my parents' house.*

At least therapy was good for something, she thought. *It gave me a goal.*

Zoey closed her eyes and breathed in the clean summer air. The shade was calming underneath the blazing sun. She stretched out her legs and put her arms behind her head.

Maybe if I close my eyes and clear my mind, I can leave everything behind. I'm not here. The world isn't here. There's nothing for me to say or do. No one is looking for me. No one is nagging me. I have no responsibilities. All I feel is calm and emptiness. Complete silence.

A loud barking dog shook her out of her fantasy. *Damn it! All I want is five minutes of peace! Isn't there somewhere I can go where I'm not constantly annoyed?*

These days, that seemed to be impossible.

Frustrated, Zoey stood up and shook the dirt off her shorts. When she looked back up, she saw the mystery boy from the other day enter the convenience store next to the park. She froze.

There he is! I was wondering if I'd get to see him again! I can't believe I've never seen him before. I thought I knew everyone in this town. And how come I only see him at convenience stores?

Zoey stood still, watching him move through the aisles.

I gotta get a closer look.

She started walking slowly towards the store, carefully staying out of his viewpoint. When he turned around to grab a drink out of one of the refrigerators, she ran across the park until she made it to the front door. Making sure he was still facing away from her, she opened the door as quietly as she could.

RING-A-LING!

Idiot! You forgot about the bell above the door!

Zoey ducked behind the first shelf, but the boy didn't even turn around.

Jesus Christ, you are such a dork. People come and go from the store all the time. Why would he turn around for that? And why do you care if he did? Why are you hiding?

Zoey didn't have a good answer for any of her own questions. She felt completely out of her element. She'd never stalked a boy alone before, not that this was stalking exactly. But there were no clear motives as to why she was sneaking around the store, watching him.

It was the kind of thing she and Laura would do whenever they saw a good-looking guy. If they felt he was out of their league, they would simply follow him around for a little while, trying not to giggle and give away their cover. They called themselves the "Boy Crazy Ninjas." Zoey smiled from the memory.

All of a sudden she realized he wasn't standing in front of the refrigerators any more.

Crap! I broke the first rule of the ninja code. Never lose your focus!

She quickly walked into the next empty aisle, frantically looking around for him. She hoped no one was watching the store cameras. *I probably look like I'm about to steal something.*

"Can I help you, miss?" called out the cashier. "You look lost."

Oh great. Now I look like an even bigger dork, seemingly lost among shelves of candy, toilet paper, and potato chips.

"No, I'm fine," she said hastily, praying the cashier would stop talking and leave her alone. *Can't he see I'm trying to be stealthy?*

That's probably why he noticed you, dumbass! Could you be any more obvious?

Zoey planted herself in front of the ice cream case, pretending to browse all of the flavors. In reality she was taking advantage of the viewpoint she had of the entire store in the glass door.

Where the heck did he go?

After another minute of scanning the store, she decided to give up. It was beginning to feel silly anyway, without her partner in crime.

As she turned around to leave she bumped into him, knocking the package of cookies he held onto the floor.

"Holy shit!" she exclaimed, more out of shock than anything else. He grinned.

"It's ok," he said, reaching down to pick up the package. "They're only cookies. I was planning on buying them anyway, so you're off the hook for the whole, you break 'em, you buy 'em policy."

Zoey was speechless, feeling her cheeks flush with embarrassment. She hadn't actually planned on meeting the boy. That would be awkward.

Case in point.

"I, uh, I'm really sorry."

"Like I said, it's ok."

"No, I should've been watching where I was going."

"All you did was turn around," he said. "I should've been paying more attention."

"No, really, I'm just retarded." *Oh my god, dude, shut up! He doesn't need to know that!*

He smiled, and for the first time she noticed his light hazel eyes. They were beautiful, piercing, as if he knew everything about her in one glance. His sleeve grazed against her arm and she shivered, suddenly realizing how close she was to him.

She had to get out of there.

"I gotta go," she stammered, turning in the other direction.

"Wait. It's no big deal, really. You don't have to..."

Zoey didn't wait to hear the rest of his sentence as she flew out the door.
RING-A-LING!

CHAPTER TWENTY-FIVE

"So, Zoey. It's almost September. Have you spoken with your parents about going back to school?"

Zoey was amazed at how quickly three months of therapy sessions had passed, now that the summer was coming to an end. Her parents were pleased with her progress, and to her surprise, Zoey could see it too. It was only once a week so it wasn't as constant as her parents nagging, and she was able to talk to someone about her parents annoying behavior.

"We sort of came up with a compromise."

"Oh? What's that?"

"I'm taking a year off to re-evaluate what I want to do with my life. My parents' words, not mine. Anyway, I told them I'd keep coming here so they don't think I'm losing focus or whatever."

Dr. Stephens set her notebook down in her lap and clasped her hands together. Zoey knew what that reaction was by now- concern.

"It almost sounds like we've come back to the drawing board then."

"What do you mean?"

"Well, it sounds as if therapy is once again your parents' idea and that you neither need nor want to be here."

Zoey looked down at her feet, trying not to give away how she truly felt. She found it almost comical that she didn't want to admit to her therapist that the sessions were helping her to cope with her life. It would mean that her parents were right all along, that she really did need help beyond what they could give her.

"That's not true," she said quietly. "I do want to be here. It just goes against everything I thought, and Laura thought, about therapy."

"And what was that?"

Zoey tried not to grin.

"You know, uh, we thought that, people who come here just whine about their daily lives because no one else wants to listen," she said. "And those same people are always saying, 'Well my therapist says' because they're unable to think for themselves. All they believe in is the current self-help propaganda that really only has a foundation because so many people are looking for a quick fix."

"Do you still think that?"

"I guess not," Zoey answered. "I mean, at first I almost felt like I was letting Laura down or something by coming here, like I was betraying that private joke we had. But now, I'm kinda realizing this has become my Laura. Not like a replacement for her or anything. I just needed something healthy to fill the void for a while, ya know?"

"I do know," Stephens said. "You're right. Sometimes people come here because they're hoping for a simple answer to get their life back on track and this seems like an automatic place to go. But everyone feels that way at one time or another, no matter how strong or capable they think they are, and it's my job to help them find the right path.

"On the other hand, there are those who honestly need someone to talk to, someone who can help them hash out their problems in, as you say, a healthy manner," she continued. "And there's no shame in either one of those reasons."

"I know."

"Good. Then I think you're ready to take responsibility for scheduling your next round of sessions. Sound good?"

Zoey nodded.

"Ok then. What would you like to talk about today?"

Oh good, it's going to be one of those sessions, she thought. No mention of her dream journal today.

"Well," Zoey paused. "There's this guy."

Dr. Stephens picked up her notebook. "Ok. There's a guy."

"No, not just a guy. This guy."

"Ah, I see. What makes him 'this' guy?"

"This guy, he is the most beautiful person I've ever seen," Zoey exclaimed, trying not to gush. "He's literally tall, dark and handsome. I mean, not handsome in the traditional sense I guess, but he's hot."

"Are you referring to him as 'this guy' because you don't know his name?"

"Yeah. I've barely even spoken to him. There was that one time in the convenience store and it was a complete disaster."

"Why is that?"

"Because I wasn't planning on talking to him!"

"Why not?"

"Because I knew it would be a disaster!"

"So it's almost like it became a self-fulfilling prophecy."

"No no, nothing like that. That's just how I am around guys. It's inevitable."

"Have you ever been in a relationship?"

"I wish. I've never even been on a date alone with a guy before. I always double dated with Laura."

"So now you're on your own, and you're not sure what to do."

"Something like that," Zoey agreed. "I mean, I figured someday I might find a guy on my own. But I thought when that happened, I'd at least have Laura there to back me up. You know, help me decode the secret guy speak and everything."

"But so far it's only been 'disaster speak.'"

"Well yeah, because I wasn't prepared."

"Prepared? For what?"

"For talking to him. You have to have a plan before you can approach anyone new, especially a cute guy."

"You can't just say the first thing that comes to mind?"

"The first thing I said to him was 'holy shit.'"

Dr. Stephens stared at Zoey, who nodded her head.

"Ok, a plan is good."

Zoey giggled.

"We bumped into each other at the convenience store, after I followed him around for a while. I wasn't expecting to meet him that way."

"Well, Zoey, people meet that way all the time," Stephens said. "You always hear those stories of meeting in the grocery store or the library or wherever. It doesn't always have to be a bar or some other party setting."

"Laura always met her boyfriends at parties."

"That's pretty typical in a college environment."

"I just don't know what I'm doing," Zoey sighed. "I mean, I've only seen him twice. I'll probably never see him again and that short two minutes is all I'll get. I can file his image away with the rest of the guys I never had the guts to talk to."

"I'm curious about something," Stephens said, looking at her notebook. "You've talked about going out to parties and hanging out with various people with Laura all the time. I'm surprised you never ended up meeting a new guy to hang out with."

"Are you kidding? I met plenty. But they were always into Laura, never me. She was the outgoing one, the social butterfly. I was basically along for the ride."

"And you were okay with that?"

"That's how it always was," Zoey shrugged. "Laura was so pretty."

"What did she look like?"

"She had dirty blonde hair, which meant she could dye it darker or lighter depending on her mood and it always looked great," she began. "She was taller than me, so clothes always hung much better on her than on me, even though we were the same size. And she had really pretty blue eyes, everyone thought so. It's like they became mesmerized by them or something. She had this spark about her, I don't know. Some people have that way of walking into a room and putting everyone at ease. That was Laura."

"And how would you characterize yourself?"

"Me? I don't know. Boring brown hair, brown eyes, dark clothes, dark everything."

"You know what it sounds like to me? It sounds like Laura put in all the effort to present her best version of herself, which meant you didn't have to put forth any effort," Stephens explained. "Laura took care of the initial meeting, and you were able to sit back and enjoy the experience."

Zoey looked at Dr. Stephens quizzically. Not since their first meeting had Dr. Stephens said something that made her feel uneasy. The fact she approached things from an objective manner was the single reason Zoey was beginning to enjoy their sessions. But this, this sounded like a judgment again, and one she was not going to like. She felt a knot begin to form in her stomach.

"You make it sound like I was using her."

"I didn't say that. It just sounds like Laura automatically drew attention to herself, because as you said, she was the social butterfly. She enjoyed all of the attention. But you, you were simply content to be there, even if you were just sitting on the sidelines."

"That's just how it was. Laura was stunning and people responded to that. I'm not stunning. I'm not anything but realistic. I know how the world works. Beautiful people get treated differently. It's a fact of life."

"It sounds like you put a lot of stock in that popular idea."

"Are you saying it gave me some sort of an advantage?"

"You're telling me you were the follower; that was all that was expected of you," Stephens said. "You projected a certain image based on the image that Laura sent out. You didn't have to do anything, essentially. You let Laura take the reins on everything and let the rest come to you."

Zoey stood up from her chair suddenly, causing Dr. Stephens to look up, surprised. She had assumed that since Zoey and Laura had been friends for so long that the description of this dynamic would not be news to her. But gauging by Zoey's defensive reaction, she realized she may have crossed a line.

"I can't believe you're belittling my relationship with Laura. She was my only true friend. I loved her! How dare you talk about her like that!"

Dr. Stephens put down her notebook and gestured for Zoey to sit down.

"Zoey, I'm not judging anything about Laura or your relationship," she said calmly. "I'm simply looking at the different roles you girls had. Please, sit back down and we can discuss this."

"I don't want to discuss this anymore," Zoey shook her head, holding back tears of frustration. "You said we don't have to talk about anything if I don't want to. Well this, we are not talking about. I'm outta here."

Zoey expected Dr. Stephens to stop her, or at least try to talk her into coming back. When she reached the door, she heard nothing.

Fine. She doesn't care if I leave, I'm gone. Screw my parents and this stupid arrangement.

Zoey stormed out, slamming the door behind her.

Dr. Stephens set her pen down and looked over her notes, trying to find the catalyst that set Zoey's anger in motion. Many of their conversations about Laura had been reminiscing about all the fun they had growing up and discussing their close relationship. But Dr. Stephens had yet to learn why it was such an important part of Zoey's life.

It wasn't the first time a client had stormed out of her office. She was used to that. But Dr. Stephens really hoped she would see Zoey again.

CHAPTER TWENTY-SIX

Deirdre walked along the sidewalk in her old neighborhood, the place where she and Ben had lived for 5 years. The sun played peek-a-boo with her in and out of the maple trees that lined either side of the street, creating a semi-circle of leaves that Deirdre thought of as comforting arms wrapped around their small community. She had always felt safe, secure, like they lived in their own little world where the things she wrote about couldn't touch them. It was their own peaceful haven, the perfect place to call "home". Deirdre breathed in the comforting scent of fresh air.

The sidewalk brought her past the playground, past the baseball diamond, and around the corner towards their old house. But as she came closer to it, she realized there were no kids out playing baseball, or parents tending to their lawns. There were no cars driving by, no dogs barking or birds chirping. There was nothing but the road, the trees, and the houses, and even they seemed empty, almost like cardboard cutouts. A slight breeze rose up through the air, sending a chill down her spine. Something wasn't quite right in their own slice of tranquility.

Up ahead, Deirdre could see their old house, looking the same as when they left it over three years ago, chipped paint and all. She stopped at the walkway to the door and looked around the front yard. A brand new red tricycle sat off to the side, with brightly colored ribbons coming out of the handles. Deirdre walked over and sat down next to it, running her fingers along the handlebars. It felt strangely familiar.

"Isn't she beautiful?"

Startled, Deirdre looked up to see her mother standing over her. Her father stood next to her.

"Mom? Dad? What are you doing here?"

"She's been wanting this for a while now," her father said, seemingly ignoring her.

"What? The bike?"

"I hope she knows it's only a start," Rebecca said. "She'll have to learn to ride on two wheels eventually."

Deirdre let go of the bike and stood up to face her mother.

"I have no use for this bike any more, Mom. I'm too big. It's too late."

"She has to start somewhere," her father replied.

Deirdre shook her head.

"You're not listening to me, Dad. I don't need this bike."

"And then when she becomes a mother she can pass it onto her child."

"Mom, I'm not having kids, remember? I can't."

"Rebecca, how do you know she'll even want children?"

"Oh, Samuel, she'll want children. She wants to be like her big sister."

Deirdre felt the tears start to well up in her eyes as her lips began to tremble. She turned away from her parents.

"Why don't you understand, Mom? I can't have kids!"

"Then we can't be a family," said Ben's voice.

RING! RING!

Deirdre sat up suddenly at her desk. She looked around, confused, until she realized she had fallen asleep while typing up some of her notes. Tonight she was focusing on a story out of Boston from the 1990s, where people from the community had worked together to decrease the amount of teenage violence in the area by the end of the decade. Deirdre discovered a book on the case called *Murder is No Accident* which offered a detailed account of the citywide movement which included members from the school system, police, hospitals, and families who had been affected by such violence. It was one of the few things she came across that offered any of the solutions she was searching for.

But now it seemed the long string of restless nights surfing the Internet and reading extensive books on violent teenagers had finally caught up with her. She looked at the clock and saw it read 9:46 pm.

RING!

She leaned over and looked at the caller ID. It was Haley. She picked up her cell phone.

"Hello?"

"Finally! I've been trying to reach you for like, an hour now!" Haley exclaimed over the noise in the background. "Nina and I finally left for the bar without you. What are you doing?"

"I was sleeping actually," Deirdre admitted. She left out the part about the strange dream. *I don't need to give Haley any more fuel than she already has.*

"Sleeping? Are you sick?"

"No, no, I just have a headache. I think I'm gonna skip tonight."

"Aw, come on. Just take some aspirin and you'll be fine. You need to get outta the house, Deirdre."

"Haley, going out to a bar is not going to make me feel better. I'm going back to sleep."

"Deirdre…"

"Haley, no."

"Ugh. Fine. But we're coming over and dragging you out tomorrow, you hear me?"

"Yeah, yeah," Deirdre mumbled. "I'll talk to you tomorrow."

Deirdre hung up the phone and rubbed her eyes. She hadn't dreamt anything that vivid in years, since just after the shooting. And back then they all took place in the courtyard. It had taken over a year for her to get past those dreams, with Ben bearing the brunt of her waking up screaming night after night. But being back in her old neighborhood, where she hadn't been back to visit since she left, it didn't make her want to scream. It simply filled her with a sense of sadness, knowing she would never be able to go back.

Her phone rang again, snapping Deirdre back to reality a second time. Annoyed, she snatched the phone without looking at the caller ID.

"Jesus, I said I'm staying home!"

"Uh, ok," said Ben. Deirdre froze. "Is this a bad time, Deeds?"

"Ben. God, I'm sorry," Deirdre said, mortified. "I was just on the phone with Haley, telling her I wasn't coming out tonight. I thought you were her calling again."

"Honestly, I wasn't sure you'd be home. And if you were, I wasn't sure you'd pick up the phone. You seem to be avoiding me."

They hadn't talked since Ben left the divorce papers at Deirdre's place. He had thought it was best to give her some time to look over the documents and make sure everything was in order. He knew that was how Deirdre handled any kind of conflict in their relationship. She had always needed more time than he did to recover from something, no matter what it was. The fact that she threw herself into her work to avoid confrontation had never helped either.

But she couldn't avoid this, not forever, and he hoped to clear up any confusion that was left over from their previous conversation.

Unfortunately, Deirdre didn't have any answers either. She tried to think of something to say when he spoke again.

"So, uh, has your lawyer had a chance to look over the divorce papers yet?"

"I'm sorry. Am I taking too long to get your divorce through?"

The minute she said the words Deirdre regretted them. She didn't want to get into another involved and messy fight with him. She didn't have the energy anymore.

"Ben, uh, that was uncalled for," she stammered. "Things are taking a little bit longer than I was expecting them to." *Just not with the lawyer,* she thought, suddenly feeling guilty.

"Oh." Deirdre could hear a hint of disappointment in his voice. "Well, that's ok. This is a big step and I don't want to rush you into anything."

"I appreciate that."

The silence on the other end suggested Ben had nothing else to discuss with her. She remembered the days when they would talk on the phone for hours, since she often worked late. Whenever she had felt writer's block she would call him, and he would always have something to say that kept her going. But not anymore.

"Well, then…" Ben said, clearing his throat.

"Ben, wait. I know our last conversation didn't go the way either one of us hoped it would. Well, actually, I don't think it could have gone any of the ways I'd hoped it would. But that aside, we need to talk about it."

"Ok."

Deirdre took a deep breath. She wasn't prepared for this discussion tonight. She had a feeling Ben wasn't either. But after her dream, she realized she was beginning to fall back into old habits.

"I'm really sorry we had to get into all of that stuff again," she began. "It happened over three years ago, and if I'm still having trouble dealing with it, that's not your fault. I've been going around and around in my mind about this, and I keep coming back to the same conclusion. It's just not one that I like."

Before Ben could respond she continued.

"And that's my problem. We had our time to figure things out, and it's not like we didn't try. I'm just so angry and disappointed that things ended up the way they did. I feel so helpless sometimes, and it's not a great feeling."

"I know," Ben replied. "I didn't come to this decision lightly either. I mean, there were times I had no idea what was happening to us, which meant I had no idea how to fix things. I only knew we were both unhappy, and there was no right way to change that."

Deirdre sat back in her chair and closed her eyes. She felt like crying, but she wasn't sure she had any tears left for their marriage. She could hear Ben sigh on the other end.

"You know, it's almost ironic," he continued. "We both knew what the other person was going through, for the most part, yet it was that same thing which kept us apart. It's like we were both the best and worst person for each other during that time. I guess you never know how you're going to react to some things until they actually happen."

"For better or worse," she said sadly.

"It sounds a lot easier than it is."

"But there are plenty of couples who stay together through all that. Look at both our parents."

"Deeds, they never went through anything like what we went through. At least nothing that directly affected their potential for staying together."

"Hey, my parents almost lost their daughter, like you almost lost your wife."

Ben paused.

"I hate to say this, honey, and I mean no disrespect, but they both would've gone through the same pain of losing their daughter. There was nothing either one of them could have done. But the fact that you were in that courtyard and I wasn't meant we were never going to fully understand what the other person was going through."

Deirdre had never thought about it that way. She knew they had handled things differently, but she assumed that's where their differences began. This was a completely new perspective, something she didn't believe still existed.

"Was I out of line there?" Ben asked, breaking her train of thought.

Deirdre smiled slightly.

"Oddly enough, no. That actually makes sense, what you said. I guess we always had a different take on the subject, from beginning to end."

"I guess so."

Deirdre glanced over at the coffee table, where the divorce papers had been sitting ever since he left that night. They were the one thing holding them together and keeping them apart, which is why she didn't even want to touch them. They were in limbo, yes, but they were still married and still a part of each other's lives. Those papers were going to change everything.

But now she realized that she was the one keeping herself from getting what she really needed- closure. She took a deep breath.

"Ben, I'll sign the papers over the weekend and get them back to you for Monday."

"It's ok, Deirdre, if you need more time…"

"No. I've already used up too much of that. We need to get this done."

Ben paused, not wanting to say the wrong thing. Deirdre helped him out.

"No matter what happens after this, I want you to know that I'll always love you," she said. "You were such a big part of my life, it's not easy to let you go. But I know we have no other choice."

It was the first time Deirdre felt okay with that statement, and Ben knew it. He breathed a sigh of relief.

"Deeds, I want you to realize that this is the best thing for you too," he emphasized. "We were very quickly devolving into people we didn't even recognize any more. And I know you felt it too. Unfortunately, the only way to save our relationship was to go our separate ways."

"I know. It just really, really sucks."

Ben chuckled, and Deirdre joined in.

"This life stuff is hard," he said, smiling.

"No shit."

"Well, I guess I should let you get back to work."

"How'd you know I was working?"

"Because you're home on a Friday night rather than out drinking with the girls."

"Damn, both you and my mom. Am I that predictable?"

"Afraid so, kid."

Deirdre smiled, glad that he still remembered such personal things about her. Those were the good memories, and they would always remain that way.

"And Deeds?"

"Yeah?"

"You know you will always be my first love, right? No matter what, nothing will ever change that."

Closing her eyes, Deirdre leaned back in her chair. She realized after all the fights, all the hard work, and all the love they had given each other, that was all she was going to get. For the rest of her life, that was going to have to be enough.

One day at a time, Deirdre. One day at a time.

"I know," she finally answered.

"Good," he replied. He wasn't sure he believed her, but it was a start. "It's important to me that you realize that."

"Ok," she said, opening her eyes again. "Good night, Ben."

"Good night."

CHAPTER TWENTY-SEVEN

All right. Time to give this park another try.

Zoey sat under the same tree at the same park across from the same ill-fated convenience store. From there she could keep an eye out for "mystery boy" in case he came back to it.

Not that he would while I'm here. That's just my luck.

Staring across the field, Zoey watched the kids on the playground. A little girl with long blond hair climbed the monkey bars under the careful watch of a woman with similar blond hair. Zoey smiled.

That's Laura right there, she thought. Her parents were always worried about the reckless way she climbed everything- playground equipment, trees, some of the boulders along the river that ran through town. She never stopped to figure out the best way to the top, she simply ran for it, with Zoey close behind her. Even though it had gotten them into trouble numerous times, it was one of the things Zoey had loved about her best friend. She would always run straight ahead and never look back, grabbing Zoey's hand to bring her along for the ride.

She would've gladly taken Laura's hand in the car that day. But Laura didn't offer, and without a word she was gone.

Zoey shook her head, wiping a tear from the corner of her eye. Those thoughts were relentless, sneaking up on her no matter where she was. Everything reminded her of Laura. The whole town held memories of the two of them, and Zoey would never get away from that, not as long as she stayed there.

But even worse than that, Zoey couldn't get her last therapy session out of her head. It was one thing for her parents to misunderstand her relationship with Laura- they were always looking at it from the wrong angle. But her therapist? She was supposed to look at things objectively. *How could she get it wrong too?*

Zoey couldn't figure out why it bothered her so much. She was never concerned with outsiders' reactions to their relationship before this. Why should it matter what her therapist thought? There was nothing wrong with their relationship.

Still, she couldn't help but wonder if there was some truth to what Dr. Stephens said.

It was all so confusing without Laura there to talk to. At least Zoey could bring up most subjects with Dr. Stephens and have a rational conversation about it, unlike with her parents. And her parents still wanted her to go to therapy while she was trying to figure out her next move. She didn't know how she felt about any of that. All she knew was that she would never get over Laura's death, not by herself.

"I can't believe you left me," she whispered, looking toward the ground.

Suddenly, a shadow fell over her. She looked up hopefully.

"Hi, again."

Mystery boy! Zoey couldn't believe it.

"Sorry to bother you. It looked like you might be deep in thought," he said, looking down at her. "But I saw you sitting here and thought, the last time I startled her was such a huge hit, I should try it again. So here I am. Hi. I'm Tristan."

Zoey stared at him as he offered his hand to her. She blinked a couple times, making sure he was actually standing there. Slowly, she reached out and shook his hand. His fingers slid against hers, and she could almost see the sparks ignite from their touch.

"So, you know who I am. Who might you be?"

"I'm Zoey," she breathed, not wanting to let go of his hand. She wondered what touching the rest of him would feel like. The idea made her blush.

"It's nice to meet you, Zoey," he said, letting go of her hand. She had never heard anyone say her name like that before, as if he gave it new meaning by saying it out loud. "Mind if I join you?"

Zoey nodded, then abruptly shook her head.

"Of course not. Please, sit down," she stammered.

Tristan settled onto the ground next to her, the chain hanging out of his pocket tapping her arm as he sat down. He wasn't wearing his studded belt today, but Zoey admired his Nine Inch Nails T-shirt. Laura had bought her a similar one at the last concert they went to.

I like his style, she thought. She hoped to learn more.

"So, what are you doing out here?" he asked, running his fingers through his hair as he leaned back against the tree.

"Well, uh, basically I needed to get out of the house. My parents place is right down the street, but my mom thinks I went to work early."

"You're not in school?"

Zoey bit her lip. Answering that question from adults was tough enough. She wasn't expecting other people her age to be asking. That was part of why she didn't want to go back.

"I'm, well, actually I'm taking a year off. I needed a break for a while."

"That's cool," he nodded. Zoey breathed a sigh of relief. "I just graduated myself."

"Oh. You don't look that old." Realizing how that sounded she tried to back pedal. "I mean, not that you look like anything in particular…"

"It's okay. I graduated a couple years earlier than most people. I'm only 20," he said, smiling.

"Oh. Wow. That's impressive."

"I've always been in accelerated programs," Tristan shrugged. "It's no big deal."

Good-looking, smart, but not too cocky. I like where this is going, Zoey thought.

"So, are you working now?"

"Nah, not yet. I'm kinda taking a break myself, until I figure out where I wanna go next," he replied. "Right now my parents are footing the bill for an apartment as a graduation gift. They aren't particularly thrilled with me taking a break, but they can't really say anything since I just graduated early with honors. It's not like I'm a problem child or something."

"If I did that, my parents would probably still be disappointed in me," Zoey sighed. "Like, why didn't I have a $100,000 job waiting for me after graduation? They can find any excuse for me to do more, to be more."

"I'm sure the break thing went over well with them then, huh?"

"Ugh. You have no idea. I didn't get an apartment out of the deal anyway."

"Yeah, I totally lucked out there. Parents can be such a drag," he said sympathetically. "So, where do you work?"

"At Benjamin's Restaurant, on the corner…"

"Of Main and Harris Street. I know the place."

Zoey was surprised. It was a small restaurant where mostly older locals hung out for lunch.

"Did you grow up around here?" she asked, confused.

"Sort of," he said. "I skipped a couple grades, so by the time I hit junior high and high school I was taking all sorts of honors courses that were several grade levels above where I was supposed to be. Then once I graduated I was off to college in the big city. So I never really got to know anyone my age around here."

"Wow, I can't even imagine. Just the pressure alone to keep up with everything. It must've been hard."

131

"The social stuff was the hardest part. The school stuff was almost boring at times, but being with older kids was fascinating. They were dealing with things I hadn't come across yet, which was thoroughly intriguing. I felt like a spy."

Zoey giggled.

"So you got quite the life lesson too, huh?"

"Totally. Of course, I wasn't really accepted by people until I got to college. Up to that point, everyone else thought I was a nerd who had no friends because I was too smart for them, like I thought I was better than them. But just because I was doesn't mean we couldn't have been friends."

Tristan looked over at Zoey, grinning. She laughed.

"Gee, you're so modest."

"It goes with my good looks."

Zoey laughed again.

"I like your laugh," he said, glancing at her sideways. "It's honest."

"What do you mean?"

"Well, you don't laugh just because you're supposed to, because it's polite or whatever. You laugh because the situation deserves it."

"Huh. No one's ever complimented me on that before," Zoey said, thinking it over for a moment. "It's kinda weird."

"Gee, thanks. I was going for different, not deranged."

"I didn't say you were deranged!"

"Ah, you were thinking it though."

Zoey shrugged playfully. It had been a long time since she had bantered with anyone like this. It felt good.

Suddenly she realized she had no idea what time it was. She grabbed her cell phone out of her pocket.

"Are you late?"

"No," she said, sighing in relief. "Thankfully any place in this town only takes 10 minutes to walk to, and I have exactly that."

"Oh, ok." Zoey thought she heard a hint of disappointment in his voice. It made her shiver. "Well, maybe we can run into each other again some time."

Absolutely.

"Uh, sure," Zoey said, trying to sound casual. In reality, her heart was pounding so hard she could hardly hear herself talk. "It's a small town."

"That it is. Well, then, until next time I guess."

Tristan stood up, holding his hand out to her again. As she took it, he helped her up, brushing some dirt off her shoulder.

"Ok, next time." Slowly she started walking across the field, past the kids and the playground. She was dying to turn around.

No. I want to remember him just as I left him, she thought. *Perfect.*

CHAPTER TWENTY-EIGHT

Gisele Robin sat on her bed with her head bowed, tears staining the pages of her journal. She held a package of frozen peas against her eye, hoping her mother wouldn't notice them missing from the freezer. Her split lip had finally stopped bleeding, but the bruises on her arms and legs were still fresh. She tried to ignore the pain in her ribs as she began to write.

I knew it was them. I can't believe it. My two best friends, the ones I trusted with my life, my secrets, betrayed me.

How could I have gone from the top of the cheerleading pyramid to the ground so fast? I couldn't even do anything. My entire life changed in one day.

I guess that's how it works. They're the ones who build you up, place you on the pedestal. And you accept it because that's the only way to make it through high school. At least, the only sane way.

But once they've had their way with you they don't need you anymore, and they knock you down the first chance they get. Sometimes you don't even have to do anything. It's their choice, and you get to be the pawn they get rid of.

I hadn't even seen the video. He told me he destroyed it. I can't believe he let something like that get out! I thought he loved me.

But then I found out he was dating Heather too. So much for being exclusive. How could I have been so stupid? I really thought he was the first guy to date me for me, not my reputation. I guess I was wrong.

And how could Tara pass the video around school like that? Then she went ballistic and called me a slut in front of the whole squad. It's like she had to find the quickest way to distance herself from me, without even thinking about my feelings. Has our friendship all these years been a lie?

Unfortunately that wasn't even the worst part. Today they all jumped me after practice. I've never been beaten up before. I couldn't do anything but curl up in a ball as they kept

133

kicking and hitting me. It was the most horrible experience of my life. And the fact it was people who are supposed to care about me… that hurt most of all.

I've tried so hard to fit in with them. I went to the parties, I drank the beer, I did the drugs. I screwed the right guys and made fun of the wrong girls. And I kept my mouth shut when I didn't agree with the general consensus. That was the hardest thing.

And for what? So they could call me names? Beat the shit out of me? Toss me aside like I wasn't even a person?

I don't know what to do anymore. I played by their rules and I'm still exiled. There's no way to spin this where I come out on top. I've already lost.

I'm nothing to them anymore.

Gisele heard the front door close. She froze. *I didn't think she'd be home so soon.*

Hastily she closed the journal and shoved it under her pillow. Looking around, she saw her pajamas on the floor next to her bed. She reached down and grabbed them, wincing with each breath. She took off the bloody cheerleading top and slid into the ratty T-shirt she wore to bed. The pants were a bit tougher, since it was difficult for her to lean forward.

"Gisele? Baby, are you home?"

Shit. She managed to remove the short skirt and slide on the pajama bottoms, just in time to hear her mother knock on her door.

"Hang on a sec!" she called out. She hid her cheerleading outfit under her backpack and slid under the covers, stifling her screams of pain. She turned off the light and set the frozen peas under her bed.

"Ok, Mom."

Betsy Robin opened the door slightly and stuck her head in. "Are you asleep already, babe?"

"No, it was just a long day," Gisele answered, trying to keep her head out of the light coming in from the hallway. "I just needed to lie down."

Betsy opened the door further, far enough to see her daughter's black eye. She gasped.

"Oh my god, honey, what happened?"

"It's no big deal, Mom, really."

As Betsy walked further into the room, Gisele's split lip became visible.

"No big deal? You look like you were in a gang fight."

Well, you got the gang part right.

Gisele had been hoping her mother would have to work her usual double shift as a housekeeper, giving her all night to heal. In the morning she could've gotten away with some cover-up. No such luck now.

"It was just a fight with some of the girls that got outta hand."

"Out of hand? Sweetheart, look at you! You look like you should be in the hospital!"

"I made it home fine, Mom."

"Fine? Your eye is swollen! And," Betsy pulled back the sheets which Gisele had been clinging to. "Look at your arms. Is your whole body like this?"

"Sort of," Gisele mumbled.

"Who did this to you? Because we are going to the hospital and calling the police."

"No, Mom, you don't understand!" Gisele exclaimed. If she ratted out the cheerleading squad, she would never again be able to set foot in her school. *Hell, I'd probably get beaten up all over again.*

"I don't need to understand, Gisele. I can see with my own eyes. Now tell me who did this."

"I can take care of it myself, Mom. I've been doing that for years now. I know what I'm doing."

Betsy sat down gingerly on the edge of the bed.

"Baby, now is not the time for that discussion," she cooed. "I know you think I haven't been around, but I had to pick up extra shifts after Bobby left us. There was nothing I could do about that, honey, and you know it."

"Well, it wasn't my fault," Gisele said, exasperated. "He tried to force himself on me, Mom! Or don't you remember that?"

"That was a misunderstanding," Betsy said matter-of-factly. "And he's not the first of my boyfriends you tried to pin that on either, young lady."

Gisele couldn't believe what she was hearing. Ever since she had developed breasts at age 12, she had to deal with inappropriate comments and gestures from older men, which made her father distraught. He was often embarrassed by his daughter's curves, and he resented having to defend her honor from those who would flirt shamelessly with her. Gisele didn't know what to do with those advances, but she knew her mother loved the attention and was very proud of having a beautiful daughter. So she followed her mother's lead and returned the flirtation. It wasn't long after that her father walked out on them. And suddenly their front door became open to a number of men in town, all looking to get in good with Betsy's daughter.

But of course, her mother never saw it that way. She was only around enough to see her newest boyfriend being a solid role model for her daughter. On the nights she worked, however, they wanted to "get to know Gisele better", and she was still young enough to listen when they told her it was their own way of showing affection. Once she grew older though, and started dating boys her own age, she soon discovered what their advances meant.

"I can't believe this! You're still taking their word over your own daughter's. And you wonder why I don't come to you about this stuff," Gisele exclaimed. "You have the worst taste in losers!"

"Hey, it's not easy finding someone to go out with these days," Betsy said, her voice rising. "I'm not in my twenties any more. These guys have stable jobs and they're willing to date a woman with an 18-year-old daughter. They're sweet to me and they're sweet to you."

"Yeah, because they want to screw your 18-year-old daughter. Did you ever think that's why they go out with you? To get to me?"

"You know, just because you sleep around with the football team that doesn't mean every guy wants you," Betsy fumed. "Ever since your father left you've been getting sympathy lays from half the guys in town. At least I have long-lasting adult relationships. You're gonna have to grow up sometime too, princess."

"Do you hear yourself? You've been using dad's leaving as an excuse to whore yourself out to any guy who'll do you!" Gisele yelled. "Great role model, Mom! Meanwhile, I've had to keep it together for the both of us so people don't think we're running a brothel here. I've been able to keep up the good grades and the cheerleading so that the whole town doesn't know our business. Or should I say your business?"

"You are way outta line, Gisele!" Betsy said, standing up. "Look at you! Obviously something happened to break this little bubble you claim you've formed around us. I have to work three jobs just to keep this household together. You've done nothing to contribute any money to this family! If you're gonna sleep around you could at least make yourself useful and bring in some cash!"

"Get out!" Gisele screamed, fresh tears running down her face. "Get out you bitch!"

"Fine!" Betsy yelled back. "You'll get no sympathy from me, little girl. You're gonna have to learn sometime that there are consequences to your actions. You might as well start now!"

Betsy turned and stormed out of Gisele's room, slamming the door behind her. Gisele began sobbing, clinging to her ribs as her heavy breathing grew worse. All she had wanted was some time to heal. Instead, all of her mistakes had been thrown back in her face, by her own mother no less.

Who is she to lecture me? she thought angrily. *I didn't chase her boyfriends away because I was an angry little girl who wanted her daddy back. I had to defend myself! Why can't she see that?*

Gisele reached under her pillow and brought out her journal. Wiping her eyes, she started a new entry.

This is for all those people who never knew the real me. I leave this journal in the hopes that someone will find it and read it. Because that is the only way my true story will be told. My life has been surrounded by lies and rumors and stories, and only this book contains the truth. It is uncensored and unedited, and it is my life the way I lived it. No one can take this away from me.

Gisele set her pen down for a moment, trying to slow her thoughts. Looking down at her bruised and broken body, she realized what she needed to do.

People won't understand. They'll say, what a shame. She was so young. What could have driven her to such violence? And her poor mother, struggling to make ends meet on her own. What a tragedy.

But the real tragedy is trapped within these pages. Day after day I struggled to make ends meet in my life. Stay in shape so I could be part of the group that runs the show. Keep up good grades so I could get out of this hellhole. Paint on the smile I could never maintain on my own, all so people would find me pleasing. Nothing belonged to me- they owned me.

Well, not any more. I'm taking back what's rightfully mine, and no one's going to stop me. This time, I get to say and do whatever the hell I want. Because I'm not going to let them walk all over me anymore. It's my turn to run the show. And it's my turn to choose the pawns.

They're never going to control me again.

CHAPTER TWENTY-NINE

"Here's your order, ma'am."

"Uh, thanks."

Deirdre took her coffee from the young barista behind the counter at the one coffee shop in town that offered Wi-Fi. As she sat down she set her laptop on the table and put her coffee down next to it.

Ma'am. Since when did I stop being a Miss?

Opening her computer, Deirdre yawned and took a sip of her black coffee. It was barely 8 a.m., and she had been up until 3 a.m. reading a new book written by a psychologist who dealt with troubled teens. She didn't want to put it down, since the last few chapters had titles which suggested there were solutions on how to handle that part of the population. But since she couldn't switch her 9 a.m. meeting, she forced herself to go to bed before reaching the book's general conclusion.

Like I want to meet at 9 in the morning with a politician who won't want to talk to me about this controversial bill. Man I hate this job sometimes.

As Deirdre searched online for articles about the bill, she noticed a couple in their mid-50s sitting across from her, discussing a newspaper article. The woman began reading aloud to the man next to her.

"Tragedy struck the fields of Jackson High School yesterday, as senior Gisele Robin, 18, shot and killed two classmates, Heather Strout and Tara Leichfield, both also 18."

Deirdre lifted her head suddenly, and glanced over to see what newspaper they were reading. She recognized it as one of the national papers sold at the coffeehouse, and stood up to grab a copy. She left the change for it on the counter and sat back down quickly.

On the front page, three yearbook pictures, all girls, took up one corner, and the middle picture showed a body being wheeled into an ambulance. The headline read, "Local senior murders two schoolmates before taking own life." Deirdre began to read.

"According to local police reports, Robin confronted the two girls after cheerleading practice. Other students said they saw Robin yelling at the two girls, who often stayed after practice to clean up the field. Both girls seemed to dismiss her until she pulled out a handgun and shot Strout in the head.

'Heather fell to the ground and that's when Tara screamed,' said cheerleading captain Phoebe Newburg, who saw the whole incident from across the field. 'Gisele then shot Tara in the chest. Once she collapsed, Gisele turned and started walking away, real slowly like she was in a trance. But then she stopped and turned around, and that's when she shot herself in the head. It was the most horrible thing I've ever seen.'

Newburg said all three girls have been on the cheerleading squad since freshman year, and were rarely seen apart as they rose through the ranks.

'They were a tight group,' Newburg said, wiping tears from her eyes. 'They were the best on the team. They were responsible for the last two years of titles we've won. And to think Gisele turned on them. I don't know what happened. It's so unreal.'

As the coroner took Robin's body from the scene, it was noted she had several bruises on her body, along with a black eye and split lip. Newburg said she had no idea where the marks came from, since there was no struggle during the confrontation.

'Gisele often got into trouble with guys,' Newburg claimed. 'She told us some of her mother's boyfriend's tried to rape her but she never had any marks on her body. We all thought she was trying to get attention, since she never filed any charges, and neither did her mom. But maybe something actually happened this time, and she got in over her head.'

Teachers from Jackson said Robin was a straight A student, and that she had been looking at various colleges for after graduation.

'She could've made it into any college she wanted, what with her good grades and exceptional cheerleading skills,' said Sam Hughes, Robin's calculus teacher. 'She had asked me to write a recommendation for her for several schools she was looking at. It seemed like she had a bright future ahead of her.'

Strout and Leichfield were average students, Hughes said, and were both looking to cheerleading scholarships to help further their education.

'I think they applied to a couple of the same schools even,' he said. 'The three of them seemed inseparable, except in their college choices. Gisele applied all over the place while the other two girls said they wanted to stay in the area.'

When asked if he or any other teacher had noticed any tension among the girls, Hughes said he was unaware of any trouble.

'All three of them were very well-behaved. They took cheerleading very seriously,' he said. 'They saw themselves as representatives of the school and they acted as such.'

Robin was raised by her mother, Betsy, after her husband left them shortly after Robin turned 13. Mrs. Robin was inundated by the press yesterday evening, after police informed her of her daughter's actions. She broke down in tears and begged to see her daughter's body. Police brought her back inside the house so they could search Gisele's room. One detective emerged carrying what looked like a book in an evidence bag, with Mrs. Robin following him.

When asked why she thought her daughter did this, she stopped and turned to face the group.

'My daughter is dead!' she exclaimed, tears streaming down her face. 'She was a good girl. She was just confused sometimes that's all. All teenagers are confused. She wasn't a killer! My baby wasn't a killer!'"

"It's so horrible," Deirdre heard the woman say at the other table. "I never really imagined something like that could actually happen in such a small school, but Jackson is about the same size as Zach's school."

"I was just thinking that," the man said. "It's crazy."

Deirdre noticed the story continued on another page, and opened the newspaper to find the rest of the story. She continued reading.

"According to police reports, Mrs. Robin claimed she last spoke with her daughter the night before, and saw that she had been beaten. When she asked who did it, Gisele refused to tell her, saying only that a fight with 'some of the girls' had gotten out of hand. But when the rest of the squad was questioned, none of the other students had any idea why she would have bruises on her body.

'Then we had an argument,' Mrs. Robin stated. 'She was upset that I wasn't home as much as I used to be, now that I'm working three jobs. And she was upset over some of my previous boyfriends. She was never supportive of any of them. I think she never really got over her father leaving.'

At press time, reporters were still awaiting word from the police on the contents of the book that was confiscated."

Deirdre set the paper down again and reached over to grab her notebook out of her bag. When she turned back she noticed the couple stand up and walk around their table past hers. The woman glanced down at Deirdre's newspaper open to the second part of the article and gestured to it.

"Isn't it terrible? Even smaller towns can't escape this level of violence anymore," the woman said to Deirdre, shaking her head. "Whether it's an adult or a teenager, people get killed everywhere."

"It does seem like kids are going crazy these days," the man agreed. "I thought suicide rates in this country were bad enough. But now kids are taking others with them."

"I hate to say it, but I suppose it could've been worse," Deirdre replied. "The last two shootings that happened, those kids took out dozens of people, complete strangers. At least this seems like an isolated incident."

"I just can't believe how much we're hearing these stories," the woman commented. "It seems like every other week we're hearing about students beating up or shooting each other."

"Welcome to the age of technology," the man said. "With 24-hour news channels and the Internet, never mind the newspaper, we're getting the news as soon as it happens. We never used to have that kind of coverage before."

Deirdre nodded.

"Maybe kids are finding they have a new medium to express their anger. Now they don't have to lock themselves in their room anymore and go quietly. They can show the whole world how repressed they are now."

"Well, we do have all these reality TV shows that involve people arguing and getting in each other's faces, and that's what they call entertainment. Heck, we've had the show Cops for years, and Jerry Springer, and those contain plenty of violent behavior," the woman said. "It's almost like kids are used to it these days."

"Yes, but is it TV reflecting life or life reflecting TV?" the man asked.

Hmmm. Interesting question, Deirdre thought.

"I think they grow together," the woman answered. "Think about life in the 1950s, and the kinds of entertainment there was. Times change, and entertainment changes with it. People find they have to continuously push the envelope to keep people entertained. Everything has to be bigger or more extreme. Why wouldn't kids change that way, too?"

"I don't know. I think people blame the media because they're easy scapegoats," the man replied. "But unfortunately they have to keep up with what people want, as with any other business. And these stories are always noticed. Hell, I needed to know what happened."

"It's human nature, people slowing down while passing a car accident. It's not good or bad. Just the stories are horrific."

"I guess. Still, it makes me afraid to think of the kind of world our grandkids will be growing up in."

"I know, honey, I know," the woman sighed, rubbing his arm. That's when she glanced down at Deirdre and saw her work bag. "Anyway, we should let this poor girl finish her coffee."

Deirdre smiled. *She called me girl.*

"Thank you for the stimulating early morning conversation."

As they turned to leave the coffee shop, Deirdre quickly wrote down a few notes from their conversation before she noticed the time.

Damn it! I don't have time to look this up online. There must be so much more available by now. Ugh, but I have to get going or else I'll miss this meeting. Stupid article.

With all of the books Deirdre had bought over the last couple of weeks, she barely had time to focus on anything else. Her nights were consumed by new and interesting studies that seemed to pop up everywhere she looked. It was exhausting, but she knew she could never talk to Neil about it. The only thing she could do was tell him everything was fine and keep up as best she could with her other stories. She was thoroughly bored by them, but they required time and effort just the same, hence the early morning meeting.

Finishing up her notes, Deirdre quickly packed up her bag and grabbed her coffee. Her curiosity would have to wait until later.

CHAPTER THIRTY

Zoey sat in the waiting room of Dr. Stephens' office, staring at the open magazine in her lap. For the first time since her initial visit, she felt nervous.

Why am I nervous? It's not like I did anything wrong, Zoey thought to herself. *If anything, she was the one who was outta line.*

But what if she doesn't see it that way?

It had been three weeks since her last session, during which time Zoey went back and forth trying to decide if she would continue with therapy. On the one hand, she had grown accustomed to their weekly visits. It was usually an open forum to talk about Laura without the conversation turning into an argument. But the end of the last session reminded her of previous fights with her parents, and she didn't need her father to pay for one of those.

Still, she was never able to be that honest with her parents, who were expecting her to continue with the sessions as part of their agreement.

There's just no easy way out of this.

"Zoey. I'm so glad you called," said Dr. Stephens, walking out of her office and startling Zoey. "Please, come in."

Zoey slowly followed her into the office and sat down in her usual chair. She had spent the last week trying to figure out how she would start this conversation. As upset as she was about their last session, she still didn't know if it was because what Dr. Stephens said was wrong or right.

Dr. Stephens sat down in the chair across from Zoey, without her notebook or pen. Zoey looked at her quizzically.

Is this not a regular session?

"I would like to start by talking about what happened at the last session," Stephens began. "Is that ok with you?"

Zoey nodded.

"All right. My main question is, what got you so upset that you felt you had to leave?"

Oh man, Zoey thought, her discouragement deepening. *She really doesn't have any idea what happened.*

"No offense, but as a therapist shouldn't you already know why I was upset?"

"I'm not a mind reader, Zoey. That's why I ask certain questions. Because I don't know all the answers. All I know is what you tell me, and from that I come up with certain conclusions as to why things happen the way they do, or why people feel the way they feel. Mostly, I'm here to listen."

"That's it. That's why I was so angry. You weren't listening to me."

"What do you mean?"

"I was trying to tell you about hanging out with Laura, and you came out with all these assumptions that I kept telling you were wrong," Zoey said, exasperated. "But you kept going on about them like I had no idea what I was talking about."

"Zoey, I never meant to insult you or undermine your relationship with Laura," Stephens said. "But as an outside observer, I may notice certain things. You and Laura were friends for a long time, and you established habits and routines that became a part of your everyday life. I was simply offering my interpretation of things from an objective point of view."

Zoey looked down at the floor, trying to put into words why she was still so upset. Dr. Stephens waited patiently for her response. After a minute Zoey shook her head.

"I just don't like people talking about Laura when they didn't really know her."

"Why is that?"

"Because, she was the most important person in my life."

"So you're very protective of her and her memory?" Stephens asked, grabbing her notebook.

"Yeah."

"Why do you place Laura as the most important person in your life above your parents?"

Zoey knew it was time, time to stop holding back the truth. She lifted her head and looked at Dr. Stephens.

"Because my dad didn't even want to have me, and my mom has no idea who I am."

Dr. Stephens sat up in her chair a bit. *Here it is. Now we're getting somewhere.*

"Go ahead, Zoey."

After all of their conversations about Laura, deep down Zoey knew her parents were to blame for all of her anxiety. Her last session with Dr. Stephens made that abundantly clear.

"I overheard an argument my parents had one night when I was in first grade. The thing I remember the most about it is hearing my dad say he never wanted a kid in the first place."

"Do you know the context of their argument?"

"No. I couldn't hear a lot of it. It's like they were trying to be quiet and it just escalated."

"So you don't know what they were arguing about."

"Well, for him to say something like that I assume they were arguing about me."

"I don't know if that one sentence is enough to assume anything."

"What else could they have been talking about?"

"Well, I'm sure you've had enough fights with your parents to know that arguments can often start out one way and then morph into something else. It's always best to try and stay on topic, of course, but when emotions are involved that's not always easy."

"Yeah, but to say something like that is pretty straightforward," Zoey insisted. "He didn't want to have kids. He didn't want to have me. But obviously something happened, so here I am, a kid he has to put up with. Up to that point I thought I was 'Daddy's little girl.' That's what my mom always called me. But that was just a lie to try and protect me from knowing the truth."

"Do you feel your father doesn't love you?"

Zoey bit her lip. She had spent her entire life trying not to think about that question.

"I don't know. Maybe. Only when I get really angry at him I guess, or when he gets really angry at me. It's like he doesn't get me sometimes, like he's not even trying."

"You know, Zoey, there are many people who feel like they don't want to have kids, or that they aren't capable of raising a child," Stephens said. "But if they do have a child, they often find that nothing else in the world matters to them as much as their child does."

"Huh. If that's the case then my dad has a funny way of showing me how important I am to him."

"What do you mean?"

"He's always off in his own little world," Zoey said. "Half the time my mom has to interrupt him whenever she wants to talk to him about stuff. I try not to do that because I know how annoying she can be. But even between books, it's like we can't talk to each other anymore. We used to be close, but now everything is so serious. And I don't just mean Laura's death, I mean even before that."

"What did you guys talk about?"

"Mostly it was about my future, and what I wanted to do, and how my relationship with Laura might interfere with all that," Zoey replied. "And I know as a dad he feels that's his job or whatever. But I'm not even 20 yet. I don't know why I have to have everything figured out right now."

"I think most parents worry that their child won't have any direction," Stephens explained. "It's the parents' job to teach their children about making it in the real world, which also means at a certain point they'll wonder if they've done their job. And there's no real way to tell that, so I think some parents look to how well their child does when they move out of the house."

"So the fact I'm still in my parents' house worries him?"

Dr. Stephens shook her head.

"I doubt that. As you said, you're only 19. However, dropping out of school does fall into the worry category. All these conversations you've had with your parents are pretty typical. Plus, I think it shows how much your father cares about you and your well-being."

"But all those talks we've had about Laura? He just doesn't get it."

"I think the way you relied on your relationship with Laura was a concern only in the context of making your own way in the world," Stephens replied. "I think it's difficult for some parents to accept when outside influences begin to have sway in their child's life. They start to lose control. And Laura has been a part of your life from very early on, which means your parents almost had to accept her as part of your family as well."

"Do you think my dad thought of her as another daughter that he had to take care of? Maybe that's why he resented our relationship so much."

"I wasn't thinking about that," Stephens said. "I was thinking that his main concern was that she had more influence over your actions then he did. It's important for your child to have a social network, and he may have perceived your strong ties to Laura as a hindrance to forming other relationships."

"But I've told him that she's the one who introduced me to all these new people and new experiences."

"Did you carry anything with you from these experiences? Maintain ties with the people you met?"

"Well, we hung out with the same people all the time."

"But as you said before, that was all with Laura. Do you still keep in touch with the same people now?"

"No," Zoey admitted.

"Maybe your father is concerned that you were limiting your choices when you felt that you were opening them," Stephens suggested. "It was a completely different point of view on the same situation."

Zoey pondered that statement for a moment. She assumed her father didn't understand why she and Laura were so close because she had never talked to him about the argument she had overheard. It never occurred to her that he had a different perspective simply because he was her father.

"Still, that idea goes completely against his statement of not wanting kids. I don't know why he would say something like that."

"Have you ever thought about asking him?"

"Are you kidding? Our relationship is strained enough as it is."

"Or maybe you're afraid of the answer."

"I don't know."

"Zoey, I don't think finding out the answer to that question would make things worse. You already think the worst- that he didn't want to have you. What have you got to lose in asking him?"

Zoey bit her lip as she tried to hold back tears.

"The possibility that I might be wrong."

Dr. Stephens stopped writing and looked up at Zoey.

"What do you mean?"

"Right now there's still the hope that I'm wrong, that he wanted to have me," Zoey said, wiping the tears that fell down her cheeks. "That's all I have."

Dr. Stephens set her notebook down in her lap and grabbed the box of tissues from her desk. She handed it to Zoey.

"Zoey, listen to me. I know it's difficult, but from what you've told me I think your father has shown a great concern for your well-being," she began. "That's not something to take lightly. But only you can make the decision on how to handle something like this."

Zoey nodded, blowing her nose. Stephens picked up her notebook from her lap.

"Are you okay?" she asked, concerned. This was the first time Zoey had cried during a session. Zoey nodded again and set the box back on the desk.

"All right. We talked about your father. What about your mother? You said she doesn't know who you are."

"I don't think my mom knows much about anything to be honest."

"Why is that?"

"Because all she does is talk about stupid, mundane stuff. She talks in clichés. Any time anything happens it's such a tragedy and what is this world coming to and tsk tsk. She never actually has anything real to say."

"You feel she mostly engages in small talk?"

"That's all she does. Even when we argue, she uses all these outdated phrases, rather than just telling me how she feels."

"Do you tell her how you feel?"

"It's almost impossible, because she always finds some other cliché to answer it."

"And that's why you think she doesn't know you?"

"Yeah. I really can't talk to her. We have nothing in common."

"Do you feel that way because your parents grew up in a different generation?"

"That has something to do with it, sure."

"But your parents were kids and teenagers once too," Stephens pointed out. "So they would have a different perspective on things now that they've grown up and had their own experiences. You might be surprised if you talked to them about their childhoods."

"You don't know my mother. Having a real conversation with her hurts my brain sometimes."

"Well, I've certainly had some mind numbing conversations with my mother," Stephens sighed. Zoey laughed.

"Still, communication is important for any relationship," Stephens continued. "Unfortunately that's not always easy."

"You're telling me."

"I think spending some time with your parents might help you to reconnect with them. I know that's the last thing you want to do, hang out with your parents, but it might help you to see things from their perspective. You said you used to have a good relationship with them at one point. There's no reason why that should change just because you're older."

"I guess."

"Honestly, Zoey, I'm very glad we talked about your parents. I think they've been at the root of many of your feelings of anger and resentment. I think everything that's happened has brought to light some of the anxiety you've had regarding your relationship with them."

"To be honest, that's the only reason I came back here," Zoey admitted. "I didn't really have anyone to talk to about, well, anything, and my parents were making things worse."

"Well, I'm glad you felt you had a place to turn to here. I hope we can continue our sessions as we have been?"

"Yeah," Zoey agreed. "Especially now that I've actually talked to mystery boy."

"You saw him again?"

"Yup."

"And you spoke to him?"

"I had no choice. He approached me."

"Did you say something besides holy shit?" Stephens asked, smiling. Zoey laughed.

"Yes, thank god!"

"Well then, that's definitely progress."

CHAPTER THIRTY-ONE

Sigh. Another family dinner. Just another event for my family to blame my job for my lack of relationships. Yay.

Deirdre wove her way through the various small neighborhoods near her parents' home, keeping an eye out for kids playing in the street. Her parents still lived in the house where she grew up, along with the same neighbors she grew up next to. Their kids had also moved out, but returned for the holidays for what Deirdre expected was the same grilling process she endured every time.

And not the fun barbecue kind.

Ugh. Why should I have to constantly defend my life choices to these people? My dad seems okay with everything, but my mom and sister, Jesus Christ. Talk about the Spanish Inquisition! Nothing is good enough for them.

At least I have a job. Ellen is a housewife who lets her husband work the 40-hour week while she runs after two kids. Sure, that's a lot of work too, but that's the life she chose. No one made her do that. And no one antagonizes her about that choice. But me, who actually works to expose all the injustice in the world, I'm the one with the mixed-up priorities. And all because I don't care the cost. Is it really so wrong for me to want to get these things right?

But the one thing Deirdre couldn't do was balance her obsession for the truth with the rest of her life. It had become the convenient excuse she needed to get past her own tragedy. She could see that now.

For some, that would be enough to change their work habits. Not me. That seems to be the only way I can function these days. But that's just my natural-born personality, she thought smiling, thinking back to her interview with Dr. Stephens. *There's obviously nothing I can do about it. Hmmm. I'll have to try that on my mom some time.*

149

Deirdre saw her sister's minivan in the driveway and pulled in behind it. Taking a deep breath, she walked to the front door and knocked loudly twice before turning the handle.

"Hello?"

She was met by the sound of two young children chasing each other around the house. She could hear them getting louder and louder until Brad bumped into her leg, followed by Karen.

"Hi Auntie Deider!" Karen yelled. Deirdre wondered at what age they would get her name right. But it was cute for now.

"Deider! Deider! Deider!" Brad chanted. *Hmmm. Maybe not so cute.*

"Brad! Karen! What have I told you two about running around the house?" Deirdre heard Ellen call from the other room. The kids giggled as they galloped into the living room.

"Goodness, I can't get those two to calm down," Ellen exclaimed as she walked over to hug Deirdre.

"Have you tried tranquilizers?"

"Ha ha."

"Who's laughing? I'm serious."

"Is that the other daughter?" their mother called out from the kitchen. "Did she bring the wine?"

"Got it right here, Mom!" Deirdre called back as she walked toward the kitchen. She was grateful her only contribution was alcohol- it was the one thing that helped to get her through these dinners.

"Hello, dear," Rebecca greeted her, kissing her on the cheek. "How was the traffic?

"There's never any traffic, Mom. There are more farm animals in this town than people."

"Is that Deirdre's sarcastic wit I hear?" asked Samuel, wandering into the room.

"Hey, Dad."

"Still antagonizing your mother I see?"

"They say the best defense is a good offense."

"So I can be offensive too?" Rebecca asked, raising her eyebrows.

"Nope. You're my mother. You're supposed to set a good example."

"I can see it's too late for that."

"Ah, family," Samuel grinned, patting Deirdre on the shoulder. "Isn't it good to be home?"

"It's something all right," Deirdre said as the kids raced by them again.

"Hey! What did I just say?" Ellen yelled as she ran after them. "Peter! Why aren't you watching them?"

Just as Ellen left the room her husband entered it.

"Was she calling me?"

"Hey, Pete," Deirdre said, giving him a hug. "How's the game going?"

"I have no idea. I haven't been able to watch it with the kids screaming like hyenas."

As if on cue, Brad and Karen came barreling into the kitchen. Pete leaned down and caught Brad under one arm and Karen in the other arm.

"Ok speed racers, the sprint is over. Dinner's almost ready so let's figure out where you're going to sit."

The minute he let them go they ran into the dining room, almost knocking Rebecca over in the process. Samuel reached out to steady her.

"Isn't it nice having little kids in the house again?"

"Sorry, Mom," Pete said sheepishly. "I'll see if I can find some straps to tie them down for dinner."

"Dee Dee, honey, can you set the table for me?"

Deirdre nodded as she suppressed a sigh and walked into the dining room. Ellen was setting up the high chairs for the kids while Pete tried to calm them down in the other room.

"Are you guys staying the night?"

"Yeah. It's much easier than trying to get the kids to go to sleep after we get home."

"I see. So how come you guys couldn't come over on Thanksgiving?"

"Some of Pete's co-workers are single and couldn't make it back to their families for the holiday," Ellen replied. "So we offered to throw our own little Thanksgiving dinner. Mom said they didn't care if we had our family's dinner on the weekend, as long as we got together at some point."

Deirdre nodded as she placed the settings around the table.

"What are you doing on the actual day?" Ellen asked.

"Probably working," Deirdre answered automatically. She cringed, realizing she had now given Ellen the open invitation to begin the criticism.

"Working? On Thanksgiving?" Ellen said, shaking her head. "Why don't you come over to our place if you have nothing better to do?"

That is something better to do, Deirdre thought to herself.

"I don't know. We'll see."

"No one should have to work on Thanksgiving, Dee Dee. And you shouldn't be by yourself. Isn't that part of why people end up going on those shooting sprees you're writing about?"

Ha! I get that feeling sometimes after leaving here.

"I'm writing about teenage suicide shooters," Deirdre reminded her. "Most of whom have families to sit down with at the holidays. You're talking about people who are generally older. And no, I don't think being by myself on a random Thursday will make me suicidal."

"It's not a random Thursday."

"It will be if I think about it that way."

"I'm just saying, you have a place to go."

"You're right. I do have a place to go. I call it my apartment."

"You know what I mean."

Before Deirdre could reply, Rebecca walked in carrying a tray of salads and began placing them on the table.

"Could one of you bring in the dressing?"

Without a word Deirdre quickly walked into the kitchen, glad to be done with the first interrogation. She grabbed the salad dressing from the counter and went back into the dining room. Samuel followed her carrying the bowl of mashed potatoes.

Once the table was set, everyone sat down in their usual places. Even after the kids were born, their seats simply moved down by two.

"A toast," Samuel said, holding up his glass while everyone else picked up theirs. "To friends and family, near and far, and to this wonderful meal we're about to devour. Salute!"

"Salad!" Karen yelled, throwing her milk cup onto the table. Deirdre giggled as Ellen groaned and retrieved the cup.

"Don't encourage her," she said, sitting back down in her chair.

"It was funny!"

"Who wants some mashed potatoes?" Samuel asked abruptly.

For the next few minutes the conversation focused on the food- who could reach what, who had enough gravy, who needed a roll. Deirdre settled in her chair, hoping to at least get a good meal out of the visit. The leftovers alone would last her about a week. But once everyone was set, the conversation turned to the daughters.

"So, Ellen, how was Brad's last doctor's appointment?"

"Really good. He's in the ninetieth percentile for height and his language skills are right where they should be."

"Good job, Brad!" Samuel said.

"Gampy!" Brad called out.

"And Karen? Have you been able to set up play dates?"

"There are a couple kids in the neighborhood who are her age. But I rarely see them outside which suggests to me their parents let them watch a lot of TV. We're trying to keep the kids away from that."

"What's wrong with a little TV?" Deirdre asked. "We watched TV all the time when we were younger."

"But we also played outside at the playground and ran around the yard and used our imagination," Ellen stated. "I don't want the kids learning any bad habits this early on."

"Like running around mom and dad's house?"

"Well, they are toddlers, Dee. They'll do that."

"That was kinda my point."

"I think Ellen just wants to be careful about who we let the kids play with," Peter chimed in quickly. "We're just getting to know the other parents in the neighborhood right now."

"I'd never let my child into the house of someone I didn't know extremely well," Ellen said.

"Well duh," Deirdre said, rolling her eyes. "I wasn't saying you should drop her off at a stranger's house."

"Plenty of people do that," Ellen replied. "It's called day care. And that's not something I could do."

"Oh please! That's a bunch of bull. Day care is a licensed operation regulated by state laws. You just don't want to go back to work so you use that as a convenient excuse to stay home."

"Deirdre!" Rebecca exclaimed.

"I choose to stay home so that my children are actively raised by a parent. I don't want someone else raising them."

"So all the people who have their kids in the day care system because they need two incomes to support their family are doing a disservice to them? That's the norm, Ellen. And most of those kids grow up to be just fine. Those who don't often have their parents to blame for that."

"And you know this how, Dee Dee?" Ellen shot back. "You don't have kids."

The room went silent. Deirdre glared across the table at her sister, who leaned back in her chair and looked down at the table.

"Dee, I didn't mean…"

"Forget it," Deirdre said through gritted teeth. "You're the only one who can have the correct opinion on the subject because you have two little kids. You know the best way to maintain a household and a marriage. You always have the right answer because you're older, and I have no idea what I'm talking about."

"I never said that…" Ellen stammered, looking up surprised.

"You don't have to. Your attitude says it all!"

"All right girls, that's enough," Rebecca said exasperated. "I can't believe I still have to separate you two. Can't we get through one family dinner in peace?"

"Sorry, Mom," Ellen muttered.

"Yeah, Mom. Sorry."

Both sisters dropped the conversation. Karen began banging the table to signal she was done. Brad followed suit. Ellen stood up to let them down from the high chairs, and followed them into the living room. She set them up with blocks and walked back into the dining room, keeping an eye on them from her chair. She continued to eat quietly.

Samuel looked around the table, his eyes stopping on his wife. He could see she was struggling to remain calm as the tension hung in the air between their two daughters. He cleared his throat.

"So, Pete, how's work?"

As her brother-in-law talked about his job at the bank, Deirdre still fumed about their previous conversation. *God, if it's not one thing it's something else. I'm too obsessed with work. I don't have a family of my own. Even my personal opinion is wrong.* Feeling flushed, she suddenly excused herself from the table and walked upstairs to the bathroom. Ellen watched her leave.

Standing in front of the sink, Deirdre stared at the running water. It made no difference how many times she tried to prepare herself for the inevitable agonizing conversation. It caught her off guard every time. Trying to stop her hands from shaking, she splashed some cold water on her face.

God, I'm a grown woman! Why do I let her get to me like that?

As she reached for a towel, she heard a knock on the door.

"Deirdre? It's me," said Ellen. "Can I come in?"

Deirdre stared at her reflection in the mirror. She could still see that little girl struggling to break out of her sister's ambitious shadow. A good marriage, adorable kids, a great house. The American dream that Deirdre couldn't quite achieve herself. Not that she even wanted it, but it seemed to be what everyone thought she should have also. She wiped her eyes and face dry and set the towel back on the rack. She looked back into the mirror and took a deep breath.

"Come in."

Ellen poked her head around the door and walked into the room, closing the door behind her. She sat down on the edge of the tub.

"Honey, you know I didn't mean anything by what I said. It was wrong of me to bring up that topic and I'm sorry. I guess it's hard for me sometimes to remember that you're not my little sister any more. Not like that anyway."

Deirdre turned to face Ellen.

"Old habits die hard, I guess. I didn't mean what I said about you not working. I know the kids are a full time job. Maybe arguing with each other just comes naturally."

"Remember the time we got into the pillow fight that turned into world war three?" Ellen giggled. "By the time mom found us there were cotton shreds everywhere and we had knocked over every piece of furniture that could be moved."

"Now that was a fight!" Deirdre said, chuckling at the memory. "Mom was like, 'what the hell is going on in here? Have you lost your minds?'"

"And you said, 'No, Mom. We haven't beaten each other's brains out yet,'" Ellen laughed. "Man, we got into so much trouble for that!"

"Wouldn't it be nice if all our fights could be as simple as dodging pillows?"

"Are you kidding? You knocked me onto the floor," Ellen exclaimed. "From the top bunk! I'll stick with the occasional exchange of angry words, thank you."

"Chicken."

After a moment, Ellen stood up and walked over to Deirdre.

"I heard about the divorce. I just didn't want to mention it in front of mom. Are you okay?"

Deirdre paused, thinking about the actual answer to that question. Even though the arguments with her sister had remained consistent over the years, so had their close bond as family. Despite the constant bickering, she knew Ellen still cared about her. And while they weren't always honest with their parents, they always were with each other.

"I'm not okay yet," she answered slowly. "But I will be."

Ellen put her arm around Deirdre's shoulder.

"Any time you wanna talk, sis. You know that, right?"

"Yeah, I know."

"Good," Ellen said, squeezing her. "So are we okay?"

"Well, I don't know about that, but we're good."

"Then I guess we should go back downstairs before mom thinks we're ruining another bedroom."

Deirdre followed Ellen down the stairs to find her mother and Pete clearing the table. She could see her father in the living room stacking blocks with the kids as the football game continued in the background. She smiled at the familiar scene.

"There you are," Rebecca said as they reached the first floor. She was relieved to see her daughters walking side by side again. "Don't think you're getting out of doing dishes."

"I wouldn't dream of it, Mom," Deirdre replied.

CHAPTER THIRTY-TWO

"Well, this is lovely."

It was Zoey's 20th birthday, and she sat with her parents in her favorite restaurant, a diner across town that made the best burger she'd ever eaten. Against her better judgment, she decided to take Dr. Stephens advice and suggested they go out to dinner to celebrate. Since Friday was her father's night off from writing, everything fell into place.

"Oh my, are you feeling all right darling?" Connie had asked her, smiling.

Ugh. Don't make me regret this any more than I already do, Zoey thought.

"Share some cheese fries with me, Zoey?" Walter asked. Before she could answer, Connie chimed in.

"I don't know how you two do it. Just reading that on the menu gives me heartburn."

"Ah, we can handle it. Right, honey?"

"Right," Zoey agreed, trying to muster a genuine smile.

"I can't decide between the garden salad or the Caesar salad," Connie mused. "They both look wonderful. I just don't know if I'm in the mood for that much cheese."

Oh god, please help her decide so we can move on from talking about the friggin menu!

"What are you getting, Walt?"

"I'm going with the steak platter."

"How about you, honey?"

Zoey sighed. *No wonder it's been a while since we've done this.*

"The cheeseburger."

"Whoa. Going a little crazy aren't you, Zoey?" Walter teased her. "Are you surprised, Connie?"

"It's nice to know some things don't change."

I wish I could say the same thing, Zoey thought, trying not to roll her eyes in front of her parents.

"So, uh, how's the book coming, Dad?"

Walter's face lit up a bit. Zoey hadn't asked him about his writing in a long time.

"It's going very well, thanks for asking, honey. I've finally reached the point where I have a good idea of how I want the story to end."

That always made Zoey smile, the way her father began a book without knowing how it was going to end. He once told her that his characters were the ones who revealed the killer to him. He simply had to find a way to convey the same thought to his readers.

"So was it the butler in the study with the candlestick?"

"That's what we should do when we get home," Connie interrupted. "Play a board game."

Zoey couldn't keep from rolling her eyes this time as her father continued talking about his book. That was the last thing she wanted, more family time. Gazing around the diner she saw the front door open. A couple entered, with a tall boy about her age with dark hair. He looked around the room, his gaze landing on Zoey. It was Tristan.

Oh my god. It's him again! Zoey felt her cheeks grow warm as he winked at her.

"Honey? Are you ok? You look a little flushed. It is kind of warm in here," Connie said, feeling Zoey's forehead. Zoey jerked her head back, embarrassed.

"Mom, I'm fine!" she exclaimed, looking down at the table. When she looked back up the hostess was seating Tristan and the two people he came in with. She seemed to know them well.

"All right honey. I'm just saying you feel warm."

Of all the times and places to go out to dinner with my parents, it had to be here, it had to be now.

Zoey tried to keep her gaze fixed on her father sitting across from her. When the waitress came to take their order she blocked Tristan's table, which helped Zoey to remember what she wanted to eat. But once the waitress left, she could see him out of the corner of her eye.

That's when she saw him turn toward her and smile.

Oh my god! He noticed me! Before she could react, he motioned for her to meet him near the bathrooms. Zoey nodded.

"Um, I have to go the bathroom," she said, standing up. She saw Tristan say something to the couple as he also stood up and followed her. She stopped at the end of the hallway where the restrooms were and turned around to face him.

"Are you stalking me?" he asked jokingly.

"I was about to ask you the same thing," she accused. "First the store, then the park, and now this? Very suspicious."

"Damn, I thought I was being subtle. Maybe I should stick to driving by your house ten times a day."

"Gee, you're really good at this stuff," Zoey giggled.

"It's a gift."

"So, is that your parents you're with?"

"Yup. You?"

"Yeah. I had this terrible idea of trying to have a normal conversation with them over dinner. Big mistake."

"At least you had a choice in the matter," Tristan replied, rolling his eyes. "Every Friday my parents insist on going out to dinner to keep the 'family dynamic' alive. But who says all family dynamics should be kept alive?"

"Totally."

"So, do you come here often?"

"Wow, if that isn't the oldest pickup line in the book."

"Hey, give me a break," Tristan exclaimed. "We've already had our first official meeting. Well, I guess we had two. So that can't be considered a pickup line. In this context it's an actual question."

"I guess I can accept those terms. To answer your question, we used to come here all the time when I was younger. It's my favorite restaurant."

"This place is your favorite?" he asked incredulously. "Out of all the restaurants in the world, you think this diner is the best?"

"Well, I haven't eaten at all the restaurants in the world. Actually, I haven't eaten in any restaurant outside this area in a long time. So I can only go by the ones where I have eaten."

"When you say area, do you mean this state?"

"Um, more like this county."

Tristan gasped, leaning against the wall and melodramatically holding his chest.

"Holy shit woman, are you serious?" Zoey nodded, trying not to giggle.

"Well, that's something we shall have to remedy then," he said in a garbled Scottish accent.

"Nice Braveheart impression. You sounded like a drunk Sean Connery."

"Same difference, right?"

"Not for Sean Connery."

"Ah, lassie, that's a matter of opinion."

"I hope you don't do impressions for a living."

"Wow, kick a guy while he's down why don't ya."

Zoey found herself grinning again, unable to stop as the conversation continued. The immediate ease of their repartee was almost natural, and she was surprised at how comfortable she felt. It was a complete transformation from her nervous, stammering self at the convenience store. *Maybe I'm not such a hopeless case after all.* She didn't want the moment to end.

"A great laugh and a great smile," Tristan said. "I'm sorry, but I'm gonna have to ask for the digits."

"The digits for what?" Zoey joked.

"Boy, you're not gonna make this easy for me, are you?"

"All right. I'll make you a deal. I'll show you my digits if you show me yours."

"Are we still talking about numbers?" he asked with a sly grin. Zoey blushed.

"While we're standing in public? Yes," she responded, trying to keep her heartbeat from rising. Tristan smiled, pulling a pen out of his pocket. He grabbed her hand and turned over her palm, writing his phone number on it. He handed her the pen.

"Your turn." She touched his wrist to steady his hand, and wrote her phone number on it. Reluctantly she let go, trying not to linger, and gave him back the pen.

"There. Now I can stalk you over the phone too."

"At least this evens things out. I can equally stalk you."

"I've always been a firm believer in women's equality," he replied. Zoey laughed.

"Good to know."

After a few seconds of silence, Tristan looked over his shoulder.

"Well, I guess we should go back before our parents think we were kidnapped or something. So, it was nice stalking you. I'd shake your hand but some chick just gave me her number and I don't want it to smudge."

"Good call. Maybe I'll see you around sometime, like at the park, and the convenience store, and the restaurant where I work, and the supermarket."

"Hey, thanks for those last two options. I was running out of ideas."

Tristan stepped aside, gesturing for Zoey to go out first. She walked past him and made her way down the hallway back to her parents' table. She saw him rejoin his parents a few seconds later. Once he sat down he glanced over at her and smiled.

"Everything alright kiddo? You were gone for a while," Walter said. Zoey smiled back.

"Everything's great, Dad," she replied, looking down at her hand. *Happy Birthday to me!*

CHAPTER THIRTY-THREE

Zoey lay in her bed, staring at the piece of paper on which she had re-written Tristan's phone number. It took every ounce of strength she had not to pick up her cell phone and dial it. Her laptop sat open in front of her, but that one piece of paper continued to hold her attention.

Her thoughts returned to their last chance meeting. Even though her dating life was short, she knew this was somehow different, he was different. She recalled every conversation she had with Laura about the various boys she dated, and the way Aaron eventually became a constant in their daily lives. Zoey had a feeling Tristan was that boy for her, and even though she didn't believe in a particular god, she prayed their flirtations were just the beginning.

I can't stop thinking about him. I don't even know him that well. All I know is that I want to get to know him- I need to.

KNOCK! KNOCK! Zoey jumped. It was one of many jolting reactions she had that day to any kind of noise which shook her from her daydreams.

"Zoey? Honey? Can I come in?"

Ugh. Can't you leave me alone for a day? I'm waiting for an important call! Not that Zoey could tell her mother that. Besides, she fully expected to have to suffer through the male-standard three-day waiting period.

"Yeah, come in."

As soon as Connie pushed open the door Zoey's phone rang. She jumped off the bed in surprise, startling her mother in the process. Zoey grabbed the phone and turned toward Connie, holding up her hand.

"Sorry, Mom, can we do this later?" she asked suddenly, pushing Connie back out the door.

"What? Honey, what are you doing? Who's calling you?"

"Hello?" Connie heard her daughter say as the door shut in her face. She strained to hear the conversation, putting her ear up to the door, when Zoey

160

opened it again. Connie stood up abruptly, trying to look down the hallway. Zoey glared at her as she put up her hands.

"Ok, ok, I'm going," she whispered. Zoey waited until her mother disappeared down the stairs before going back into her room.

"Sorry about that," she said, closing the door. "You were saying?"

"I was just saying I tried to wait the standard three days to look cool, but I couldn't do it. I hope one day doesn't make me look like too much of a dork," Tristan said.

"I'll try to overlook it." *YES! He called!* Trying to keep her breathing steady she laid down on the bed.

"You're a pal," he replied. "So, what'cha up to?"

"Surfing the Interwebs."

"Find anything interesting?"

"Only if you consider monkeys playing the piano interesting."

"That depends. Are they reading music?"

"I don't think so."

"Oh. Then yeah, that's not very interesting."

"Well, what are you doing?"

"The same actually."

"You're watching monkey pianists too?"

"No, I hadn't settled on anything in particular yet," he said. "I literally was clicking on random sites looking for something to catch my eye. I find myself surfing more than doing anything else other people might call useful, those other people being my parents mostly."

Zoey giggled.

"I know what you mean. I remember one day a friend of mine and I were watching videos on YouTube and my mom had no idea why we would spend time doing that."

"It's the same with mine. It's like they don't get all the different things you can do online, including watch any kind of entertainment you want."

"I think my parents just have a different idea of what it means to be 'entertaining.'"

"That could be too. Generational gap I guess."

"Tell me about it. My parents understand the TV and their cell phones, and maybe how to do email," Zoey said. "Oh, and of course my dad uses the computer to write his books. But ask them to download an attachment or send a photo? Blank stares."

"When I told my parents I started a blog they asked me what kind of a group that was," he sighed. "I told them we meet once a week to complain about our parents' lack of technological savvy."

"Please tell me they realized you were being sarcastic?"

"Thankfully, yes. But they still have no clue what a blog is so they've never seen it. Which might not be a bad thing, considering some of the things I have on it."

"Porn?" Zoey asked jokingly.

"Oh, that's a given. I think people expect that to be on a public blog."

"Naturally."

"Nah, it's not quite that racy. Although I might get more hits if it were."

"I would check it out," Zoey grinned.

"Really? All right. My kind of girl."

"But if it's only boring entries about your life then forget it."

"Nice. Real nice."

"What can I say? I'm a media snob."

"I guess I'll have to work on that. But until then, I'll have to find some other way to impress you."

"Hmmm. Sounds intriguing."

"Not really," he admitted, drawing another smile out of Zoey. "All I got is an invitation to go hear a cool local band."

Finally! I thought I was going to have a heart attack. Zoey held her hands up toward the ceiling and mouthed, *thank you!*

"A cool local band, huh? Well, I guess I can't pass that up," she replied, trying to sound casual. "Where are they playing?"

"Lou's Lair. Ever been?"

It was a name Zoey hadn't heard in over a year. It used to be Laura's favorite hang-out a couple years ago, when she was dating one of the club's DJs. Zoey hadn't been back since the two had broken up, nor had she ever been there with someone other than Laura.

She thought the idea of going back without her best friend should seem strange. It wasn't.

"I've been there a few times," she said, offering no further explanation.

"So, does that mean you'd be willing to go again?"

"Sure. As long as it's for a cool band."

"Oh, you have no idea. Unless you hate totally awesome metal fused with some punk rock and industrial overtones."

"Aw man, I was with you until you mentioned metal, punk, and industrial," Zoey joked.

"Damn it! I knew I should've gotten tickets for the Backstreet Boys."

"Are they even still together?"

"I don't know. I don't listen to that crap."

"Good. Me either. In fact, I like all those things you mentioned before the Backstreet Boys."

"Sweet."

"So when is the concert?"

"Next Friday. That's not too soon is it? I didn't know if you would have plans already."

Too soon? Hell, no. Zoey felt like she had been waiting her entire life for this moment.

"No. Sounds good to me. I'm on Willow Street, the third house on the right."

"Awesome. So, what's your view on motorcycles?"

"However you roll," she said. Tristan laughed.

God, I love making him laugh, she thought, proud of herself for saying something clever.

"Cool. I'll pick you up at 8 then."

"Ok. I'll see you at 8."

CHAPTER THIRTY-FOUR

It was the perfect fall night to be wrapped in a blanket, sitting on the couch and sipping hot chocolate, which was exactly what Deirdre was doing. Work was done for the week and she had managed to publish all of her assignments on time without any hassle from Neil. Not that it was difficult- most of the stories had been town meetings and budget concerns that were very straightforward and required little research. But nonetheless, she had earned her paycheck for the week, and even arrived home earlier than usual.

This is so weird, she thought, warming her hands on the coffee mug. *I actually have some free time.*

Deirdre looked around her living room for something to do that required little to no effort. She glanced at the remote, but realized one of the good things about Friday nights was that she rarely missed any good TV. Those shows were on during the week. She could take a nap before the weekly card game with Nina and Haley in a couple hours, but her mind was too busy to fall asleep that quickly.

Scanning the room, her eyes settled on the pile of books sitting on her coffee table. The title on top read "The Serial Killer Files." It was one of the books she had bought on a whim, because it had information similar to the sheets she had taken from Professor Tate's class. She didn't plan on reading the entire book, only the parts that pertained to psychopaths.

This shouldn't take too long. Reaching down she grabbed the book and opened to the front page.

Hours later, Deirdre was highlighting whole paragraphs about killers in their 20s or younger, some who were considered psychopaths, along with chapters about the public's reaction to these murders. She was surprised at how far back the book went in terms of the killers and the public's interest in such violence, back to the days of the guillotine and public hangings. *Looks like humans really have been interested in violence forever. Does that make me less weird for being intrigued by all this stuff? God I hope so.*

KNOCK! KNOCK! KNOCK!

Deirdre didn't realize how late it was until her friends knocked on her front door for the card game. She sat up and looked at the time on her cell phone.

"Deirdre! Are you gonna let us in or what?"

"Damn it," she muttered to herself. "Hang on a second!"

Deirdre stood up quickly, throwing off the blanket and knocking over the pile of books sitting on the table. She reached down and scooped them up, running over to throw them onto her bed, and raced back to the front door. Smoothing her hair, she took a deep breath and grabbed the handle.

"Sorry about that, guys," she said, opening the door slightly out of breath. "I was in the bathroom."

"Uh huh," Haley said, walking past her. "If I touch your laptop, will it, per chance, be hot?"

"Ha! Go ahead." Haley narrowed her eyes and began to search the room.

"So you've turned to reading actual books? Ok. Where's the stash?"

"Stash? There's no stash. You make me sound like a drug dealer."

As Haley made her way toward the bedroom, Deirdre ran over and blocked the doorway.

"Oh sure, there's no stash," Haley said, batting her eyelashes. "Just don't go in my bedroom."

"I, uh, don't want you to see my vibrator," Deirdre said, trying to keep a straight face.

"Oh please. You don't think every woman in America has one of those? I have the Rabbit."

"Ewww," Nina groaned.

"What?"

"All right, so I'm reading some books," Deirdre admitted, steering Haley away from the bedroom and toward the couch. "It's no big deal."

"Fine. To be honest, I'm kinda glad you're off the Internet kick. I was afraid you were going to start visiting teen chat sites next."

Deirdre paused. It was the final step she considered to complete her research.

"Ha! I told you, Nina! Pretty soon she's gonna be sexting."

"Dude, that's disgusting!"

"Uh oh. Dude? They're already wrangling her in with the teen slang."

"You're the one who brought up sexting."

"I saw it on the news."

"Or on your phone!" Deirdre said, grabbing Haley's purse. Haley snatched it back.

"A lady never tells."

"All right, all right," Nina said, grabbing the purse and setting it down on the coffee table. "I thought you guys wanted to play cards, not re-enact a Laurel and Hardy routine."

"What kind of friends would we be if we weren't constantly antagonizing each other?" Haley asked.

"My favorite kind?" The three of them laughed.

"Ok. Let's get this game going," Haley said, changing the subject. "What'll it be tonight, ladies?"

"I was thinking rummy," Deirdre suggested. "I don't want you cheating at poker and taking all my money like last time."

"Oh, please. You've got no game. It was like taking candy from a baby."

"Got no game? Who are you, Spike Lee?" Nina retorted

Deirdre laughed as she opened up the folding table in the living room. She was thankful they didn't ask why the room wasn't set up for the game yet. It might have been a bit awkward to explain the kind of book she was reading; not that her friends would have been surprised. *I'm such a nut case.*

Haley walked over to the refrigerator to grab the soda, when she noticed a DVD sitting on Deirdre's counter. She squinted at the title.

"What the hell is 'Gunning for America?'"

"Oh, that's this great documentary on gun control I watched. It got rave reviews at the Sundance Film Festival and..."

Haley groaned before Deirdre could finish.

"Ugh! I'm sorry I asked! Just tell me you haven't been hanging out at the shooting range too."

"No seriously, it was really interesting," Deirdre pushed. "I mean, did you know that there are over 250 million privately owned firearms in this country? And that number goes up over 4 million every year."

"I'm gonna become one of them if you talk about this issue all night," Haley muttered through gritted teeth.

Deirdre looked over at Nina, who held up her hands in surrender.

"Don't look at me! This is your thing, not mine!"

"That's just it though. It's everyone's issue," Deirdre insisted.

"Oh for god's sake!" Haley exclaimed, rolling her eyes. "What are you, running for mayor? Give it a rest, Deirdre!"

"What? You make it sound like we can't have an intelligent conversation about a controversial topic."

"On Friday night? No! Suddenly we're back in college, listening to a friggin lecture on guns in America. After a long week of work and family obligation, I'd like some mindless entertainment."

"Ok, fine," Deirdre said. "You can make the same inane comments as you would during any conversation we have. How about that?"

Sighing, Haley realized she was fighting a losing battle.

"All right, tell us about the damn movie. But after we start playing cards!"

"Thanks for the enthusiasm, Hale."

"No problem, OCDeirdre."

Deirdre stuck her tongue out at Haley as she walked over to her desk drawer to grab the cards. Nina shook her head as she brought three chairs over to the table.

"It's nice having two mature friends."

Haley stuck her tongue out at her as she set down the soda and bowl of potato chips.

"Case in point."

Deirdre placed the cards on the table and sat down as Nina and Haley joined her. She wrote their names on a piece of paper for the scorecard and began to shuffle the cards.

"All right girls, rummy to 500."

Dealing the cards, Deirdre set the rest of the deck in the middle of the table and checked out her hand. She was dying to hear what her friends would think about the documentary, but she also knew to be careful when to bring it up during the game. Everyone had to be settled and having a good time first.

"So, did you survive Thanksgiving dinner?" Nina asked, picking up the first card.

"Ugh, barely," Deirdre answered, as she leaned forward in her seat.. "Ellen and I had to have it out again on the whole kids issue."

"Are hers still holy terrors?" Haley asked, as she took her turn.

"Sort of. But they're still cute holy terrors."

"Give 'em a few years."

Deirdre tried not to spit out her soda.

"What about at your house? Tell me your brother-in-law wasn't there."

"Trust me, I had no choice in the matter," Haley said, rolling her eyes again. "Family's family, right?"

"I hear that."

"Well, I had a perfectly lovely evening with my family," Nina interjected.

"Uh huh. And how many people asked if you were dating anyone?" Haley smirked. Nina glared at her from across the table.

"I plead the fifth." Deirdre patted her on the shoulder.

"See? No one's family is perfect."

"No kidding."

The banter continued through the first game, each one doing their fair share of trash talking as they took their turn. Nina won quickly, and Deirdre noted her score as she passed the deck to Haley. When they began the second game, Deirdre leaned back in her chair and sighed contentedly. She would never admit it to her friends, but she enjoyed the nights they stayed in the most. Going out was fun on occasion, but lately she had been so drained from work that a relaxing night in with friends was exactly what she needed.

Haley's right, she thought. *I really have to find some down time. I guess they are looking out for me.*

But as the night wore on, Deirdre realized she couldn't shut off her brain completely. She was so immersed in the subject matter that it seeped into every thought and free moment she had. She knew the serial killer book was a bit much for casual conversation, but the gun control documentary was perfect for an adult discussion. And now that she had her friends' attention in a quiet environment, she was eager to share her ideas.

I have to tread lightly though. I don't want them to think I'm completely consumed by this whole thing. Even if it is true.

Deirdre waited for a lull in the conversation, when Nina stood up to get more soda. Deirdre cleared her throat.

"Sooo, did you guys hear about the most recent gun control case in the Supreme Court?"

"Wow, real subtle, D," Haley said sarcastically, as she began shuffling the deck. Nina sat back down and playfully punched her in the arm. "Ow! Totally uncalled for! Jesus. Fine, Deirdre. Why don't you tell us something about the movie?"

"All right, I will," Deirdre answered smugly. "So obviously it's all about the Second Amendment, which is mostly controversial because of how it's written. It says, a well-regulated militia, being necessary to the security of a free state, the right of the people to keep and bear arms, shall not be infringed."

Both of her friends nodded.

"They spent their time talking with people from groups like the National Rifle Association and a group called the Brady Campaign, who wants tougher gun control laws. So they basically go back and forth between those who think owning guns is an American right, and those who think it's a misrepresentation of the amendment."

"That's an understatement," Haley interrupted as she dealt the cards.

"Yeah, but usually these issues don't come up until there's a major gun-related incident. These people are saying that gun control should always be discussed until there's some kind of resolution to help prevent another incident, especially when it's happening everywhere in the country."

"Meaning it's not solely gang-related."

"Yeah," Deirdre replied. "It's not just in the inner cities anymore, and the kinds of guns used are getting more and more advanced. Like this one mother, whose son was killed during a drive by, she was asking why these weapons should even be allowed on the street."

"Which goes back to the constitutional right," Nina said.

"Exactly. But people ignore the fact that the second amendment begins with the phrase 'a well-regulated militia.' I know when it was first written, it was important for the public to be able to defend themselves against a hostile government. But that's long gone now that we're an established country. I think it means our military should be allowed to use guns to protect us."

"Sure, you can read it that way," Nina commented. "But other people say the law allows the public to arm itself to fight against its own government. And if the military is this well-equipped, then the public should have the same access."

"But we have a system of checks and balances in place to prevent that kind of a corrupt government from happening," Deirdre said, as she put down the first set of cards. "I don't think a hostile takeover of the government would be necessary because that kind of abuse of power would never happen."

Haley snickered.

"Try telling that to the homeless, or unemployed, or uninsured."

Deirdre ignored her comment and continued.

"Look, I don't think people shouldn't be allowed to own some kinds of guns, like hunters. I think they have a right to use their rifles for that kind of thing. And there are those who feel they need to protect themselves and their families. But you don't need AK-47s to do either of those things."

"Seriously though, Americans love their guns," Haley countered. "You can't just change that."

"True. But there was this one group who wanted to try and change public perception before trying to change the gun laws."

"By doing what?"

"Well, really all they had were statistics," Deirdre admitted. "The U.S. Department of Justice did this study which shows homicides are most often committed with handguns, especially teen and young adult homicides. But at the same time, there's a new FBI study that says violent crime is at a 35-year low and murder is at a 43-year low, while gun ownership is at an all-time high."

"Let me guess. That one group said in homes where a gun is present, there's a three times greater chance of a homicide and a four times greater chance of a suicide?" Haley interjected. Deirdre looked over at her in surprise.

"Yeah. How'd you know that?"

"Are you kidding? I always hear that statistic, any time they bring up gun control on the news."

"Oh. I didn't know you paid attention to that stuff."

"Of course I do. I have kids, and anything that has to do with their safety I listen to. But of course each side is gonna have their facts, and they're gonna spin them however they want."

"I do agree with one thing," Nina said, putting down more cards. "Those kids you've been researching wouldn't have been able to do that much damage if they didn't have such advanced guns."

"Didn't the Columbine kids have pipe bombs or something?" Haley asked.

"Yes they did, and they got all the information they needed on the Internet," Deirdre answered. "In fact, several of their bombs never even went off, or else the carnage would've been even worse."

"Still, their primary weapons were more powerful guns, correct?"

"Yes."

"Well, there you go," Haley said. "I agree with those people who don't see a need for those kinds of guns to be available to the public."

"But again, it comes down to the argument of keeping up with our military," Nina said.

"Oh please. Our military has friggin nukes," Haley snorted, shaking her head. "If they wanted to take us out, they could, very easily."

"But we'd still need some kind of advanced weapons to survive the Apocalypse, wouldn't we?" Nina smirked.

"Yeah, like you would survive the Apocalypse."

"And you would?"

"Of course I would. I've always been the toughest out of all of us."

"What?" Deirdre exclaimed. "You can't even tell your own husband to stop letting his deadbeat brother crash at your place."

"Hey, that's family. That's a totally different thing."

"You're saying the Apocalypse is easier to deal with than your family?"

"Absolutely."

"You have serious issues," Deirdre snorted.

"See? Another side effect of having a family."

"You're such a loving mother."

"I'm a realistic one."

"And that's why you feel these guns should not be in the hands of anyone, let alone teenagers?" Deirdre asked.

"Nice tie-in to the previous conversation."

"Thank you."

"It's not solely because of my kids. It's for everyone. I mean, just because I want to shoot you guys sometimes doesn't mean it's right."

Nina threw a chip at Haley, hitting her in the head. Deirdre laughed as Haley threw one back at Nina.

"See all this violence you guys subject me to?"

"Well, prepare to be dominated bitches, because I'm out!" Haley exclaimed, setting down her cards.

"Whoa. When did that happen?"

"Just now. I finally picked up the one card I needed."

"You suck," Deirdre replied, writing down her friend's score.

"All right, my turn to deal," Nina said, grabbing the deck to shuffle. She turned toward Deirdre.

"Ok, so I just have one question. That movie, *Bowling for Columbine*, said a lot of other European countries have lower death rates from gun violence. Is that true?"

"Yeah, actually. There was a paper they cited in the movie which compared several European nations that owned more than double the amount of firearms of other nations. And the first group with more guns had one-third the homicide rate of the second group."

"Wow. Crazy."

"Yeah. And the same paper said just because gun ownership is high and crime is low, that could mean those countries always had low rates, so they never needed to create strict gun laws. You can't automatically draw a direct correlation between the two."

"Well, if you think about it, the people you need to keep away from guns probably can't buy them legally anyway," Haley commented. "But they always find a way around that."

"It's true. But what scares me the most is that people 18-24 have almost always had the highest violence rates, including homicide."

"Well of course it's going to feel that way when you're completely immersed in the subject. That's all you see right now is teen violence all over the place."

"Hey, the studies I'm looking at come from state and federal departments," Deirdre said defensively. "I'm not looking to be another news source that spreads information through fear mongering. I'm trying to approach this from a purely objective standpoint."

"Either way, it's pretty sad," Nina murmured. "And scary. You don't know who's going to have a gun these days. It's hard to feel safe anywhere really."

"I know," Haley agreed. "I don't even want to think about anything like that happening to my kids."

All three women sat in silence, mulling over the entire conversation. Deirdre tried to remember the last time they had a lengthy discussion about such a solemn topic. They seemed to be fewer and fewer as they grew older, their real world issues often taking precedence over intellectual discourse. It was a productive dialogue, but Deirdre knew it would have felt more satisfying if the subject matter wasn't so somber. She looked at her friends, catching Nina's frowning expression. She glanced over at Deirdre, and then at Haley, who was glaring at both of them.

"See? I said this was a bad idea! Now I'm totally depressed. Thanks a lot!"

"Hey, I didn't make the movie," Deirdre exclaimed. "I blame society."

Her friends laughed as Deidre mockingly put the back of her hand to her forehead.

"That may not be far off," Haley said.

CHAPTER THIRTY-FIVE

"Bye guys."

Zoey came charging down the stairs, hoping to avoid a conversation with her parents. Friday night had finally come after the longest week of Zoey's life, and Tristan had called to say he was waiting outside. The thought of spending several hours with him was thrilling, but the thought of him meeting her parents was horrifying.

"You don't need to come in," she had told him hastily.

"I don't mind. It is the tradition."

"No, no. I'll be right out."

As Zoey hit the last step, Connie turned her attention away from the TV to notice the short tank top that rose above her daughter's low slung jeans and studded belt under her jacket.

"Honey, are you going out?"

"Uh, yeah. Bye!"

This time it was Walter's turn to face his daughter.

"You have plans? On a Friday?"

"Yes, Dad. I gotta go."

"Whoa, whoa, hang on there," he said, eyeing her outfit. "Where are you going?"

Zoey sighed, stopping in front of the door.

"To Lou's."

"Lou's Lair?" he asked incredulously. He had never known Zoey to go there without Laura.

"That's the one."

Walter and Connie glanced at each other, trying not to overreact. On the inside they were reeling from the thought of their daughter finally having weekend plans with someone, anyone. They were dying to know who it was, but they also knew to tread lightly on this particular topic. Zoey shifted her feet impatiently.

"Who are you going with, honey?" Connie asked gently.

"Geez, Mom, do we have to do this now?"

"Before you walk out the door? Yes."

Zoey looked out the side window to see Tristan leaning against his motorcycle. *I gotta get this done before he tries to come in here!*

"I'm going with Tristan, okay?"

"Tristan? Is that the boy on the phone from the other night?" Connie exclaimed. "Wait a second. When did you two meet?"

Oh god. I am back in junior high.

"A couple weeks ago, Mom. It's no big deal. I gotta go. He's waiting for me."

The minute the words left her mouth she cringed.

"What? He's here?" Walter asked, getting up out of his chair and walking towards her.

"Ok, I'm out!" Zoey rushed out the door, slamming it behind her. She tried not to look back at her father, who she knew was looking out the window at Tristan and his bike.

"Hey," she said breathlessly. "I'm ready to go."

"Is that your dad sitting like a dog in the window?"

Zoey rolled her eyes.

"Yes, which is why we totally need to go!"

"Ok, ok," he laughed. "Should I drive the bike up on the sidewalk and peel out for effect?"

"Ha! I'm sure my parents would have nothing to say about that!"

"Don't worry," he said, handing her a helmet. "I'm a big hit with the parents."

"Oh yeah? Why's that?"

"I make excellent pot brownies." Zoey snickered.

"Do you mention that before you hand them out?" This time it was Tristan's turn to chuckle.

"Absolutely. So, shall we?"

"Uh, sure," she said, looking at the motorcycle.

"Don't worry. Most people I know have never ridden one." Zoey sighed in relief.

"It's not a big deal. You just have to be careful to keep your feet up. And of course, hang on tight."

Gladly, Zoey thought. She nodded.

Tristan put on his helmet and got onto the bike, motioning for her to get on behind him. She swung her leg over and sat down. *God, I hope he can't feel my heart pounding.* She tried to slow her breathing as she wrapped her arms around his waist.

"Here we go." She could barely understand his muffled voice, but when he started the engine she knew it was time to tighten her grip.

Tristan led the bike slowly away from the curb and gained speed heading down her street. Zoey was thankful that, in their town, there were no major highways they had to go down to get anywhere. And Lou's Lair was right on the town line.

Riding with Tristan through those familiar streets gave Zoey a sense of visiting for the first time. The street lamps radiated a celestial glow, drawing them into a forest of neon signs shining on people buying their last items before the shops closed. Teenagers hung out in groups on the street corners and in parking lots, creating the illusion that something would soon be happening there. As they got closer to the club the crowds became a bit older, a bit dressier, with a hint of frenzy.

For the first time in months, Zoey was beginning to feel alive again.

Tristan pulled into the parking lot of Lou's, finding a spot easily where his bike could fit. Zoey reluctantly let go and stood up. Taking off her helmet, she shook her hair in the hopes it wasn't too messy. When Tristan removed his helmet, she saw him watching her.

"You look great." Zoey tried not to blush at the compliment. She found that was a natural reaction just being around him.

"Thanks."

"All right, let's go."

As they walked toward the door, Zoey could see a line forming that reached to the end of the building. She could see a sign for a live band next to the bouncer who kept watch over the front door.

"Ugh. We're never gonna get in with this crowd."

"Not to worry."

She watched as Tristan walked to the front of the line and said something to the bouncer. The bouncer patted him on the back and waved for Zoey to join them. He opened the front door to let them in as everyone at the front of the line began to complain. Zoey tried not to look behind her as they slipped into the front hallway. Once inside, she turned to Tristan.

"Uh, what just happened?"

"It's good to know certain people. DJs, bartenders, bouncers. Those people can get you in anywhere."

Wow. I'm dating the male version of Laura, she thought. It made her smile.

Even though it had been a couple years since the last time Zoey had been to Lou's, the place hadn't changed much. The stage was the highest point in the front of the room, with the dance floor directly across from it. In the back of the room was a raised platform with several tables and the bar. After weaving their way through the small crowd on the dance floor, they found an empty table and sat down to watch the band finish setting up onstage.

"I heard these guys were good," Tristan said. "Think Rob Zombie meets Trent Reznor."

"That's cool. I like both of them."

"Yeah? Me too. There just aren't that many new metal bands out there I can get into."

"Tell me about it. There's a lot of dance and pop music out there that doesn't say anything. There's no real depth to it. Even those bands that call themselves metal are more Emo than anything. It's like all the great stuff has been done already, like no one has anything original to say any more. I think we can blame American Idol."

"Why do you say that?"

"Well, in the old school days bands had to struggle to be discovered, and once they were they had to continuously prove their worth to maintain a record deal," she explained. "Now, people can just go on a TV show to get a recording gig, a show that's mass producing the same kind of musical artists like a factory."

"Pop robots?"

"Exactly."

"Sounds like the name of a sci-fi book."

They stopped talking as the band finished their sound check and began playing their first song. The people on the dance floor and those sitting at the tables immediately stood up and began moving and headbanging to the harsh tones of the guitars and drums. The singer's voice, although deep and raspy, blended with the chords that tore through the crowd. Zoey looked over at Tristan, who was leaning forward as if trying to absorb as much of the music as he could.

He's really into this. That's awesome, she thought as she began to relax. The more they talked, the more she realized they had many similar interests. She watched as Tristan closed his eyes, seemingly oblivious to anything but the music. She smiled, turning her attention back to the band.

A figure out of the corner of her eye caught her attention a few minutes later. She glanced over to see an older looking man make his way toward them and tap Tristan on the shoulder. Tristan turned and stood up to give the man a fist bump and short hug. They talked for a couple minutes, Tristan with his back to Zoey, until the man shook his hand and walked back toward the bar. Tristan sat back down and waved to a group of people who also seemed to know the man. They looked a bit more hardcore metal than he did, with a couple thin girls wearing short plaid skirts and fishnet stockings who blew him mock kisses. Tristan laughed and returned to listening to the music, not saying a word to Zoey. She thought it was strange he didn't introduce her, but it was only their first date so she hoped it was because she didn't have an official title yet.

After the fourth song, Tristan leaned over and touched Zoey's leg to get her attention. Being engrossed in the music she jumped slightly.

"Oh. Sorry about that!"

"No, no, it's ok," she giggled sheepishly. "It's just hard to concentrate on anything else in here!"

"I know what you mean. It's like the music takes over the whole place, the whole crowd, and we have no choice but to give into it."

"Totally. It feels like there's nothing else but the beat and the singer's voice."

"And us," Tristan added, taking her hand. Zoey felt her cheeks growing warmer.

"So, um, what were you going to say?" *Maybe something about who those other people are?*

"Oh yeah. I was thinking how this reminds me of the lead guitar in 'Enter Sandman'."

"Oh," Zoey replied, trying not to sound too disappointed that he didn't want to introduce her. "Uh, yeah. I was thinking that too. I haven't heard that song in a while."

"It's a classic. Back in the heyday of Metallica, when they friggin rocked."

Over the next few songs, the two of them discussed the various influences of the band, and how many of the songs reminded them of their favorites. Tristan often turned to Zoey as she would turn to him to say the same thing. The loud music forced them to sit close to each other, knees touching, creating intimate moments throughout the hectic scene. It had been a long time since Zoey had such an extensive conversation in an enjoyable atmosphere.

As the drums began to beat faster and faster, the crowd on the dance floor began to flail around and collide into each other, forming a mosh pit of headbangers surrounded by other headbangers. Zoey watched as more and more boys jumped into the controlled chaos, causing the circle to grow wider. By the start of the next song, the mosh pit covered the entire dance floor. Tristan tugged lightly on Zoey's arm.

"Do you mind if I go mosh? I didn't know if you liked that or not."

Zoey shook her head.

"I don't do it myself, but I wouldn't mind getting a closer look."

Tristan nodded and stood up, helping her out of her seat. He took her hand and led her towards the dance floor, which was lower than the rest of the tables in the back of the room. Zoey could feel the bass from the speakers start to pulse through her entire body. Tristan let go of her hand.

"I'll see you on the other side!" he joked. He turned and jumped off the platform and into the fury.

Zoey stood on the edge with the other girls who didn't mosh, but rather danced to the music in their own way, or watched the person they came with mosh. It wasn't until then that Zoey began to feel a bit strange without Laura there. The only time Zoey danced at concerts was with her best friend, and as the show went on they would get sillier and wilder. She had a feeling this would be a completely different experience with Tristan. He seemed to be more serious about the music.

As the night wore on, the music grew heavier and heavier, and Zoey watched as Tristan thrashed around with the rest of the moshers. She had never been in a mosh pit before, but she admired those with the guts and endurance to withstand the violent nature of moshing. Tristan was tall and thin, but his confidence gave him a certain strength that Zoey found intoxicating. She would've given anything to join in the frenzy, if only to push up against him time and time again.

The band played one long set with no intermission, and by the end of the concert the singer was screaming into the microphone for their last song. Zoey found herself thrashing around with the rest of the crowd, completely carefree. When the band played its last encore, she applauded and hollered as they left the stage. Once people began to clear the dance floor, Tristan emerged from the mosh pit, sweaty and flushed and breathing as heavy as she was.

"Ready to go?" he asked, his chest heaving.

Zoey nodded, disappointed to leave. *This was the best night of my life. Who knew it could happen after Laura's death?*

They joined the mob as it filed out of the club. Walking behind Tristan, Zoey struggled to keep him in her sight. He turned around to see her getting further behind and waited for her to catch up to him. That's when he took her hand to lead her through the crowd. It was a small gesture, but one that Zoey had never experienced before this. He made her feel special in a way no one else ever had, not even Laura.

As they rode back to her house, the lights throughout the town had dimmed, leaving only the stars and a full moon to light their way. Riding on a loud motorcycle, coming back from a metal concert, Zoey reveled in the dark romance surrounding them.

Now she wished the club was located beyond the town limits. The ride home wasn't enough time.

Tristan pulled in front of the house and turned off the engine. Zoey stepped off the bike and took off her helmet, turning to face him.

This is it, she thought. *He wouldn't take off his helmet if he wasn't going to kiss me. Finally!*

"This was great. I had so much fun," she said. "It's been awhile since I've been to Lou's."

"It's the best place for that kind of music. I'm glad you enjoyed it."

Zoey didn't know what else to say. *Am I supposed to prompt him in some way to show him it's okay to kiss me? Should I make the first move? And what the hell would that be?*

"Can I call you again?" Tristan asked, suddenly filling in the blanks for her.

"Absolutely," she said breathlessly.

"Great. I'll talk to you soon then. Good night, Zoey."

Tristan put his helmet back on and turned on the bike. Zoey stood on the sidewalk, confused as she watched him drive out of sight.

What just happened, she wondered. *Was I supposed to do something else? Why didn't he kiss me?*

But despite her disappointment, Zoey couldn't help feel relieved at the same time. This was her first real date with someone she wanted to see again. She didn't want anything to ruin her memory of the night.

I'll know when the moment is right.

CHAPTER THIRTY-SIX

"He didn't kiss me."

"Does that bother you? Were you expecting him to?"

"I was kind of expecting it. But at the same time, it was almost a relief that he didn't. I've never really had that kind of a kiss before."

"What do you mean, 'that kind' of a kiss?"

"You know, one that matters. One that's not outside the gym at a junior high dance or in the back seat of a stuffy car. It's that one you have with someone you know will change your life forever."

"And you think Tristan is someone who can change your life forever?"

"I know it sounds extreme, but I feel like we have this connection, like he gets me. He's not like any of the other guys I've met, and I mean throughout my entire life!"

Zoey felt relieved to have a therapy session so soon after her date. Her parents asked how it went but she couldn't be as open with them as she was with Dr. Stephens. She felt like a little kid trying to explain to her parents feelings that they would probably call "puppy love." It was a derogatory term she had always hated; one she felt was completely dismissive of true emotions. *Isn't that the point of emotion? To feel alive?*

She felt alive just knowing someone like Tristan was real.

"So how was the rest of the date?"

"Awesome."

Zoey described the date in great detail- what she wore, what he wore, the exhilarating ride to the club, their various conversations about bands, the way he led her out of the club, and the final moment in front of her parents' house. She decided to leave out the mystery group by the bar, since she felt silly even worrying about it. Dr. Stephens sat and listened, barely writing down anything.

"And that's when he drove away."

"It sounds like you had a great time. First dates can be tough, and I know you had some reservations after your very first meeting."

"I know. I thought it was going to be really awkward at first," Zoey admitted. "But he made me feel at ease immediately, which isn't an easy thing to do! Our conversations happen so naturally."

"That's great."

"Yeah. I wasn't expecting that."

"Why not?"

"Well, normally I'm not that great at meeting new people, or going to places where I can meet new people. But with Tristan, he made the first move and kept things going, and now I'm actually dating someone that Laura had nothing to do with."

It was the first time Zoey had said that out loud. She hadn't thought about that until this moment. She suddenly realized how sad it made her feel. Dr. Stephens could sense a change in her demeanor.

"Zoey? What are you thinking about?"

"I always thought my first real date, my first real anything, would happen with Laura's help," she said quietly. "It never occurred to me that my best friend wouldn't be involved somehow. At the very least she would've been the one person who understood what I was going through. But now I'm telling a therapist instead. Once he gets to know me he'll probably think I'm a loser."

Dr. Stephens set down her notebook and leaned forward.

"You said you feel as if you already have a lot in common. That's a great jumping off point for developing a relationship. And problems often arise when the communication is lacking, which doesn't sound like the case here."

"That's just it though. We have basic things in common, like music or places we like to hang out. But that's all superficial stuff, ya know? Beyond that my life doesn't offer much else."

"You seemed to think everything was going well until you mentioned Laura. What changed?"

"I don't know. I still feel like she was the one solid thing in my life, the one thing that made sense. Without her, I don't know what's real anymore," Zoey replied. "Hell, I even thought about Tristan as being a male version of Laura because of his social connections!"

"Well, that makes sense. There's a direct parallel there."

"Yeah. But I feel like I don't know how to do this kind of stuff on my own. I never had to before."

"That part of growing up can be frightening," Stephens admitted. "You feel ready in some ways to be out on your own, but you never really know what's going to happen until you're out there. But even as adults we go through the same routine any time we come across something new. All we have is the wisdom from past experiences to guide us."

"And when you don't have that wisdom yet?"

"Then you learn as you go."

"Great. Meanwhile the best opportunities in your life could pass you by if you make the wrong choice."

"They could pass you by either way. There's no guarantee that even if you pick the so-called right choice that everything is going to work out as you planned."

"God. Life sucks."

"Is that what you were thinking in the club the other night?"

Zoey glanced over at Dr. Stephens and grinned.

"No."

"There it is then. We all have those moments of loss and regret, where we think everything is over or that nothing will be the same again. But we also have those moments where we wouldn't change a thing. And that's the delicate balance of living."

"It just feels like there are a lot of days where people only go through the motions- working, taking care of the kids, doing chores. There's so much responsibility to deal with all the time," Zoey said. "Sometimes I'm amazed at how my parents can go through their daily routine and not want to scream by the end of it."

"I think some people are more satisfied with a simpler life. They're content with their situation."

"What do you mean?"

"Well, they enjoy having a family and working to provide that family with a good life. It can be very gratifying. And then there are those who choose not to have a family and pursue other things to keep themselves content."

"So that's what we should be striving for? Being content?"

"As I said, for some people that's enough. For others, they need excitement or chaos to feel happy."

"I'm not sure I like either one of those choices," Zoey said, wrinkling her nose.

"Then choose your own way of measuring happiness. Everyone is different, so your idea of how you should live your life won't be the same as someone else's idea."

"Yeah, like my parents."

"But ultimately you're living life the way you wanted to, right? You're working, you're not in school, you took charge of what you wanted to do."

"Well, with a cost."

"There's always a cost."

"I guess."

"You could say you took a risk by going out with Tristan. He represents an unknown in your life."

"Totally."

"And how did you feel afterwards?"

Zoey didn't even have to think about that question.

"Awesome."

"So you would say it was worth the awkward meeting and feelings of nervousness?"

"Yes."

"So then, maybe you can think about this as a new chapter in your life," Stephens suggested. "Laura was a very important person in your life, and through that relationship you learned a lot about friendship and trust and loyalty. That's knowledge you will carry with you for the rest of your life."

The idea was oddly comforting to Zoey; it was the only one that made sense in comparison to others' words of wisdom on how to cope with Laura's death.

"I guess I never thought about it like that. I mean, it's still not as good as having her here. But I didn't think I had anything to help me handle my first relationship. No offense."

"None taken," Stephens smiled.

"So, I guess this is the part where I shouldn't ask you if I should call Tristan or if I should let him call me because I should already know the answer, right?"

"Women have been asking that question for years, Zoey. I don't think it ever has a right answer," Stephens replied, laughing. Zoey joined her.

"So there are some mysteries even therapists don't know about, huh?"

"All I can tell you is to go with what feels right."

"Chicken," said Zoey jokingly.

"Hey, you could always ask your parents what they think."

Zoey groaned at that prospect.

"Fine. I'll go with my gut."

As Stephens finished writing in her notebook, Zoey thought back to the blog entry she had written about relationships. It seemed so long ago, but she had finally attained that one thing that had eluded her for so long. She realized then that she truly was learning as she went along. It was terrifying but exciting to her at the same time, as things were progressing really well with Tristan. Of course, the relationship was still in the early stages, but she hoped the bliss would continue for a bit longer.

So much has happened since then. It seems more like years ago than months now. It's crazy how much can change in so little time. I almost feel like a different person.

Except I have the same insecurities. Ugh. Will those ever go away?

"Zoey? You seem somewhere else again."

"What? Oh, sorry. I was just thinking about how our whole conversation mirrors this thing I wrote in my blog."

"You have a blog?" Stephens repeated, writing something down. "What do you like to write about?"

"It's nothing profound or anything. It used to be about how boring my life was. Then after Laura's death it was all about how lonely my life was. Now, well, I guess it's about how different my life is."

Stephens nodded for her to continue.

"I mean, it's so weird. I always thought the Internet was the only way I could interact with people other than Laura, but now I realize I wasn't really 'interacting' with them," Zoey mused. "We exchange ideas sometimes on the blogs, but I don't know any of those people. We're all just randomly throwing thoughts into the void and seeing who else is doing the same. After hanging out with Tristan, I realize all this stuff I've been missing out on."

"Well, the Internet *can* make people feel isolated from the rest of the world, especially if they're on it alone," Stephens said. "But at the same time, a lot of people connect with others through online gaming, chatting, email, or sharing videos, and others make comments on each other's blogs. It can bring people together just as easily as it can separate them."

"I guess so."

"Do you talk to these other people who read your blog?"

"Nah, we would usually just communicate through blog comments. Tristan is the only person I actually know who reads it, but obviously we didn't meet through that. But it's funny, because we totally could've met that way, since he has one too."

"As I said, people meet in all kinds of interesting ways. Technology adds a whole new dimension to the process."

"Yeah, totally."

As the session began to wind down, Stephens looked over at the clock and set down her notebook.

"Well, it looks like our time is up. Would you like to keep going with once a week?"

Zoey shifted in her seat, looking down at the floor. As much as she hated to admit it, the sessions had been a big part of helping her to get past her initial depression after Laura's death. Even now, she felt unsure of where her relationship was going with Tristan, if it was going anywhere. She realized she still needed guidance, but at the same time she was enjoying the new territory she was entering with Tristan. She was beginning to see the potential he had to help her as well.

"Well, um, I was thinking maybe we could do every two or three weeks now," she mumbled. "I mean, not that I don't like coming here, but I just feel like I'm starting to do a little better on my own. I guess."

This time it was Stephens turn to smile.

"Zoey, these are your sessions, remember? You can schedule them however you like."

Looking up, Zoey breathed a sigh of relief. She liked Dr. Stephens, but she truly appreciated the fact that she could say anything to her without judgment.

"Ok. Let's try two weeks."

CHAPTER THIRTY-SEVEN

Deirdre sat at her desk at work, tapping her foot nervously. The day had arrived for her to meet with Neil to discuss her article in full detail. She looked down at her notes, scribbled all over dozens of pages.

It had been eight months since she began researching this topic, and she was finally ready to show Neil some results. Just as everyone had predicted, the subject matter was overwhelming and took up more time and energy than Deirdre ever could have anticipated. And as much as she didn't want to admit it, the cheerleader shooting, as most people recognized it, was the one thing keeping her story alive in Neil's mind. Deirdre was thankful to still find articles about the incident online, although many of them were only interviews with "experts" who hypothesized about what could have happened between the girls involved. But the article she found the other day shed some light on a possible motive.

"In a new development, investigators say they've discovered a sex video that had surfaced at the high school prior to the shooting, showing Robin with a previous boyfriend, Tyrell Davidson, senior quarterback for the football team," the article read. "Students who knew Gisele said she was furious once she heard about the tape, but was even more upset that it was distributed throughout the student body.

'I saw it on someone's phone,' said junior Isaac Pringle. 'And they told me it was posted online by [Gisele's best friend] Tara Leichfield.'

Police questioned Davidson about the tape, and according to reports, he claimed he was not responsible for uploading the video onto the web. He said another cheerleader, Heather Strout, found the tape when they were hanging out in his room, and thought she must have stolen the tape and showed it to

Leichfield. He added that he did not know why Leichfield would show it to anyone else.

'Gisele cornered me that morning and asked me about the tape. She was really upset,' he said. 'I told her what happened with Heather, and she asked why I didn't destroy the tape. I wish I had now.'"

Even though this incident was a bit different from the others, in that it was an attack against specific people, it was still a teenage suicide shooting. Deirdre had taken extensive notes from the beginning, only to find new details emerged every day, disproving previous theories. But this article provided a "why" for the incident, one that was consistent with the rest of the confirmed details. It also mentioned Gisele's journal.

"According to the police chief, the night before the shooting, Robin had written in her journal that members of the cheerleading squad attacked her after school. That would explain the bruises and internal damage found during the autopsy," the article continued. "The entire squad has since been questioned, and police say five students have been charged with aggravated assault and battery. This has some parents outraged, claiming that the incident could have been in self-defense, knowing now that Robin was 'clearly disturbed.'

The five students were arrested and released to their parents after they posted bail. The hearings have been set for Wednesday, at which time it is expected the district attorney will submit Robin's journal into evidence."

Deirdre picked up the article and placed it in the folder. Taking a deep breath, she walked over to Neil's open doorway and knocked on the frame.

"Hey. Are you ready for our meeting?"

"Sure, come on in."

Deirdre sat down in the nearest chair and set her file down on his desk.

"Wow, that looks like a lot of information," he said, eyeing the bulging folder.

"Well, I still have a bit more research to do, but I'm making plenty of progress. My next move is to talk to some local teenagers."

Neil opened the folder and began to leaf through the articles and papers. One of the top pages listed her earliest findings for mass suicide shootings and shootings done by teenagers.

One of the earliest suicide shootings I came across online is Charles Whitman at the University of Texas in 1966, although he was 25. He killed 14 people and wounded 31 others after a shooting rampage in one of the school's administrative buildings. In that case he had requested in his suicide note that an autopsy be done. That's when they discovered he had a brain tumor. He was also on prescribed medication for depression, although they didn't know if he was on the medication during the incident.

After that, I found information on a school shooting in 1979, where Brenda Spencer, 16, had a rifle and shot at the Grover Cleveland Elementary school in San Diego. She killed two adults and wounded eight students, although she did not kill herself. When asked why she did it she said she didn't like Mondays. She's also one of the very few female shooters, suicide or not. The other two incidents I found were in 1985, when Sylvia Seegrist, 25, killed 3 people in a shooting spree at the Springfield Mall in Pennsylvania, and in 1988, Laurie Wasserman Dunn, 31, shot 6 kids and killed 1 at Hubbard Woods Elementary School. Afterwards she broke into a nearby home and killed herself.

Of course, the majority of mass shooters are male, although their ethnic backgrounds are different.

There are some suicide shootings from the 1980s, all school shootings, but only one was a freshman in high school. In 1983, David Lawler, 14, brought 2 pistols into school and opened fire, killing one other student. He then committed suicide. There were two other suicide shootings but both of those people were 30. The remaining school shootings involved teenagers who were apprehended.

Detailed information on those shootings was limited at best, except for what I could find on Wikipedia about Whitman. The ones from the 80s only had a couple lines on different web sites.

It's much easier to find information on the more recent cases, mostly from the late 90s and on. That's why my main focus is on the last two decades, where there is a general explosion of information through increasing use of technology, mainly 24-hour news channels and the Internet.

Hopefully that is the key to understanding all of this. If the onslaught of news media contributes to the cause of this mass violence, maybe it can also play a part in its solution. Taking the time to research each story and obtain all of the facts can only prove useful.

Several newspaper and online articles describing the aforementioned events followed Deirdre's notes. Neil glanced over each one, reading the headlines and looking at the pictures. They only took up a small portion of the entire file, and he soon found more of Deirdre's general thoughts written down.

In my current research, the general idea I get from each story involves a sense of isolation. Evan Little didn't appear to have many friends and had a rocky relationship with at least his father. He was put on medication to help with anger management, but he didn't seem to have much of a support group besides a psychologist.

It was the same with Philip Smith. He was oppressed by his religion for being gay, and was denied his first love. He was surrounded by many people in his community, but they were the wrong people.

As for Gisele Robin, she was very popular, until something happened to change that status. Her mother didn't believe her claims of rape, and her friends ultimately abandoned her. Of course, she did not commit a mass shooting, which seems to fit with the idea that women are far less likely to commit such an act.

From a discussion I had with Dr. Carla Stephens, for a teenager, social acceptance is a large part of growing up and discovering who you are and what your place is in the world. It seems all social beings need a delicate balance of family and friends to grow up in a safe and nurturing environment. Are parents oblivious to their children's needs? Are they unable to be there on a regular basis like many parents were 50 years ago? Or are outside circumstances, environmental factors, more to blame for these incidents?

It seems to be both. So what, then, is the answer?

Turning over more pages, Neil came across several articles about Columbine and the shooting at Virginia Tech. These made up the bulk of the pages in the folder. He began to read Deirdre's notes found at the end of the stack.

Let's look back to previous events, the two major ones being Columbine and Virginia Tech. In both cases there were warning signs. The Columbine shooters were in a disciplinary program, and had written some violent school assignments. Same with the Virginia Tech shooter, who was in his 20s, but close enough. He had written some very disturbing work and had been seen by a counselor. How did they slip through the cracks?

Their parents had no idea the kind of violence their child could commit. That is definitely a common thread throughout this whole topic, the shock of the family. Is it because teenagers are desperately trying to break away from their parents' guidance? It obviously doesn't make things easier. These kids are going through physical and emotional changes, and they need this guidance they are pushing away more than ever.

Of course, I can't ignore the fact that some of these kids may honestly be imbalanced. They've determined one of the Columbine shooters was a psychopath, while others had been diagnosed with depression and prescribed medication. These days, the definition of "normal" is always changing.

But why? What's changed in the last 50 years to see this rise in violent behavior in our youth? It's not like any of this is new. Back in the days of beheadings, spectators could go home with a souvenir program or guillotine earrings and toy replicas for kids. In the late 1880s, people would read "broadsides," or one page accounts of news that often involved the most gruesome of crimes. As for music, never mind gangsta rap- before widespread literacy we had "murder ballads," which were crudely composed songs of a gruesome killing that were passed down from village to village. And in 1872, when 13-year-old serial killer Jesse Pomeroy was arrested for the murder of 2 younger children, critics immediately pointed to the "dime novels" read mostly by children after the Civil War, even though there was no evidence he had ever read one.

All these individual stories and cases and I still don't see the rise or fall of anything social that's directly connected to them. I mean, people have their theories, but each of them has an "other side".

Am I asking the right questions? Am I looking in the right places? Am I missing something important which ties this all together? Why do I feel like I have a lot of information but not a lot of answers?

Neil sat back in his chair, shaking his head at the last paragraph. He set the folder back on his desk.

"There is a lot of information here Deirdre, but I'm not seeing what your interpretation of it is. Do you have an opinion on any of this yet? A message of any kind?"

"An opinion? Sure. It's horrible. That's what I think."

"Deirdre, if this is going to be an opinion piece then we need to see your opinion. If this is going to be an article, then you need to have both sides of the argument. Politicians, gun lobbyists, law enforcement, they'd all have a place."

"Well, at this point I've got a column in mind."

"Well, good. You've been working on this for the better half of this year. I'd like to see something eventually."

"I've been publishing other stories, Neil. I'm keeping up with my monthly assignments."

"Yes, I know. Keeping up with them is a good way to put it," Neil sighed. "Deirdre, I know this issue is a monster and there's a lot of good stuff here, but like you said, you have other assignments. And lately those assignments have become smaller and smaller. You said you could handle this."

Deirdre looked up, surprised. Neil had never before mentioned a problem with her writing. She shifted in her seat.

"You think I'm slipping?"

He paused.

"I think you're preoccupied. If you recall that was my main concern at the beginning of all this."

"I know, I know. I really thought I was balancing things ok," she said nervously. "If you need me to step things up a little bit I can do that. Now that I know, it won't be a problem anymore."

Oh please, do not take me off of this.

Neil leaned forward in his chair. He could see Deirdre silently pleading with him to allow her to continue.

"Boy, you have a terrible poker face."

"I'm just really dedicated to this issue. And I can show that same kind of dedication to everything else..."

Neil held up his hand.

"Ok, ok, you're not interviewing for your job again. I just wanted to remind you of your job description, that's all."

"Duly noted."

Gathering the rest of her notes off the desk, Deirdre placed them in her folder. Before she could thank Neil for understanding, he leaned forward and touched her arm gently.

"Since we're on the subject, how are you dealing with all of this research?"

"Fine." *Come on poker face.*

"I heard about Ben."

Deirdre paused, looking down at the desk. She had been hoping to keep her personal life as private as possible, but working for a newspaper in a small town made it fairly impossible. She cleared her throat.

"Yes, well, that's something he wanted. He proposed to his new girlfriend."

"That can't be easy, to have that thrown in with everything else you're dealing with."

"Neil, I'm not dealing with anything. I'm doing research."

"Hey, we've been friends for a long time. You don't have to feed me that middle-of-the-road bullshit."

Deirdre sighed, sitting back down in the chair.

"All right, all right. It friggin sucks. I know we've been separated for a while, but actually going through the motions takes its toll."

"I know. That's why I haven't said anything to you until now. I didn't want you to think you were losing your job or something too."

"I didn't think that at all! Jesus, Neil, thanks for putting that idea in my head!"

"Stop. You know I'm not saying that!"

"You've got a funny way of consoling people."

"Must be why I never married."

"That, and you're a bear in here in the morning."

"Hmm. Maybe your job security is slipping a little."

Deirdre laughed.

"So much for honesty."

CHAPTER THIRTY-EIGHT

"Hello?"

"Hey Idol-hater," said the voice on the other end. *Yes! I didn't even have to survive the week to hear from him again.*

"Hey yourself."

"So, I was sitting here, trying to come up with another inventive date idea. But our first date was such a good time I'm having some trouble. Wanna help me out?"

I was hoping he'd ask that.

"Well, I don't know about you but I'm pretty bored right now," she said slowly. "We could go for a walk. You know, test our conversational skills."

"A challenge already, huh? You're definitely gonna keep me on my toes."

"Is that a bad thing?"

"Not at all. It's a rare thing actually. I like it."

"All right then. Meet me in the park in 15 minutes?"

"See you then."

As Zoey hung up the phone she looked down at her outfit. *Hmmm. Now I've given myself the challenge of what to wear on a casual date. It shouldn't be that difficult. I bet boys don't worry about these things. Ugh. Great idea, Zoey.*

After settling on a plain fitted shirt and ripped jeans, Zoey walked downstairs and grabbed her leather jacket out of the closet.

"I'm going for a walk," she called to her parents before closing the door. She stepped out into the cold night air, her breath a foggy cloud in front of her. Trying to blow smoke rings, she turned toward the park.

As she came closer to the playground, she saw Tristan leaning against "their tree." She thought that had a nice ring to it, until she noticed the two men standing on the other side of him. *Geez. Tristan can't go anywhere without being noticed!* Zoey paused, wondering whether or not to walk over to him, until the two men shook his hand and turned to walk away in the other direction. Tristan twisted back toward her and caught her eye. Beaming at the sight of her, he stood up straight.

Ok, I guess that's my answer, she thought. She made her way over to him.

"Funny meeting you here."

"Hey, stranger. Long time no see."

Zoey turned and began walking. Tristan joined her.

"So, were you talking to someone else just now? It seemed like there was someone else with you," Zoey mentioned tentatively.

"What? Oh yeah. It was a couple guys I knew from this band back in the day. So, I guess this is the part where we get to know each other, huh?"

Zoey tried not to frown at his vague answer, followed by the change in topic. *Come on, it's no big deal that he didn't want to introduce you. You guys aren't even serious yet.*

"Uh, yeah, I guess so. I hope you can handle it."

"Bring it on."

"Ok. First question. What's your favorite color?"

Tristan stopped to look at Zoey.

"Seriously? This is the frightening interrogation I'm supposed to have trouble with?"

Zoey grinned mischievously.

"I'm just buttering you up, lulling you into a false sense of security."

"Oh, I see. Of course," he said, walking forward again. "Sorry to have questioned your methods. Blue."

"Huh. I thought you would've said black. That's mine."

"Well, I hope you won't hold it against me."

"No, it's ok to be wrong sometimes."

Tristan raised his eyebrows.

"How is my favorite color wrong?"

"Ever seen Monty Python's Holy Grail?"

Tristan laughed.

"Hmmm. Good call. Ok, what else?"

"Favorite movie?"

"Oh, see, that's a tough one. I have favorite movies for all different genres."

"Seriously? Like what?"

"Well, like the first Die Hard for action," he explained. "For sci-fi, I like the original Star Wars trilogy. Fantasy is Lord of the Rings. Fight Club for, well, a psycho-drama I guess. Classic kung fu would be Legend of the Drunken Master. Old School for comedy. And House of a Thousand Corpses for horror."

"That's quite the list."

"What've you got?"

"Pulp Fiction."

"A classic. Cool," he nodded. "Are we gonna talk about my favorite food now? Where I would go on my dream vacation?"

"Nope. Now the real torture begins. Let's move on to family. What do your parents do?"

"My mom's a doctor and my dad's a philosophy professor."

"That's an interesting pairing."

"Interesting doesn't even begin to describe it," Tristan groaned, rolling his eyes. "You should hear them sometimes, my mom lecturing on the benefits of some new scientific discovery, while my dad argues its harmful social ramifications. I don't know how they possibly got together."

"It's better than the conversations my parents have. Although, now that I think about it, they don't have a lot of conversations. My mother covers both the pros and cons of something while my father sits there and thinks about his next book."

"Your dad's an author?"

"Yeah, mystery novels."

"That's cool. At least your dad publishes things people read. I don't think anyone reads my dad's papers."

"Not even your mom?" Zoey asked jokingly. "Or you? Or your siblings?"

Zoey expected a simple yes or no answer, but Tristan didn't say anything. He looked away from Zoey and into the distance ahead of them. She felt a knot begin to form in her stomach. The conversation had been seamless until that last question, which obviously made Tristan uncomfortable. They continued walking in silence.

After a few minutes of listening to the frozen grass crunching under their feet, the growing tension became too much for Zoey.

"Um, I was just kidding before," she said nervously.

Tristan stopped walking and turned to face her.

"It's just me," he replied softly. "I had a twin sister. She was killed almost five years ago."

Zoey gasped as she stared back at him. This was not the kind of conversation she was expecting, nor did she feel ready for it. She hadn't planned on delving into the past; that was a subject usually left for months into the relationship. But she had no choice now. She was immediately sent back to just after Laura's death, when everyone around her fumbled to say something, anything, that was even slightly comforting. Her mind was reeling.

"Oh my god, Tristan, I'm so sorry. I feel so stupid."

"It's ok. You didn't know."

"I, uh…" Zoey felt herself begin to stutter. She had to say something else. "My best friend was killed eight months ago."

Oh god. I can't believe I blurted that out, especially right after he told me about his sister!

"Jesus, I'm sorry again. I don't know what the hell is wrong with me."

Tristan scanned the park, looking for something. He nodded towards a bench at the edge of the grass, and Zoey followed him over to it, sitting down next to him. Tristan looked up at the stars, while Zoey looked down at the ground, uncertain of what to do next. Neither one of them spoke.

Finally, Tristan sighed.

"What happened to your friend?"

Zoey looked up at him. His head was tilted towards her curiously. She took a deep breath.

"We were driving somewhere, me behind the wheel and Laura in the passenger's seat," she began. "We were stopped at a red light, and when it turned green I started to go. It wasn't until the last second that I saw the truck. A drunk driver ran the red light and hit us from the right. They said she died instantly."

"I'm sorry. How long were you friends?"

"Since first grade."

"Wow. That must've been awful."

"The most terrifying moment of my life," she said, fighting back tears. "There was nothing I could do."

Tristan nodded. "I know what you mean."

"Were you there when your sister died?"

"Yeah," he said. "Her name was Chastity. We were 15. I convinced her to ditch school to go into the city with me. She was reluctant at first, but I told her nothing bad would happen as long as we stuck together. We were inseparable. She trusted me. So we took the train in and wandered around, looking up at all the tall buildings and making fun of all the crazy outfits and people we saw on the street.

"At one point we went into this convenience store to get drinks. While we were in the back, a guy came in with a gun and pointed it at the cashier. He said no one would get hurt as long as he got the money. So the cashier opened the drawer and started giving him the cash, when the robber asked about a safe. I thought he was distracted enough, so I grabbed Chastity's arm and tried to lead her quietly towards the door. But I accidentally knocked a box onto the floor with my arm. We froze, but the guy turned around and shot at us in surprise."

Tristan paused. Zoey could see him struggling to control his anger as he remembered the rest of the story. She knew how difficult it was to recall something so horrible without reliving it. She waited patiently for him to continue.

"It was my fault," he said, his voice breaking slightly. "But the bullet hit Chastity in the chest and she fell backwards onto the floor. That's when the guy freaked out and took off with the money. I yelled for someone to call 911, and I grabbed some paper towels to try and stop the bleeding. I told her she was okay, that everything would be okay. But there was too much blood. She took my hand, looked into my eyes, and said, 'It was a good day, Tristan.' She died in my arms.'"

Zoey had never known anyone else with such a tragic story. It used to be something she only saw or read in the news. She knew that if she had met Tristan earlier, she wouldn't have known what to say. But she knew now. She reached over and took Tristan's hand.

"There's no way to get over something like that, no matter what anyone tells you," she said softly. "Your life is changed forever."

Tristan looked at Zoey, looked into her eyes, as if only now realizing who she was. Without any hesitation, he reached behind her neck, leaned over and kissed her.

The feeling behind his kiss was one of recognition, as if he had finally found someone who understood his pain. His reaction took Zoey by surprise, but she found herself settling into the safety of his embrace. The moment wasn't what she imagined at all- it was better.

After a minute, Tristan pulled back, his arms still around her.

"You truly believe," he whispered, sounding almost hopeful.

"What?" Zoey asked, trying to regain her composure. Tristan let go of her and reached for her hand, squeezing it firmly.

"You believe it's not possible to recover from something like that, that we shouldn't recover. No matter what you do, nothing can ever bring them back to us. We're all just helpless animals in the universe, with no say over our own lives."

"It's a terrible feeling."

"But it's more than that," he persisted, standing up suddenly. "To realize you have no control over your own life, your own happiness, to know there's no permanence to the people around you, it's excruciating. And as humans we have this terrible ability to comprehend the horror without knowing the reason why it has to be that way."

Zoey studied his profile in the moonlight. She could see his frustration tightening every muscle in his body. *Wow, I've never seen this much anger over death before,* Zoey thought. *Hell, the people I know don't even talk about it. That's why it's been so difficult to deal with Laura's death. He must feel the same way about Chastity.*

Standing up, Zoey moved closer to him and carefully took his hand. She recognized the pain on his face all too well.

"I'm so sorry, Tristan. I wish there was more I could say."

Her words seemed to shake him out of his trance. He shook his head.

"No, I'm sorry. I get so wrapped up in my own head sometimes."

"It's okay. Everyone does."

Tristan gestured for them to start walking again, and Zoey took her place beside him. As they continued across the park, she began to realize how close they had become after only two dates. She hadn't planned on discussing such intimate details of her life, or learning such details about his life. She wondered how much more there was under the surface.

Glancing over at her, Tristan cleared his throat.

"So, did you take a break from school because of what happened with Laura?"

For the first time, Zoey was confident to answer that question without fear of judgment.

"Yeah. We had this daily routine that I just couldn't continue without her."

"I know what you mean."

"Was it hard for you to go away to college?"

"Well, I had never been out on my own before, so that was pretty tough. My parents were really worried that I would zone out or distance myself from them, so they threw a lot of money at me to get me through school," he began. "But I was 16, ya know? And all I had was an advisor looking out for me, along with the dorm's RA. So I kinda went crazy. I partied a lot with the so-called 'wrong crowd', tried a lot of drugs, drank. But in the end it didn't change anything. I realized I'd always be devastated."

"Wow."

"Yeah, it was pretty intense. And now I'm just here."

Zoey didn't know how to respond. It was yet another side of Tristan she had not expected, and she knew nothing about living that kind of lifestyle. It seemed to be behind him now, but it made her feel even younger than she already was. Tristan stopped and brushed her hair behind her ear.

"Is something wrong?"

"No," Zoey answered quickly. "It's just, I've never been through what you've been through. I've never lived anywhere else, and I've only had two years of community college. It's kind of a lot to process on a second date."

Tristan walked in front of Zoey and turned around to face her, kissing her gently.

"I wasn't planning on talking about any of these things either," he said, taking her hand again. "But I'm glad we did. We share something that I've never had with anyone else. You know how I feel about Chastity, and we can talk about Laura. We can help each other."

After everything that had been revealed in their conversation, Zoey knew she could trust him. It felt good to have that kind of trust with someone again, someone who wasn't paid to have it, like Dr. Stephens. She nodded.

"I'd like that."

"My new partner in crime."

CHAPTER THIRTY-NINE

I can't believe it's only two weeks until Christmas. Time really does go by faster as you get older. I should get started on my Christmas shopping at some point. I wonder what horrible marketing fads Brad and Karen are into these days? I'm so out of the loop.

Deirdre sat at her desk in the living room, staring at the Google home page. She went back and forth between looking up teenage chat sites and ideas for gifts. While Christmas was always one of the few fun holidays with her family, it also reminded her of a celebration she would never have at her own home. She and Ben had always talked about combining the traditions of both of their families into their own holiday tradition with their kids. The memory caused a lump to rise up in her throat, and Deirdre stood up to get a glass of water. Sitting back down, she set the glass next to the computer and took a deep breath.

Back to work.

Deirdre began entering various key words until she found the kinds of sites she was looking for. Some of the names seemed like something out a B 80s movie, such as "Teen Dish" or "Let's Hang". Being in her late twenties, she couldn't help but feel a bit like a child stalker.

Oh Jesus, Deirdre, it's not like you're looking for a relationship with one of these kids! You'll be telling them outright that you're a reporter, which will directly imply that you're older. Of course, at that point they may not want to talk to you anymore.

God, has it really been that long since I was a teenager? I can't believe it's already time for my ten-year high school reunion.

Just wait until it's your 20th. Or your 50th. Oh, God.

Shaking her head, Deirdre tried to concentrate on the task at hand. She clicked on the first link, simply titled "Teen Chat".

It's been years since I've been on one of these things. I usually only IM with my friends. I think in this case I'll need a more clever IM name than dhart28.

Before she could chat, Deirdre had to set up a free account. After typing her actual name she came to the blank line for her chat name. Deirdre thought for a moment and smiled.

"hartonhersleeve"

She hit the Enter key and a new page came up with lists of chat names already involved in conversations. There was an open chat forum where everyone could see what was being written, as well as private chats between two users. Deirdre decided to start with the open forum.

hannahsux: that movie was way too emo for me.

Lautnerlover: shut up! that movie f'n kicked ass!

hannahsux: wtf? vampires and werewolves and moody chicks, oh my! like we've never seen that before!

Lautnerlover: you so don't get forbidden love.

hannahsux: boring!

Deirdre recognized the references to the Twilight series, but not having read the books or seen the movies, she decided to try another conversation.

Maybe one where kids are talking about reality. Not that I haven't had my share of conversations about what movie Brad Pitt looks hottest in, but I don't think I'm up-to-date on who the new Brad Pitt is.

jdk16holla: it sucked! he tried to sext me last night when we were eating and my mom grabbed the phone and saw it!

poprincess: OMG. what did she do?

jdk16holla: she took my phone and my laptop. can you believe it? i'm at the library right now. it's so embarrassing!

poprincess: more embarrassing than your mom reading your sexts?

jdk16holla: LOL! ok maybe not!

livinlarge: you can sext me anytime holla!

jdk16holla: I ain't no holla back girl!

livinlarge: yeah you are. it says it in your name!

Wow. They're actually talking about sexting. Did Haley call that one! I am definitely not telling her about this! I think this might be out of my league anyway. I can't just drop myself into their conversation. Damn. This is going to be harder than I thought.

All of a sudden a small box appeared on the screen. Deirdre realized someone had clicked on her name from the list of those online for a private chat. The name read socalbro1.

socalbro1: hey what up?

hartonhersleeve: Hi.

socalbro1: never seen you here before.

hartonhersleeve: It's my first time.

socalbro1: a virgin? nice!

Deirdre shook her head. *I can't believe I wrote that! I'm such a dork.*

hartonhersleeve: Ha ha. Yeah, guess so.

socalbro1: don't worry, I'll go easy on ya.

hartonhersleeve: Uh, thanks.

socalbro1: so how old are you?

Damn. I was hoping I wouldn't get that question until much later.

hartonhersleeve: Well, actually, I'm in my 20s. I'm a reporter and I wanted to chat with some teens about an article I'm doing.

socalbro1: wtf? your not supposed to be on here.

hartonhersleeve: I know, I just wanted to talk to some kids upfront about this thing I'm writing about youth violence.

socalbro1: dude that is messed up.

Shit. I was afraid this would happen.

Before Deirdre could finish typing her response, she saw socalbro1 post a general message to everyone in the room.

socalbro1: hey, don't talk to hartonhersleeve. she's not a teen, she's a reporter writing about youth violence or somethin.

livinlarge: serious dude? someone should report her.

Great.

hartonhersleeve: It's ok. I'm leaving now. Sorry to have disrupted your chats about sexting and vampire movies.

But before Deirdre logged out, another individual box came up on her screen. The name read angelandme.

angelandme: what are you writing about youth violence?

hartonhersleeve: Well, I'm focusing specifically on teenage suicide shooters.

angelandme: wow, heavy topic.

hartonhersleeve: Totally. What I wanted to do here was talk to some actual teenagers about their lives and what they think about or worry about. Then maybe I could get some insight into what today's kids are dealing with.

angelandme: you should read blogs then. kids say a lot more on those than they do here.

hartonhersleeve: Do you have any suggestions?

angelandme: sure. i'll paste a couple links for you.

hartonhersleeve: That would be great. Thank you so much.

angelandme: no prob. it would be nice to see some real representation instead of older people assuming they know how teens think and act.

hartonhersleeve: I'll do my best to represent. ☺

angelandme: LOL. nice. see ya

Deirdre copied and pasted the three links sent to her onto a blank page so she could continuously reference them whenever she wanted. She then logged off of the chat room to avoid any further problems.

I've never felt so old in my life. Nina and Haley were right.

She pasted the first web site into the address bar and hit Enter. A black page came up with red and white lettering, along with symbols and CD covers from various metal bands on the sides. The blog was titled "Teenage Wasteland."

Huh. Nice reference to The Who. I'm surprised. That band isn't really modern. Maybe they just heard the phrase somewhere. The song Baba O'Riley was pretty mainstream after the movie American Beauty came out in the 90s. That's the first time I heard it.

Scanning the page, Deirdre saw lyrics from bands such as Type O Negative, Korn, and Mudvayne. This one she recognized from the song "Closer" by Nine Inch Nails:

You can have my isolation
You can have the hate that it brings
You can have my absence of faith
You can have my everything.

Deirdre recognized a number of the bands, but she needed more than merely pages of lyrics. She wanted to read what kids today thought of those lyrics, thought about life, and where they fit into it. She copied the second web address and hit Enter.

The second blog wasn't as heavily decorated with art as the first one, but it seemed to have more variety to its content. There were some song lyrics, mostly from girl bands, but the majority of posts seemed to be written by someone known as "that girl you used to know."

"I woke up today and the sun was blinding. Can there be too much sunshine? These days it seems like there's not enough, even though I wake up to it all the time. How did I get so jaded that even things like sunshine hurt? I know it's another beautiful day but I can't feel it. Can't feel the warmth on my skin or the cool breeze through my hair or the light rain on my face. Nothing feels the same anymore. Even me."

Deirdre scrolled down the page.

"Another kid got shot outside school today. I skipped last period so I didn't see it, but some of my friends heard the shots and went running for cover. I didn't know the kid, but the guy who shot him obviously did. They must've been on opposite sides or something since they wore rival colors. His red bandana matched his blood spilled all over the sidewalk. I hope he was ready to die for the cause, whatever it was. I hope he knew what it was."

Wow. This was the first time Deirdre thought about gangs and their impact on teenagers. She hadn't thought about anything except the typical social cliques. This was a more severe kind of teen violence. She made a mental note to research gang violence in schools, and continued to read down the page.

"I was invisible today. He walked right by me and our arms almost touched. But that's the closest I'll ever get to being with him. No one wants to be with someone invisible. How can they ever think you matter if you don't?"

Deirdre sat back in her chair and sighed. She wished she could write to this person and tell them that it would get better as they got older, that things would get easier.

Unfortunately, it isn't true. We spend so much of our childhood trying to grow up, and the rest of our adulthood trying to find what it was we used to enjoy. Is there ever anything we used to enjoy?

Looking at the third web address, Deirdre hesitated. She thought reading teenage blogs would bring her back to her days in high school with nostalgia. Instead, it reminded her of how much anxiety she continued to cope with as an adult. She shook her head and entered the last address.

The third site came up with the title "Two Become One," with the author's name listed as "melancholyteen". Again, it seemed to be individual entries, although this one included some poetry as well. It was nothing Deirdre recognized, although the Internet search engines might prove otherwise. She began to read the latest entry.

I entered, crying, screaming,
knowing nothing but thrust into everything.
The world's chaos came crashing down
until you took my hand.
And all was calm.

We faced the world as boundless forces,
blind to any fear or flaw.
And time and space would bend for us
to hasten us away.

But life knew not the bond we forged
and one day ripped the cord.
I turned to catch your falling grace
and lost mine in return.

So by myself I was again
and crying just the same
for now my light had turned to grey
and in its place, a darkened hole.

Was this to be my fate I feared-
To wander deep in woods so cold?
Oh no, said Fate, continue on,
for she will come again.

You must believe her soul's at rest,
but not her place with you,
another will be soon along
to bring the circle full.

And I have found her, shining through,
I see her now in you.
My light burns bright again, my love,
your life and mine always entwined.

And all is calm again.

Deirdre sat back in her chair, pondering the meaning of the poem. She had assumed the title meant two people making love, but the poem seemed to indicate that a lost love had caused the author to become one. It was certainly different from the other two blogs.

Along the side of the page, Deirdre noticed links to other blog web sites, and decided to bookmark the page so she could return to it. Looking more closely at the poem, she noticed a place where people could write comments on the entry. She thought for a moment and clicked on it.

"Very intriguing imagery," she wrote. "I truly felt it."

CHAPTER FORTY

Zoey woke up Christmas morning to her favorite scene- a bright sky and snowy ground. She could hear the sizzling breakfast her father cooked every year on one of the few days he took off from writing. Classic Christmas songs sung by 1960s artists spun on the record player- still the only way her mother listened to music. And the pine smell from the tree they decorated the night before hung light in the air as a gentle reminder that presents sat underneath it, ready to be opened.

All of the traditions were in place save one. There would be no morning call from Laura, wishing her a happy Pagan winter solstice. It was one of their private jokes, after a night of Googling revealed that Jesus wasn't born on December 25th, and Christmas Day corresponded with the Pagan winter solstice. It was a tradition she couldn't carry on with anyone else.

"Happy Pagan winter solstice," she whispered, looking out the window.

"Zoey! Are you up? Breakfast's almost ready!" Connie yelled from downstairs. Zoey wiped the single tear that fell down her cheek.

"Coming!"

Making her way downstairs, Zoey could see the smoke from the bacon floating out of the kitchen towards the smoke detector. Hardly a year went by when it didn't go off, and she wondered if her mom didn't take out the battery because it was a part of the tradition as well. She waved her hands above her head and opened the front door to let out some of the smoke.

"Hey Dad, are you cooking breakfast or preparing us for a fire drill?"

"Nothing like killing two birds with one stone," he called back to her.

"Zoey, my goodness, close the door!" Connie exclaimed, walking into the hallway. "It's freezing out there!"

Zoey shut the door and walked into the kitchen, snagging a piece of bacon from the plate on the stove.

"Hey, careful there, that's hot," Walter said, flipping over the pieces in the pan. He moved over to the eggs, scooping them onto another plate.

"Honey, can you check on the toast?"

While Zoey waited for the toast to pop up, Connie set the dining room table. It was the one time all year they sat down to eat with no TV. Since it was part of the tradition, Zoey didn't mind it one day out of the year.

"Ok, Connie, I think we can start bringing some stuff in!"

Zoey and Connie grabbed the plates of food and set everything out on the table, while Walter put his cooking utensils in the dishwasher. Zoey sat down and eagerly awaited her favorite tradition of the day- her father's toast.

"Clean-up is done!" he announced. As he sat down he grabbed his coffee mug, looked at the two women in his life, and raised his arm.

"Let us all raise our glasses to another successful Christmas breakfast, and the hope of many more."

"Happy Birthday!" they replied in unison, clinking their glasses together. It was the second part of the toast, which had become tradition ever since Zoey, age 5, called that out after watching *Frosty the Snowman*.

"Good toast, Dad," Zoey said, setting him up for their usual Christmas joke.

"Thanks, but I can't take the credit. The toaster did all the work."

"Every year? Really?"

"It's tradition, Mom. You love tradition!"

"Sure," Connie said, rolling her eyes. Zoey grinned at her mother, which caused Connie to return the expression. It had been a long time since she had seen Zoey display an honest sense of joy.

The conversation fell into a lull as the three of them ate to the sound of silverware scraping their plates and Nat King Cole in the background. Zoey stopped to look around her, taking in every moment of her favorite holiday. Her family didn't celebrate any other holiday- even for Thanksgiving they ate at a restaurant. But this one, they reveled in the tradition.

"It's nice to have one day to remind us of how every day should be," her mother always said.

"Except no one wants to put that amount of effort into every day," Zoey would reply.

"Well, that's why it's only one day," her father would add, completing the sentiment.

Once everyone finished their breakfast it was time to move into the living room for gifts. Connie took down each of their stockings and placed them on the couch. Even though Zoey couldn't stand to hold a conversation with Connie for more than a few minutes at a time, she had to admit her mother bought perfect gifts.

"All right, iTunes gift card! Thanks, Mom."

"Honey, how did you know I wanted this software?" Walter asked, holding up a computer package.

"Are you kidding? I hear you grumbling in your office all the time about how your current writing program sucks."

"What did you get, Mom?"

"I got some very delicious and horribly bad for you chocolates."

"Those are the best kind."

"I wouldn't have it any other way."

After the stockings they moved onto the few presents under the tree. As Zoey was about to open her last one her cell phone on the table rang.

"I'll be right back," she said, standing up to grab the phone. "Hello?"

"Hey, merry not Jesus's birthday," said Tristan. A chill went down Zoey's spine.

Close enough.

"Happy Pagan holiday to you," she smiled. Connie looked over at her quizzically as she walked out of the room.

"I hope I'm not interrupting some big family holiday thing."

"Nah, we just finished opening presents. We don't go anywhere on Christmas, since my dad takes the day off from writing. We basically hang out here and watch Christmas specials."

"Huh, that actually sounds pretty cool, right up to the part about the TV specials."

"That's because you don't know how we watch them. We spend the whole time making fun of them."

"Oh, now I get it! Okay, that does sound kinda fun!"

As Zoey continued her conversation in the hallway, Connie strained to hear what they were saying.

"Honey, what are you doing?" Walter asked, looking over at her.

"Eavesdropping, of course."

"And you wonder why Zoey has trust issues."

"Oh hush."

"You know, you could just ask her about him."

"Yes. I could also get a root canal. Which one do you think would give me better results?"

Walter chuckled.

"Okay, point taken."

Suddenly Connie stood up from the couch and walked over to Zoey in the hallway.

"Honey," she whispered. "Invite Tristan over for dinner!"

Zoey placed her hand over the phone, mortified.

"What? No, Mom!" she whispered back.

"Yes! He's your boyfriend and we want to meet him."

This time it was Walter's turn to strain to hear what his wife was saying to his daughter.

"Mom, not now!"

"Why not now? This is the perfect time!"

"No!"

"Uh, Zoey, is there something going on I should know about?" Tristan asked.

"What? Oh, no, it's nothing," she replied, taking her hand off of the phone.

"Tristan, we would love to have you over for dinner some time!" Connie yelled in the background.

Oh my god. She needs a mute button!

"I assume that was your mom?" Tristan chuckled.

"Unfortunately, yes."

"Ok, I never say no to a free meal. Assuming it is free."

"Trust me, you always pay a price around here," Zoey muttered.

"Honey, that's terrible!"

"All right, Mom, he said he'll come over. You can go back to eavesdropping from a farther distance now!"

"Thank you," she said, as she turned around to go back into the living room.

"Sorry about that," Zoey sighed.

"No problem. So, about this not-so-free meal. When should I come over?"

CHAPTER FORTY-ONE

Oh man, Tristan's gonna be here any minute. I have a feeling today will be my very first lesson in humility.

Zoey sat in front of her mirror brushing her hair for the twelfth time that day. She had changed outfits three times and moved things around her bedroom twice in case they ended up there. If she couldn't control her parents' behavior, she could at least control the appearance of herself and her environment.

It's something.

"Zoey! Can you come down and help me set the table?"

What? We're eating at the dining room table? We never eat there! Now we'll be forced to have a detailed conversation without TV to save me! This is so gonna suck!

Zoey came bounding down the stairs just in time to see Connie emerge from the kitchen in a striped linen dress. She wrinkled her forehead, trying to decipher the image her mother was attempting to portray.

"Uh, Mom? Have you been watching 'Leave it to Beaver' reruns again?"

"What are you talking about?"

"What am I... uh, how about that linen tablecloth you're wearing?"

"You don't like it?"

"I've never seen you wear it before."

"That's because it's new," Connie beamed, smoothing out the front of it. "I haven't gone out and bought a new dress in years."

"That's pretty obvious," Zoey muttered.

"What, honey?"

"Uh, nothing. You didn't have to do that just because Tristan's coming over. In fact, I think it might be kind of, um, intimidating for him," Zoey said, trying to find any excuse to get her mother to change. "I told him this was a casual dinner, and if you're all dressed up he might feel underdressed."

"You really think he'll be uncomfortable?"

"Yes, Mom, terribly so," Zoey persisted. "Please, will you change into your normal, I mean, casual clothes? I think we'll all be way more comfortable."

Connie frowned, looking down at her new ensemble. Zoey noticed her disappointment.

"Another time, Mom, okay? Please?"

"All right. I'll put on something else. In the meantime can you finish setting the table?"

"Yes. Absolutely." *Anything to get you to change!*

Zoey breathed a sigh of relief as Connie turned to walk up the stairs. Once her mother disappeared, she took a quick look around the downstairs to make sure everything was clean, and walked into the dining room. After she finished the place settings, she turned toward her father's office. *Now to find Dad to make sure he doesn't look like a dork.*

Before she could take another step the doorbell rang.

Great. I guess I'll just have to have faith in my father's ability to dress himself properly for the occasion. Taking a deep breath, Zoey walked over and opened the door.

"Hi," said Tristan, holding out two bouquets of flowers. "One is for you and the other is for your mom."

"Wow, trying to score points already, huh?"

"You know it. I told you I was good with parents."

"Dude, my mom's gonna see right through that."

"Oh, is this Tristan?" Connie asked as if on cue. Zoey turned to see her mother wearing a flower-print skirt and white blouse. *Apparently she's become Donna Reed now. Oh well. It's better than the full-size apron.*

"Hi, Mrs. Young. It's nice to meet you. I brought you some flowers for a centerpiece."

"What a wonderful gift! Thank you so much!" Connie exclaimed. Tristan glanced back over his shoulder and winked at Zoey. She shook her head, trying to suppress a laugh as she took his jacket.

"Uh oh. Who is this young man giving flowers to my wife?" Walter asked, entering the hallway. Zoey was relieved to see he was wearing simple khakis and a plain blue button down shirt.

"You must be Mr. Young. It's nice to meet you, sir."

Wow, he does have this parent thing down, Zoey thought.

"Same to you, Tristan. Welcome to our humble abode."

"Dinner will be ready in a minute. I'm just going to put these beautiful flowers in some water," Connie said, beaming.

"Well played, son."

"Uh, thank you."

"I think I'm gonna give Tristan a tour of the house," Zoey interrupted.

"Good idea, honey. We'll call you when dinner's ready."

Zoey grabbed Tristan's arm and led him into the living room, out of earshot to her parents.

"Sorry about that. I wish I could say it'll get better, but it won't."

"What are you talking about? Your parents are fine."

"Yeah, well, we'll see if you still think that when you leave."

Tristan glanced around the living room, eyeing the various picture frames hanging on the wall. One set of photographs looked to be taken on a family trip at an amusement park, while others depicted the Young's wedding. He noticed there were no recent family pictures.

Walking over to one of the vacation pictures, Tristan asked how old Zoey was in the photo.

"I think I was ten."

"Ten, huh? Have you not taken any more family trips since then?"

"Well, we've gone on short weekend trips here and there, but nothing like that one. That one was two weeks traveling all over New England."

"That sounds cool."

"Yeah," Zoey said, looking over the collection of pictures from the trip. "That was back when I could stand to be with my parents for two weeks straight."

"Sometimes I think that's the only reason I can still talk to my parents, having been away at school."

"That does sound nice."

"Ah, you won't be living with your parents forever."

"It sure feels that way sometimes!"

At that moment, Connie called out for them to join her and Walter in the dining room. Zoey tried not to show her growing trepidation as Tristan turned toward the sound of her mother's voice.

"Short tour."

"It'll give us a good excuse to leave the dinner table," Zoey replied.

She led him into the dining room where Connie set down the chicken and pasta dish she had prepared. Walter took his place at the head of the table and gestured for Tristan to sit down on his right. Zoey took the chair across from Tristan as Connie settled into the fourth chair at the other end of the table.

"A toast," Walter said, picking up his glass. The other three joined him. "To meeting new friends."

"To meeting new friends!" Zoey and Connie repeated. Tristan grinned as he clinked his glass with everyone else's.

"That's cool. My parents just sit down and start eating. I don't think they've ever toasted a dinner, even one for a formal event."

"Walter has always been big on toasts," Connie said, passing the plate of chicken around the table. "It's been a tradition in his family forever."

"We used to be fairly close when we all lived near each other. We would all get together for the holidays at my parents' house," Walter said. "But then my parents passed away and my sister and her family moved to the west coast for her job. So the tradition sort of faded, as did the relationship with some of my older cousins unfortunately."

"What about your family, Mrs. Young?"

"My parents have also passed on, both from lung cancer," Connie replied. "Goodness, they smoked like chimneys. Anyway, I'm an only child, and we were never really close with my mom's side of the family. We would see my father's siblings occasionally when they were in the area, but you know how it is. Everyone has their own traditions to keep up with, which makes it difficult to get everyone together. What about you, Tristan? Are you close with your family?"

Zoey cringed. She wasn't expecting to come across the topic of his family situation so soon.

"I am fairly close with my parents," he answered. "But my sister passed away almost five years ago."

"Oh my, I'm so sorry to hear that," Connie gasped, touching her chest. "That's terrible."

"It was," Tristan said quietly. "For a couple years after that we didn't see my relatives very much for the holidays. But now my parents are getting back into the old traditions, and we have most of our extended family over for Thanksgiving and Christmas."

"A close family can certainly help in times of tragedy," Walter acknowledged.

"Oh yes. I've always wished we were closer with our cousins. Nothing is more important than family," Connie said. "That's why we're so happy to introduce you to ours."

"Dad, can you please pass the pasta?" Zoey asked, trying to break up the sappy conversation she felt was unfolding.

"Here you go, kiddo."

"So, Tristan, are you in school right now?" Connie asked, picking up on Zoey's desire to change topics.

"Actually, I recently graduated with my bachelor's degree in Sociology."

"Sociology? That sounds interesting," Walter said. "Do you have any future plans for that yet?"

"Not exactly. My parents agreed I could take some time off for a short break."

"We're hoping Zoey decides to go back to school soon," Connie said.

"Mom!"

"What? An education is very important," she insisted. "I'm sure Tristan can tell you that. Right, Tristan?"

"Don't put him in the middle of this!"

"Zoey, your mother is only trying to include our guest in the conversation."

"He was already a part of the conversation," Zoey replied through clenched teeth.

"I do think education is important," Tristan said quickly. "But I also think you have to be ready for it. College can be pretty demanding, and if you're not in the right frame of mind you might as well not even be there."

Zoey tried not to smirk as she looked down at her plate. *Of course he would know the perfect thing to say.*

"I agree with that, of course," Connie said. "It's just that Zoey was already involved in college, with a scholarship to boot. They don't hand those out willy-nilly."

"That's true," Tristan said. "But taking this route, Zoey can go back whenever she feels she can give it her all again. If she's distracted then she's just wasting the money."

Walter grunted. Connie saw Zoey glare at him.

"Well, we'll just have to see what the future holds," she said. Zoey turned back to her food.

"So, uh, Mr. Young, Zoey told me you're working on another book? Is it with Detective Teller again?"

A wave of relief washed over Zoey as Tristan turned the attention away from her and toward her father's work instead. His eyes lit up slightly.

"Why, yes, it does involve him," he answered. "But I've got a twist to this one, because it doesn't solely feature him. I brought in another detective, a woman, who I introduced a couple of years ago. They worked on a case for the government together, and I hinted at a romantic connection by the end of the book. Now I'm bringing her back to explore that idea."

"Sounds like a great gimmick," Tristan said.

"I think so."

As Walter continued to discuss his new ideas, Zoey glanced over at Tristan. He was turned toward her father, listening intently as if he actually cared about the book. *He is good,* she thought. She began to relax as the conversation turned to more casual topics of what made good literature.

Once they finished eating, Zoey offered to bring Tristan's plate into the kitchen. Connie stood up to help her clear the dishes.

"Do you need any help with the clean-up, Mrs. Young?" Tristan asked.

"Oh no, you're a guest. You stay right there."

The two of them walked into the kitchen and began to rinse off the plates. Walter leaned forward in his chair, realizing he had the perfect opportunity to talk to Tristan about his intentions with Zoey.

"So, Tristan, you're taking a break from school right now. But I assume you'll be looking for a job in the near future?"

"I'll have to do something, yeah," Tristan answered simply. Walter shifted in his seat and waited for a more complete answer. When Tristan didn't offer one, he searched for a follow-up.

"Something? Like what exactly?"

"Well, I haven't quite decided what that is yet. I still have some decisions to make. But I think Zoey and I are going through some similar things right now, which is why I really like spending time with her."

Hearing the last statement made Walter relax a bit. *Things seem to be going well between them. That's good. I like this kid. He's polite and respectful. I know he isn't working yet, but he seems like a bright guy. Reminds me of me when I got out of college.*

"Well, I'm glad you two are taking the time to get to know each other," he nodded in response. "Zoey hasn't made up her mind on her career path, but we hope at some point she finishes her English degree. I know she's constantly writing on her blog. Have you seen it yet?"

"I've read some it," Tristan replied. "It's pretty good. Who knows, Mr. Young. She may follow in your footsteps."

Walter beamed at the thought.

A minute later Zoey emerged from the kitchen nervously, hoping her father wasn't embarrassing her in any way. She was relieved to hear the conversation had returned to the topic of writing.

"Ok, Dad, Mom said we could be excused," she interrupted, taking Tristan's hand. Walter nodded toward Tristan and stood up to join Connie in the kitchen. Zoey led him up the stairs to her room and closed the door behind her. He sat down on the bed, taking off his shoes.

"That was relatively painless."

"Hold still a second," Zoey said, walking over to him and raising her hand. "You've got a little something brown on your nose."

Tristan laughed as he playfully swatted her hand away from his face.

"Hey. That's how you win over parents! It's called being polite."

"Uh huh. You wanna ask my mom out dancing too? Maybe go to a poetry reading with my dad?"

Tristan reached over and grabbed Zoey's arm, pulling her onto the bed next to him.

"I'd like to do something with you."

Before Zoey could ask him about his discussion with her father, Tristan leaned down and kissed her. She put her arms around his neck and settled into his embrace as he positioned himself on top of her. She forgot all about the awkward dinner conversation as the kiss deepened. Tristan pulled back and looked down at Zoey in admiration.

"I'm glad I got the chance to come over tonight. I feel like I'm more a part of your life now, you know?"

Zoey nodded as Tristan laid back down next to her.

"So you realize now that I've met your parents, my parents are gonna want to have you over too?"

"Yeah, I figured that would be the case."

"Well, my parents want to be even dorkier than yours. They want to have you over for New Year's Eve."

"Seriously? Wow," Zoey said, propping herself up on the bed. "That does trump my parents' dorkiness."

"So you'll be there then? If for nothing else then to experience something worse than dinner with your parents?"

Zoey smiled at the thought of becoming more involved in Tristan's life. She had been afraid her parents' invitation was too early in their relationship, but Tristan's visit proved otherwise. He seemed perfectly at ease, in her home and with her parents, without any hesitation at the rate which their relationship was growing. And now he wanted to bring her further into his world, without the slightest hint of uncertainty. It was finally happening.

"I guess it's only fair," she replied, her heart beginning to beat more rapidly. Her answer was sealed with a kiss.

CHAPTER FORTY-TWO

"Thank you for your time, Senator."

Deirdre hung up the phone after yet another unsatisfying interview. *God, I'm so bored writing this story. No one's gonna care about this. Of course, I can't say that to Neil. He'll just give me the editor's response that it's my job to make it interesting.*

Deirdre threw her notebook and pen onto her desk and sat back in her chair. She looked around the room at all of the other reporters busily making phone calls and typing up their notes into articles. Neil sat in his office, clearly arguing with someone on the phone.

I should be writing this political article right now. It's due in two days. But it won't take up too much time if I check out one or two blogs. It's not like I have any other interviews to do. I just need a break. Besides, I do have to write this column at some point. The more research I do, the better.

As much as she didn't want to admit it to herself, Deirdre was becoming addicted to reading these pages. Each site offered new thoughts and images that shaped a young person's life, and she wanted to read it all. It wasn't just a violent topic she was researching any more- these were kids growing up with the same peer pressures she had. She was beginning to identify with them.

Does this mean I could identify with the shooters I'm researching? That's a scary thought. Then again, they are just people. Even the boy who shot me...

Deirdre had never really thought about that until now. The idea made her feel queasy. She had refused to read anything written about the shooter after the incident- he didn't deserve all the press in her mind. But her need for information on other shooters was breaking her own rule, and possibly adding to the public feeding frenzy that occurred every time one of those stories hit the news.

It was the first time Deirdre considered the possible impact her column could have on her readers.

I imagine this is how people who lost someone on 9/11 feel when it's suddenly mentioned on TV. No one can escape these tragedies, not with the amount of media surrounding us these days. I can pretend I'm not still haunted by what happened to me, but the mere mention of the mall's name on the news and I have to change the channel before I have a panic attack. Will my column have the same effect on other shooting victims?

No. My piece will be different, she tried to convince herself. *This won't be a sensational piece on the life of killers. There's so much more to this topic than just a person's background. I'm looking at this from every angle possible so I can offer solutions; my contribution will be a productive one.*

Shaking her head, Deirdre tried to turn her thoughts back to her research by going online to her favorite teen blog, "Two Become One." The author seemed to be building a new relationship, writing about a girl who came from the same place he did. She wasn't sure if that meant from the same town or the same place emotionally, or perhaps both. Either way, it was one of the few blogs where the author seemed to be working toward something.

When the page finally loaded, Deirdre read the title of the newest entry- "It's Almost Time."

I've waited so long for this moment, and it's almost time. All the pain, anxiety, and anguish, they will soon come to an end, and I will be ruled by them no longer. I kept my promise to her. I finished our dream for her. I waited as long as I could for her. And now I can finally let go of the anger and resentment that have haunted me since she left.

For I have found the one I was truly meant to be with- the one who will complete my journey with me. I'd hoped and planned and kept the momentum going as long as I could by myself, until I could almost bear it no more. But then she came along, my purpose, my muse; and I knew that my time, our time, had come.

She is everything I was looking for- loyal, understanding, and passionate. She has felt the same pain and cried the same tears and screamed the same words, and has never apologized for it. She knows there is nothing she can do to change the past and it fuels her anger and sadness just as it fuels mine. We are of one mind- my search has ended.

Now I merely have to show her there is only one path for us to take. There is no other solution to end our suffering other than to use our devotion for a greater purpose. It will be our most memorable achievement, one that nobody can ignore. And we will do it together.

For it's time to forget the world and all the hurt it has caused us. It's time to express what we've so desperately needed to express. It's time to cast aside society's notions of what is acceptable. And it's time to be free of this burden.

It's our time.

Deirdre sat back in her chair, reading the entry again. A feeling of apprehension washed over her as she stared at the last sentence. Many of the previous entries, foregoing the very first poem she read on the blog, were simple and upbeat. He would write about what he had learned that day about his girlfriend, or what they talked about, or what they did. It seemed to be a normal teenage relationship in its beginning stages, one that Deirdre hoped all teens could read about and emulate.

But this entry, filled with anger and frustration, and wanting to end things, it didn't sound like a typical young romance.

What does he mean by a memorable achievement that nobody can ignore? It sounds like he's talking about staging a final event, one that will help to end their suffering. These were all topics Deirdre had been reading about, and many of the articles written about the suicide shooters, along with the notes they left behind, used those very same words. Reading it again made Deirdre shudder.

It almost sounds like he's trying to recruit this new person into some sort of plan he's had ever since he lost that special someone. But I don't know. It seems a bit strange that he would talk about a violent plan on a public blog. Then again, statistics show that many teenage shooters, school and suicide, told someone about what they were thinking of doing in some way. But he doesn't list anything specific here.

God, Deirdre, you're just being paranoid, that's what everyone will say. I'm too obsessed with this topic to be objective about something like this. Either that, or I'm so immersed in it that I'm recognizing the warning signs of a potential teen shooter.

Ugh. I sound like something out of a cheesy cop drama.

I need to talk to "angelandme" in that chat room, see if anyone knows more about the person who writes this blog.

Deirdre typed in the address for the teen chat site and waited for it to load. She kept an eye out for anyone walking by who might be able to see what was on her computer screen. Once the page came up, Deirdre signed into her account and scanned the list of screen names until she found it: angelandme. She clicked on it to begin a private chat.

hartonhersleeve: Hi there.

Deirdre hit Enter and waited for a response. After a minute of silence she continued typing.

hartonhersleeve: I don't know if you remember me…

Before she could finish typing she received a reply.

angelandme: hey, it's lois lane. ☺ how's the article coming?

Deirdre smiled.

hartonhersleeve: It's going pretty well. I've got a lot of good stuff.

angelandme: so when do me and all my friends get to read it?

hartonhersleeve: Hopefully soon! Sometimes I feel like I'll never find all the information I'm looking for.

angelandme: it's a pretty big topic.

hartonhersleeve: No kidding! Thanks again for the blog suggestions.

angelandme: no prob. find anything useful?

hartonhersleeve: I did actually, plenty of things. But I did want to ask you about one in particular.

angelandme: k.

hartonhersleeve: melancholyteen, you know, the one who writes Two Become One. Do you know anything about him?

angelandme: like what?

hartonhersleeve: Like anything about who he is, aspects of his real life, stuff like that.

angelandme: oh sure. i chat with him all the time. he's pretty popular on here. he calls his blog that cuz his sister was killed a few years ago.

hartonhersleeve: Wow. So that's who he's talking about losing then?

angelandme: yup.

hartonhersleeve: That's terrible. Does he have any other siblings?

angelandme: not that I know of. he only really talks about her. he still seems pretty messed up by it.

hartonhersleeve: do you know how old he is?

angelandme: 19. although he might be 20 now

hartonhersleeve: You said he's pretty messed up about his sister. What makes you say that?

angelandme: he just talks about how angry he still is and stuff, and how he's pissed at his parents for moving on with their lives. i told him that's what people do when someone they love dies and he really went off on me, saying if we truly loved someone we would never get over their death. i said then we'd never be able to love anyone cuz we all die, and he said that's when we finally learn how pointless life is

hartonhersleeve: I'm surprised to hear that. I mean, much of his blog that I've been reading has been about how he met this new girl he seems to be in love with.

angelandme: the only reason he writes that is cuz she lost someone too, so he feels like she knows what he's going thru

hartonhersleeve: That makes sense then, the two of them being "of one mind."

angelandme: yeah

hartonhersleeve: I don't know. His last entry seemed so, harsh I guess, especially near the end. It sounds like something's about to go down, ya know?

angelandme: you sound like a cop on tv. ☺

I knew it sounded silly!

hartonhersleeve: lol. Yeah, I guess so.

angelandme: i wouldn't freak out about it. i think he's just an intense person

hartonhersleeve: Ok, thanks. Good to know.

angelandme: no prob. but i gotta go. there's this guy i've been trying to chat with forever on here.

 hartonhersleeve: Ok, good luck with that. Thanks again!

angelandme: later

Deirdre signed out of the site, just in time to see Neil come walking out of his office toward her desk. She quickly closed the browser window and opened up a new file for her article.

"Deirdre, you got a second?"

"Sure, Neil. I'll be right there."

She watched him go back into his office and breathed a sigh of relief. *That was close.* Grabbing her notebook, she made a mental note to call Dr. Stephens to follow up on the blog. She knew it might be silly, but it also might be something dangerous. Intense or not, she couldn't help but be concerned about the potential of something serious unfolding.

CHAPTER FORTY-THREE

"Welcome to the 9th circle of hell," Tristan greeted Zoey as she walked into his parents' house.

"And a happy new year's eve to you too. Thanks for putting me at ease by the way."

"No problem," he said, kissing her. "Happy new year to you."

Zoey smiled and entered the hallway as Tristan slid her jacket off her shoulders. Unlike her home, which was covered in bright colors, Tristan's parents' interior was painted a plain cream color, with nothing hanging on the walls. Zoey got the impression that everything in the house had its place.

"What? No flowers?" Tristan asked.

"Nah. Flowers are so last season. Ha! Get it? Fall? Last season?"

"So you've got nothing to appease the demigods, huh?"

"My charm's not enough?"

"Not unless you plan on making out with my dad," Tristan said, making a face. "Ugh. Let's never talk about that again."

"Agreed!" Zoey sputtered. "I was thinking more along the lines of these brownies I made. Don't ask me where I got that idea from."

"Well played."

"Thanks, Walter."

"Tristan? Is that Zoey?"

"No, Mom. It's the stripper I hired for the evening," Tristan called out behind him.

"Tristan! That is highly inappropriate!" his mother exclaimed as she entered the hallway. Zoey giggled.

"Oh, Mom, Zoey says much worse. I'm just getting you ready for her vulgarity."

"Tristan!"

His mother shook her head, sighing.

"I'm glad I'm not the only one appalled by my son," she said, walking over to Zoey and extending her hand. "Hi. I'm Sandra Wright. It's lovely to finally meet you, Zoey. Happy new year."

"You too," Zoey said, shaking her hand. "I brought some brownies for dessert."

"Oh, thank you! You didn't have to do that."

Zoey glanced over at Tristan with a melodramatic wink. He laughed.

"Ok, enough winning over my mother. How about the grand tour?"

"Wow, you've really got nothing original to offer, huh?"

"Take it or leave it."

"I'll be in the kitchen if you guys need anything," Sandra said. "Oh, and if you happen to find your father tell him dinner will be ready in 15 minutes."

"Ok."

Tristan took Zoey's hand and led her into the dining room.

"Here's the lovely table where we'll be dining shortly," he announced, sweeping his arm around the room. "And if you'll follow me, we're walking, we're walking, and we're stopping in the living room. Notice the charming fireplace with a luminous fire spreading warmth and love throughout the entire house."

"Is that what that is? I thought maybe it was your insanity lingering."

"Ah, that's my girl. You always know what to say to break a guy down."

Zoey grinned.

"Now, let's see how much you can make fun of me in my own room."

As he led her up the stairs, Zoey noticed another person emerge from the other end of the hall.

"Oh, don't look now, it's the master philosopher, emerging from his cocoon of ideology," Tristan said. As his father came closer he held out his hand.

"It's nice to know all that money we paid for your education was well spent. It certainly sharpened the wit. But he is correct about the philosophy. Hi, I'm Alan. Nice to meet you, Zoey."

"You too."

"Mom says dinner will be ready in 15."

"Sounds good. See you down there."

Once his dad was out of sight, Zoey turned to Tristan.

"So, are you gonna tell me the key to getting out of this Twilight zone episode or do I have to figure it out on my own?"

"What do you mean?"

"What do I mean? Your parents are totally normal. They haven't embarrassed you once yet."

"Remember your parents before dinner? Yeah, this is just the beginning," Tristan explained, turning her around by her shoulders and leading her into his room. "Wait until the real dinner conversation starts."

Zoey looked around at the walls of his old room. She noticed his high school diploma first, framed and hanging near the doorway. He was the only person she knew who had it out on display. Next to it hung his bachelor's degree, with a gold honors tassel hanging from one corner.

As she turned around she glanced at the several movie posters from his favorites list, along with a small poster of Albert Einstein and one of a female Japanese anime character holding a sword.

"Ah, I see your weakness is hot animated women with weapons."

"Actually, I prefer real hot women with weapons. But the animated ones have ridiculous, curvy bodies, shown off by even tighter outfits."

"You know, I have seen some anime where the women almost look realistic and wear flowing robes."

"I don't believe you."

"It's true."

Tristan sat down on the bed, glancing around the room with her. He noticed her looking at a picture of him and Chastity sitting in a tree in their back yard.

"I don't know why my mom keeps that picture out. We used to have a tree house, just for the two of us, no parents allowed. But it fell down during a nasty thunderstorm. It was right after she died."

"I would've liked to have seen it."

"It needed to go anyway," he said matter-of-factly. Zoey turned to look at him.

"What do you mean?"

"Well, we didn't need it anymore. It lost its purpose."

Before Zoey could ask him anything else, Sandra called up to them that dinner was ready. Tristan stood up abruptly and walked past her, heading down the stairs. She followed him out and down into the dining room.

Unlike at her house, the dining room table here was large and round. Alan brought in the mixed vegetable plate and placed it next to the leg of lamb sitting in the middle of the table. Zoey had only tried lamb once in her life during one of her father's book parties.

"Tristan said you ate meat, right?" Sandra asked, noticing Zoey staring at it.

"Uh, yeah," Zoey replied, trying to regain her composure. "I don't like enough vegetables to be a vegetarian."

"Oh well, you need to have a balanced diet mixed with both meat and vegetables," Sandra lectured, handing her the salad bowl. "I hope you take a good helping of salad at least."

"Sandra, she's a guest. I don't think we need to force her to eat vegetables."

"I'm not forcing her," she replied, still holding out the bowl to Zoey. "I'm just offering."

"I will take some salad, thank you," Zoey said, quickly spooning some onto her plate. Sandra smiled, handing her the homemade dressing. Tristan rolled his eyes and turned to Zoey.

"You don't have to do that to please her."

"Tristan, I think Zoey can decide for herself."

"Not if you make her feel uncomfortable."

"You're the one making things uncomfortable here."

"Honey, can you pass me the rolls?" Alan asked, breaking up the conversation. Sandra glared at him as she passed him the bread basket.

"Zoey, would you like one?" he offered with a forced smile.

"Yes, please."

After taking a roll, she noticed the conversation stopped. She felt her shoulders begin to relax as she focused on eating her dinner.

"So, Zoey, are you in school?"

"Mom, I told you, she's not in school right now."

"Oh, that's right. You're working at some restaurant, correct?"

"Yes."

"Is that something you plan to do for a while?"

"Uh, I'm not sure yet," Zoey answered, looking down at her plate. "I haven't figured out anything that far into the future."

"Ah. Just like Tristan," Sandra sighed. "He seems to be doing just fine, coasting along without a care in the world. But soon he'll have to figure out the next step. Everyone does."

"It takes time to find your true passion though," Alan interjected as Sandra groaned. "What? It's true. I don't know why you have trouble accepting that."

"Alan, that's something people say when they don't want to put the effort into getting a job, or moving on with their life. I see it as a cop-out."

"Honey, just because you knew what your calling was right out of high school doesn't mean everyone else does. Not everyone has that secure feeling so early on in their lives."

"Ugh, I hate when you use that term, 'calling'. You make me sound like a priest. You know I don't believe in things like destiny. I chose to be a doctor because I'm interested in the body and how it functions and how we can keep it functioning through technology. I didn't choose my profession as part of some divine plan."

"Well, there are those who would disagree with you."

"And they would be incorrect."

"Honey, your lack of imagination is really disheartening sometimes. There are plenty of things in the universe that we don't understand, science be damned. So why is it so difficult for you to accept that such things as destiny may exist?"

Zoey looked back and forth between Tristan's parents when her gaze settled on Tristan. His face grew redder as he stared down at his plate. She began to feel uneasy with the daggers he was silently shooting from his eyes.

"Because, Alan, I know what I can see with my own eyes, and touch with my own hands. Science is always developing and changing, yes, but as it does, it brings us closer to the fact that things in the universe cannot be pre-determined."

"Really, Mom?" Tristan interrupted, suddenly looking up at her. "Because I predicted that you two would get into one of your stupid arguments tonight with Zoey sitting here."

"Tristan, we're not arguing. We're having a healthy debate," Sandra replied. "You two can jump in at any time."

"Can't we have a normal conversation about everyday things for once, instead of making everything out to be the weight of the world?"

"We started this whole thing talking about Zoey's job. That's pretty average," Alan said.

"Yeah, and look where we ended up!"

"Well, Tristan, I'm sorry we like to have intellectual conversations once in a while," Sandra said. "Would you rather we talked about football instead?"

"You don't have to patronize me!" Tristan said sharply, dropping his fork onto his plate. The loud clatter resonated throughout the dining room, matching his anger. The whole room went quiet.

"Let's change the subject," Sandra said calmly, picking up her knife. "Zoey, what do your parents do?"

"Well, my mom sells real estate and my dad's an author."

"Oh? Anything we would have read?"

"I don't know. Do you like mystery novels?"

"I mostly read non-fiction."

"Oh. Then probably not."

Before Alan could add anything, Tristan stood up suddenly and took his plate into the kitchen. Sandra watched him leave out of the corner of her eye as she continued eating. She glanced over at Alan, who raised his eyebrows in confusion. She shook her head.

What is going on? Zoey wondered. *Should I go into the kitchen after him? Is there even proper etiquette for leaving the dinner table where you're eating with your boyfriend's parents?* She continued eating quietly until Tristan walked back into the room.

"We actually have to leave soon," he said, looking at Sandra. "Zoey hasn't seen my apartment yet and I thought tonight would be a good time."

223

"We're in the middle of dinner, Tristan," Sandra said, placing her silverware down on her plate. "Why would you want to show her the apartment when you knew she was coming here for dinner?"

"It was the only time we could fit it into her schedule," he said. Before Zoey could refute him he added, "And because it's New Year's Eve. I wasn't expecting to spend the whole night with my parents."

Tristan turned and left the room again, leaving Zoey awkwardly sitting between his parents. His strange mood and sudden outburst left her confused as to what was happening with him. She looked down at her plate, wondering if she should finish her meal.

"Well, I'm sorry we had to cut things so short, Zoey," Sandra said quietly. "It looks like we don't even have time to try your brownies."

"Oh, well, uh, you can keep them for later. Dinner was delicious. Thank you."

As she stood up to bring her dish into the kitchen Sandra touched her arm.

"I'll take that for you," she said, pushing her chair back from the table. "Why don't you get ready to go with Tristan."

Zoey nodded, letting go of her plate. She tried not to show her embarrassment over Tristan's behavior.

"It was really nice meeting you both. And happy new year."

"Yes, you too, Zoey," Alan said, returning the forced sentiment. "Hopefully we'll get to do this again when there's more time."

At that moment Tristan re-appeared wearing his jacket and holding Zoey's.

"Thanks for dinner, Mom," he mumbled. "See you guys later."

Tristan took Zoey's hand, practically dragging her down the hallway and out the front door. As he closed it behind them, Zoey grabbed Tristan's arm to stop him.

"Uh, what the heck was that all about? We don't have to do this tonight."

"Trust me," Tristan said, turning towards her car. "This is for the best."

*　　*　　*　　*　　*　　*　　*

Zoey pulled the car into the parking lot of Tristan's apartment complex, parking next to his motorcycle which was covered with a blue tarp. The silence since they left his parents' house had been deafening, leaving Zoey feeling uneasy. Turning off the engine, she turned towards him.

"Are you ok? You haven't said anything since we left your parents' place."

"I'm fine," he said, taking off his seat belt. "I just knew that would happen, that's all."

"What would happen?"

"My parents would have the same stupid argument they always have, philosophy versus science. I have no idea how they got married."

"Tristan, it really wasn't that bad."

"That's because you didn't live with it," he muttered.

I hope this doesn't screw up the rest of the night, she thought. Before she could say anything, Tristan noticed the expression on her face and walked over to take her hand.

"Don't worry, I'll get over it. I don't wanna think about my parents anymore."

Zoey breathed a sigh of relief.

"Ok."

They walked over to the building and Tristan unlocked the outside door. They walked past a set of small mailboxes and up one flight of stairs to the first door on the right. Putting his key in the deadbolt, he opened the door and led Zoey into the apartment. When he turned on the light, Zoey surveyed the décor.

"I can see you decorated this place too, huh?" she said, taking off her jacket.

Matching his bedroom, there were even more movie posters in Tristan's apartment, except all of these were framed. Two bookshelves sat at either end of the living room, overflowing with titles from every genre. A large flat screen TV sat on a small entertainment center in the middle of the room, with three video game systems sitting on the various shelves surrounded by games.

"Video game much?"

"Oh sure, gloss over the fact I have two huge bookshelves full of books and stuff I wrote and land right on the gaming systems. Whose side are you on?"

"Side? There are sides?"

"Oh yeah," he answered, walking over to the single piece of furniture in the living room, the couch, in front of the TV. "You're either on the parents' side or the kids' side. And video games are obviously on the kids' side. You should understand that."

"I'm not a gamer. Never have been."

"But you should still sympathize with your kind over the parents."

"I see," Zoey said, sitting down next to him. "I'll try to remember that."

"Good."

Tristan leaned back against the cushions and put his arm around Zoey's shoulder. She settled into the crook of his arm, the awkward dinner at Tristan's parents' house slowly fading from her memory.

"So, what do you wanna do?"

Zoey looked around the room.

"You said you wrote 'stuff'. Can I read some of it?"

Tristan paused, seemingly unsure of how to answer her question. Zoey bit her lip.

"If you don't want me to that's ok," she said, trying to put him at ease. He shook his head.

"No, it's ok. It's just, I haven't shown anyone my work in a while. I have the blog where I post a lot of stuff, but that's anonymous to most people, ya know?"

"I understand."

Tristan stood up and walked over to one of the bookcases. Scanning the shelves, he took out a journal and brought it over to Zoey. She took it from him, running her hand over the leather cover. It had the initials TW on the front.

"Chastity got this for me for our 15th birthday," he said, sitting back down. "I was writing a lot of stupid angsty poetry, trying to be the next Trent Reznor, so she got me a journal to keep it all in one place. I never actually used it until recently. When she died I just couldn't bring myself to touch it. But then I met you."

Tristan reached up and brushed the hair out of Zoey's face. Her eyes urged him to continue.

"You really gave me purpose again, Zoey. When I realized how much you understood my pain, I knew I had found a true partner, someone who could help me cope with everything. After that, the words just flowed."

Zoey didn't know what to say. It had been a long time since she felt needed by someone, especially when she needed that someone too. After Laura's death she was afraid the feeling of emptiness would never fade, that she would be lost in her own world forever. But meeting Tristan changed everything. His understanding brought her back into the rest of the world again.

Leaning down Tristan kissed her gently, caressing her cheek with his fingertips. She felt her entire body relax as he wrapped his arms around her. After a moment he pulled away slowly, and reached for the journal in Zoey's lap to open it to the first page.

"This was the first poem I wrote after we met."

Zoey read the title: "Found"

Drowning in a sea of chaotic dreams,
Forced under by waves of memories
I would cling to the dark void that is my mind
And wait for Death to come.

But alas, Death had no pity
And Death he knew no ache,
He only laughed and rode the rain
That crashed upon my head.

So there I lay in wait of nothing,
With only time by my side,

Until her figure floating out at sea
Stretched out to save my soul.

So now we drift together
On these waters rough and high,
And as the sun sets every night
We'll ride toward our salvation.

It was a much darker poem than Zoey had been expecting. She knew Tristan was still devastated over his sister's death, but she hadn't realized the extent to which he still felt the pain. To say he was waiting to die? That thought had never crossed Zoey's mind after Laura's death.

And the last word, salvation, caught Zoey by surprise. She had felt their bond grow over time, but she never realized that he, too, felt the same thing. She wondered how soon after they met he had written the poem.

Tristan laced his fingers through hers, looking at her expectantly. She realized he was waiting for her reaction.

"Wow," she said, not wanting to articulate everything she was thinking. "It, um, wasn't what I was expecting."

Tristan frowned, letting go of her hand.

"You didn't like it."

"No, no, it's not that," Zoey replied quickly. "It's just, it's kind of dark, you know, with all that talk of death. I wasn't expecting it to be so heavy."

"But that's just it. Everything in my life was dark and heavy, until I met you. Isn't this how you felt after Laura's death?"

Zoey paused, not wanting to insult him and his interpretation of her feelings.

"I was devastated. I still am," she admitted. It wasn't a lie. Tristan smiled.

"I knew you would understand. You always do. That's how I knew I had found the one."

The one. That was the closest thing to "I love you" that any boy had ever said to her. Zoey felt chills as he leaned over to kiss her again, but at the same time she was still bothered by the poem. *Maybe I'm just not used to reading something so deep by someone my own age. He obviously still has a lot of pain stored away that he's been unable to express with anyone else. That I do get. And he's not afraid to tell me what he's feeling, which is completely different from other guys I've known. Maybe I'm just experiencing my first adult relationship.*

Tristan leaned back after a moment and picked up the journal.

"Much of this is dedicated to you. I know we haven't known each other for very long, but I feel really close to you. I hope that doesn't scare you."

Zoey shook her head. Even with the occasional apprehensive moment, she never felt scared of what she had with Tristan. She knew with her first relationship she would be nervous and confused. But Tristan put her at ease

227

almost immediately, and the bond that had formed since was born out of true acceptance. That, she would always be grateful for.

"I feel close to you too."

Just then, the clock on the living room wall struck midnight. Tristan leaned toward her again.

"Here's to our new year," he whispered into her ear. She shivered as he kissed her again.

Our new year.

CHAPTER FORTY-FOUR

"Thank you for meeting with me again, Dr. Stephens."

It had been a week since Deirdre had read the blog entry and her anxiety still lingered. She couldn't get the wording out of her head. All of her research online, all of the books and newspaper articles she read, all of the information she had collected over the past year, was all reflected in that one blog entry. She just couldn't ignore it.

And Nina and Haley were no help. At this point they were done listening patiently every time she brought up her "obsession" as they called it. They couldn't have a conversation any more without Deirdre instinctively adding a statistic or two that vaguely fit the topic. She knew she was testing the boundaries of their friendship, and was surprised they hadn't completely shut her out yet.

It was time to get a professional opinion.

As Deirdre sat down she realized how long it had been since her last visit. *I can't believe I'm still working on this thing. No wonder my friends have given up on me.*

"So, Ms. Hart, what can I do for you?"

"Well, I'm still working on the teen violence article," Deirdre replied, trying not to sound too sheepish. "And right now I'm checking out teen blogs online. I've come across a number of fairly detailed ones, at least in terms of the entries people write, but there was this one blog that really caught my attention."

"Ok."

"At first I was interested in it just because it was different from a lot of the other blogs. It had a new entry almost every day, mostly about a growing relationship, and the poetry had a lot of great imagery. It was much more detailed than most of the pages I've seen. But the most recent entry made me, well, pause I guess."

"What do you mean, pause?"

"Well, it was something about the wording he used. He was talking about this new relationship as usual, but it sounded like he wanted to recruit her for some 'final' event."

"Final event?"

"He starts off talking about finally finding that one person who understands him, and then says he needs to 'get her to see the only path' there is for them to take. Then he writes about this one memorable achievement that no one will be able to ignore."

"That's verbatim?"

"Pretty much. It's called "Two Become One," which at first I thought was about sex. But as I read more entries I discovered the author was talking about losing someone close to him, which I now believe was a sister."

Stephens raised her eyebrows.

"Does he say that specifically?"

"No, but I spoke with a girl who had chatted with him in the past. She was the one who directed me to his blog. Anyway, she said he spoke about a sister who had died a few years ago. Apparently he's still very angry about it, because he said if you truly love someone, you never get over their death."

Deirdre paused, waiting for Dr. Stephens to comment. She seemed lost in thought.

"Dr. Stephens? Is something wrong?"

Stephens looked at her, trying not to frown.

"Can you show me the blog?"

"Sure." As both of them stood up, Deirdre could feel that something about their conversation had changed. Dr. Stephens was seemingly distracted, making their discussion awkward and stilted. It took her slightly aback, given that their very first conversation, when they were complete strangers, went much more smoothly.

Is something going on here?

Deirdre followed Dr. Stephens over to her desk and stood behind her as she sat down. Stephens opened her laptop and turned it towards Deirdre to put in the address. After checking out the page every day, Deirdre had it memorized.

"Here. It's this entry."

Stephens began to read it to herself, squinting her eyes every so often. When she finished reading she began scanning the page, stopping on the last poem that was written. Deirdre waited impatiently, trying to read her expression. *Is this a big deal or not?* She shifted her feet nervously.

Finally, Stephens looked up from the screen.

"I can see why that last entry raised some flags. You're right. It sounds like he has some plan for, or with, a new girlfriend that she is currently unaware of. Whether it involves violence or not is debatable, but it does seem like he's building toward a finale of some kind."

"So I'm not being overly paranoid then?"

Stephens smiled.

"I don't think so."

"Thank god!" Deirdre exclaimed, feeling validated. "I thought I had gotten so lost in this topic that I was seeing it everywhere!"

Stephens lack of response made Deirdre even more curious. She was now convinced there was more to the story.

"So, is there anything we can do?" she asked, trying to prod Dr. Stephens into telling her what she was thinking. Stephens turned back to the blog.

"Can we communicate with the author in some way?" she asked, scrolling over various links on the page.

"I've left comments after some of the entries before," Deirdre said, pointing out the icon. "He's never replied, but I assume he could."

"Well, I suppose that's an option for the future, in case his entries escalate into something more. For now, I would just keep an eye on it. There's nothing specific for us to go on or do anything about."

"Are you sure, Dr. Stephens?" Deirdre asked. She knew she wasn't getting all of the answers. "It seems like you have something else on your mind."

"Well, I might be able to do some research on this. I don't know for sure if I'll be able to find out anything more, but I'll certainly let you know if I do. Thank you for bringing this to my attention, Ms. Hart."

Before Deirdre could say anything else, Dr. Stephens stood up abruptly and began walking toward the door. Deirdre frowned slightly, grabbing her purse and following her.

"Of course. I just didn't want this to turn into one of those situations where someone close to the person knew something was wrong, but didn't do anything about it. That was definitely a common thread I found throughout my research."

"It is pretty common. I know with school shootings specifically there's evidence that at least one person, usually a peer, often knows something about the attacker's plan. Unfortunately, that information rarely reaches an adult's attention, or it's not taken seriously enough."

"But this is pretty blatant, don't you think? I mean, to actually post something like that online for everyone to see?"

"If he's cocky enough to think he can get away with it? I would say yes. Then there are those who are convinced that no one is paying attention, and often times they're right. They're proving a point by showing the whole world how ignored they are."

"Well, he made me sit up and take notice! How could you not?"

"That's generally the idea. As you said, though, it was more of an uneasy feeling from some of the language rather than anything he mentions specifically."

Stopping at the door, Deirdre turned to face Dr. Stephens.

"So, keeping an eye on the site is our only option for now?"

"Unfortunately, that's all we have to go on for the moment. We would need a lot more information before we could bring anything to the authorities. And by information I mean names, dates, times and places."

Deirdre frowned.

"All right. Well, if you're able to make some headway into this, you'll call me?"

"Absolutely. You were the one, after all, to bring this to my attention. Hopefully it's nothing, but as you said you never know. These warning signs have been ignored too many times."

"Thank god I came to the right place. You've been a tremendous help, really."

"That's my job, helping people."

"You do it very well."

"Thank you. I'll be in touch."

Stephens watched as Deirdre left the office and got into her car. Once she drove off, she walked over to her filing cabinet and opened the second drawer. Thumbing through the folders, she found the one she was looking for labeled "Consults". Sitting down, she began to read her notes from a meeting a few years ago with Dr. Loring.

"Was asked for a consult because the client exhibited possible sociopathic tendencies. Client lost a close sibling and his parents wanted him to go through therapy because he couldn't get over his anger. Then after only two months the client was acting almost completely different, saying his feelings had changed and he was able to move on from the incident. This made Dr. Loring fairly suspicious, so he asked for the parents' permission for a consult. They agreed, but never actually scheduled an appointment. After that Dr. Loring never heard anything more from the client."

Sitting back in her chair, Stephens thought about her limited discussions with Dr. Loring concerning his client. Because of patient confidentiality, he had been unable to divulge any information until the parents agreed to a consult. But since it never materialized the discussion was dropped, forcing Dr. Loring to drop his concerns as well.

This seems too similar to be a coincidence, Stephens thought. *But at the same time there's not a heck of a lot to go on right now. I mean, could the boy really be from around here?*

The only thing Stephens knew for sure was that the whole situation bothered her.

She thought back to all of her sessions with Zoey so far. When Zoey had first mentioned Tristan, there was no talk about his background. But the more Zoey had learned about him, the more Stephens had learned about him, which made her more concerned that he was the same boy. Of course, the boy she had heard about was 15 years old, and it was now five years later. And she had no idea why the parents had stopped scheduling sessions for their son. Anything could have happened, including the possibility that he really hadn't needed therapy to deal with his sister's death.

For Zoey's stories about him told of a sweet, patient, well-adjusted boy. He treated her well, and had gotten her to emerge from the shell she developed after Laura's death. Ever since Zoey met him she seemed more comfortable talking about her feelings, and even more comfortable with herself in general. She was starting to overcome the low self-esteem that initially held her back, which was a huge step in her development. So it did seem that Tristan truly was a good thing for her, that he was helping her to get past Laura's death.

It all makes sense. The blogger said he finally found the one person who understood, so of course that someone would have to have suffered a similar loss.

Of course, he's also her first love. Her view of him and the relationship could be skewed. There's really no way to tell without seeing them together. And Zoey will definitely get upset if I make any insinuations that Tristan is dangerous. I mean, I imagine she hasn't seen this blog, plus there's no definitive evidence that he's the author. Ugh. This is where it gets tricky, especially now that Zoey isn't scheduling as many sessions. God, I thought that was a good thing, that she was finally moving on with her life in a healthy manner. Now, I don't know.

Stephens picked up her calendar book and flipped to the next week of appointments. It had been a couple of weeks, but Zoey had her usual afternoon time slot coming up in a few days.

I guess I'll have to wait until then, she thought. *Hopefully I can get some answers.*

CHAPTER FORTY-FIVE

I can't believe it. I'm hanging out in my room with my boyfriend of six months, and he's reading my quote board. Laura would be so proud.

"I've never seen anything like this before," Tristan said, sitting next to her on the bed. "It's pretty cool."

And he still thinks I'm cool, even after all this time.

"Yeah? Thanks. It's just something I put together after Laura gave me this book of quotes for my birthday. I'm always quoting other people. I mean, they say everything worth doing has been done already, so why not quote someone who's already done it, and explained it better than I ever could?"

"Hmmm."

Uh oh, Zoey thought. *I think my coolness factor just dropped.*

"What?"

"Well, I don't know," he said cautiously. "I mean, I don't want to seem insulting or anything. I just think that's kind of a cop-out. Like, maybe you're afraid you have nothing to offer, so you repeat things that have already been approved by others."

Zoey felt her heart drop into her stomach. She had never analyzed her interest in quotes that way. She simply thought it made her look knowledgeable to be able to quote famous people, as if she could talk about any subject intelligently. She didn't respond to his statement.

Tristan turned toward her and saw the look of disappointment on her face. He reached over and touched her arm.

"I'm sorry. That was really rude to blurt that out," he said softly. "I didn't mean that you didn't have anything to offer. It just seems like sometimes you don't give yourself enough credit. I guess what I said before doesn't help your self-esteem. You can throw my ass out now if you want."

Zoey smiled.

"Nah, you can stay. You're right. I've never really been someone who was able to say what I wanted to say. I mean, sometimes I don't know what I think about things, ya know? Someone will tell me something that seems true and makes sense, and then I hear the other side and I think that makes sense too. And that makes me feel stupid."

"That's not stupid," Tristan reassured her. "That makes you open-minded. You're willing to listen to both sides of an issue, rather than just making up your mind after only hearing one side. And sometimes both sides have a point, and there's no right or wrong, only gray area. Seriously, I think most issues in the world are like that."

I really like that about him, Zoey thought. *He talks to me in a way that I can join in the conversation without having to turn into my mother. We talk about things that matter.*

Zoey suddenly realized she was off in her own world, and that Tristan was studying her.

"I'm sorry, I totally zoned out."

"It's okay. I like watching you."

Zoey blushed.

"So, um, what were you saying?"

"I asked you what you thought of the media going crazy about this girl who shot her friends at school a couple months ago. I can't believe they're still talking about the students who were put on trial for beating her up."

"Yeah, that was a while ago. But what does anyone really think when something like that happens? People wonder about the person and why they did it, then the story usually fades into obscurity after about a week until the next shooting happens. Why? What did you think?"

Tristan paused, formulating his answer carefully.

"I'm always intrigued by the way the media goes after each story, like they're trying to find some rhyme or reason for what happened," he began. "But everything they find is just speculation. I mean, even if they come across a journal or a blog or even a suicide note, that's not the real story. But they keep plugging away at the 'truth' until they think they've covered every 'angle' and move on. Like it's that easy for those involved to 'move on.'"

Zoey agreed with the last part. She had been feeling that way ever since Laura's death. Once all of the reporters moved onto something else and the news stories about the drunk driver and the car accident had stopped, Zoey felt she finally had a moment to breathe. But that also meant she had the rest of her life to process that one moment that had changed things forever.

"I agree with some of that. But isn't it the media's job to research all the facts about a news story? I mean, when the shooter dies, how else are they gonna put a story together except with the bits and pieces they left behind?"

"That's true," Tristan agreed. "But what I'm talking about is how they try to figure out the motive. I mean, that's all anyone ever cares about, the why.

Like it's some kind of puzzle where, if they could get the whole picture, they would solve the mystery. But why do they need to solve the mystery?"

"Um, again, isn't that their job?"

"No, that would be a job for the cops or a detective when they're trying to find the killer," he explained. "In this case they already have the killer, and he's dead. No, the desire to solve the case here is purely for, I don't know, a way to link it to other cases to figure out why it's happening as a whole. Like it's an epidemic or something that can be cured if they could just figure out why it's happening. But it's not like that at all. There's no one reason or cure."

"What do you mean?"

"Oh, you know, all those bullshit issues they bring up every time something like that happens," he said, rolling his eyes. "It's divorce! It's lack of gun control! It's violent video games! It's all the preservatives in our food! It's R rated movies! There was even one study done on the link of candy to violent behavior. It's always gotta be something. That's what they're really searching for when they 'investigate' these things. They're looking for an easy scapegoat."

"Well, you gotta admit, it would be pretty scary if these things were just random."

"That's life," Tristan replied casually. "It's not like people haven't been killing each other since they discovered they could throw rocks and swing clubs. We blow people up with nuclear weapons for wars that supposedly have a purpose, but it's those who kill a select few that are murderers. I think it was Voltaire who said, 'It is forbidden to kill, therefore all murderers are punished unless they kill in large numbers and to the sound of trumpets.'"

Suddenly, Zoey felt uncomfortable with Tristan's nonchalant attitude toward the conversation. She understood his point about war, of course, but she thought the term murderer was still an apt one for those who killed innocent people. Then again, he had brought up a valid point about the subjective nature of a war's "purpose". *I'm sure he's just playing devil's advocate.*

Mostly, she wasn't used to having such an intense discussion, especially with someone her own age. Tristan was unlike anyone she'd ever met which, in turn, made her want to rise to his level of conversation. He challenged her, but in a good way. It made her stop and think about how she truly felt, who she really was. It was refreshing, but nerve-wracking at the same time.

Again, Tristan could sense her trepidation.

"It's okay. You can tell me what you really think."

"Well," she began tentatively, "war *is* a part of society, but at least there are rules, sort of. I mean, we've set up parameters for that kind of thing so it won't be so, ya know, barbaric. That's a conscious thing. But I don't know how conscious some of these kids are of the consequences of their actions."

Tristan frowned and sat back against the wall. Zoey could tell immediately that he disagreed with her. After a minute of silence he sat up and shook his head.

"No, I think they're more conscious of it than you realize," he countered. "I think people would feel more comfortable if they weren't, because then it would be easier to label them killers. They wouldn't be seen as human any more. People don't identify themselves with these kids because, being different from them, they would never do something so violent. But when it comes down to it, I think anyone can be pushed beyond their so-called limits."

This time Zoey shook her head immediately.

"Now that I don't agree with. I know it's cliché, but I agree with those who say, even though you can't control everything in life, you can always control your reaction to things."

"You sound like a therapist," Tristan snickered.

Zoey didn't like his sarcastic tone, but before she could respond he turned back to the quote board.

"I think you should put up one from Voltaire," he said, chuckling. "'Men will always be mad, and those who think they can cure them are the maddest of all.' What do you think?"

"I think my therapist would disagree with you," she replied angrily. Realizing she just admitted she was in therapy, Zoey turned red. *Shit. I just became "one of those" people.* Tristan tilted his head quizzically, waiting for her to voice her apparent frustration. When she didn't continue he placed his hand on her arm.

"Zoey, I'm sorry if I said something to offend you. I know we were having a serious conversation, but I was just teasing you. I didn't mean to insult you by mentioning therapy."

Tristan's response didn't help to make Zoey feel any better, even though she understood his point of view. She had never taken therapy seriously before either, until she began seeing Dr. Stephens. But she recognized now that the sessions had become a huge part of her healing process, and she felt more like herself than she had in months. She was returning to the way she was with Laura, and she didn't feel the need to defend that.

When she didn't answer, Tristan tried a different approach.

"I went to Dr. Loring," he admitted. Zoey looked up at him, surprised. He smiled sheepishly.

"Oh yeah, I did my time. It was after my sister. My parents decided I wasn't dealing with anything, so they paid for me to go."

Zoey felt her embarrassment begin to subside, while her sudden anger turned to curiosity. She tilted her head toward him and nodded.

"That's what mine are doing."

"I think it's a rite of passage these days," he said, as he noticed Zoey's attitude start to change. "You know, having your parents pay for someone else to listen to your problems. Very modern."

Zoey giggled, and Tristan knew the tense moment had passed.

"Do you go to Dr. Loring too?"

"No, I see Dr. Stephens." She felt better knowing he had experienced therapy for himself. It was almost a relief.

"Yeah, I guess there's only two to choose from, unless they send you to a specialist. Thankfully my parents weren't that concerned. That would've really sucked."

"How long were you in therapy?"

"It didn't take me that long to figure out the system, so I got out of it pretty quickly. I can help you out if you want."

Zoey paused, unsure of what he meant. They had just gotten through their first argument and she didn't want to return to it. She worded her answer carefully.

"Oh. Well, I'm kinda getting used to it now. It's not that bad anymore."

This time it was Tristan's turn to be surprised.

"Really? I thought it was more bullshit. But hey, to each his own, I guess."

Again, Zoey felt her coolness factor drop another notch. She quickly tried to back-pedal.

"Well, I mean, I thought the whole 'homework' thing was retarded. But now we really are just talking about everyday stuff."

"Then what do you need her for? Seriously. It's like that quote. No one can be cured, so why waste your time?"

This time, Zoey didn't have a response. She disagreed with him, of course, but after Tristan's reaction to the subject of therapy, she decided to keep that thought to herself.

"Like I said, it was my parents idea," she mumbled.

"Yeah. I guess if your parents are paying for it then who cares, right?" he said. Zoey nodded, feeling numb.

"Yeah. Who cares?"

Zoey glanced over at Tristan as he stared at the ceiling, wondering what he was thinking. She wanted to move past this subject, but didn't know what to say that wouldn't sound awkward. Slowly Tristan brought his head back down and looked over at her.

"So, you think with the help of therapy that people can control their emotions?" he asked curiously. Zoey wished at that moment she had thought of something to say.

"Well, sort of. I guess some people have to learn to control them that way. But I don't think everyone needs therapy to do that."

"So after Laura's death, you were able to keep yourself from being depressed?"

Zoey frowned, wrinkling her forehead.

"That's not really what I meant."

"Well, I think that's the level of thinking that sets people off," he said, turning toward her. "Thoughts are one thing, but emotions? That's what makes them emotions. You have no control over them. They can be pretty strong, don't you think?"

"Yeah, I guess so."

"That's all I'm saying. Some things you can't let go, nor should you. My sister, your best friend, they're a part of us, and they always will be. There's no letting go of that loss, and sometimes you have to act out before it consumes you. You know what I'm saying, right?"

Tristan gazed into her eyes, and Zoey recognized the same fervor every time he talked about his sister's death. She understood it, and felt it along with him, but the intensity was a little overwhelming at times. Even after all these years he seemed to be consumed with the same anger he had felt when he was 15. Still, she knew very few people who could sympathize with her situation, and he was one of them. She didn't want to insult him, especially when he was confiding in her.

"I do understand. I do."

Reaching out, Tristan touched her face and kissed her gently. The softness turned into a deeper embrace, as he wrapped his arms around her and pulled her close. His touch was always calming, allowing her to let go of all of her anxiety. After another moment, he loosened his grip and leaned back to look at her.

"I knew you would. That's why we're perfect for each other."

Zoey nodded, trying to catch her breath.

Tristan leaned back against the wall as Zoey nestled against him. They sat there in silence for a moment, letting their breathing settle. After another minute, Tristan looked over at the quote board again.

"That's an interesting one," he noted, reading the quote out loud. "'All the art of living lies in a fine mingling of letting go and holding on'. Havelock Ellis. Who's that?"

"I think he was a British doctor or something."

"Wait, you don't know? What if he was some psychopathic killer and you have one of his quotes on your board?"

"So what? I'm sure some of history's darkest characters had some great quotes about life."

"So if Hitler said something brilliant you'd put it on your board?"

"Well, not if it was something about how to eliminate an entire race of people or anything."

Tristan grinned and let go of Zoey. He stood up and went over to the computer on her desk.

"Let's look him up."

"Who? Hitler?"

"No, Havelock Ellis."

Zoey got up and stood behind him, leaning toward the screen. After putting Ellis's name in the search engine, Tristan clicked on the first link that came up in the list.

"Oh nice. The first line says he was a British sexologist."

"And a doctor, and a social reformer," Zoey added hastily. Tristan scanned the rest of the entry.

"It says here he was impotent until 60 years old, when he realized he got excited by watching a woman urinate," Tristan sputtered. "Ellis named the interest in urination "Undinism" but it is now more commonly called Urolagnia. Oh shit, you have a quote from the guy who came up with the golden shower! I wonder if that's what he means by 'letting go and holding on!'"

Zoey felt herself blushing again as Tristan laughed even harder. She was too embarrassed to tell him that it was her favorite quote, especially when she knew nothing about the person who said it.

Damn Internet.

"Hey, he also defended homosexuality," she pointed out, reading further down the entry. "That makes him a guy ahead of his time."

"Oh, you're just pissed off you have a quote from a guy who liked to be pissed on," Tristan said, still laughing.

"Ewww, gross! He never said he liked being peed on!" Zoey exclaimed. "Ugh. Can we stop talking about peeing, please?"

"Ok, ok, I'm sorry," Tristan said, trying to control his breathing. He could tell she was embarrassed again. "You're right. Whoever the guy was, it is a good quote."

CHAPTER FORTY-SIX

Dr. Stephens sat at her desk, staring at the clock. She had been anxiously awaiting her next session with Zoey, over a concern she hadn't felt for a client in a long time, maybe ever in her 25 years as a therapist. In that time she had dealt with many troubled and violent teenagers, and each client taught her something new about the teenage psyche. But in every case she had dealt with the potentially dangerous person directly, which meant she had some control over the situation. This time, she didn't even know the full extent of the problem, never mind what she could do to change it.

As a professional, she hoped being the outside observer would continue to be helpful in Zoey's case. Jumping to conclusions was never a good idea, and it was important to maintain Zoey's trust.

I have to be careful not to ruin the relationship we've built up over these last few months. That's a given.

When it was finally time for the session, Stephens went out into the waiting room to find Zoey looking through a magazine.

"Hi, Zoey. Are you ready?"

"I am," she replied, standing up. "Let's do this."

At least she seems to be in a good mood, Stephens thought.

As Zoey sat down, Stephens grabbed her notebook and looked over her notes from their previous session one more time. She had a specific plan to follow.

"Ok, Zoey. Before we begin, I was thinking about something from our last conversation that I would like to explore. Time ran out on us unfortunately."

"Sure."

"Great. I wanted to discuss your blog, since that was a new piece of information you shared with me. Do you share your name on the blog, or is it anonymous?"

"It's anonymous for the most part. I call myself 'Z' and I talk about other people by the first letter of their name to make things easier. But that's about it."

"But you said you shared your blog with Tristan, which suggests to me you're not concerned about those thoughts being anonymous with him?"

"That's true. I'm not nervous about opening up to him, since he's not concerned about opening up to me."

"You feel you share things freely?"

"Definitely."

"And you mentioned he has a blog also. Has he shared that with you?"

"Yup."

Stephens paused. With the ease in which Zoey answered the question, Stephens had a sinking feeling it was a different blog than the one she had read. She had to phrase the next couple of questions very carefully.

"Do you write about each other on the blogs?"

"Sometimes. He doesn't use my name, like I don't use his. But his is mostly about general stuff in his life, rather than specific things we do together, same as mine."

"I see."

Stephens paused again, looking over her notes. As Zoey sat there, she wondered why Dr. Stephens was so interested in the content of their blogs. There didn't seem to be anything noteworthy to this conversation, but she assumed Stephens had brought it up for a reason. She waited to see what that reason was.

After another minute of silence, Zoey cleared her throat.

"Um, was there anything else with the blog thing?"

Stephens lifted her head from her notes. *Shoot. I don't think there's much else I can do here.*

"I don't think so. As long as there isn't anything you're concerned about."

"With the blog? Like what?"

"Well, when you're with someone else and you talk about them in an open forum, trust issues can arise. Putting everything out there for the world to see in a blog can be a concern for some people."

"Oh. Well, it's not like that with us," Zoey replied. "I mean, we don't get that personal in the blogs. They're really more for fun now, especially since we both have one. It was another interest we shared that brought us closer together."

"I see. Well, that's great, Zoey."

Zoey heard the words Dr. Stephens was saying, but her tone seemed cautious. Their conversation didn't flow as casually as others had in the past.

Even during the times Zoey was upset, Dr. Stephens seemed to know what to say every time to bring the conversation back down to a calmer level. Today she simply seemed preoccupied.

I guess therapists can have a bad day too, she thought.

"Am I in trouble or something?" Zoey joked, attempting to break the silence.

I wish I knew, Stephens thought. It took some effort not to cringe at Zoey's question.

"You know I take all my cues from you, Zoey," she answered, forcing a smile. "Why don't we move onto something else then. What would you like to talk about today?"

As Zoey changed the subject Stephens listened intently, but in the back of her mind her concerns still nagged at her. *Zoey's responses didn't answer any of the important questions. But I can't introduce new information into our sessions. It would disturb the sense of trust I've worked so hard to establish with her.*

Stephens shifted in her seat as she continued to take notes.

Who knows. Maybe Zoey isn't in danger, she wondered. *There are a number of possibilities, and Zoey being directly involved with this blogger is only one of them. It's quite possible that nothing will come of this.*

Now all Stephens had to do was convince herself of that.

CHAPTER FORTY-SEVEN

"Come on, Walter, I'll be at the house in five minutes. That's plenty of time to finish writing your page. Then you can come out to help bring in the groceries."

Do we have to have this conversation every time? Connie wondered as she talked to her husband on her cell phone. *It's bad enough I have to go grocery shopping by myself, especially since Walter's always home working. He claims he can never "tear" himself away from the book until it's finished, which I can understand when it comes to other household duties. But grocery shopping takes up the most time, damn it!*

"You just finished a book for Christ sake! Can't you take a break in-between projects for once?" Connie asked, exasperated. "Seriously, honey, if you could for once help me out with this I would greatly appreciate it."

"Connie, is it really that much to bring them from the driveway into the house?"

"After a full day of showing properties and then wandering around the grocery store for an hour? Yes!"

She could hear Walter sigh on the other end of the phone.

"Fine. See you in a minute."

Click.

"Bye!" she said loudly into the silent phone. Shaking her head she put the phone back in her purse.

"God, you'd think I was asking him to move furniture or something," she muttered out loud. A minute later she pulled into the driveway, looking for Walter. He was nowhere in sight.

"Ugh!" she exclaimed, putting the car in park. As she stepped out of the car she noticed a flyer taped to the front door.

What could that be for?

Walking to the back of the car, Connie opened up the trunk and grabbed several bags of groceries. She fumbled with her keys in case the front door was locked and made her way up to the house. Before trying the handle she read the piece of paper hanging at eye level.

"A memorial will be held for beloved student Laura Simmons at 11 a.m. on April 11, the first-year anniversary of her death," it read. "Students who attend at the campus quad are encouraged to bring photos of Laura to celebrate the life of a young girl who was tragically taken from us too soon."

I wonder if Zoey has seen this yet.

Connie unlocked the door and walked into the house, loudly placing the numerous bags on the kitchen table.

"Walter? There are a lot more bags in the car!" She could hear the sound of his chair moving in his office, followed by the door opening.

"Yes, darling, I'm coming," he called sweetly back to her.

"Thank you, my love," she cooed as he entered the kitchen.

"Mm hmm." He walked out to the car, with Connie close behind him.

"Walt? Did you see this flyer for a memorial for Laura?"

Walter grabbed two armfuls of bags from the trunk and looked toward his wife, shaking his head no. Connie carefully pulled the paper off the door and brought it inside. She placed it on the counter and began putting the groceries away. Walter joined her.

"A memorial, huh?" he asked, glancing at the sheet. "I wonder if Zoey has seen this yet."

"I was wondering the same thing. She didn't say anything to me. I thought maybe she mentioned something to you."

"Nope. I imagine if she did see it she would've taken it down. And I doubt she would talk to either one of us about it, seeing as she never talks about Laura anymore."

"That's true. Maybe when she gets home I'll show it to her, in case she wants to go."

"I think I already know the answer to that."

"I don't know, Walt. She seems to be doing much better, especially now that she's dating Tristan. He seems like such a nice boy. And so smart too! I think he'll be a great influence on Zoey. You know, keep her out of that funk she was in for a while."

"I hope so."

Just as Walter finished his sentence they both heard the front door open and close.

"Well, I guess now's as good a time as any," Connie said, grabbing the flyer off the counter.

"Zoey? Honey, can you come into the kitchen, please?

Geez, I just walked in the door. What did I do now? she wondered, walking into the kitchen.

"Hey."

"Hey, kiddo," Walter said, sounding a bit too upbeat. "How was work?"

"Fine," Zoey answered cautiously. "What's up?"

"Well, honey, when I came home from grocery shopping I found this flyer taped to the door."

Connie handed the paper to Zoey and waited for her to read it. She couldn't tell immediately what Zoey's reaction was- all she saw was a blank look on her face. She glanced over at Walter who was also trying to gauge his daughter's reaction. After a moment Zoey placed the paper on the kitchen table.

"Is that it?"

"Yes," Connie said. "Do you think you'd like to go to the memorial?"

"For what?"

Connie paused, looking to Walter for help. He put his hand on Zoey's shoulder.

"Being the anniversary of her death, it might help to be with other people who knew Laura. It might help to remember the good times you had, rather than grieving for her. It's part of the process of moving on with your life, honey."

"Dad, I really don't know any of those people," Zoey replied, walking away from him. "My memories of her don't often include them. She and I had a much more special relationship than she had with anyone else. So I really don't see what good it would do to sit there and watch a bunch of strangers talk about things that have nothing to do with me or my relationship with Laura."

"Zoey, I think your father is right. Besides, Laura was such a social butterfly that getting everyone together is the perfect way to honor her memory."

"But I don't need a memorial once a year to 'honor' her memory, Mom. I think about her all the time."

"I know, honey, I know. That's why it might be easier to gather with other people and share those thoughts, rather than keeping them bottled up inside."

"It's the perfect forum to express your feelings," Walter added.

"Isn't that why I'm in therapy?"

"This is different," Connie said. "It would be a much more personal experience than talking to Dr. Stephens."

"I share plenty with her."

Connie looked to Walter again, raising her eyebrows. He shrugged.

"That's great, honey. I'm really glad to hear therapy is going well," she said quietly.

"So is that it?" Zoey asked, inching closer to the doorway.

"Just think about it, okay Zoey?"

"Ugh. Fine," she said, turning toward the stairs. "I don't know why you guys are making such a big deal about this."

Walter waited until he heard her footsteps enter her bedroom and the door close. He turned back to Connie.

"I told you."

"Hey, it didn't hurt to ask!"

"Not for her. But we got to have yet another mini-argument about how best to grieve her best friend's death. I guess the fact she hasn't been talking about this with us is a good thing."

"Walter! That's a terrible thing to say!"

"Come on, Connie. Is this something you'd like to discuss with her on a daily basis? She claims to be letting it all out in therapy, but I don't think anything has changed over this past year."

"Well, now you know how I've felt all this time! The more I try to communicate with her, about anything, the more she pushes me away. Even during dinner with Tristan she acted as if we were the bane of her existence."

"I know."

Connie sat down at the kitchen table, frustrated by her daughter's negative response to yet another good idea. It was a trend that seemingly no one could break.

"Is this something we have to ride out?" she asked, sounding tired. "Because if so, I don't know how much longer I can do that."

Walter joined her at the table and took her hand.

"It feels like a lot, I know. Every day it's a struggle just to get her to say two words to us. But it's important for her to know we're always here, whether she wants us to be or not. She still needs guidance, even if she's resistant to it."

"I know. I just wish it wasn't such a battle to communicate with our own child."

"Ah, the wish of every parent with a teenager," Walter said. "If I was able to figure that out, I could write a book on that and really be rich!"

Connie laughed.

"We'll have to work on that."

CHAPTER FORTY-EIGHT

It had been more than a week since her parents mentioned the memorial service, and Zoey was grateful it hadn't become a daily reminder. Even though she hated to admit it, she already thought about the memorial- a lot.

I can't believe it's been a year already, she wrote in her journal. *I didn't think I would survive this long. I mean, I knew the world wouldn't stop turning, I just didn't think I'd still be as much a part of it as I am without her. Maybe I am stronger than I thought.*

Of course, there's still that part of me that's waiting for her to return, as if life will suddenly realize it made a terrible mistake and bring her back to me somehow. I don't know if that feeling will ever go away. And do I really want it to? Some days I feel like that's the only thing keeping me going.

But that's not something I can tell random people. Dad seems to think since we all knew Laura that we have this common bond, but some bonds are stronger than others. I was always the sidekick, the girl who accompanied Laura wherever she went. And I was okay with that, because what Laura gave me in return was far greater than just numerous acquaintances. She was what made life bearable.

Even now, being with Tristan, I realize there's still a part of me missing, a part of me that will always be connected to her. I thought he would be able to fill the void that opened up when Laura died, but no one can do that. She was my true soul mate, if that concept even exists.

Thankfully, though, Tristan did bring something back into my life that I desperately needed- understanding.

He feels the pain that comes along with losing someone you thought you couldn't live without, until one day you have to. He endures the constant struggle of waking up every day knowing she won't be there, and getting out of bed anyway. He realizes that time can do nothing but continue on, as if there's nothing to stop for, when he knows very well there is. And he consoles me whenever I need it, because he knows the kind of consoling he needs in return.

He's the only thing in my life that would make me believe in God.

Zoey studied her last thought. It had been a long time since she even thought about the existence of God. She used to read books and articles on the subject all the time before Laura's death. But in the last year or so she had been fairly convinced she knew the answer.

I know there's plenty of tragedy in the world, which is my main argument against the existence of god. All that "God works in mysterious ways" bullshit doesn't do it for me, nor does "we can't understand his plan." The only way I can rationalize it, if I can even use that term, is that we all have to suffer through a short life so we can make it to a really kickass afterlife as a great reward. If that was indeed true, then I could almost understand the Catholic god. I just think the idea of an afterlife is complete crap, which pretty much refutes that whole rationalization.

Before she could write any further her cell phone rang. Zoey waited a few seconds to answer it. It was all part of the "I'm not that eager" persona she was trying to maintain in the early stages of their relationship. It was a Laura thing.

"Hi."

"Hey," he said. "What'cha up to?"

"I was writing in my journal."

"Anything hot and sexy?"

"Yeah, I was writing about my other boyfriend and me having a threesome with a stripper."

"Damn! I miss all the good stuff!"

"You know me and my wild side."

"Totally. So, anything you can share with your real boyfriend?"

"Actually, I was just writing some stuff about Laura. It's the one-year anniversary coming up and there's this memorial thing they're having at the college next month."

"Are you going?"

"I don't know. My parents think I should."

"What do you think?"

"I think that kind of thing is pointless. I don't need to sit there with a bunch of people to remember Laura. I always think about her. I mean, if it helps other people that's fine, but I don't need help."

"I know what you mean. For the first couple years after Chastity's death my parents would always do something special, you know, stuff that she liked to do, on the anniversary of her death. It made me feel stupid. Nothing's gonna bring her back so why even bother?"

"At least they had a more fun idea than people standing around in one place looking at pictures. I can appreciate the sentiment, I guess."

"Just because it was tailored to her doesn't make it any more meaningful," Tristan scoffed. "Either way it's pointless. I don't want to be reminded of what happened that day by supposedly 'celebrating' her life on an annual basis after she's dead."

Zoey paused, not knowing what to say. She agreed wholeheartedly, but Tristan often became angry when talking about Chastity's death. She never knew how to respond without making it worse.

Her pause must've lasted longer than she thought.

"Zoey? You still there?"

"What? Oh, yeah, sorry. I was, um, lost in thought."

"You know what I mean though, right? About there not being a good way to honor someone's memory?"

"Sure," she said, trying not to sound awkward. "The memories should be a daily thing."

"Well, not only that, there's no way to get over something like that. It's dishonoring their memory, going on as if they never existed. But that's what my parents think was the 'right thing to do.' It's ironic. That's the one thing they agree on and it's totally wrong."

"What do you mean, wrong?"

"I mean just that. It's wrong. It's disrespectful to my sister, to treat her death like it doesn't change their lives. Mine will never be the same again."

"But they grieved, right? I mean, they went through the grieving process?"

"Please. Grieving process. That's such a clinical term. My grief will never end," he said defiantly. "I mean, think about Laura. Will your grief ever end?"

Zoey thought about what she had just written in her journal. Sure, she was still hurting from the loss of her closest friend, but she was still living day to day. Meeting Tristan had given her a new outlook on life. And even if her life was completely different without Laura, she knew Laura would want her to live it any way she could.

But the word grief stuck in her mind. *Is that something people carry around forever for their loved ones and just try to hide it? Does it exist in different levels depending on the day or place? Will it always be this weight on my back?* Zoey didn't know. All she knew was that she was surviving.

"Honestly, I don't know. Everyone tells me it will lessen over time, that things will get easier. It still hurts, but I'm also still here."

"Yeah, but how much of you is still here?"

"What do you mean?"

"Don't you sometimes feel like only a certain part of you is still carrying on, like you're split into several personalities who handle different aspects of your life? I feel completely torn apart, where only a handful of tattered pieces survived and are being held together by thread."

"Well, that I understand. I felt completely lost without Laura here, like I didn't even exist as a person without her anymore."

"You said felt, as in past tense. You don't still feel that way?"

"Well, not in the same way, no. I mean, once I met you, I began to feel like more of a whole person again."

Zoey was met by silence on the other end. *Oh no, I blew it. We were finally starting to connect and I blurt something like that out without even thinking how it would sound! Think, Zoey, think!*

But it didn't take long for Tristan to put her at ease.

"You strengthened some of my threads too," he said softly. "You're the one who allowed me to finally reach this point in my life. And for that I will always be grateful."

Zoey breathed a sigh of relief.

"But no one will ever take the place of my sister."

"Oh, no, of course not!" Zoey exclaimed. "I didn't mean…"

"I know, it's okay. You understand."

"I do."

Tristan paused.

"When is this memorial thing?"

"April 11."

"You know, maybe you should go. Maybe we both should. I think we're ready. We don't need this life anymore, you know? We have a way to deal with our pain and we don't need anyone else. It's time for a change, and I know the best way to do that."

"Yeah? What's that?" Zoey asked, surprised by Tristan's change of heart.

"You know how I told you some of my friends are in a band?" he asked. "Well, the night before the memorial they're having a big jam session at their practice space in the city. There will be lots of people there from my college days. You should come with me. It'll be a celebration of our lives, the way we live them, not how our parents think we should. Then we can have our final stand at the memorial. What do you say?"

Zoey didn't have to think about it for a second. The idea of finally getting to meet his friends, letting go of all her inhibitions, was so exciting that she didn't even question what he meant by their "final stand".

"I'm in!"

CHAPTER FORTY-NINE

Zoey stood in front of her mirror, surveying her outfit. Tristan's invite finally gave her the opportunity to wear her leather pants, along with the boots Laura had bought her. After buckling them up, she adjusted her fitted shirt and reached for her chain necklace and leather bracelets.

Now this is an ensemble.

Checking her hair one more time, she grabbed her cell phone and walked downstairs. Her parents had gone to an overnight party thrown by her father's agent, allowing her to leave the house without any disapproving parental stares. Zoey had never cared about her appearance before, which had been a great relief to her parents. They never had to have the talk with their daughter about what was and wasn't appropriate to wear in public.

But now there was a boy involved, and it happened after Zoey was old enough to buy and wear what she wanted. They didn't know which was worse.

Jesus, they're such hypocrites, Zoey thought. *I've seen a number of pictures of my mom from the seventies, miniskirt and all. What's the difference? At least I'm not wearing pants with the word "juicy" on the ass.*

Outside Zoey could hear the engine of Tristan's motorcycle roaring down her street, right on time. Not wanting to appear too eager, she decided to wait for him to come to the door and knock.

"Just a second," she called out from the kitchen. Trying to look confident, she sauntered to the front door and opened it.

"Hey," she said, a small grin parting her lips. Tristan took a step back, deliberately looking her up and down as Zoey tried to remain cool. He stepped toward her again and leaned into her neck.

"Nice," he whispered. A shiver ran down her back.

"Thanks. You're not so bad yourself."

"Well, sexy, you ready to go?"

"Absolutely."

Zoey was getting used to the bike, so much so that she didn't have to hang onto Tristan as tightly as she used to. It didn't stop her from still doing so, but it helped to boost her confidence riding on the highway. Racing through the April night, it was unusually warm as a slight breeze blew over them. They soon left the town behind them, Zoey's sense of excitement growing along with the office buildings.

I'm free.

But soon the neon lights began to dim as Tristan brought them deeper and deeper into the city, entering a realm that Zoey had never believed existed outside of TV and movies. Office complexes and shopping malls became seedy video stores and abandoned warehouses. The crowds changed from professionals rushing home in business suits to professionals whose business took place on the street. Headlights were fires in trash cans, policemen turned homeless, and the rush of commerce, now a faint murmur.

Zoey realized her life was now entirely in Tristan's hands.

Turning the corner, Tristan led the bike down a small alley and stopped alongside an old brick building. She could hear the faint guttural sounds of guitars and heavy drums through the helmet. Tristan turned off the engine and waited for Zoey to let go of him. Reluctantly, she loosened her grip.

"Are you okay?" he asked, taking off his helmet. Zoey removed hers, trying not to show her feelings of trepidation. The music grew louder.

"Uh, yeah. I was just kinda wondering where we are."

"We're here."

"This is their jam space?"

"Yup."

"Um, this doesn't seem like a very safe neighborhood."

Tristan chuckled.

"Don't worry. People know this is my bike."

"Okay," she said, unsure of what he meant by that statement. Before she could ask, he took her hand and led her toward one of the buildings.

"Come on. The party's inside."

Tristan walked over to a steel door and opened it, revealing a dark hall with two flights of stairs. As they got closer to the bottom, Zoey could hear the thumping sounds of the drums grow louder and louder. By the time they reached the second steel door her entire body was pulsing.

God, I hope I don't spontaneously combust.

Grabbing the handle, Tristan turned it and opened the door to the rabbit hole.

With that first step, it appeared to Zoey that she had tumbled down a seemingly black abyss. She strained her eyes to see darkened figures lingering against the brick walls, their faces occasionally lit up by a flickering cigarette lighter. Others relied on hoodies to keep their identity hidden. Zoey coughed from the thick haze of smoke that hung as heavy in the air as the chords being struck somewhere in another room. As Tristan led her through the fog, the crack addicts and meth heads turned to study the obvious newbie.

"Let's find the beer!" Tristan yelled over the music.

Zoey nodded in an attempt to stifle her growing anxiety as they wandered around an endless assortment of drug users, groupie strip teasers and wannabe thugs. Tristan seemed to recognize a number of them from each group, something that made her both relieved and uneasy.

After what seemed an eternity to Zoey, they found a large cooler filled with beer in the corner of the third room, the same room where they discovered the band playing. Tristan handed her a can and reached in for another one. Zoey popped it open and took a long drink.

"I feel like we wandered into a Nine Inch Nails video!" she shouted. Tristan grinned and took her hand again.

"Let's find an open spot somewhere!"

"Okay!"

Zoey followed as he turned to the other side of the room. Avoiding the growing circle of groupies in the middle of the floor, he chose the line of pot smokers for a less invasive path and found his way to an empty bench along the wall. Zoey felt relieved to sit down away from the numerous clusters of dark shadows covering the room.

Tristan looked over and noticed her nervous expression for the first time.

"It's a lot to take in, huh?"

"You know, I thought after going to some crazy frat parties that I would be totally fine. But this. This is a whole world I've never seen before."

Tristan leaned back as he gazed across the room.

"Welcome to my kingdom."

"Kingdom?" Zoey asked, smiling. "Isn't that a bit much?"

"Not at all."

Even with the deafening music, Zoey could hear the gravity in his voice. She didn't know what to say. She sipped her beer to avoid a reply and turned her attention back to the band.

Suddenly, out of the throng of groupies, a blonde high schooler emerged from the crowd and made her way over to Tristan. Her outfit barely served the purpose of covering her taut body. As she came closer, Zoey recognized her as one of the girls from Lou's Lair. She stared as the girl blatantly ignored her presence and tried to sit down in Tristan's lap.

"Hey, baby. You going to the afterparty tonight?"

Tristan held up his hand, abruptly stopping her before she could sit down.

"Not tonight," he said, emotionless. "I'm not hanging out with the band after this."

"What? Why not?"

One look from Tristan and the girl began to back up slowly. Zoey watched her expression turn from coy to apprehensive.

"Ok. No problem," she said nervously. Without another word she disappeared back into the crowd. Zoey turned to Tristan, confused.

"Fuckin groupies," he said, rolling his eyes. "Sorry about that. That's Brandy. She got kicked out of her house or something so she stays here sometimes. She knows we party here a lot and that I'm friends with the bands, so she's always trying to get closer to them to have a place to crash."

"Oh," Zoey said, trying to mimic his nonchalant attitude. Inside she was still reeling. "I see."

"You'll find all kinds here. That's the price you pay for acceptance."

As he continued to describe other individuals he knew, Zoey began to feel the same apprehension as the blonde. She knew Tristan was bringing her to a place where she could throw off all social constraints and expectations, but there was no order of any sort, only the four walls that hid all of the drug use and homeless teenagers. She couldn't relax and be herself if she felt like a stranger among other outcasts. This place wasn't a relief- it was frightening.

And Tristan had claimed it for his throne.

Another look toward Zoey made Tristan suddenly pause from his storytelling.

"You're really uncomfortable, aren't you? What's wrong?"

"I just..." Zoey trailed off, not knowing how to explain her anxiety without sounding like a scared child. Tristan wrinkled his forehead.

"Are you feeling claustrophobic?"

"Yes," she answered quickly. *That sounds plausible.* "It's just kinda stuffy in here."

"Don't worry. I know someone who can help with that. I'll be right back."

Before she could object, Tristan stood up and immediately vanished into the void, leaving her alone against the brick wall.

This is supposed to help my anxiety?

Zoey tried not to panic as she sat there by herself. People walked by on their way to another room, some of the guys nodding their heads toward her. She gave them a tight-lipped smile so as not to appear nervous. She knew she looked the part enough so no one would think she was a narc, but not knowing anyone else made her stand out as the one loner. *How ironic,* she thought, *to still feel like a loner in a place like this. God, where the hell is Tristan?*

It seemed like an hour had passed before he returned, but her phone claimed it was only 10 minutes. In his hand he held a small sandwich bag with 4 pills.

"Here. Take one of these," he offered, handing her the bag.

"What is it?"

"It's just a little something to take the edge off. You'll feel great in no time."

Zoey paused. *So he does still do drugs?*

"I, I've never done drugs before."

"It's okay. This is small stuff, really. Don't you trust me?"

Zoey thought she knew the answer to that question, until now. She had been ready for Tristan to take her anywhere that night, as long as it was away from the confines of the small town that had been her sole existence. But the anticipation she felt at the beginning of the night had turned into uncertainty, in a place where she felt even more isolated than in that small town.

But looking into Tristan's eyes Zoey was reminded of their first date, and how he had reached back to take her hand. She felt that same euphoria any time he touched her, and she believed he would always protect her. Even in the darkness surrounding them she wanted to be with him, wherever he was. It was Zoey's first experience with this kind of emotional struggle, where her desire began to eclipse her common sense.

God, I wish Laura was here.

Tristan knelt down in front of her, waiting for her answer. She knew this moment could either make or break the rest of their night.

"Well... of course. I trust you."

"This will help tremendously, I promise. It's like nothing you've ever experienced before. You're gonna feel so good, you'll never want to come back down."

Zoey knew he wasn't going to let it go until she at least tried it. *How bad can it be*, she began to rationalize. *People do this kind of stuff all the time, right?* She opened the bag and popped one of the pills in her mouth, taking the beer Tristan held out to her and swallowing. Handing the bag back to Tristan, he took one out as well and downed it with a swig of beer. She tried not to gasp.

"Shouldn't you stay sober? You have to drive!"

"It's fine. I'll be over one pill and one beer by the time we leave."

Never having taken drugs before, Zoey had no choice but to believe him. He put the bag in his pocket and sat down next to her.

"So, did I miss anything exciting?"

"Not that I know of," Zoey replied. She was almost afraid to ask what would be considered exciting in this place. Tristan put his arm around her and she tried to settle into his embrace without showing any more anxiety. Resting her head lightly on his shoulder, she drank her beer, assuming it wouldn't have any adverse effects with the drugs. *Maybe it'll even help.* She hoped so.

As the night wore on, the two of them watched as the crowd grew bigger and began to mosh. Pretty soon their private nook wasn't so private any more, and it seemed everyone knew Tristan. He continuously took his arm off of her to fist bump someone or stand up and hug them. He introduced Zoey to some of them, while others, especially girls, he simply caressed their arm and sent on their way.

But after he kissed one girl lightly on the lips, Zoey opened her mouth to protest, only to pause as she felt the effects of the pill start to kick in. As she looked around the room she began to see more shapes and colors in the dark outlines of the people. Her fears began to subside as she lifted her head back toward Tristan, who was waving bye to the scantily dressed girl. She giggled as he sat back down next to her.

"How ya feeling, baby? Better?"

"Yeah," Zoey sighed, forgetting about the girl.

"You wanna go into another room?"

"Okay!"

Zoey jumped off the bench and grabbed Tristan's hand. Pulling him up, she started to walk into another room when Tristan stopped her.

"I know a better one, babe."

Zoey nodded and followed him in the other direction. A heavy curtain hung in the corner of the first room near the front door, and Tristan pushed it aside to reveal a smaller room with a futon and cushions on the floor. One couple was already kissing on the futon, so he led Zoey over to the cushions and pulled her down onto him. Zoey giggled as she tumbled onto the floor.

Tristan rolled on top of her and covered her mouth with his. A rush of heat washed over Zoey's entire body as she pressed against him, running her hands along his arms and chest. Tristan's kiss deepened, and Zoey felt pockets of electricity under his fingertips as he trailed them down her back. He reached down to unzip her pants when three more couples came barreling into the room, tripping over them.

"Hey! What the fuck?" Tristan yelled as he pushed one of the couples away from them.

"Sorry, man," the guy said, sitting down next to them. "There's nowhere else to go."

Tristan grunted as their floor space became even smaller. He looked over at Zoey who instinctively leaned in for another kiss. He shook his head.

"Let's get outta here," he said gruffly. Zoey nodded.

CHAPTER FIFTY

Zoey and Tristan came falling through the door of his apartment, completely entangled in each other. The room spun along with them as they landed against the wall. Zoey had never before felt such a surge of emotion mixed with physical pleasure. She couldn't remember anything about the ride home, except for the intense fever she felt all over her body as she held onto Tristan. He was all that mattered.

Tristan slammed the door behind them and held her against the back of it, kissing her as if it was the last time. He pulled her shirt over her head and threw it on the floor, licking her neck and biting her earlobe. Zoey could barely breathe as she clung to his back. He unhooked her bra and let it fall beside them, gently cupping her breasts. The sensation seared through Zoey's body as she tore the shirt over his head.

Kissing her again, Tristan pulled her further into the room, causing them to fall onto the couch. Zoey landed on top of him and began to laugh. He flipped her onto her back and kissed her as he tugged at the buttons of her leather pants. He trailed his tongue down her chest to her navel, peeling the pants off on his way down. Zoey lifted her hips and legs instinctively.

That's when Tristan found his way down to her boots. He grabbed them and tried to pull them off, but the buckles held firm. Zoey wiggled her feet.

"Do you like my boots? They're new."

"Sorry, baby," he answered, pulling the buckles open. "They gotta go."

Throwing them aside, Tristan fell back on top of her, and Zoey fumbled with his belt and jeans. He helped her remove them, along with his boxers, and stood up, staring down the length of her almost naked body. She could feel his eyes wash over every inch of her as he leaned down and pulled her off the couch.

"Bedroom."

Tristan turned on the lamp next to his bed as Zoey pulled him onto the mattress. He pulled off her final piece of clothing and began to gently massage inside her. It was amazing, until she felt an intense pressure she'd never experienced before now. She grabbed his wrist.

"Tristan, I've never done this before," she uttered breathlessly, suddenly very aware of what was about to happen.

"I know," he said, matching her breath for breath. "I'll take care of you."

Before she could reply, he leaned down and kissed her very gently. Her heightened sense of touch allowed her to forget about her anxiety as he returned to pleasuring her.

Suddenly she realized how hard he was, and she leaned back to look at it. She had seen penises in pornography before, but this was the first time she was seeing one in real life. It was then she realized there was no turning back–he was ready.

"Do you have something?" she whispered.

Tristan paused, then leaned down to open a drawer on the nightstand. Taking out a condom, he slid it on and turned back to her. She breathed a sigh of relief as he kissed her again. Now everything was perfect.

"Are you ready?" he asked.

"Yes," she whispered, without hesitation.

He parted her legs and entered her slowly. At first it was just uncomfortable, but when she saw the blood trickle down her leg she suddenly felt the tearing agony. She dug her nails into his back as she cried out in pain.

"Don't worry, baby," he said, kissing her neck. "Hold on. It's okay. Everything's okay."

As he rocked in and out of her, his deliberate motion helped to ease the initial aching, while her intoxication turned her cries of pain into moans of pleasure. She clung to him as he went a bit deeper, a bit faster, and after a few minutes of heightened pleasure, he finally climaxed. Zoey wasn't sure what she felt until he stopped, and the rush of pain returned. She tried to take a couple of deep breaths.

Tristan collapsed, holding himself up by his elbows so as not to crush her. He buried his head in her shoulder as he tried to slow his breathing. Zoey didn't know if she should say something or let him speak first. She chose the latter.

After a minute, Tristan raised his head to look into her eyes.

"That was amazing. It was like you brought me back to my first time. The anticipation, the excitement, the passion, it was perfect."

Zoey felt relieved as she caught her breath.

"It was perfect."

"How about I change the sheets while you go clean up in the bathroom," he said, sitting up slowly.

"Okay."

Zoey stood up very carefully to try and alleviate the soreness she was beginning to feel. Making her way into the bathroom, she stood in front of the sink and looked at her reflection in the mirror.

I'm no longer a virgin.

The idea seemed strange to her. Laura had always shared her stories after each time she had sex, and now that Zoey had her own story, there was no one to share it with. Shaking her head, she tried to put the thought out of her mind.

I have Tristan to share things with now.

After drying herself off, Zoey walked back into the bedroom to find Tristan lounging on fresh sheets. She climbed back into bed with him and turned around so he could spoon with her. He stroked her hair as they lay together.

"I wish Laura was still here. She'd be so proud," she sighed. "This is exactly the sort of thing we would analyze to death."

"Life can be pretty cruel," Tristan replied. Zoey paused, surprised by his response. It wasn't the answer she was expecting.

"This wasn't."

Tristan propped himself up on one elbow to look over her shoulder.

"There are things in life that can dull the pain for a while, sure, but it never goes away. Time doesn't heal anything. It just reminds us how much longer we have to deal with the loss. You know that."

"I guess that's true. But I think that Laura would've wanted me to move on and make the most of my life. You don't think your sister would've wanted you to do the same?"

Tristan glared at her.

"My sister's dead. She doesn't get to wish for things anymore."

"I, I know. I just meant when she was alive."

"You sound like my parents."

"So you don't agree?"

"I don't have that luxury, Zoey. I mean, think about it," he said, abruptly letting go of her and getting out of bed. "We're born completely innocent, thinking things are beautiful, only to find out we're going to die and we have no control over it. What's the point? To live through a series of sometimes good, sometimes painful experiences until we die in one of them? Even if you live to see old age you still have to deal with a dying body! What kind of reward is that? There's no meaning to any of it, so why bother? I'm not surprised there have been all of these suicide shootings lately."

"Whoa, wait a second," Zoey said, turning to look at him. His sudden outburst was unsettling. "I can understand the suicide part, wanting to take yourself out of the equation. But why do they need to take others with them?"

"Come on, why do you think?" Tristan sputtered. "They've been repressed. They've been forced to deal with a life of complete shit, so why should they do life a favor? This is how they bring meaning to their existence. It's their final stand to show the world that they're not gonna be shit on any more. Most people are sheep, and this is their way of distinguishing themselves from the herd."

Zoey stared at him incredulously.

"So going down as a murderer of innocent people is what they want their last act to be? That's how they want to be remembered? I will never understand that. But by the way you're talking, it almost sounds like you do."

"After what I've been through, you better believe it. And I really thought you did too."

"What? Why would you think…?" Zoey began, completely taken aback. "I mean, I understand their pain, their feelings of hopelessness, but I could never take that out on someone who has nothing to do with me. That's insane."

"No. What's insane is all the various ways in which these kids are being alienated," he said, pacing back and forth next to the bed. "It's bad enough this is all meaningless, but then to go through that, too? The only way to deal with it is to give in to the chaos, let it wash over you until the waves pull you under."

"But, with so much chaos already, why would you want to willingly add more?"

Tristan sat down next to Zoey, solemnly taking her hand.

"Because, that's the only way for people to see, for people to understand, what's going on around them," he explained, his eyes searching hers for any hint of acceptance. "Most people wander aimlessly through life unaware of all the pain and suffering that happens on a daily basis. You don't think their oblivion adds to that? Of course it does! These kids are born into a world that's so caught up in its own destruction that this is their only way to join in. That's just reality."

Zoey felt her head begin to spin. The passion she felt surrounding them was quickly collapsing into anger and resentment. She couldn't comprehend why Tristan was suddenly defending teenagers who killed people, citing the reason "to prove a point." Her drug-induced state began to fade, along with her desire to continue such an irrational conversation with him.

"I, uh, I need a glass of water."

"Water? That's all you have to say?"

"I think I'm coming down from the high. I'm really thirsty."

Tristan snorted as he stood up and walked out of the room. Zoey could hear the tap running as he filled up a glass of water for her. She tried to gather her thoughts so as not to upset him further. She hoped he was simply coming down from his high as well. He returned and handed her the glass.

"Thanks."

"So, what's your final opinion?"

"Final opinion?" she asked, taking a sip of water.

"Yes, Zoey."

"I'm sorry, Tristan. I know you're upset about your sister, and I understand that, I do. You know I do. But I could never condone murder over it. And I can't believe you could either."

Tristan stared at Zoey for a moment, as if they were suddenly strangers, before turning away from her. She noticed his whole body shaking.

"Then you don't know me at all."

"What?"

"I thought you understood. I thought we were of like mind." Zoey could hear the disappointment in his voice.

"Tristan, please, tell me what's going on."

He turned around slowly, as if it hurt to look at her.

"You've really changed. When we talked about life and death before, you recognized my pain as if it were your own. You felt what I felt, like no one else has. We were soul mates because neither one of us believed in souls. But now, it's like they've drawn you back in with their standard social conventions."

Zoey bit her lip.

"Tristan, I do recognize your pain," she began carefully. "Every day without Laura still hurts, just as much as it did a year ago. And life will never be like it was when she was here. But I would never disgrace her memory with the death of more innocent people."

"That's just it, Zoey. None of them are innocent. They're all to blame for how things have turned out in this world, whether they want to admit it or not. And if you're okay with living in that kind of a society then I feel sorry for you."

"Well then, I feel sorry for you," Zoey shot back. "If all you see is death and destruction in the world then you're living no life at all. You might as well already be dead."

Tristan mumbled something Zoey couldn't hear.

"What?"

"Nothing," he said, calmly turning back to face her. "We have a busy day tomorrow. Let's get some sleep."

He walked over to the bed and slid under the covers, turning away from her. She watched him for a while, until his body finally relaxed and his breathing slowed to a calm, steady pace. She didn't want to stay there, but she was afraid to wake him up by moving. She was too tired and too frightened to go through another conversation like that.

It was the first night in a long time that she couldn't fall asleep.

CHAPTER FIFTY-ONE

Deirdre woke up early Saturday morning, squinting at the sunlight streaming in her window. She groaned as she rolled over and tried to ignore it. With all of her ongoing research she hadn't gotten a good night's sleep in months. But the daylight seemed to occupy every corner of her room. She tossed and turned for a few minutes until she realized her efforts were in vain. *Stupid sun.*

Grumbling, she sat up and stretched her arms over her head. She looked over at the clock next to her bed. It read 10:33 am. *Ugh. Might as well get up.*

Deirdre stood up and made her way to the coffee pot to set up her caffeine fix. Yawning, she picked up the remote and turned on the TV as she plopped down on the couch.

"It looks like it's going to be a gorgeous day out there today, with no April showers and early May flowers," the weatherperson was saying. Not having had her morning coffee yet, Deirdre didn't have the stomach for such commentary so early in the day and turned off the TV. Looking around the room, she walked over to her desk and turned on her computer.

Hopefully my daily blogs will be more interesting.

When the web browser finally loaded, Deirdre opened her bookmark list and clicked on the link for "Two Become One". As she looked at the page through blurry eyes she noticed it was only one line. She rubbed her eyes to look again.

"Oh my god."

Deirdre bolted out of her chair and grabbed her purse, searching for Dr. Stephens' card. After throwing a number of items on the counter the card fell out onto the floor. Deirdre bent down and scooped it up, reaching for her phone in the process. She dialed Dr. Stephens cell phone number.

"Hello?"

"Dr. Stephens, hi," she said breathless. "It's Deirdre Hart. I hope I didn't wake you."

"No, not at all. I'm sorry I haven't gotten back to you. It took a few days to get in touch with everyone I wanted to talk to and…"

"I'm sorry, Dr. Stephens, but that's why I'm calling," Deirdre said hurriedly. "There's a new entry this morning, and I'm afraid it's the one we were fearing."

Deirdre waited for Dr. Stephens to tell her what to do, but she only got a one word response.

"Zoey."

*   *   *   *   *   *   *

Zoey opened her eyes to a hazy world. She couldn't seem to focus on anything immediately. She closed her eyes again, trying to ignore the pounding inside her head, and opened them slowly. This time she was able to see more clearly. She looked at the clock beside the bed and saw it was 10:09 a.m. She turned to see Tristan sitting across the room at his computer.

"Hey," she said, propping herself up on her elbows. He quickly closed the Internet browser and turned to face her.

"Hey."

He didn't say another word as he stood up and left the room.

Shit. He's still upset from last night. I wish I knew what the hell happened? One minute we were rolling around in each other's arms, and the next he's yelling at me about teenagers killing people. Am I remembering that right?

Zoey rubbed her eyes and blinked a couple times. She remembered bits and pieces of their argument the night before, but much of the conversation was fuzzy at best. All she knew now was that he was still angry with her. She frowned.

This is not how I wanted Laura's memorial day to start.

Tristan came back into the room and grabbed a duffel bag out of his closet. He turned to face her.

"You better get up or we'll be late."

"What's that?" she asked, gesturing to the bag.

"Something for the memorial," he replied, walking out of the room again.

Zoey slid out from under the covers and stood up, suddenly remembering she was naked. She looked around for her clothes from the night before, but couldn't find them.

They must be in the living room. Great.

Before Zoey could make it that far, Tristan walked into the room carrying different clothes.

"Here," he said, handing them to her.

"Where are my other clothes?"

"Does it matter? You weren't going to wear them to the memorial, were you?"

"Well, no, but, where did you get these?"

"I bought them this morning at the store down the street, so we wouldn't have to waste time going back to your house."

"You didn't have to do that, Tristan. We have plenty of time to stop by my house. It's not like we have to be there on time."

"Yes we do," he snapped. Zoey jumped at his tone of voice. Tristan could see her growing uncomfortable.

"I just mean, we don't want to attract attention by getting there late."

Zoey looked down at the clothes, trying not to show her apprehension. She nodded.

"Ok. I'll get dressed."

She walked past him as calmly as she could and closed the door to the bathroom. She leaned against the sink to catch her breath.

What is wrong with him? He's freaking out or something, and he's making me freak out too. I don't know what to do.

Reluctantly, she put on the clothes that Tristan bought her. It was a simple pair of jeans and a T-shirt, but Zoey knew there was no reason for him to do that. The reason he had given made her more nervous, but there was no time to discuss it now. She just wanted to get to the memorial and get it over with.

When she came out of the bathroom Tristan was waiting for her by the door, holding the bag.

"I figured we could walk. That's why we have to leave sooner."

"Oh. Ok. I guess I'll get my other clothes when I come back for the car. Just let me put on my boots."

Tristan didn't say anything as he waited. Zoey wasn't planning on wearing the boots to the memorial, but in a way it was almost appropriate. When she stood up he opened the door for her. She walked past him and down the stairs, turning around to wait for him. He followed her without stopping to lock his door. Zoey thought better than to ask him why.

They walked along in silence for a while, Zoey stealing glances over at Tristan from time to time. He seemed stoic, his eyes focused straight ahead of them. She looked down at the ground, becoming lost in her own thoughts.

A few minutes later she felt her phone vibrate in her pocket. She looked down to see her parents' number on the screen. *It's probably Mom calling to see if I'm going to the memorial.* Zoey hit "ignore" and put the phone back in her pocket.

"I really hoped things would be different," Tristan said suddenly, keeping his gaze forward. Zoey turned her head towards him.

"What do you mean?"

"We're here."

Zoey looked to see the edge of the campus in front of them, a large crowd already forming around the small memorial that sat in the middle of the field.

Tristan began walking faster, causing Zoey to have to jog just to keep up with him.

He stopped slightly outside the group and began scanning the scene. He continued to walk slowly around the ring of bystanders until he found a slight opening into the middle. He placed the bag down on the ground as Zoey caught up with him.

"Wow, look at all these people," she said, looking at the crowd.

"Fuckin' sheep."

"What?" Zoey asked as she turned around. That's when she saw Tristan pull an assault rifle out of the bag. She froze.

"Tristan," she whispered in shock. "What are you doing?"

He looked at her, his eyes completely empty.

"I thought I'd have a partner in this," he replied, calmly. "But I guess I was wrong. Last night told me everything I needed to know. You're just as pathetic as the rest of them."

As he readied the gun, Zoey felt the ground begin to spin. She tried to steady herself as she watched him attach the clip. She looked at the crowd of hundreds of people standing in front of him, all easy targets. *Get a hold of yourself! Do something!*

"He's got a gun!" she shouted, finding her voice. "There's a guy with a gun. Get out of here! Run!"

Several people turned around surprised, and noticed Tristan with the rifle, standing there, staring at them in disbelief over Zoey's outburst.

"It's true!" someone else shouted. She began to run while others looked around, still confused. The sudden chaos knocked the feeling back into Zoey's body, and she raced toward Tristan as he raised the gun. He was only able to fire one shot into the crowd before she tackled him, knocking the rifle out of his hands. She struggled to hold him down as he tried to turn over.

"You stupid bitch! Get off of me!" he shouted, as the screaming crowd scattered. He noticed no one was left behind, bleeding from his one shot. Zoey wrestled with him, hoping to keep him subdued until everyone made it out safely. *So many people. Oh my god, please hurry!*

"You ruined everything!" he grunted, as he turned over and crushed her against the ground. He dug his elbow into her shoulder and she cried out in pain. She looked up and saw they were the only ones left.

"Tristan, please, stop!" she pleaded, trying to get out from under his weight. He straddled her, pinning her down onto the ground, and pulled a handgun out of his waistband. He pressed it against her chest.

"Don't you get it? I chose you!" he cried, his eyes boring a hole through her skull. "We both lost someone we couldn't live without! You were supposed to be the one who felt my anguish; knew that other people were too weak to do the right thing. You were my muse, the one I needed to complete this whole thing."

Zoey stared at him in horror.

"Did you know about Laura before you met me?"

"Hey, we've got a winner!" Tristan yelled into the air. "Tell her what she's won, Bob! Of course I knew. And you fooled me, gave me all the right answers, right up until the end."

"I don't understand," Zoey said, tears rolling down her cheeks. "I thought this was real. I thought we were real."

"Don't look at me, I thought it was real too," Tristan claimed angrily. "And then you screwed me over just like my parents did."

"Your parents?"

"They moved on, and so did you," Tristan snarled. "You gave me all that bullshit about right and wrong when I thought you were just like me, unable to live without the one person who meant so much to you. I spent years waiting for that one person to stand by my side, and I believed with every fiber of my being that you were the one who would help me complete my final act. But now I see you're just like them."

"Tristan, I will never get over Laura's death," Zoey said, trying to steady her voice. She had to choose her words carefully. "I'm still devastated, I always will be. But this, this is not the answer."

"You don't know anything. You're useless to me now," he answered, his finger tightening around the trigger. "And I'm not going down alone."

Suddenly, a voice called out behind him.

"Tristan Wright. Turn around slowly and place your hands on your head."

Zoey looked past him to see a woman and a police officer walking towards them, the officer holding a gun pointed at Tristan. She realized from the angle they were at that they couldn't see the handgun. Tristan looked up and turned his head, keeping his weight on Zoey's body.

"Who the hell are you?"

"I'm Deirdre Hart, Tristan."

"What the hell are you doing here?"

"I've been reading your blog, every day. And I just caught the last entry."

"You read my blog? I'm flattered. I didn't think anyone your age would be interested in something like that."

"I'm a reporter," Deirdre explained, as she and the officer slowly moved closer to them. "I started reading teen blogs for an article, and yours caught my attention."

"It's good, right?" Tristan asked. Zoey tried to move her arm out from under him and he jammed the gun harder into her chest, knocking the breath out of her for a moment. "I get compliments on it all the time from my peers."

"I know. It was one of your peers who recommended it to me. You've certainly made an impact on those kids. I wonder if any of them were the same ones who committed their own shootings recently."

Tristan chuckled.

"Look lady, if you think I had anything to do with those other shootings, you're wrong. I ain't the only one jumping on this bandwagon. We're just following the fine example of all those adults who have been doing this forever."

"I'm curious then, as to why you wrote about your plan on a public blog?" Deirdre asked. "It wasn't something you wanted other kids to read and emulate?"

"It's called a suicide note. Ever heard of that?" he replied, annoyed at the continued interruption. "Come to think of it, I never signed my name. How'd you even know I was talking about this place?"

"Son, we're going to need you to move off of the young lady and put your hands on your head," the officer repeated loudly.

"It doesn't matter," he said, turning his attention back to Zoey. "None of it does."

"Tristan, it's over," Deirdre said. "There's nothing else to do but give yourself up."

The sudden blare of sirens signaled that more police were on their way. Tristan looked up to see Zoey's therapist get out of a cop car at the other end of the park. Everything was falling apart, and there was nothing he could do about it. It was over. Tristan looked down and scanned Zoey's eyes as she stared back at him, her lips trembling. He softly wiped a tear from her cheek.

"I can't hold on any more," he whispered, shaking his head. "I have to let go."

Tristan squeezed the trigger. Zoey felt a searing pain in her left shoulder and screamed. The officer answered with his own shot, yelling at Tristan to put down the weapon. Tristan gazed at his arm as blood trickled through his sleeve, a sense of relief on his face. Slowly he turned back to look down at Zoey. She watched in a daze as he placed the gun to his temple.

"No!" she cried out. The gun blast was the last thing she heard before passing out.

CHAPTER FIFTY-TWO

"Zoey! Hey Z!"

"Laura?"

"Over here!"

Zoey looked up to see herself standing next to the slide in the community park. She breathed in deep the strong smell of the cedar chips that littered the ground. It was one of those smells that reminded her of her childhood. She smiled, feeling someone behind her. She turned to see Laura sitting on the swing, watching her.

"Laura! God, I've missed you so much," Zoey said, trying to move towards her best friend. But her feet didn't budge. Laura looked at her sadly.

"What's happening?" Zoey asked, looking around, frightened. "Why can't I move?"

"Because you're facing the wrong direction."

"No I'm not," Zoey said, struggling to lift her legs. "This is right where I want to be."

"But it's not where you belong. You have to go back."

"I can't," Zoey cried out. "Please, I can't go back there. I wanna stay here with you, where it's safe."

"I know, Z. I know," Laura said, as she stood up and began walking towards Zoey. "But you have so much more to see. You have so much more to do. You have to live for the both of us."

"I don't think I can, Laura. I'm so tired, I can't bear to go back."

Laura stopped in front of her, and looked into her weary eyes, smiling.

"You're a lot stronger than you think, my friend. All you have to do is open your eyes."

"Please don't leave me."

"Never."

"Please, Laura…"

"Open your eyes."

"Please…"

"Open your eyes."

"Zoey, honey? Can you open your eyes?"

Zoey looked up slowly to see her father standing over her, a worried expression on his face.

"Dad?"

"Yes baby, I'm right here," he said, taking hold of her right hand. Zoey tried to sit up, but a sharp pain on her left side prevented her from getting very far. Walter supported her head as she laid back down on the bed.

"Don't try to move too much. Your arm's in a sling. The doctor said it'll be sore for a little while."

Zoey looked down at her arm, not recognizing it as part of her own body. She looked back at her father, confused.

"Do you remember what happened, honey?"

Flashes of memory came back to Zoey as she struggled to remember where she was before the hospital. She could see Tristan leaning over her. She could feel the weight of his body on top of her. He was talking to her, whispering something to her. But there was something else pushing into her chest, harder and harder, making it difficult for her to concentrate on anything but the pain.

Until she heard the gun shot. BANG! The sound repeated over and over again in her mind. BANG! BANG! She jumped and cried out again in pain.

"It's ok, Zoey. You're ok," Walter said comfortingly. He stood up and took her into his arms, holding her for the first time in years. He rocked her back and forth gently until he could feel her settle against his chest.

"I didn't know what to do, Daddy," she whispered. "I couldn't..."

"Shhh, it's all right."

Zoey pulled away slightly and looked up at her father.

"Is he..."

"Yes, sweetie. He died at the scene."

Zoey put her head against his shoulder again, tears streaming down her cheeks. She didn't know which one she was crying for, the death of Tristan or the lie that was their relationship. It didn't matter anymore.

Walter held her for a few minutes until her tears began to subside. He could feel her body relax and he loosened his grip, helping her to lay back down. He brushed a stray hair out of her eyes and sat back in the chair next to the bed.

"Where's Mom?"

"She's out getting some food at the cafeteria. You were asleep for quite a while."

Zoey nodded, wiping her eyes as she settled back into her pillows.

"That's ok. I don't know if I'm ready yet for her words of wisdom on how life goes on."

Walter smiled.

"That's the difficulty of being a parent, trying to figure out what to say when something like this happens," he said. "You spend the first part of your kids' lives trying to protect them at all times, but it's not possible. Even before you have to let them go, there's always that chance something will happen. And when it does, you just pray you have the strength to not only overcome it, but also help them do the same."

"This is too much, Dad," Zoey said, wiping more tears from her eyes. "It's just too much."

"I know, honey. But you're still here, and your mother and I are so grateful for that," he said, taking her hand again. "Maybe if I had paid more attention, I don't know. The thought of losing you is…"

Walter trailed off, looking away from Zoey to hide his own tears. It was the first time she ever saw her father cry. After a minute he regained his composure and turned back to look at her.

"I guess your mother's 'life lessons' are how she deals with these things. She learned that a long time ago."

"What do you mean?"

"Well, after having several miscarriages she developed a standard response every time she had to answer people's questions about it."

"Miscarriages? What are you talking about, Dad?"

"Well, it took several years and several tries before you came along. After a while we didn't think we could even have children. We went through three miscarriages before we finally stopped trying. And wouldn't you know it? That's when a miracle happened- you."

"I never knew that."

"I imagine it's not something your mother brings up with anyone," Walter said. "Every time she would get excited and talk to people about it, and when it didn't happen she would have to answer the same questions and take part in the same sympathy conversations. She didn't even tell people about you until she was showing, because she didn't want to jinx it. She had the routine down pat by then, all of the small talk answers were ready at a moment's notice. I guess it's become her automatic defense mechanism now."

Zoey thought about all of those times she had made fun of her mother whenever she used clichés in their conversations. She had never considered that the habit might have come from somewhere. Of course, she had never thought much about what her parents were like before she came along at all.

"I didn't realize so much happened before my time."

"Well, there was a fourth one, actually, after your time, but you were still pretty young, so we never said anything," Walter replied. "We didn't want to get you excited about having a brother or sister, because of all the previous difficulties we had. And sure enough, that one failed too. After that I had a vasectomy. It was too much, wondering if the possibility still remained."

"When did that happen?"

271

"You must've been in first grade, because I think it happened right after you met Laura. Your mother saw how excited you were when you found someone else to play with, that she wanted to give you a sibling. Unfortunately, it didn't work out, again, and she finally gave up."

First grade? Zoey propped herself up on her pillows to look at her father.

"Dad? Did you and Mom have a fight about that? And I mean, like, a major blowout?"

Walter looked back at his daughter, surprised.

"Did you hear us?"

"Yeah," Zoey said, thinking back to what she had heard her father say. Walter leaned forward in the chair.

"What did you hear, honey?"

Zoey bit her lip.

"Well, the only thing I remember is you yelling at Mom, saying you didn't want to have a kid in the first place. At least, that's what it sounded like."

"Zoey, why didn't you ever tell me that?" Walter asked, shaking his head. "I had no idea you heard us. Obviously what I said was in anger, but it was because I was frustrated about another miscarriage. Your mother was so persistent, not wanting you to grow up an only child, that I finally gave in. And when it happened again, I was so upset that I took it out on her and I shouldn't have. I told your mother we were so lucky to have had you, that we shouldn't expect any more miracles. That's when I told her I was getting a vasectomy, since I didn't want to try for a kid in the first place, meaning *another* kid."

Zoey stared at her father in disbelief. All this time, all of those conversations they had in anger, she had the wrong idea about who her father was. He had wanted a family- she was a miracle.

"I just thought..." she said, trailing off as she looked down at the bed.

"Honey, I'm so sorry," Walter leaned over to hug her again. "I can't imagine what you've been thinking all this time."

Zoey closed her eyes as a wave of relief rushed over her entire body. Dr. Stephens was right.

As Walter let go of her again, Connie walked into the room carrying a tray of hospital food. When she saw Zoey sitting up, she hurriedly placed the tray on the table and rushed over to hug her daughter.

"My baby girl," she cried softly, smoothing her hair over her head. "Thank god you're all right."

Zoey felt the tears start all over again. She swallowed the lump that sat in her throat.

"I love you, Mom."

Connie looked over at Walter surprised, her own tears brimming in her eyes. He nodded and rubbed her arm reassuringly.

"I love you too, sweetheart," she said, squeezing Zoey tighter. "More than you'll ever know."

"I think I have a good idea," Zoey said, pulling away from her.

"So, how are you feeling? Does your arm still hurt?"

"A little. It's really stiff and I can't move it that easily."

"Well, the doctor said you should be resting anyway, so that's fine," Connie said, settling onto the bed next to Zoey. "Oh, by the way, you have a visitor. It's the reporter, Deirdre Hart. Do you remember her?"

"Yeah, I remember everything now."

"She said she'd like to speak with you, but only if you were up for it. Should I tell her to come back another time?"

"No. I want to thank her for saving my life."

Connie smiled and nodded. She walked into the hallway and gestured to someone standing outside the door. Deirdre followed her into the room and walked over to shake Walter's outstretched hand.

"Hi, Walter Young. It's so nice to meet you, Ms. Hart."

"I wish it could be under better circumstances," she replied. She turned towards Zoey. "Hi, Zoey. I'm so relieved to see you're doing better."

"Thanks. I'm glad no one else was hurt. Thank you for everything you did. I don't know what would have happened if you hadn't shown up."

"Walter, why don't you and I go have some dinner? We can let these two talk," Connie suggested. "Zoey, are you ok with that?"

"Sure."

Walter offered his chair to Deirdre as he stood up to follow Connie out of the room. As they shut the door, Deirdre sat down and looked at the sling on Zoey's arm. Just being there in a hospital room brought her back to her own experience after the courtyard. But she couldn't think about that right now.

"So, how did you know what was gonna happen?" Zoey asked.

"Well, it's true what I said about doing an article on teenage suicide shooters. I went on a teen chat site and one person gave me a list of blogs I should read. Tristan's was one of the more popular ones, and all of his entries had some detail about his real life in them."

"But he said he never put his real name on there."

"Well, that's where Dr. Stephens comes in. There was an entry on the blog where he talked about committing a final act, and it struck a chord in me. I had interviewed her for the article so I showed her the entry to get her professional opinion. That's when she recognized Tristan as a possible patient of Dr. Loring, who had consulted with her about his case."

"Wow. That's amazing."

"And extremely lucky," Deirdre added. "But it wasn't until he wrote his last entry this morning that we had something more serious. I read it first and called Dr. Stephens, who called your parents shortly before the memorial was about to start. Your mother guessed where you might be. I contacted the police and showed them the blog, and then they got a 911 call from someone at the memorial confirming there was a teenager with a gun."

Zoey exhaled slowly. The story was overwhelming.

"I can't believe this happened."

"There was really nothing you could've done."

"But I dated him! I spent so much time with him over the last nine months, and you and Dr. Stephens knew from reading a blog! How could I not have seen this sooner? I mean, I loved…"

Zoey trailed off, embarrassed by her sudden admission. She had never told anyone she had fallen in love with Tristan, and that she thought he had fallen in love with her. Her first serious relationship, and it was all a lie. And now, she didn't want to believe it herself.

Deirdre walked over and sat down on the edge of the bed.

"I know how you feel, Zoey," she said. "I think we've all been in a situation where what we thought was real turned out to be a lie. I'm getting a divorce because I thought my husband abandoned me. But the truth is we abandoned each other. Tristan felt he was abandoned by his sister, and then his parents. He thought he had found a kindred spirit in you. But the truth is, you're much stronger than he was. And he couldn't accept that."

"But what he tried to do today. How did I not see that side of him?"

"He kept that side hidden from everyone. It wasn't your job to break through his defenses. He fooled his family, his friends, even his therapist! He had been hurting for so long I don't think his former self even existed anymore."

"I just don't know what to do," Zoey said, suddenly feeling tired. "I don't know what to feel. It's like I don't have anything left in me."

Deirdre placed her hand gently on Zoey's arm.

"I'll tell you what you're going to do. You're going to heal."

"How can you be so sure?"

Standing up, Deirdre walked back to the chair and sat down to tell Zoey the story she had come to tell.

"Because I did it myself," she began. "I was also a victim of a suicide shooting. And it destroyed the best relationship I've ever had, along with my chances of having a family of my own. But I'm still here. I still have my family and my friends. And maybe some day I'll even be able to love again. It takes time, Zoey, and I know that sucks but it's all we've got. It's your life, your decision, and only you can make the best of your time here. You decide how you're going out."

Zoey looked at Deirdre wearily.

"Are you really a journalist? Cuz right now you sound like a life coach on one of those commercials."

Deirdre laughed.

"Sorry. I guess I got a little carried away there."

Zoey paused, thinking of the best way to ask her next question.

"How old were you when you were shot?"

"I was 23. I was also seven months pregnant."

"You lost the baby?" Zoey asked incredulously.

"Yes."

Zoey sat back against her pillows as she listened to Deirdre tell her story. She felt a strange comfort at first, knowing it was possible to survive something like that. There were others who had been caught in the same web of chaos and had broken free. There was hope.

But the realization that she could have done something to prevent this kept Zoey from being able to forgive herself.

CHAPTER FIFTY-THREE

"She failed me. My last great hope, and she failed me. I can no longer live like this. The time is now."

Zoey stared at the computer screen, struggling to hold back her tears. She had finally read the last statement on Tristan's blog. It was something she had to see, although she would never fully understand why. Just knowing it was out there was enough of a need. And now having read it, she found it hard to believe the existence of four short lines saved her life.

Next to her sat the announcement for his funeral in the newspaper, a very small obituary with no details except the where and when. Zoey wondered if that had anything to do with the article the day after the memorial, which included interviews from Tristan's parents who were obviously shocked by the whole story. Zoey had been asked to give a statement to the police, and Deirdre had offered to take a statement for the article so she could avoid a full scale interview so soon after the incident. Zoey was relieved.

I've had enough tragic news stories to last the rest of my life.

Looking out the window, she watched the clouds begin to roll in, blocking out the sun. She thought about Deirdre's story and how much she had already gone through in her life. She knew how much suffering there was in the world, just like everyone else, but she had never had to experience it until this past year. It was staggering.

A knock on the door brought Zoey out of her trance. She wiped her eyes.

"Honey? How ya doing in there?"

"Come in, Mom."

Connie opened the door and peeked her head around to see Zoey sitting on her bed, staring out the window. The newspaper sat in front of her, the page opened to Tristan's obituary. Connie had seen it earlier that morning.

"The funeral starts in half an hour. Did you want to go?"

Zoey looked at her mother and shook her head.

"They won't be talking about the Tristan I knew. I don't think anyone knew him anymore."

"I understand. Well, your father and I are here if you want to talk."

"Thanks," Zoey said, turning back towards the window. "But I think I'm gonna go for a walk."

"It's getting pretty cloudy out there."

"I know. I'll keep an eye on the sky," she said, using one of her mother's phrases. Connie smiled.

"Ok, honey."

Zoey walked past her mother and down the stairs. Walter came walking around the corner just in time to see Zoey go out the front door. He turned to see Connie on the bottom step.

"Is she going to the funeral?"

"I don't think so. She said she needed to go for a walk."

Walter sighed, looking back at the front door.

"I hope she's all right."

When Zoey came to the end of the walkway she stopped and looked around her neighborhood. Everything was pretty quiet for a weekend, no kids playing outside, no parents working in the yard. Nothing but grey clouds hanging over her. She turned right and continued walking.

I wonder if I'll ever leave this place, she wondered, looking at all of the cookie cutter houses along her block. *We used to talk about moving away somewhere, finding a place together, starting new jobs. We'd hang out on the weekends and do whatever the hell we wanted. We'd pick up guys and bring them back to our place, without having to deal with parental embarrassment. We were gonna throw awesome parties on the rooftop, since all the city buildings in the movies and on TV had open rooftops. It was gonna be totally different from where we were.*

Then everything changed.

Without realizing it, Zoey soon found herself in the park, walking towards the tree where Tristan had approached her for their first full conversation. She stopped underneath it, running her hand along the trunk while looking up into its tall branches. What used to bring her a sense of solace now only offered anger and sadness. *It's amazing how quickly your feelings can change,* she thought, *and what little control you have over that change.*

Zoey reached up to wipe the tears streaming down her cheeks as she turned to walk away from the tree. She didn't know if she would ever be able to set foot under that tree again. Her memories were so strong she was almost afraid that Tristan would find her there.

I thought life was finally being kind to me, bringing me someone new to start over with. Mom always says God never sends you more than you can handle, but what if you don't believe in God? There's no comforting statement out there that can justify all the shit going on in the world today without some figure being responsible. But that's not comforting either, believing that someone is out there pulling the strings. Because that would mean they're allowing all this shit to happen. So where does that leave me?

She continued past the convenience store and down to the river, where she walked along the rocky edge. Every year before the spring thaw, she and Laura would find the biggest rocks they could and build a bridge across the most shallow part of the water. It became a challenge to see how long they could maintain the bridge before Mother Nature took over and destroyed it completely, a challenge they had accepted right up through last year. Laura had said it was important to maintain a sense of tradition.

"That's how friendships stay strong."

"Did you read that in a self-help book or something?" Zoey had joked. She remembered Laura's laugh.

"No. You're just a heathen."

God, I will always miss that.

But it was not lost on Zoey that she and Tristan had also enjoyed similar banter. It was part of what drew her to him in the first place, the ease of their conversations. He was smart and witty and playful, something she had needed so desperately after Laura's death. She remembered thinking of him as the male version of Laura. The memory instantly made her feel sick.

I'm so sorry, Laura. I never meant to disrespect your memory like that. I didn't know.

It was becoming increasingly difficult for Zoey to remember anything about him before the memorial. It was as if all their time together didn't exist, that he was a stranger until that final day. She didn't want to believe that she could be so easily drawn into someone else's game. It made her feel weak and vulnerable; an outsider in her own body.

A drop of water on her forehead brought her back to reality. She stopped and looked up at the sky as more rain continued to fall softly. The clouds eventually grew darker and soon opened up to release their full power. Closing her eyes, she gingerly lifted her arms out to the side, letting the rain flow over her entire body. Her hair and clothes clung to her as she tried to drown the pain. But it wasn't enough; it would never be enough. No amount of water would ever wash away the memory of that day, and all the days leading up to it. The ache in her arm was just the beginning.

Zoey brought her head and arms back down and opened her eyes, watching the sky fall down around her. She wondered if it was possible to be swallowed whole in the cascading sea, never to be seen or heard from again. The idea was strangely comforting.

As if I never even existed.

Just as suddenly as the rain began, it slowed to a light shower and faded out completely. Zoey reached out her right hand to watch the final drops slide off her fingers and onto the ground. She was drenched and shaking, but she still had one more place to go. She began to walk again.

I'll see you soon.

*   *   *   *   *   *   *

Connie frowned as she looked out the window to see the rain grow heavier. The sky was much darker now than before when Zoey went out for her walk. She didn't even take an umbrella.

Don't worry, Connie, Zoey's a smart girl. I'm sure she'll be walking through the door any minute now.

As she turned to walk into the kitchen, Walter emerged from his study.

"Have you seen outside?" he asked, a concerned look on his face. "It's been raining pretty hard for a few minutes now."

"I know. I've been watching. She'll probably be back soon."

"She's been gone for over an hour now. It's getting dark."

"Let's give her a little more time. She's dealing with a lot right now, honey."

"That's what scares me," Walter said, walking over to the window. He glanced over at Connie staring out at the rain. She looked back at him.

"Ok. Let's go."

Walter grabbed the umbrella and a blanket while Connie found her car keys. Walking through the front doorway, he opened the umbrella and held it over the both of them as they jogged out to the car. Walter surveyed the neighborhood one last time before getting in the vehicle.

"I saw her go that way," Connie gestured, turning the car to the right as they rolled out of the driveway.

"Maybe she was going to the park." Connie nodded as she turned out of the neighborhood.

They drove in silence, listening to the rain hitting the top of the car. Walter continuously scanned the sidewalk on both sides while Connie kept her eyes on the road. She noticed the rain begin to subside and breathed a sigh of relief.

"At least it didn't last for very long," Connie said as they reached the park. She pulled the car over to the side of the road as they both looked around the field. There was no one in sight.

"Maybe she's down by the river. She and Laura hung out there all the time," she suggested, putting the car in park. Walter grabbed the umbrella and blanket as they stepped out of the car and made their way past the tree to the river bank. Connie noticed a set of muddy foot prints leading along the side of the river and out of the park. She grabbed Walter's arm and pointed to them.

"Let's follow them on foot," he said, taking Connie's hand. They began to walk.

The footprints led them out of the park and onto the sidewalk, where mud splotches took their place. As the two of them followed along they grew smaller until they ended halfway up the block. Walter looked ahead to where the sidewalk led and squeezed his wife's hand.

"I think I know where she was going." Connie nodded and followed his lead.

At the top of the hill sat one of the town's two cemeteries. The Young family had visited this cemetery a little over a year ago.

As they walked beyond the open gates, they saw Zoey sitting motionless in front of Laura's grave, staring at the headstone. They walked towards her slowly so as not to startle her. When they finally stood beside her, Walter reached down and placed the blanket over her shoulders. She didn't move.

"Hi baby," Connie said, squatting down beside her. "We were worried about you."

When Zoey didn't respond, Walter put his hand on her shoulder.

"Are you ok, honey?"

Zoey tilted her head slightly, the first sign that she was aware of their presence. She seemed to be thinking about the answer to her father's question. Her parents waited patiently.

"Yes."

Connie looked up at Walter as he wrapped the blanket tighter around Zoey's shoulders and knelt down on the other side of her. All three of them sat in silence as Zoey stared at her best friend's grave.

After a few minutes, she leaned forward and placed her hand on the stone.

"I promise," she whispered. "I love you."

Turning to her father, she began to stand up. He helped her up and reached over to Connie to do the same. Zoey looked back at Laura's grave one more time, then turned to walk back to the entrance. Her parents followed her.

Zoey was about to ask her parents how they knew where she was, when they came upon numerous sets of muddy footprints heading in the same direction. She smiled slightly as they continued walking.

When they reached the car Zoey brushed off her jeans and climbed into the back seat, pulling the blanket around her. Connie turned on the heat immediately even though there was a warm breeze rustling through the trees.

They rode back in silence, Zoey staring out the window. When they reached the house, Walter helped Zoey out of the car and through the front door. Connie took the blanket from her.

"Why don't you change into your PJs and get warm under the covers. I'll put your clothes in the wash."

That's a good idea, Zoey thought. But before she walked up the stairs, she turned to face her worried parents.

"I really am ok. I just had to tell Laura that."

Walter looked over at Connie, recognizing their first moment of peace in a long time.

"That's good to know, honey."

CHAPTER FIFTY-FOUR

Dr. Stephens looked at her appointment book and smiled about her next patient. Zoey had begun scheduling her appointments again, and Stephens was relieved to see how well she had been progressing over the last four months. It had taken a bit of explaining as to why she couldn't tell Zoey about Tristan's other blog. Too many unknowns mixed with Zoey's feelings might have broken the trust they had been able to maintain over the past year. And Zoey was still depressed from time to time, which was to be expected. But Stephens thought that was better than feeling numb, which had been Zoey's initial response.

Thankfully, with the help of a few breakthrough sessions, she had finally been able to open up again.

Looking out the window, she saw Connie drop off her daughter and wave to her. She waved back as Zoey rolled her eyes and shook her head. Stephens laughed as she opened the door to her office.

"She's still dropping you off, huh?"

"You'd think after all I've been through that some things would change," Zoey said, walking over to her usual chair. "But not my mom."

"Well, some day you might find that reassuring," Stephens replied, taking the chair next to her.

"Maybe."

"So, Zoey, what would you like to talk about today?"

Zoey turned to her, beaming.

"I did it. I signed up for classes. I'm going back next month."

"That's great. Congratulations!"

"Thanks. I wasn't sure at first, you know, that I was really ready to go back. But then I realized I wasn't going back. It was the only way I could go forward."

"That's a good way to look at it. And helpful too I'm sure. Are you nervous?"

"A little," Zoey admitted. "But I'm more nervous about how people are going to treat me. I mean, it's a small town and everyone will know what happened while I was gone. I just don't know how I'm gonna deal with that."

"It's not going to be easy, I'm sure," Stephens agreed. "But I think you've come a long way in dealing with your emotions and working out the next step in your life. You're ready and that will help."

"I hope so."

"Besides, you told me about that promise you made to Laura about continuing to live for the both of you. I know she would be very happy about your decision."

"I know. I just miss her still, a lot. We should be going into our senior year together right now, instead of me entering my junior year alone."

"It's difficult moving on from a plan you had with someone else. But just because she's not here physically doesn't mean that you can't finish it for her."

Zoey frowned, looking past Stephens and out the window.

"What are you thinking, Zoey?"

"That's why Tristan waited until after he finished school to do what he did," she said quietly. "He and his sister had a bet about who would graduate with their bachelor's degree first. That's the only reason he even finished school. It was basically out of respect for their pact."

Stephens put her notebook down in her lap. It was the first time Zoey talked about the Tristan she knew before the shooting.

"Tristan's sister meant the world to him, just as Laura meant the world to you," Stephens began. "And his sister's death seemed to switch on a kind of rage that eventually consumed him. But that doesn't mean he didn't have the same kind of plans that you had with Laura. I think everyone has ideas about how things will turn out with loved ones, especially if they're close enough to become part of the plan. Looking to the future is part of the human condition."

"I guess it's just hard for me to think of him as a normal person anymore. That's how I ended up getting hurt."

"I know. He was very convincing with everyone in his life. But being in any relationship can leave you vulnerable, because you're putting your trust in someone else's hands. And if you don't do that, the relationship can never flourish. It's a delicate balancing act."

Zoey nodded.

"We're all human, and at some point in our lives we all face tough decisions," Stephens continued. "It's the way we approach those decisions that makes us who we are as individuals."

"I will never become like Tristan," Zoey said firmly, looking Stephens in the eye. "That's one thing I know for sure."

"I believe you." *There was never any doubt.*

Zoey paused, thinking about Stephens' words. Relationships had always been a tricky part of Zoey's life, which was why she had relied so heavily on Laura. But even though she had described her relationship with Laura in great detail during therapy, it wasn't until recently that Zoey was able to look at it in an objective manner.

"I guess that's why I always let Laura go out and meet people and do things first. I never got hurt that way. And then when I finally did go out on my own, well, you know. This happened."

"Unfortunately, there's no magic wand you can wave to avoid tragedy. You said your dad told you that at the hospital, right? It's not an easy thing to live with, but people do live with it every day. It's all about finding your own way to deal with what's going on around you."

"I guess my original plan was to let someone else deal with it for me. And look how that ended."

"So now you find your own path. Try out different things. See which one fits best."

"You sound like my mom," Zoey giggled.

"Hey, those phrases became clichés for a reason," Stephens shot back. "They're obviously very popular."

"Mm hmm."

"All right. How about we get back to the topic of going back to school."

"Nice evasive maneuver."

"Evasive maneuver? Where did you get that from?"

"Independence Day was on TV last night."

"Ah. I thought maybe that was some new thing the kids were saying these days."

"I don't know. I haven't been hanging out in large groups lately."

"Well, once you get back on campus you'll be right back in the middle of things again."

"That's true. Guess I should brush up on my cool lingo."

"It's good to have goals."

Zoey laughed along with Stephens.

"And now back to our regularly scheduled therapy."

CHAPTER FIFTY-FIVE

Deirdre sat in her living room, lost in thought as she stared at the blank computer screen. It was finally time to finish the "process". And even though it was the same scene every time she wrote an elaborate column, it was much more personal this time. She had applied her usual approach, talked to a number of people, and conducted plenty of research. But she had discovered most of the answers months ago. The only thing left to do was decide what those answers meant to her.

She thought back to the first day she had heard about Evan's shooting, and her immediate interest in the subject. At that time she didn't know where the story would lead her, or how it would end. Her family and friends had been right to worry- she knew that now. But what they hadn't realized was how much of a necessary step this would be for her to finally move forward. She had her conclusions. They just weren't the ones she was expecting.

I told them all I'm ready, she thought. *Now it's time to prove it.* Taking a deep breath, she began to type.

* * * * * * *

"Ben! Honey? Are you home yet?"

"Yeah, I'm in the living room."

Veronica entered the room, setting her purse down on the coffee table. Ben sat on the couch, leafing through their local newspaper. She leaned down to kiss him and collapsed into the recliner.

"Rough day, babe?"

"Ugh. You have no idea," she replied, kicking off her shoes.

"Huh. Well then, I guess we have no choice but to order pizza."

"I knew I married you for a reason, Mr. Pierce."

"Boy, it's a good thing I can read your mind then. Don't get used to it though."

"Aw, come on. I bet you already know what toppings I want."

"Pepperoni, sausage, and tomatoes?"

"See? You're amazing," she said, standing up from the chair to kiss him again. "I'm gonna lie down for a bit."

"Ok, sweetie," he said, reaching for the cordless phone. "I'll come get you when they deliver it."

He watched Veronica walk out of the room as he placed the order. *I'm a lucky man.* Hanging up the phone, he picked up the newspaper again. When he reached the editorial page, he noticed it contained one large article with Deirdre's byline. He sat up and looked at the column title, "Leaving a Mark". He began to read.

"Five dead and 12 injured during a tragic wedding. Ten dead and 20 injured after a shooting at the mall. Three dead following a dispute among friends. These are all statistics from separate suicide shootings that happened over the past year, but none of them were committed by an adult who was angry over losing a job, or frustrated by a failed marriage, or let down by the government. They were all teenagers.

When I told people I was writing about the issue of teenage suicide shooters, I got a number of different responses. Some people were intrigued, others confused. "Why would I want to write about something so morbid," they asked. There were those with many questions and those who didn't want to know the answers. And a number of people didn't respond at all. They just said, 'Huh.'

But my reason for researching this topic was very clear to me, at first. There are some who would say teenage suicide shootings are not a common occurrence, and by some standards this is true. But recently it appeared to be a growing trend, the kind that breaks out and gains momentum, then fades into obscurity until the next one. As with all violent incidents, they catch our attention at first, but we eventually overcome whatever emotions we felt and continue on with our lives.

And isn't that what we're supposed to do, we say to ourselves? President George Bush urged every American to get back to their daily lives after September 11th or else the terrorists win. And still, there have been terrorist attempts that have thankfully been prevented. Each new incident has been cause for us to step back and evaluate what we're doing to ensure our safety.

So my question then to you is, why aren't we doing the same thing about teen violence?

It's true we have plenty of programs to teach kids about certain dangers, such as the police department DARE program for drug education or health classes that discuss pregnancy and safe sex. But how many schools offer programs to combat the current rise in teen violence? How many classes teach alternative non-violent ways to deal with conflict? How many institutions receive money for violence prevention programs, rather than violence response programs? It seems the only time this issue comes to the forefront is after another rampage hits the news. And by then, it's simply too late.

This led to my own set of "why" questions. Why is this problem growing? Why are these kids taking innocent people with them? Why do they feel it's their only option? And why is there seemingly little active response?

In the beginning I thought, there must be an answer to these questions. There must be something we can point to and say, this is it. This is what's causing our kids to lash out in this manner and this is what we can do for prevention. Everyone looks for answers as to why these things happen, and I was no different.

Unfortunately, though, my one answer never came.

Instead, it seems to be an escalation of numerous issues, issues which do not have any immediate solutions. First and foremost, suicide shooting is not limited to our youth. For years, kids have been exposed to shootings done by adults as a way to deal with their problems. In 1927, 55-year-old Andrew Kehoe from Bath Township, Michigan, killed 45 people and injured 58 more, most of whom were in the second to sixth grades. He set off bombs near the Bath Consolidated School, killing himself along with the others, all for a dispute over property taxes he claimed led to his financial ruin. Many have since followed the same path.

But as the years went by, school shootings became more well-known because of the younger population of students behind the guns. In 1966, 25-year-old Charles Whitman, a student at the University of Texas in Austin, killed 14 people and wounded 31 others during a shooting rampage from the observation deck of the school's administrative building. Some may remember the 1979 shooting at Grover Cleveland Elementary School, where 16-year-old Brenda Spencer killed two people and injured eight students and a police officer. When asked why she did it, she replied, "I don't like Mondays, this livens up the day."

After that, the number of school shootings drops off for a while, with only a handful of incidents throughout the 1980s. But out of the five I found, three of the students committed suicide.

Thus began the trend of suicide shootings that led us into the 1990s. Everyone remembers Columbine in 1999 of course, but throughout the decade there were several shootings that ended in the shooter taking his own life. And since entering the year 2000, there have been almost a dozen other incidents of a mass killing by a teenager or a young adult that ended in shooter suicide.

And it's not only connected to schools anymore- just this past year there was a shooting in a public mall and one during a church ceremony. Schools are where students spend most of their time, yes, but the rest of their families and communities are not forgotten.

This brings me back to my initial question, "Why are others targeted as part of their suicide plan?" There has always been a trend of teen suicides, but what causes this leap to teen suicide shootings?

My first thought was to research teen violence as a whole. Federal government studies claim a rise in teen violence, while adult violence is in decline. This led me to the number one topic related to this issue- gun control. Different groups offered different statistics, some saying guns were a growing problem in household violence, while others claimed the violent crime rate is down during the highest rate of gun ownership in the country's history.

Whatever the statistics reveal, it's clear that mass shootings have only escalated because of the advanced weapons being manufactured today. Certainly there are serial killers who, over time, accumulate that many victims, and don't even use guns. But those who commit mass murders, adults or youths, often need these semi-automatics to do so.

So what should we do? Should we take these guns off the market completely? No, because then the black market would be teeming with them, even more so than they are now. Should we implement even tougher gun buying laws? No, because criminals often find a way to buy guns illegally, while others may have no previous record to raise suspicion. So what, you ask, is the answer?

Alas, there is no simple solution, for the problem of teen violence exists much deeper within our society as a whole. Teenagers today grow up in a very different society than in the '50s, and what's known as "teen angst" has come a long way from the teen movies of the '80s. More than ever before, teens report experiencing much higher levels of depression, anxiety, stress, and various mental disorders. And every day, new therapies and medications are used to diagnose and treat these symptoms, when before it was all part of growing up.

But in today's world, society consists of "broken homes" and gang violence and prescription drug abuse. More advanced guns lead to more advanced armor which leads to even more advanced ammunition. Wars are fought by pushing buttons and shooting at an enemy with which you never come face to face. And the various news stations that report these stories often give their own political spin to them, offering very little, if any, factual information.

I haven't even mentioned the Internet yet, which both brings people together and pushes them apart by allowing communication with the outside world without actually having to step outside.

And therein lies the real problem- isolation. Although many of the factors in each suicide shooting were different, there was one similar detail found in every single incident. All of the families were completely shocked and confused that their loved one could commit such an act, even though the shooter often expressed in some previous manner a sense of anger or hatred towards whatever force they felt had wronged them. Clearly the phrase "ignorance is bliss" does not apply here.

And that's where much of the problem stems from. Sure, we could try to place the blame on things such as violent TV shows, movies or video games. We could say that today's musicians are corrupting our youth, promoting too much sex and violence to be healthy role models. I would even agree, to some extent, that the media continues to foster interest in these stories through their 24-hour news coverage of the most tragic events to achieve their best ratings.

But it's completely unfair to blame any of that, and way too easy, when every child should have at least one adult-influence helping to give the correct context to each of those factors. Every one of those issues mentioned above, save the news, comes with a warning label or rating that explains what is and is not acceptable for children to see. It's not "society's" job to censor everything because we all have a right to free speech. It is the parents' job to decide what is and is not best for their child, and they only have themselves to blame when they use these different forms of media as baby-sitters.

Unfortunately, it doesn't stop there. Our education system is failing our kids also, which is mostly the fault of our politicians who aren't fighting for the funding and training necessary to implement the best programs. Kids spend most of their formative years in school learning basic skills, and while those subjects are extremely important, other subjects such as the arts and trade skills are also necessary for a complete education. Alas, those are often the first to go in a budget crisis.

What needs to be done is a complete transformation of the way schools are run. Just as parents are responsible for the upbringing of their children, so too are educators responsible for the level of critical thinking necessary for children to resolve conflicts in the real world. The curriculum should include ways to handle violent confrontations in its health classes, and all schools should have special programs for its violent offenders. Taking them out of the educational environment does nothing to address the real problem. Instead it could place them back in the violent home from which they came.

Of course, the federal and state governments are not always equipped to offer assistance, and that's where the local community can lend a hand with funding. People cannot sit around and complain about the destruction of our youth when they themselves are willing to do nothing about it. They say it takes a village to raise a child, and in this case it's absolutely true. Kids are active members of the community too, and they deserve a place, such as an open and active youth center, where they can feel safe to nurture their need for positive social interaction.

For we were all teenagers once, and finding our place in the world was not always easy. Raging hormones, trying to grow up while at the same time being told we were too young, it's not an easy balance to find. Many kids survive that period just fine, but they often have help to do it. Others can just as easily get lost, especially if they come from a family life that is less than supportive.

Which brings up another major factor in teen violence, a violent home life. Young children learn from imitating the things they see at home and in their surrounding environment. They say violence breeds violence, and emotional abuse is even harder to see, existing outside of race or poverty lines.

And that is where we find ourselves today, a society where violence is no longer found only in inner cities or poor communities, but extends beyond heritage, wealth, and status. Many of the more recent suicide shooters came from two parent homes and middle class families. Columbine was a harsh slap in the face to everyone who believed that this kind of violence only existed in particular places.

I believe it's the escalation of violence in every aspect of our culture that has led us to teen suicide shootings. What was once deemed simple depression in suicidal teenagers has exploded into rage that can be televised or uploaded onto the Internet for everyone to see. Not only are they attacking those they feel represent the cause of their isolation, they can now show the rest of the world how repressed they were.

And with little in place to offer prevention and guidance for these troubled youth, why should this level of violence be surprising? After all, these kids are simply mimicking what they see, with hardly any adult supervision to guide them. We continuously change the rules of society, so isn't it our responsibility to teach future generations how to survive in it?

Unfortunately, as I stated before, there is no one solution to act as our guide to solving the problem of teen violence, and more specifically, these mass suicide shootings. But a good first step is the education of adults and teens alike, on issues such as gun control and gun use, identifying troubled youths, and learning how to handle a violent situation. Beyond that, kids should be able to enter adulthood with at least one, if not several, skill sets in place. Alas, that much education is too complex to fit into one column. But through the help of local, state and federal governments, emergency personnel, schools, and the media, I am hopeful the solutions will one day find their way out into the world.

But just as adults have a responsibility to guide our youth in the right direction, so too do the children have a responsibility to follow. If teens are going to continue to insist on being treated as adults earlier in their lives, they will also have to accept the same consequences.

Because even after all of this research, one thing had not changed for me. I have always been sickened by how these kids handle their anger. I am a victim of a teen suicide shooting, and I sympathize with everyone who has been devastated by such a tragic event. There is no quick way to heal, just as there is no easy solution to prevent it. These kids, and adults, always had a choice, and I find those who choose violence to be cowards, who either didn't have the courage to overcome their pain or simply end it. This conviction will never falter.

For even though I know humans have always been prone to violence, we have also been prone to survival. And the importance of our children's survival will never change. But if we are to guarantee their safety in this world, we will need to lead by example.

As Madame Anne Sophie Swetchine wrote, "Let our lives be pure as snowfields, where our steps leave a mark but no stain."

EPILOGUE

Zoey pulled into a parking space in the commuter lot on campus. Stepping out of the car, she looked around at the familiar scene.

It feels strange to be here without Laura. I guess that feeling will never go away. But I know she would be so proud of me.

Looking straight ahead, Zoey began to walk toward the campus center.

Nothing much had changed, which used to frustrate Zoey. Now it was a relief. All the buildings were the same, with students walking to and from class. She recognized a couple faculty members who waved to her. What she used to despise about the school she now found almost comforting. The usual routine was much appreciated.

The only difference this time around was that she finally had direction.

Zoey made it to the center and stopped just outside of it. She could see the chaos of back to school activity through the windows and it made her pause. She couldn't remember the last time she had done anything new alone. She wasn't sure she ever had.

Ok. Deep breath. You can do this.

Grabbing the handle, Zoey opened the door and stepped into the frenzy.

"Oof! Oh gosh, sorry!" said someone behind her, crashing into her arm. Zoey turned to see Beth Schumacher, juggling a number of books in her backpack.

"Hey, Beth."

"Zoey! Wow. I didn't know you were back here."

"Yeah. I decided to give it another try."

"That's awesome! I'm so glad. No one really knew what happened to you over the summer. I mean, you know, after the memorial and all."

Zoey nodded. She was ready for the questions.

"I needed some time. But I'm ready to come back now."

291

"I know it's not the same without Laura," Beth said sadly. "She was really cool, and I know everyone misses her."

"Me too."

"So how have you been?"

They continued the conversation as they walked toward the bulletin board with handouts for various campus clubs. Stopping in front of it, Zoey began to scan the different fliers.

"Are you looking for something in particular?" Beth asked.

"Yeah, I was thinking of joining the literary society."

"Seriously? I'm the club president this year!" Beth exclaimed. "We're desperate for new members! I mean, not that our club sucks or anything, we just had a number of people graduate last year."

"Oh yeah?"

"Yeah. We'd love to have you come check it out. I didn't know you were interested in writing."

I didn't think I had anything to say, Zoey thought, reflecting on her sophomore year. *Now I finally do.*

"It's kind of a new thing for me," she said. "I've taken a number of English courses already so I think I can get into the writing program. I just wanted to join a club that could help me with that."

"Oh, totally, we can help to get you on the right track," Beth said. "This is so exciting. My first recruit!"

Zoey laughed.

"You make it sound like I'm joining the Marines."

"Well, you could think of us as the writing Marines." Zoey raised her eyebrow.

Ok, so she's not Will Ferrell. At least she's a familiar face.

"Beth! Over here!" a voice called out above the noise.

"Oh! That's my roommate, Kaley," Beth said. "She's in the club too. You wanna meet her? We're throwing a party tonight in the dorm so we need to discuss. You should totally come!"

"Ok," Zoey answered without hesitation. She realized how big of a first step that was and smiled.

"Great! Come on, I'll introduce you!"

As Beth led her across the campus center, Zoey looked around at the flurry of activity surrounding her. For the first time in a long time, she actually felt comfortable in it.

Don't worry, Laura, she thought. *I'm gonna hold on.*

ABOUT THE AUTHOR

D.M. Roberts is a full-time copy editor and weekend writer who self-published her first novel, *Letting Go and Holding On*, in 2011. She released her second novel, *Running with Hounds…and an English Degree* in 2022, a romcom that was included in Kirkus Reviews' "36 Great Indie Books Worth Discovering" list in March 2023. Originally from Adams, MA, Roberts worked as a reporter and columnist for her hometown newspaper before moving to Worcester to be a copy editor for Gatehouse Media. When the company announced their plans to move, her boyfriend landed a job in Orange, CA, starting two weeks after her last day. So she set out on a six-day cross-country road trip to reach their SoCal home. There, she works on whatever ideas pop into her head, no matter the genre.

www.authordmroberts.com

Made in the USA
Middletown, DE
25 March 2023

27669627R00166